THE FLIGHT OF
ARNHEM

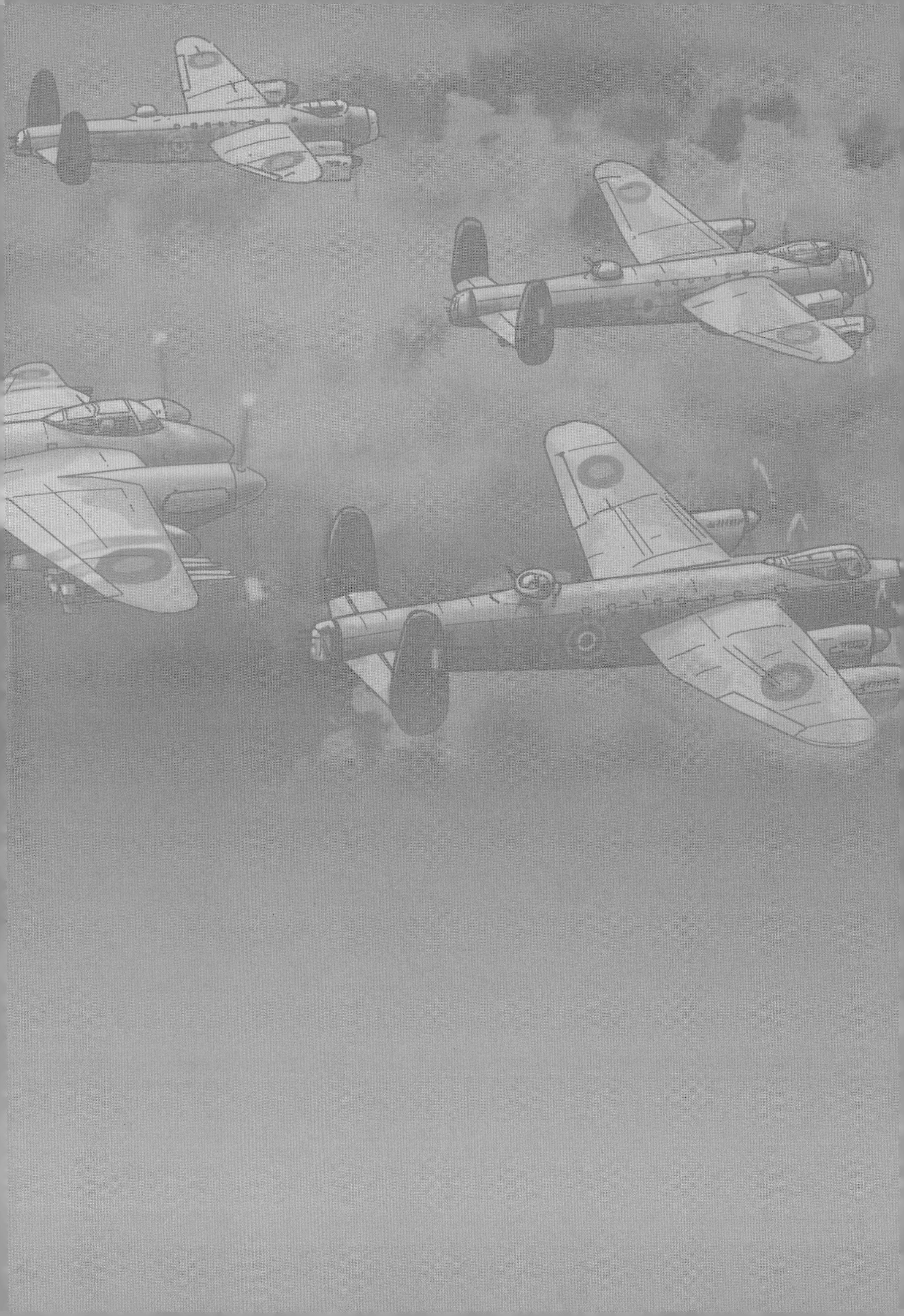

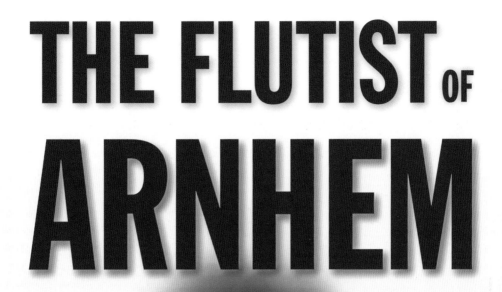

THE FLUTIST OF ARNHEM

A Story of Operation Market Garden

ANTONIO GIL

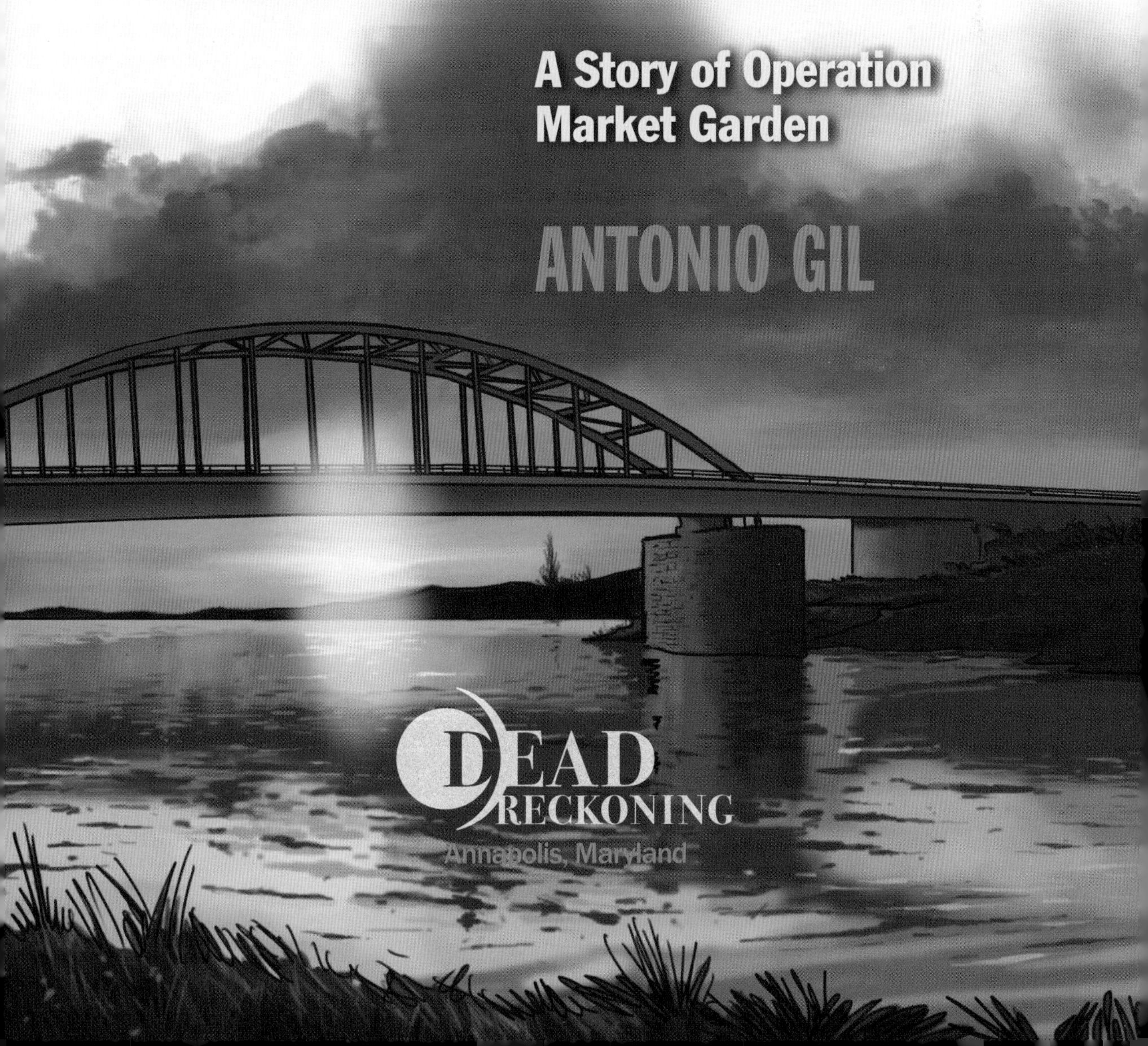

DEAD RECKONING
Annapolis, Maryland

Published by Dead Reckoning
291 Wood Road
Annapolis, MD 21402

Library of Congress Cataloging-in-Publication Data
Names: Gil, Antonio (Jesús Gil Ortega), author, illustrator.
Title: The flutist of Arnhem : a story of Operation Market Garden / Antonio Gil.
Description: Annapolis, Maryland : Dead Reckoning, [2021]
Identifiers: LCCN 2020053066 (print) | LCCN 2020053067 (ebook) | ISBN 9781682474631
    (paperback) | ISBN 9781682476406 (pdf) | ISBN 9781682476406 (epub)
Subjects: LCSH: World War, 1939–1945—Netherlands. | Arnhem, Battle of, Arnhem, Netherlands,
    1944—Comic books, strips, etc. | Netherlands—History—German occupation, 1940–1945—
    Comic books, strips, etc. | Graphic novels.
Classification: LCC PN6777.G47 F58 2021 (print) | LCC PN6777.G47 (ebook) |
    DDC 741.5/946—dc23
LC record available at https://lccn.loc.gov/2020053066
LC ebook record available at https://lccn.loc.gov/2020053067

♾ Print editions meet the requirements of ANSI/NISO z39.48-1992 (Permanence of Paper).
Printed in the United States of America.

29 28 27 26 25 24 23 22 21   9 8 7 6 5 4 3 2 1
First printing

Although this is fiction, its background is the real battle and events that happened in Operation Market Garden. It was my idea to give tribute to everyone involved in intelligence, espionage, and resistance in the hard days of the occupation, no matter the country, no matter the flag. Only that the high-risk living on the edge of the abyss, between your duty and your own life . . . was heroic.

Thanks to my friends Frank Solo, reenactor and expert in the history of the British army; Javier Yuste, who corrected my dialogue and history; and Pawel Lukasz Kolecki, who, apart from lending his image to do a “cameo,” helped me with the information about Polish troops and the Polish text.

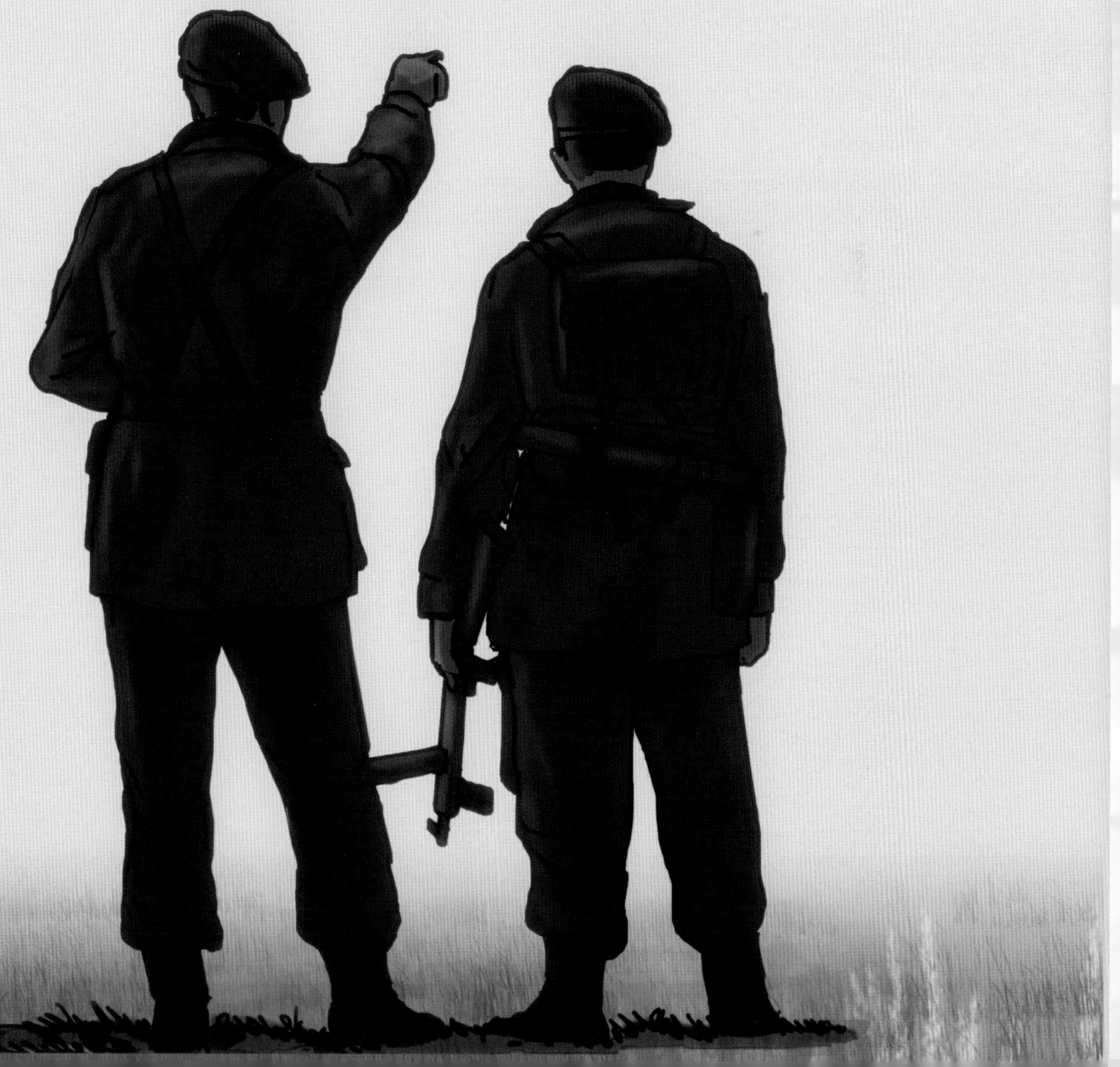

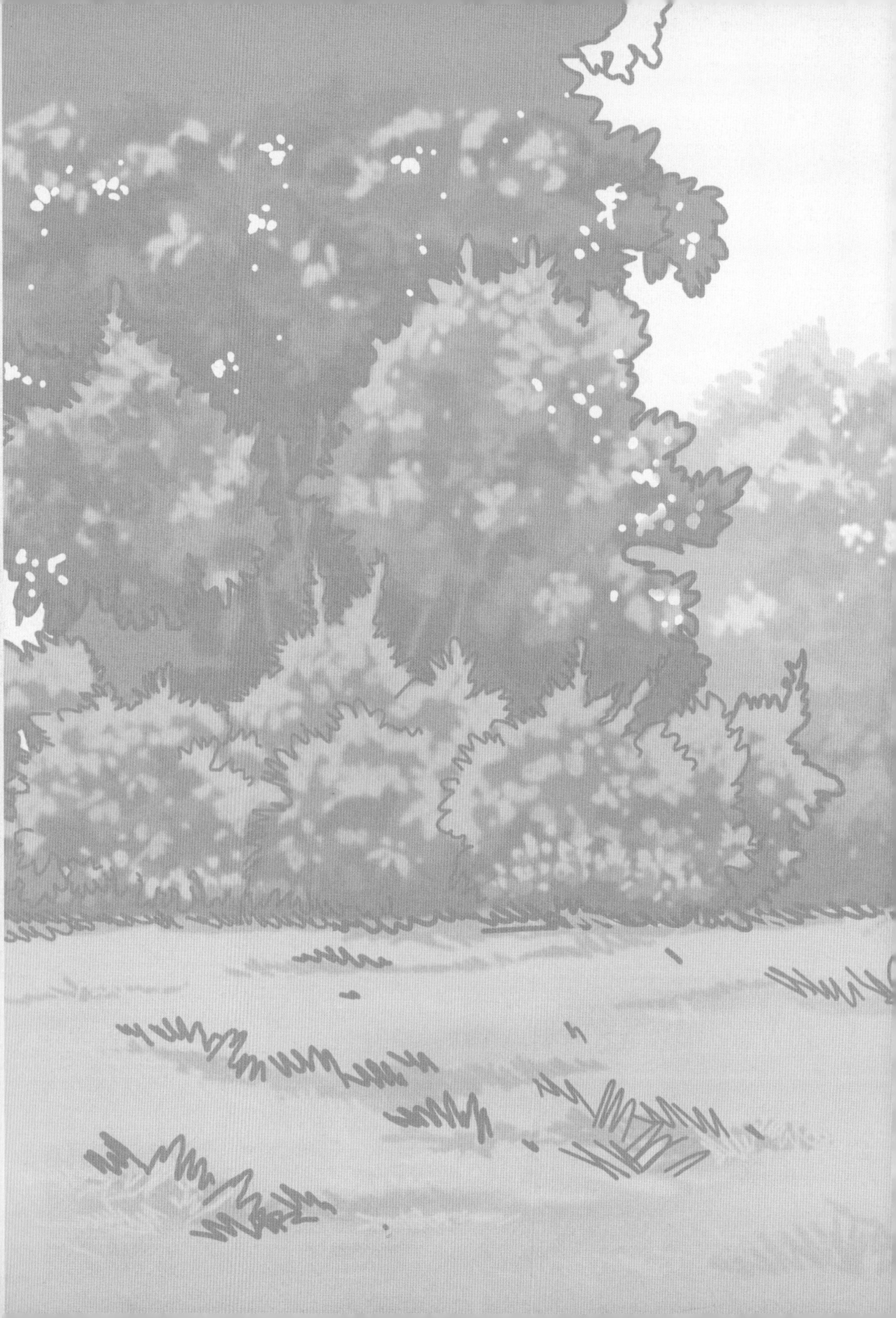

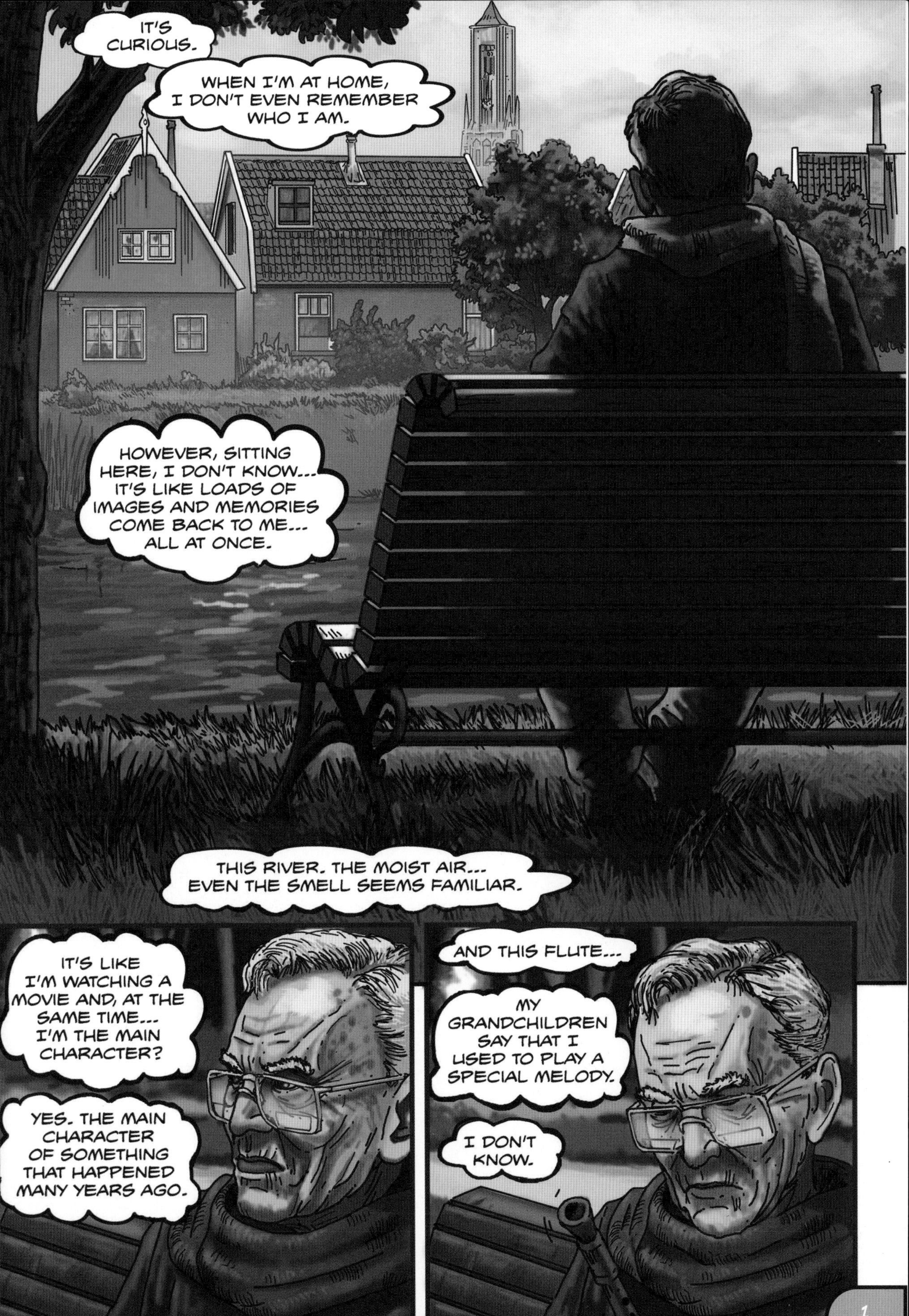

IT'S CURIOUS.
WHEN I'M AT HOME, I DON'T EVEN REMEMBER WHO I AM.
HOWEVER, SITTING HERE, I DON'T KNOW... IT'S LIKE LOADS OF IMAGES AND MEMORIES COME BACK TO ME... ALL AT ONCE.
THIS RIVER. THE MOIST AIR... EVEN THE SMELL SEEMS FAMILIAR.
IT'S LIKE I'M WATCHING A MOVIE AND, AT THE SAME TIME... I'M THE MAIN CHARACTER?
YES. THE MAIN CHARACTER OF SOMETHING THAT HAPPENED MANY YEARS AGO.
AND THIS FLUTE...
MY GRANDCHILDREN SAY THAT I USED TO PLAY A SPECIAL MELODY.
I DON'T KNOW.

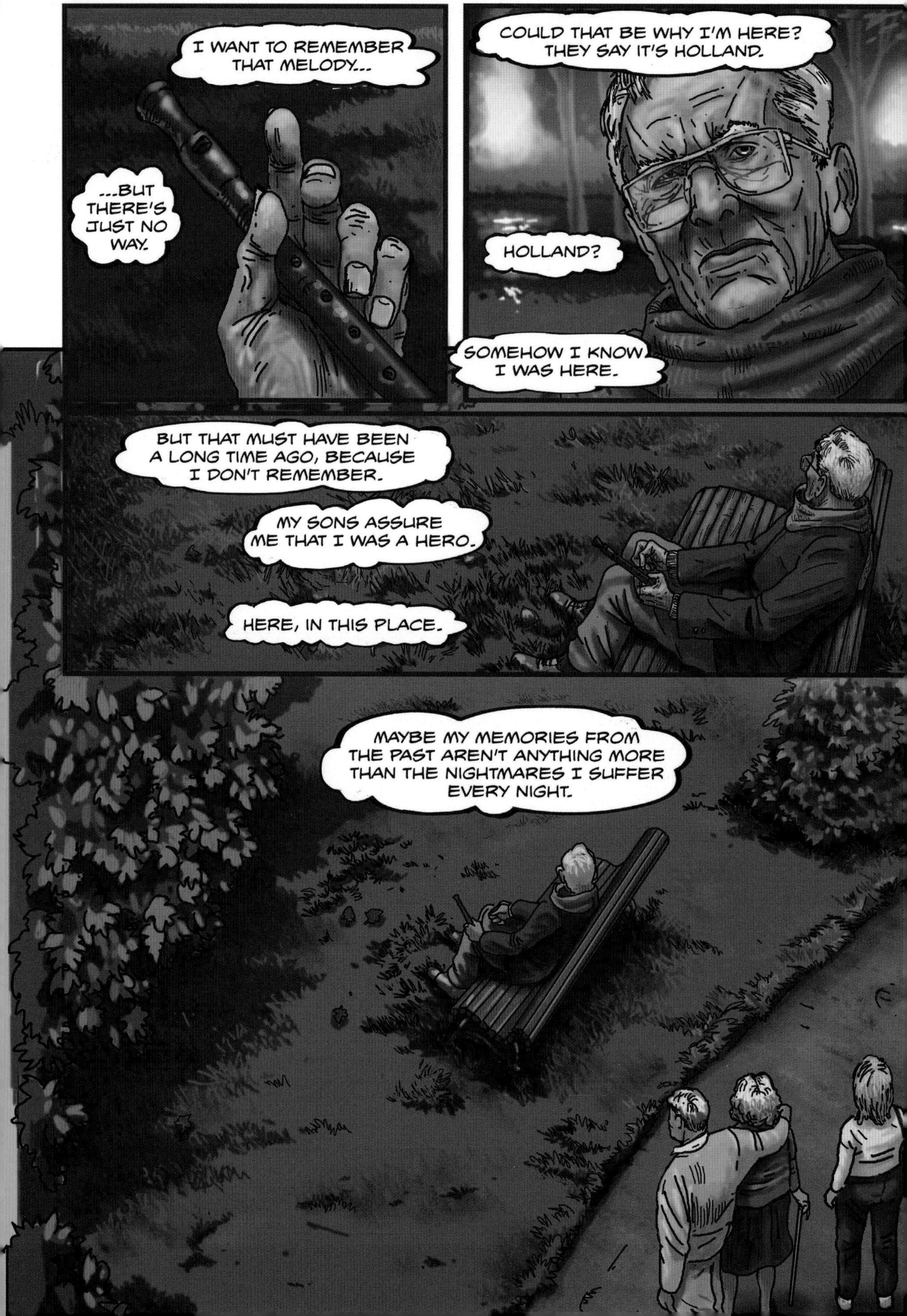
I WANT TO REMEMBER THAT MELODY...
...BUT THERE'S JUST NO WAY.
COULD THAT BE WHY I'M HERE? THEY SAY IT'S HOLLAND.
HOLLAND?
SOMEHOW I KNOW I WAS HERE.
BUT THAT MUST HAVE BEEN A LONG TIME AGO, BECAUSE I DON'T REMEMBER.
MY SONS ASSURE ME THAT I WAS A HERO.
HERE, IN THIS PLACE.
MAYBE MY MEMORIES FROM THE PAST AREN'T ANYTHING MORE THAN THE NIGHTMARES I SUFFER EVERY NIGHT.

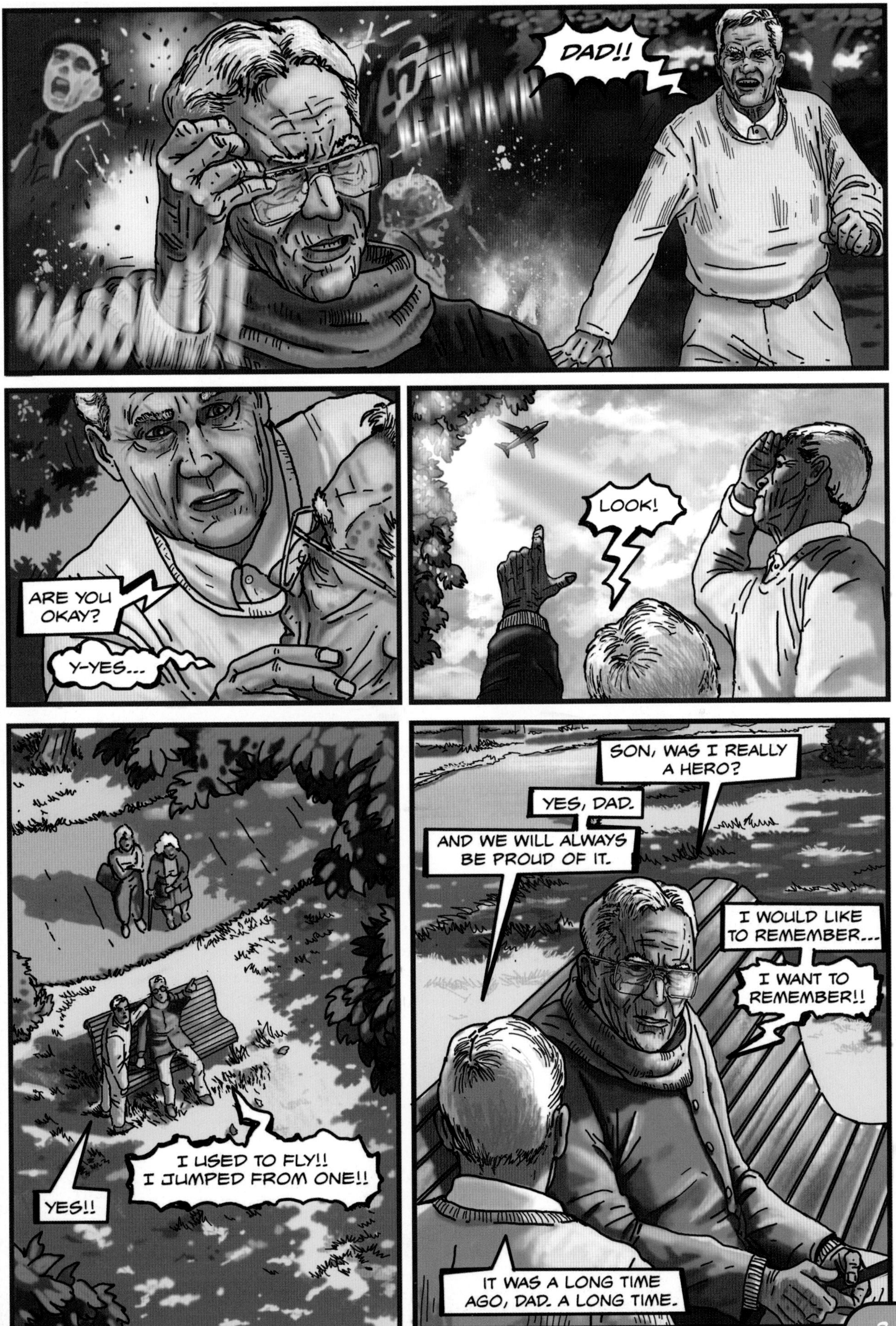
DAD!!
ARE YOU OKAY?
Y-YES...
LOOK!
I USED TO FLY!! I JUMPED FROM ONE!!
YES!!
SON, WAS I REALLY A HERO?
YES, DAD.
AND WE WILL ALWAYS BE PROUD OF IT.
I WOULD LIKE TO REMEMBER...
I WANT TO REMEMBER!!
IT WAS A LONG TIME AGO, DAD. A LONG TIME.

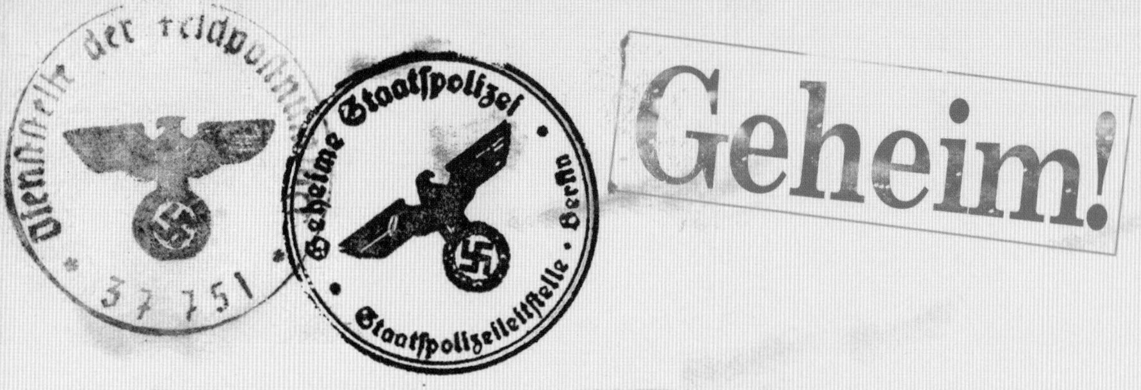
37 751
Geheime Staatspolizei
Staatspolizeileitstelle
Berlin
Geheim!

Unternehmen Nordpol "Das Englandspiel"

Operation Unternehmen Nordpol (North Pole), also called Das Englandspiel (The England Game), was one of the most successful actions of the Abwehr, the German military intelligence service.

Developed in occupied Holland during 1942 and 1943, Das Englandspiel managed to dismantle the country's entire Allied spy network, thanks to the intelligence of Oberstleutnant Hermann Giskes, one of the most prominent figures of the counterintelligence section of the Abwehr.

Giskes, who deserved his infamy for the use of some methods that were considered "not very clean," arrived in the Netherlands in 1941, where he effortlessly demonstrated his skills and abilities.

A Dutch confidant called Ridderhof gave Giskes, in exchange for money, detailed information on where British agents and supplies for the resistance forces would land. In the beginning, Giskes didn't trust Ridderhof, but the latter's tenacity convinced him. In March 1942, Giskes devised a plan to take advantage of captured agents, coercing them to work for him. Thus, Das Englandspiel was born.

In this way, Giskes was hunting, one by one, all the agents who were landing in the Netherlands and getting hold of all the codes that they used to transmit information. Giskes assumed a risk transmitting those codes while posing as an Allied agent.

Curiously, Great Britain never suspected anything.

By the end of October 1943, Giskes finalized his task, leaving the Allies blind and deaf, and adding to his account fifty-four agents from the SOE (Special Operations Executive), captured and exploited. However, Giskes was unaware of the existence of a man more dangerous than any other: John Hewson, who had in his possession documents describing, in great detail, the positions of the German army from Holland to Germany. This was vital information that the Allies could use to advance northward and continue the war until the downfall of the Third Reich.

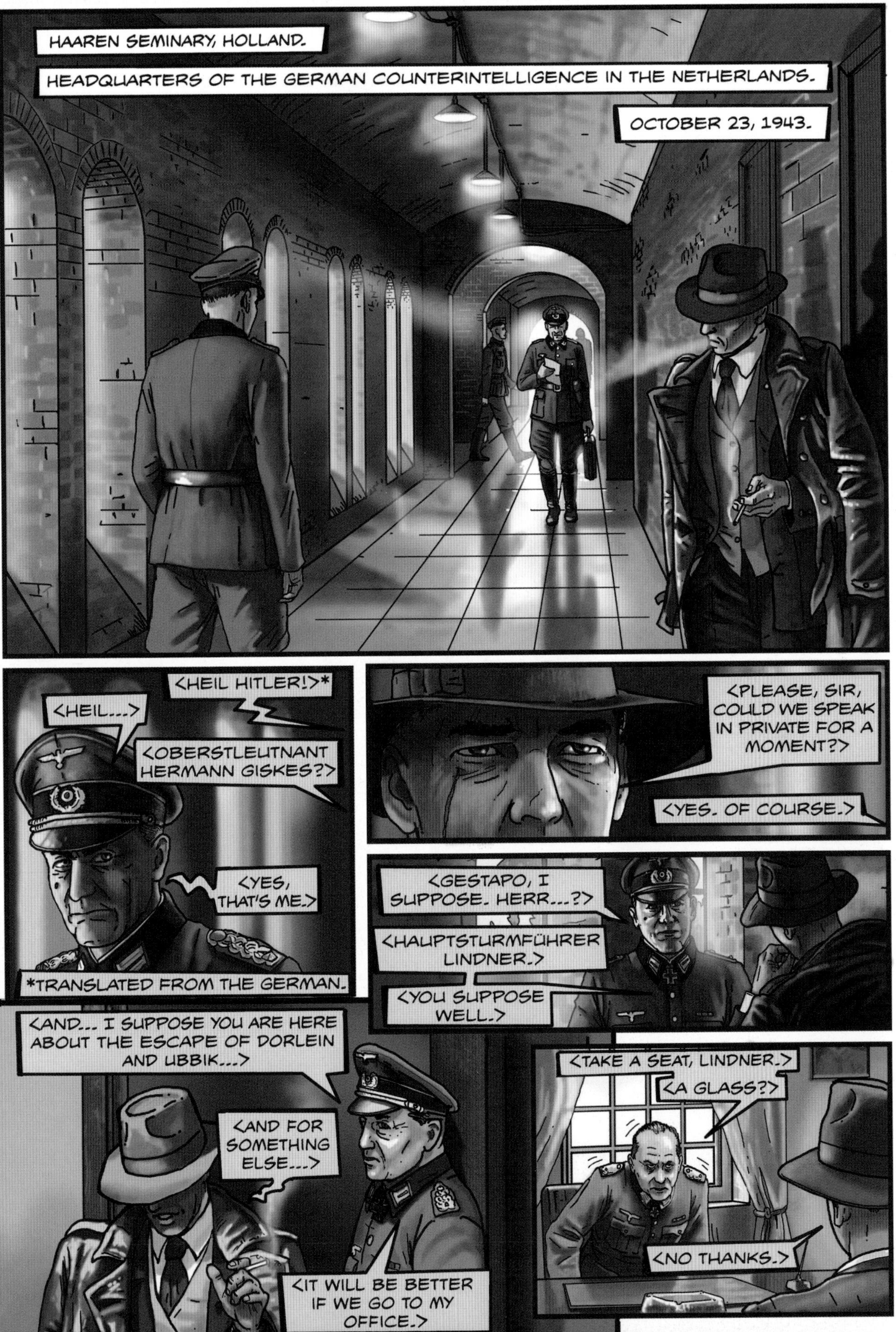
HAAREN SEMINARY, HOLLAND.
HEADQUARTERS OF THE GERMAN COUNTERINTELLIGENCE IN THE NETHERLANDS.
OCTOBER 23, 1943.
<HEIL HITLER!>*
<HEIL...>
<OBERSTLEUTNANT HERMANN GISKES?>
<YES, THAT'S ME.>
*TRANSLATED FROM THE GERMAN.
<PLEASE, SIR, COULD WE SPEAK IN PRIVATE FOR A MOMENT?>
<YES. OF COURSE.>
<GESTAPO, I SUPPOSE. HERR...?>
<HAUPTSTURMFÜHRER LINDNER.>
<YOU SUPPOSE WELL.>
<AND... I SUPPOSE YOU ARE HERE ABOUT THE ESCAPE OF DORLEIN AND UBBIK...>
<AND FOR SOMETHING ELSE...>
<IT WILL BE BETTER IF WE GO TO MY OFFICE.>
<TAKE A SEAT, LINDNER.>
<A GLASS?>
<NO THANKS.>

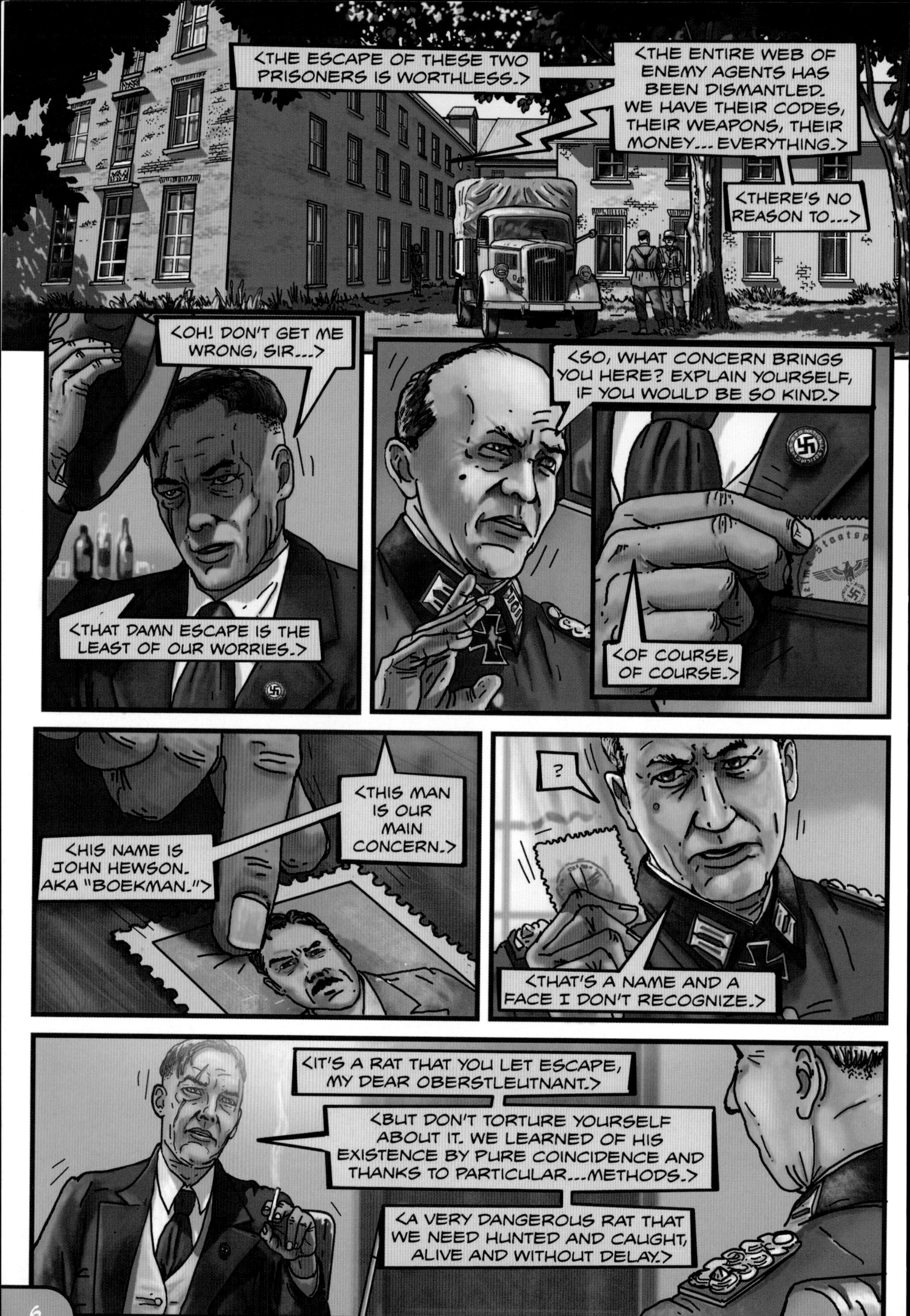
<THE ESCAPE OF THESE TWO PRISONERS IS WORTHLESS.>
<THE ENTIRE WEB OF ENEMY AGENTS HAS BEEN DISMANTLED. WE HAVE THEIR CODES, THEIR WEAPONS, THEIR MONEY... EVERYTHING.>
<THERE'S NO REASON TO...>
<OH! DON'T GET ME WRONG, SIR...>
<THAT DAMN ESCAPE IS THE LEAST OF OUR WORRIES.>
<SO, WHAT CONCERN BRINGS YOU HERE? EXPLAIN YOURSELF, IF YOU WOULD BE SO KIND.>
<OF COURSE, OF COURSE.>
<THIS MAN IS OUR MAIN CONCERN.>
<HIS NAME IS JOHN HEWSON. AKA "BOEKMAN.">
?
<THAT'S A NAME AND A FACE I DON'T RECOGNIZE.>
<IT'S A RAT THAT YOU LET ESCAPE, MY DEAR OBERSTLEUTNANT.>
<BUT DON'T TORTURE YOURSELF ABOUT IT. WE LEARNED OF HIS EXISTENCE BY PURE COINCIDENCE AND THANKS TO PARTICULAR...METHODS.>
<A VERY DANGEROUS RAT THAT WE NEED HUNTED AND CAUGHT, ALIVE AND WITHOUT DELAY.>

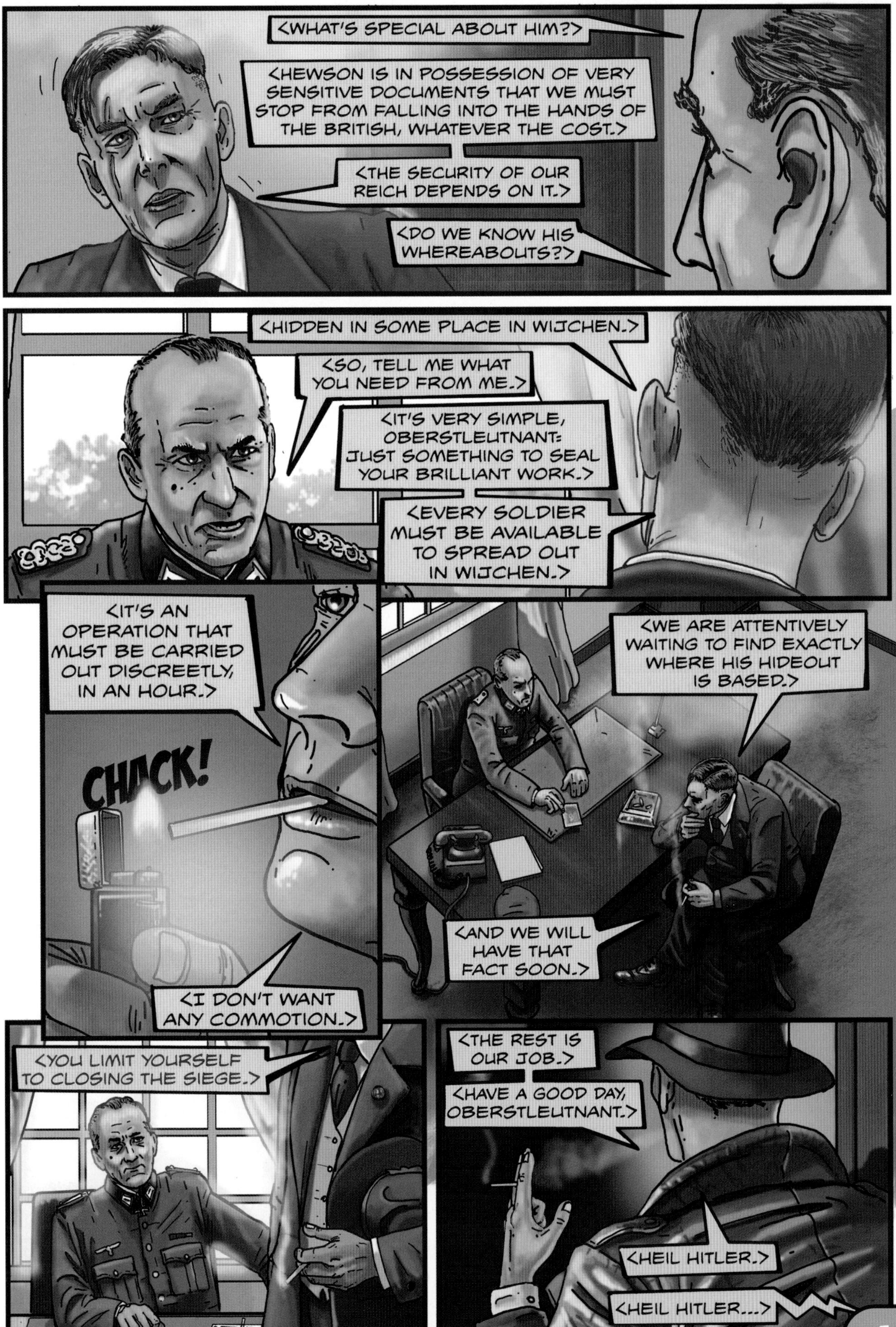
<WHAT'S SPECIAL ABOUT HIM?>
<HEWSON IS IN POSSESSION OF VERY SENSITIVE DOCUMENTS THAT WE MUST STOP FROM FALLING INTO THE HANDS OF THE BRITISH, WHATEVER THE COST.>
<THE SECURITY OF OUR REICH DEPENDS ON IT.>
<DO WE KNOW HIS WHEREABOUTS?>
<HIDDEN IN SOME PLACE IN WIJCHEN.>
<SO, TELL ME WHAT YOU NEED FROM ME.>
<IT'S VERY SIMPLE, OBERSTLEUTNANT: JUST SOMETHING TO SEAL YOUR BRILLIANT WORK.>
<EVERY SOLDIER MUST BE AVAILABLE TO SPREAD OUT IN WIJCHEN.>
<IT'S AN OPERATION THAT MUST BE CARRIED OUT DISCREETLY, IN AN HOUR.>
CHACK!
<I DON'T WANT ANY COMMOTION.>
<WE ARE ATTENTIVELY WAITING TO FIND EXACTLY WHERE HIS HIDEOUT IS BASED.>
<AND WE WILL HAVE THAT FACT SOON.>
<YOU LIMIT YOURSELF TO CLOSING THE SIEGE.>
<THE REST IS OUR JOB.>
<HAVE A GOOD DAY, OBERSTLEUTNANT.>
<HEIL HITLER.>
<HEIL HITLER...>

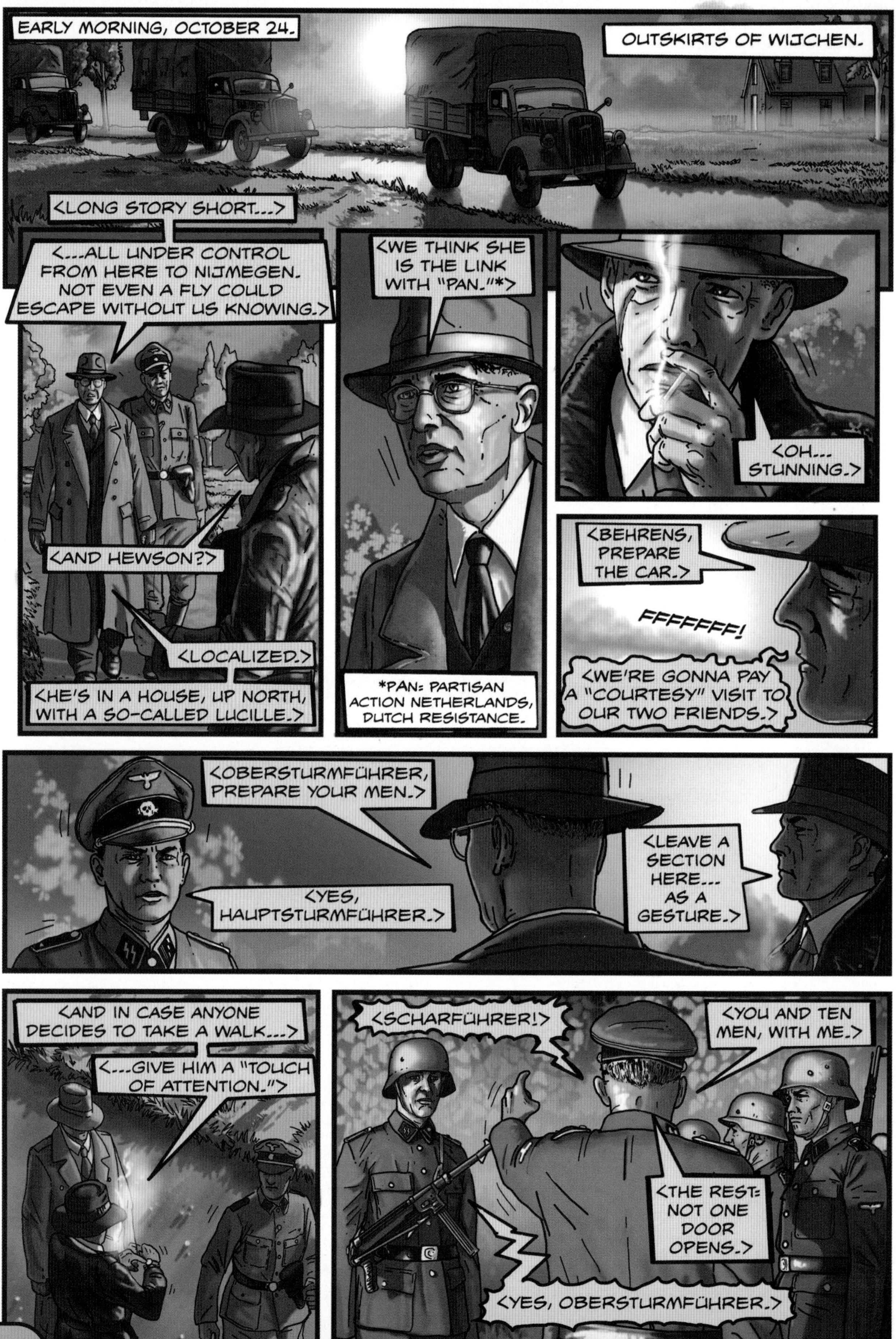

EARLY MORNING, OCTOBER 24.
OUTSKIRTS OF WIJCHEN.
<LONG STORY SHORT...>
<...ALL UNDER CONTROL FROM HERE TO NIJMEGEN. NOT EVEN A FLY COULD ESCAPE WITHOUT US KNOWING.>
<AND HEWSON?>
<LOCALIZED.>
<HE'S IN A HOUSE, UP NORTH, WITH A SO-CALLED LUCILLE.>
<WE THINK SHE IS THE LINK WITH "PAN."*>
*PAN: PARTISAN ACTION NETHERLANDS, DUTCH RESISTANCE.
<OH... STUNNING.>
<BEHRENS, PREPARE THE CAR.>
FFFFFFF!
<WE'RE GONNA PAY A "COURTESY" VISIT TO OUR TWO FRIENDS.>
<OBERSTURMFÜHRER, PREPARE YOUR MEN.>
<YES, HAUPTSTURMFÜHRER.>
<LEAVE A SECTION HERE... AS A GESTURE.>
<AND IN CASE ANYONE DECIDES TO TAKE A WALK...>
<...GIVE HIM A "TOUCH OF ATTENTION.">
<SCHARFÜHRER!>
<YOU AND TEN MEN, WITH ME.>
<THE REST: NOT ONE DOOR OPENS.>
<YES, OBERSTURMFÜHRER.>

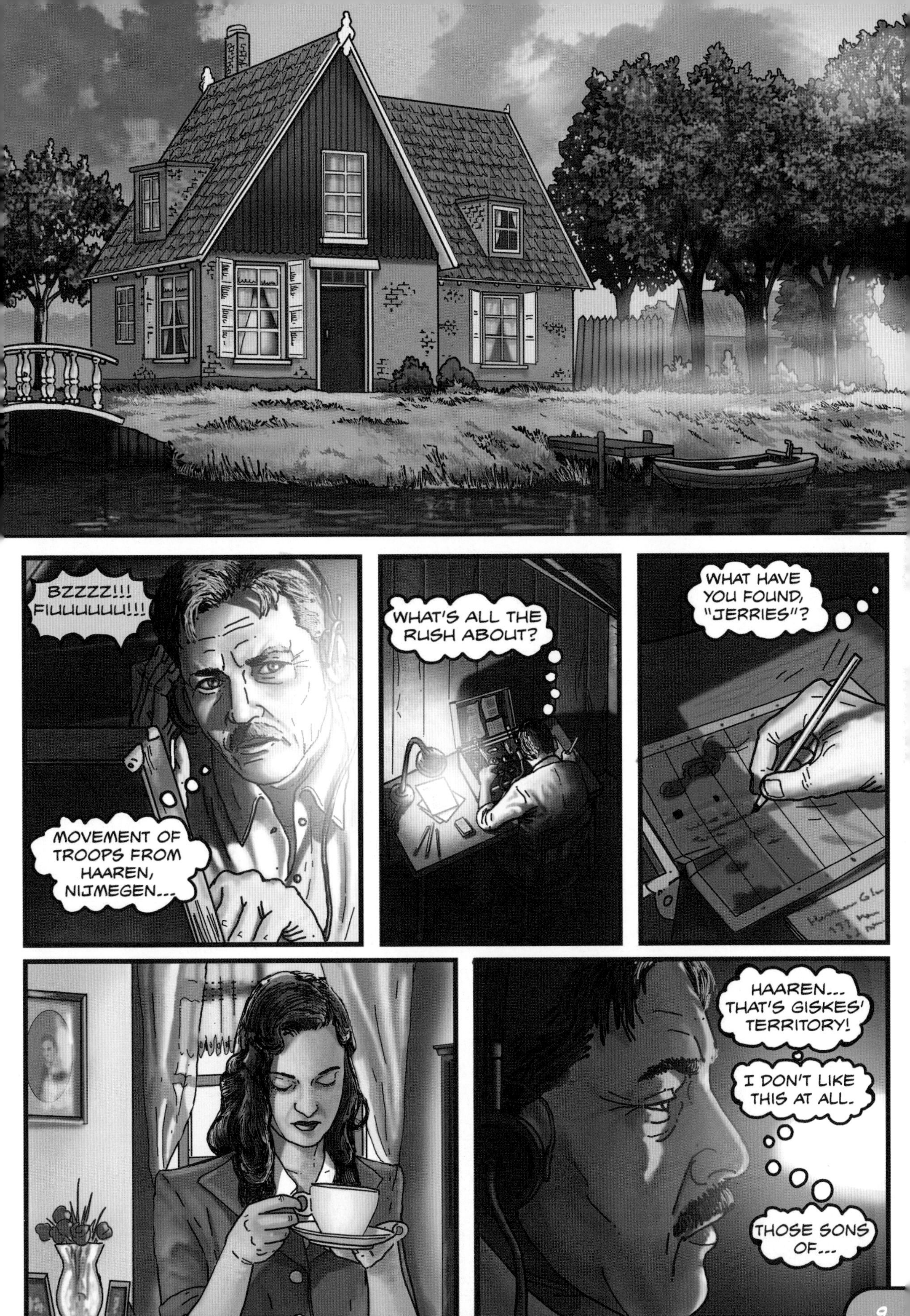

BZZZZ!!!
FIUUUUUUU!!!
MOVEMENT OF TROOPS FROM HAAREN, NIJMEGEN...
WHAT'S ALL THE RUSH ABOUT?
WHAT HAVE YOU FOUND, "JERRIES"?
HAAREN... THAT'S GISKES' TERRITORY!
I DON'T LIKE THIS AT ALL.
THOSE SONS OF...

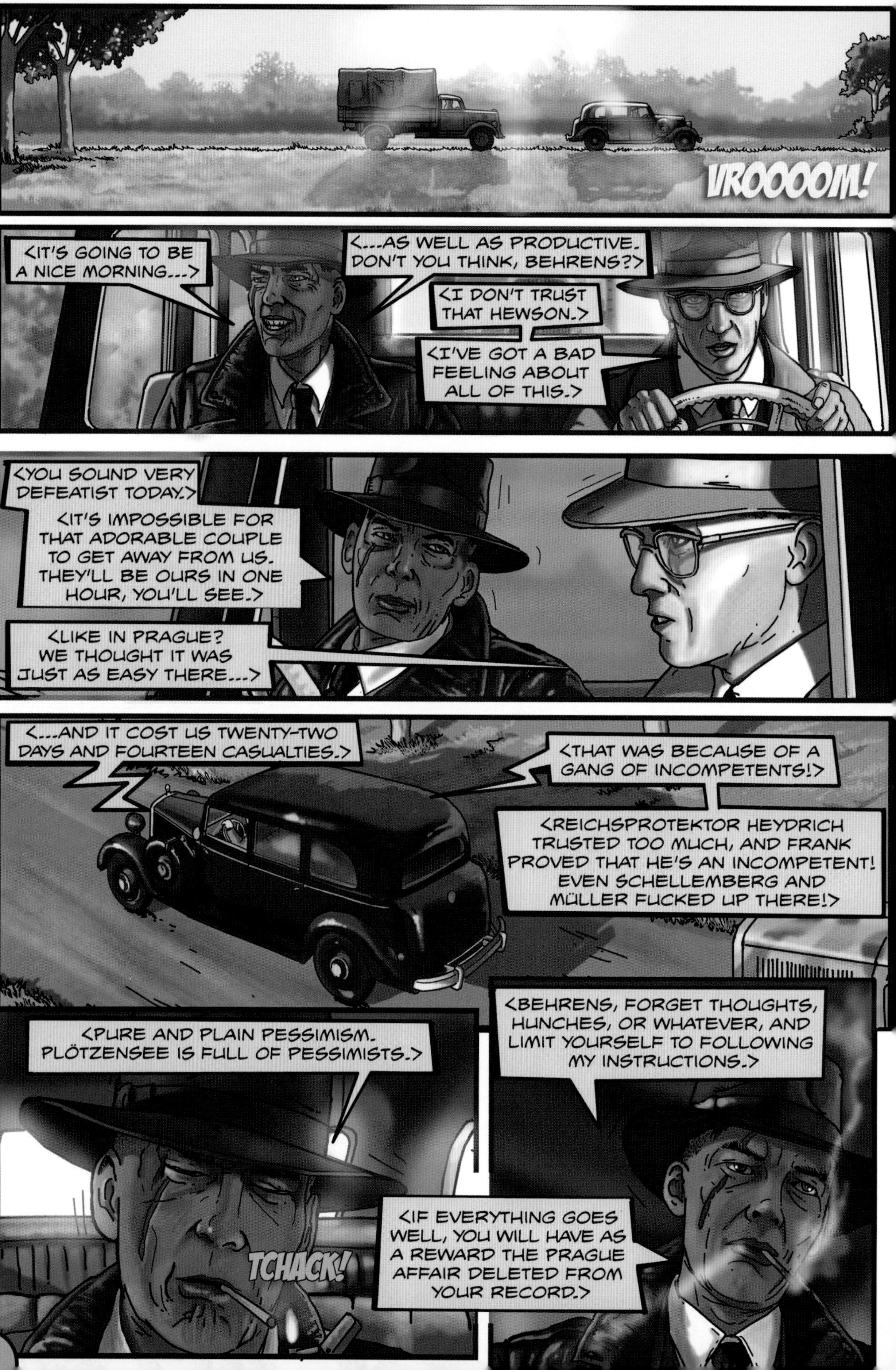
VROOOOM!
<IT'S GOING TO BE A NICE MORNING...>
<...AS WELL AS PRODUCTIVE. DON'T YOU THINK, BEHRENS?>
<I DON'T TRUST THAT HEWSON.>
<I'VE GOT A BAD FEELING ABOUT ALL OF THIS.>
<YOU SOUND VERY DEFEATIST TODAY.>
<IT'S IMPOSSIBLE FOR THAT ADORABLE COUPLE TO GET AWAY FROM US. THEY'LL BE OURS IN ONE HOUR, YOU'LL SEE.>
<LIKE IN PRAGUE? WE THOUGHT IT WAS JUST AS EASY THERE...>
<...AND IT COST US TWENTY-TWO DAYS AND FOURTEEN CASUALTIES.>
<THAT WAS BECAUSE OF A GANG OF INCOMPETENTS!>
<REICHSPROTEKTOR HEYDRICH TRUSTED TOO MUCH, AND FRANK PROVED THAT HE'S AN INCOMPETENT! EVEN SCHELLEMBERG AND MÜLLER FUCKED UP THERE!>
<PURE AND PLAIN PESSIMISM. PLÖTZENSEE IS FULL OF PESSIMISTS.>
TCHACK!
<BEHRENS, FORGET THOUGHTS, HUNCHES, OR WHATEVER, AND LIMIT YOURSELF TO FOLLOWING MY INSTRUCTIONS.>
<IF EVERYTHING GOES WELL, YOU WILL HAVE AS A REWARD THE PRAGUE AFFAIR DELETED FROM YOUR RECORD.>

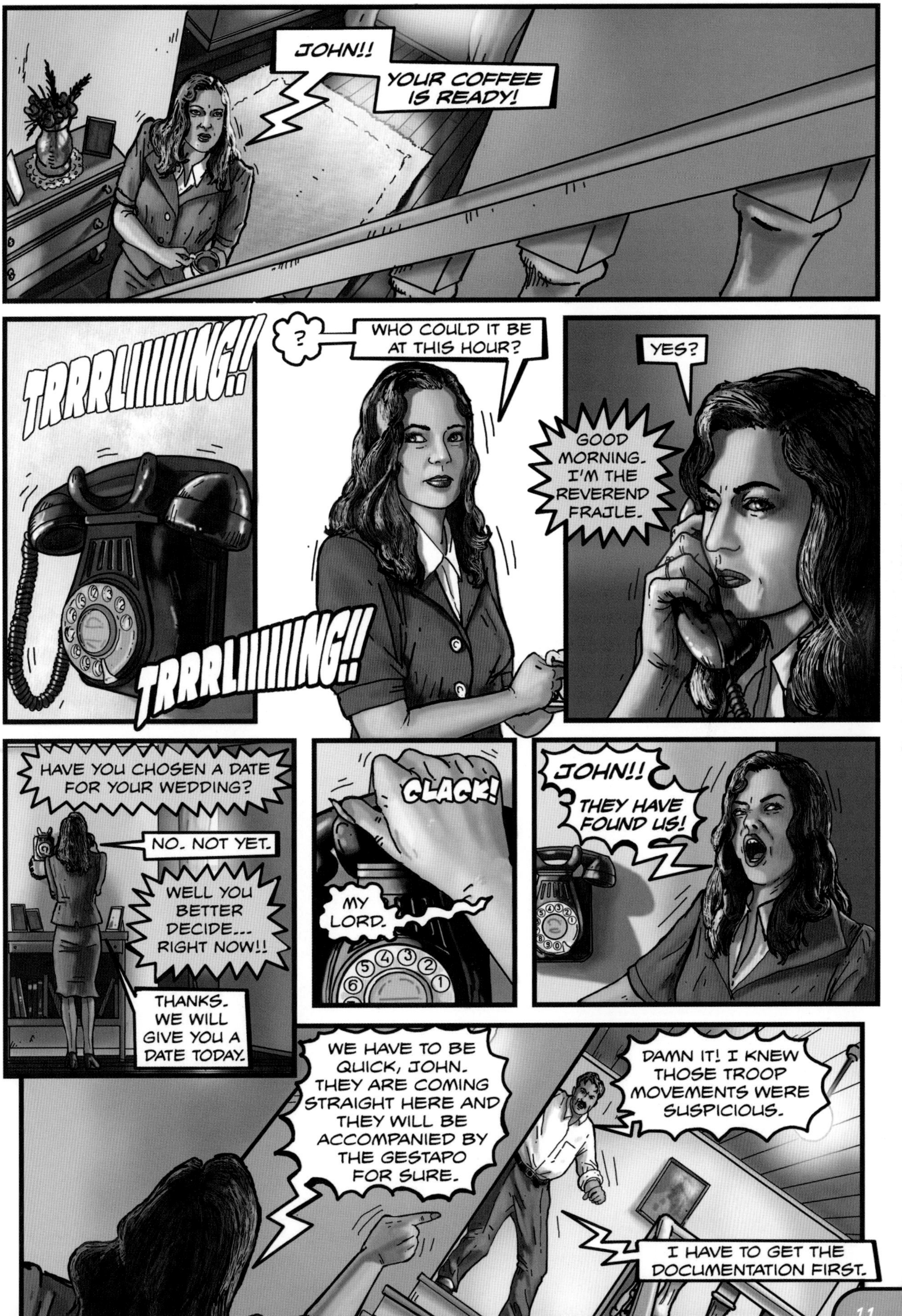
JOHN!!
YOUR COFFEE IS READY!
TRRRLIIIIIIING!!
?
WHO COULD IT BE AT THIS HOUR?
TRRRLIIIIIIING!!
YES?
GOOD MORNING. I'M THE REVEREND FRAJLE.
HAVE YOU CHOSEN A DATE FOR YOUR WEDDING?
NO. NOT YET.
WELL YOU BETTER DECIDE... RIGHT NOW!!
THANKS. WE WILL GIVE YOU A DATE TODAY.
CLACK!
MY LORD.
JOHN!!
THEY HAVE FOUND US!
WE HAVE TO BE QUICK, JOHN. THEY ARE COMING STRAIGHT HERE AND THEY WILL BE ACCOMPANIED BY THE GESTAPO FOR SURE.
DAMN IT! I KNEW THOSE TROOP MOVEMENTS WERE SUSPICIOUS.
I HAVE TO GET THE DOCUMENTATION FIRST.

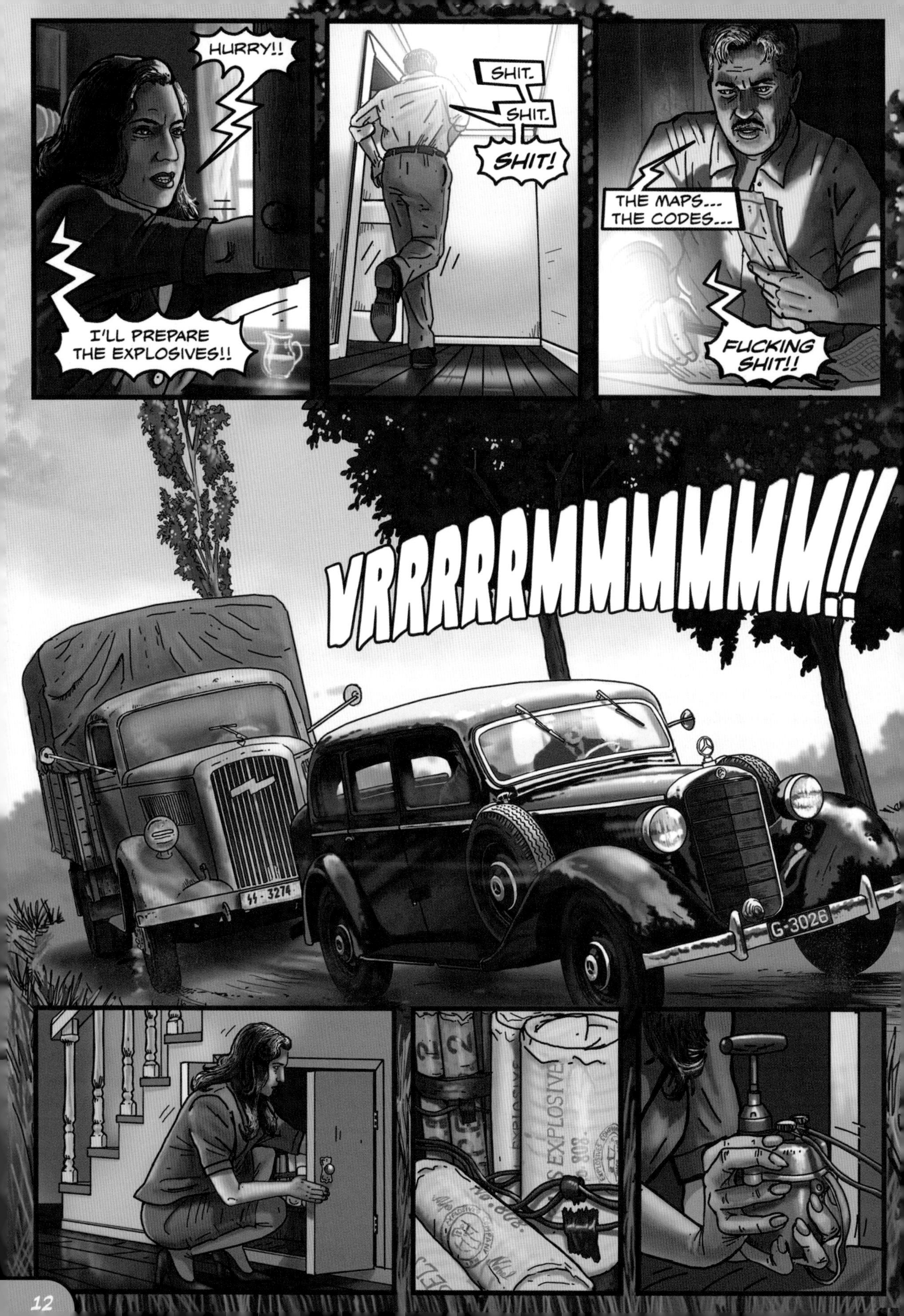
HURRY!!
I'LL PREPARE THE EXPLOSIVES!!
SHIT.
SHIT.
SHIT!
THE MAPS... THE CODES...
FUCKING SHIT!!
VRRRRRMMMMMM!!
SS-3274
G-3026
EXPLOSIVE

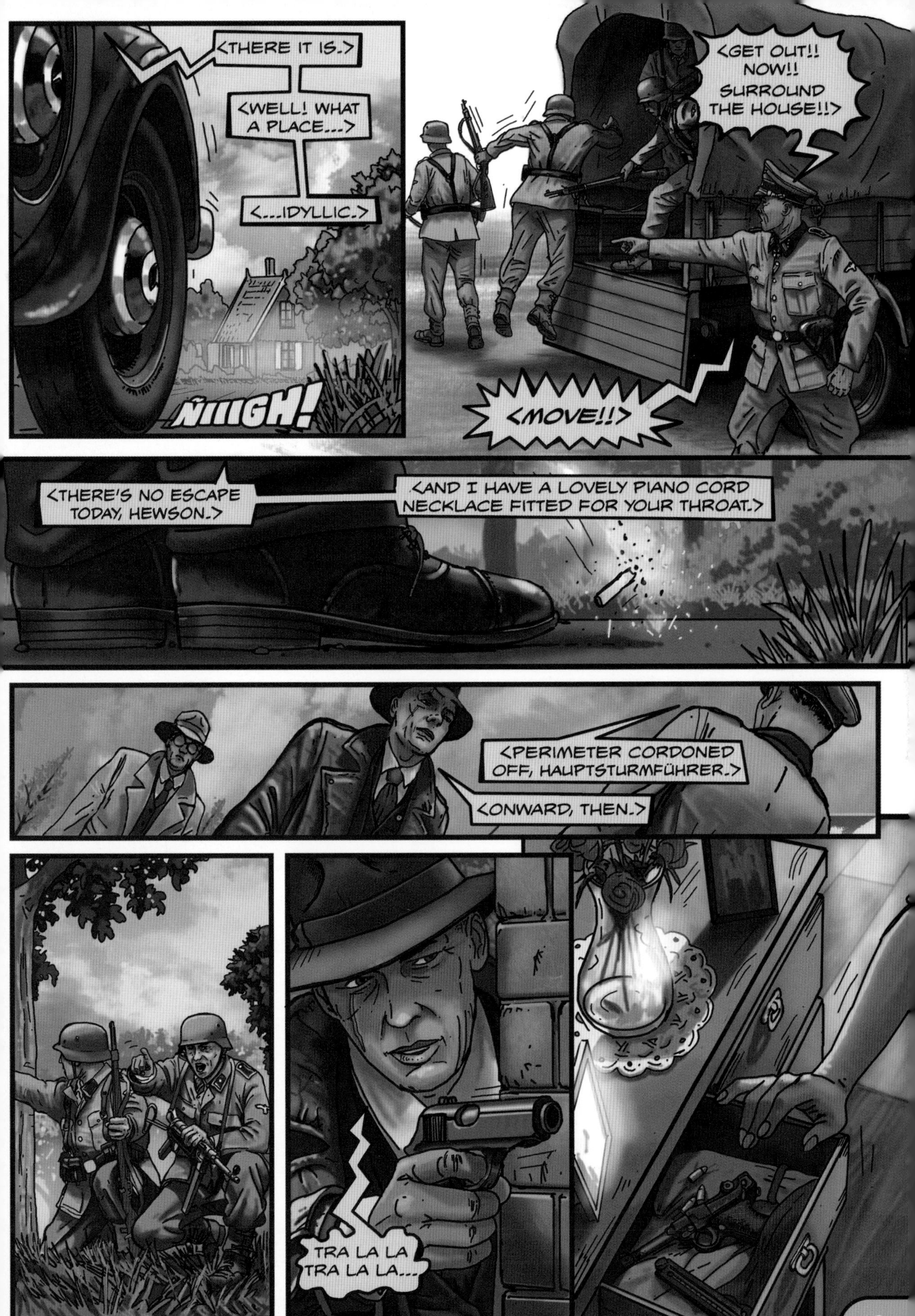
<THERE IT IS.>
<WELL! WHAT A PLACE...>
<...IDYLLIC.>
ÑIIIGH!
<GET OUT!! NOW!! SURROUND THE HOUSE!!>
<MOVE!!>
<THERE'S NO ESCAPE TODAY, HEWSON.>
<AND I HAVE A LOVELY PIANO CORD NECKLACE FITTED FOR YOUR THROAT.>
<PERIMETER CORDONED OFF, HAUPTSTURMFÜHRER.>
<ONWARD, THEN.>
TRA LA LA TRA LA LA...

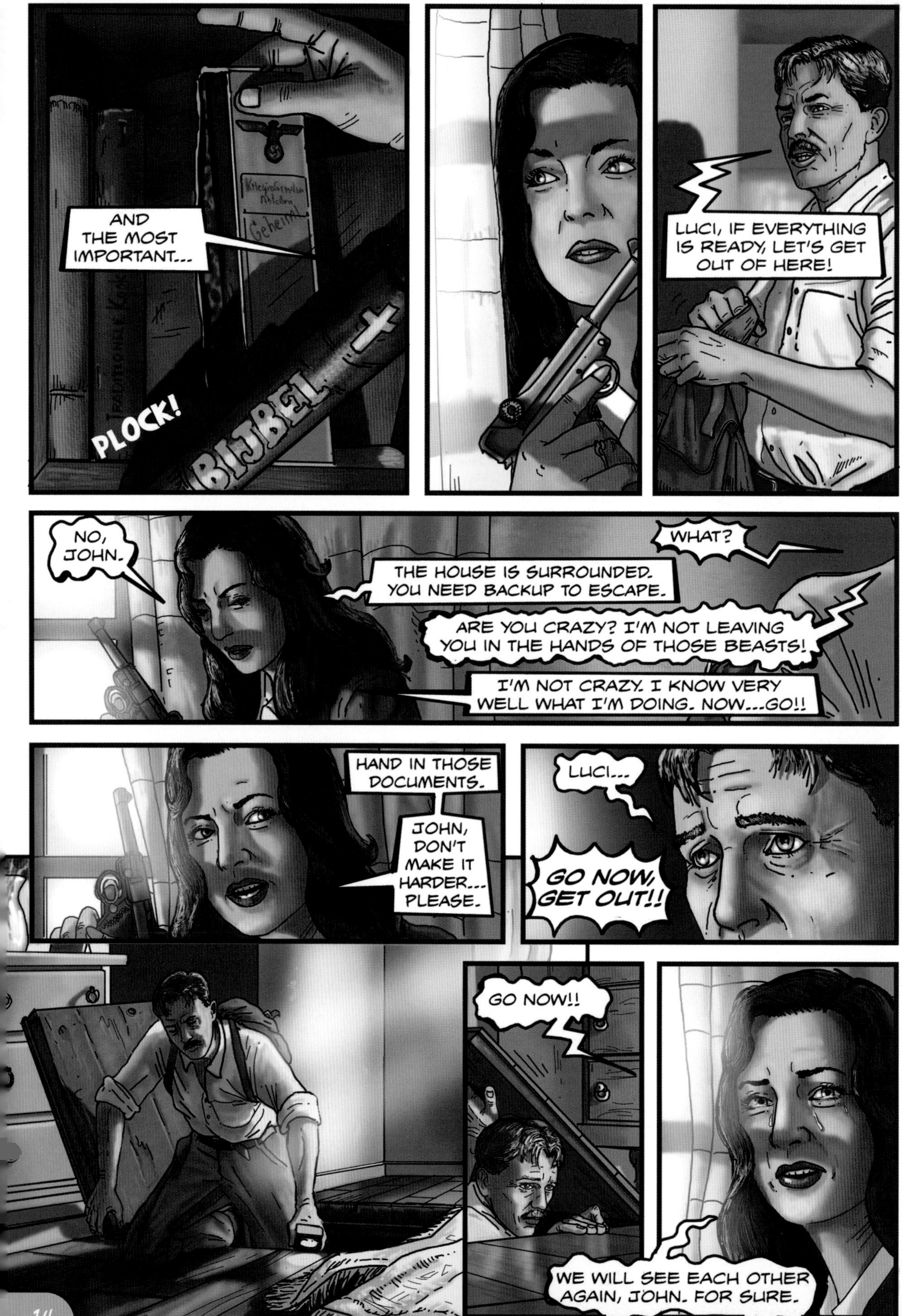
AND THE MOST IMPORTANT...
BIJBEL
PLOCK!
LUCI, IF EVERYTHING IS READY, LET'S GET OUT OF HERE!
NO, JOHN.
WHAT?
THE HOUSE IS SURROUNDED. YOU NEED BACKUP TO ESCAPE.
ARE YOU CRAZY? I'M NOT LEAVING YOU IN THE HANDS OF THOSE BEASTS!
I'M NOT CRAZY. I KNOW VERY WELL WHAT I'M DOING. NOW...GO!!
HAND IN THOSE DOCUMENTS.
JOHN, DON'T MAKE IT HARDER... PLEASE.
LUCI...
GO NOW, GET OUT!!
GO NOW!!
WE WILL SEE EACH OTHER AGAIN, JOHN. FOR SURE.

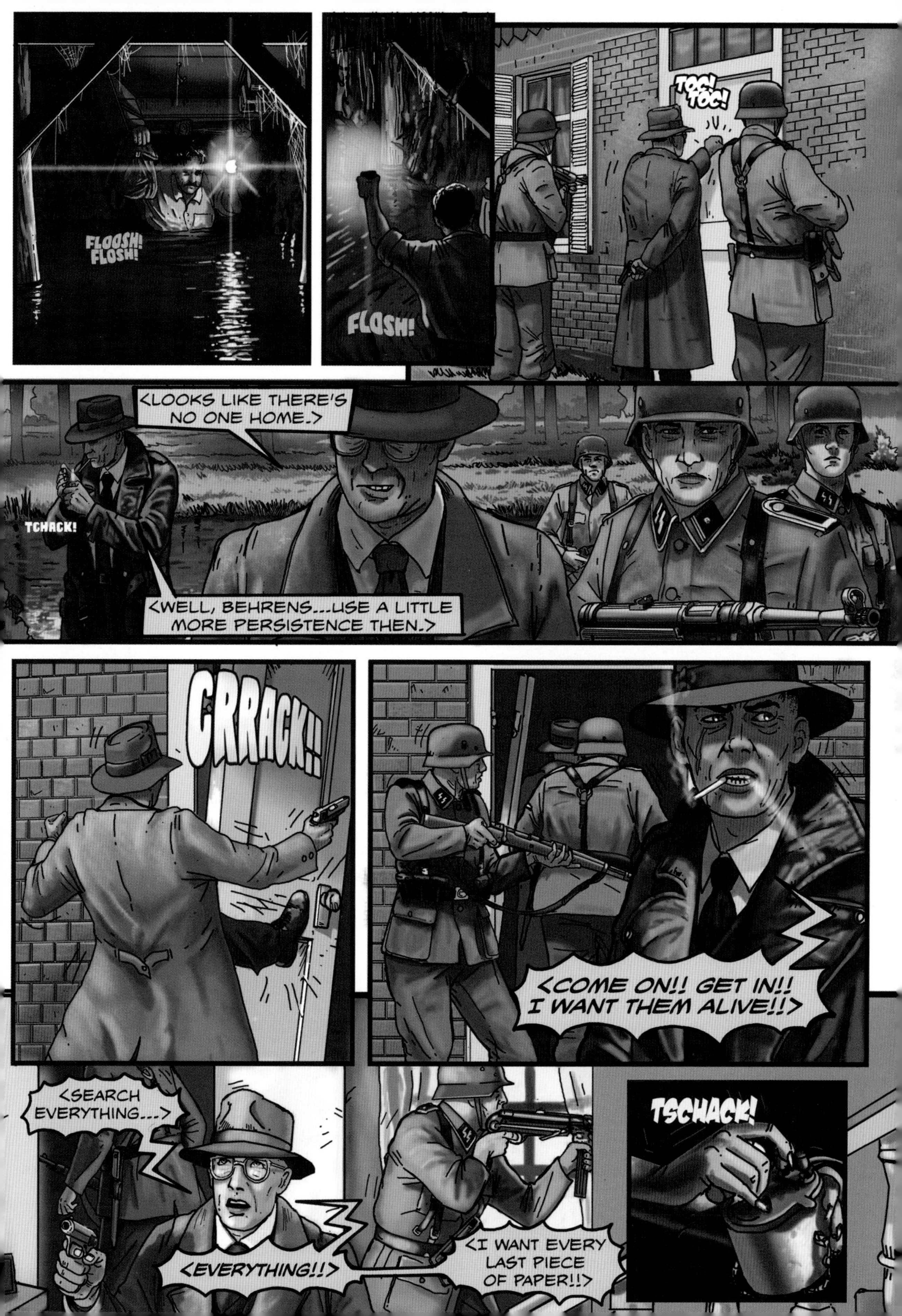

FLOOSH! FLOSH!
FLOSH!
TOC! TOC!
<LOOKS LIKE THERE'S NO ONE HOME.>
TCHACK!
<WELL, BEHRENS...USE A LITTLE MORE PERSISTENCE THEN.>
CRRACK!!
<COME ON!! GET IN!! I WANT THEM ALIVE!!>
<SEARCH EVERYTHING...>
<EVERYTHING!!>
<I WANT EVERY LAST PIECE OF PAPER!!>
TSCHACK!

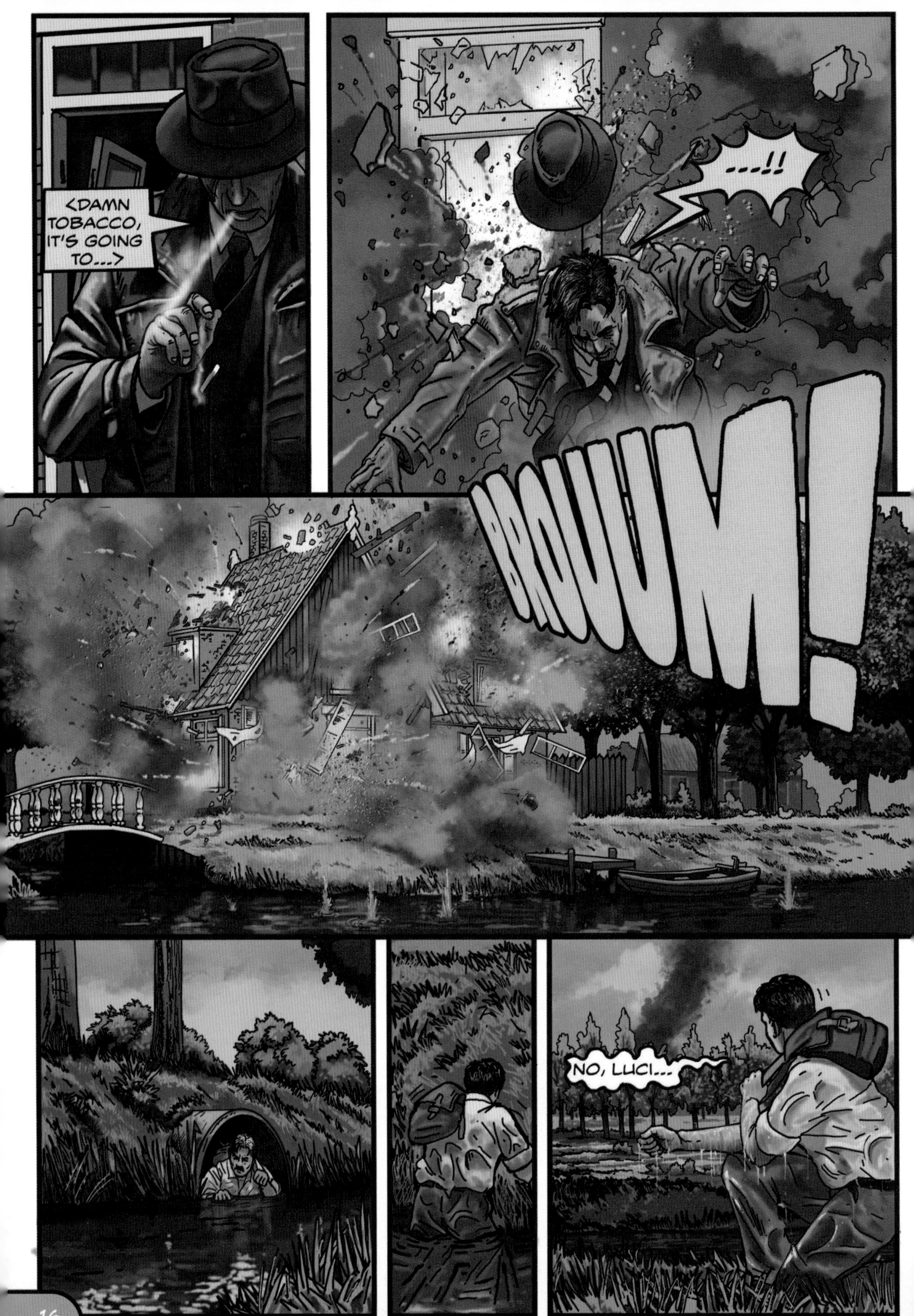
<DAMN TOBACCO, IT'S GOING TO...>
...!!
BROUUUM!
NO, LUCI...

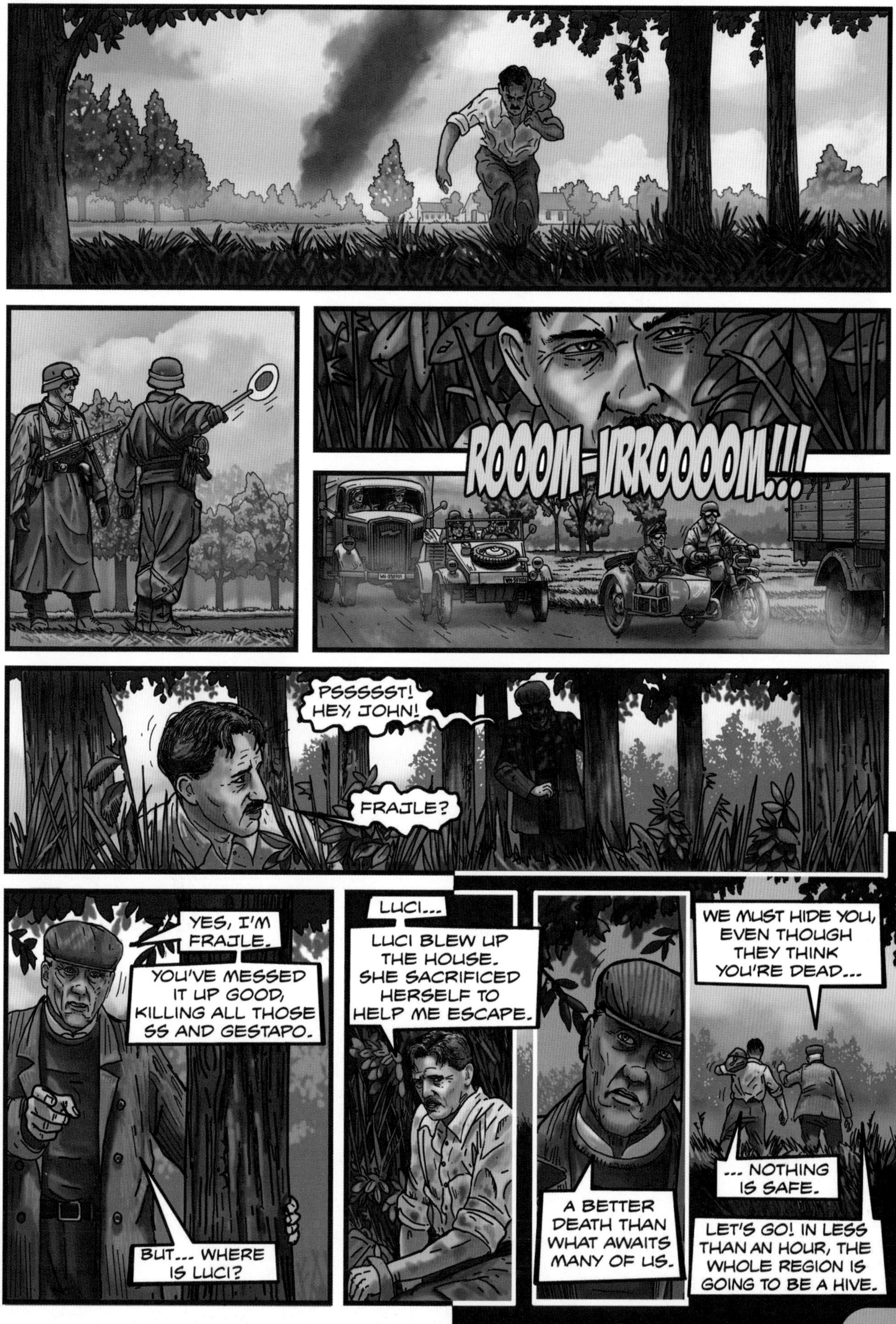
ROOOM-VRROOOOM!!!
PSSSSST! HEY, JOHN!
FRAJLE?
YES, I'M FRAJLE.
YOU'VE MESSED IT UP GOOD, KILLING ALL THOSE SS AND GESTAPO.
BUT... WHERE IS LUCI?
LUCI...
LUCI BLEW UP THE HOUSE. SHE SACRIFICED HERSELF TO HELP ME ESCAPE.
A BETTER DEATH THAN WHAT AWAITS MANY OF US.
WE MUST HIDE YOU, EVEN THOUGH THEY THINK YOU'RE DEAD...
... NOTHING IS SAFE.
LET'S GO! IN LESS THAN AN HOUR, THE WHOLE REGION IS GOING TO BE A HIVE.

The Allied Persecution

AUGUST 26 TO SEPTEMBER 11, 1944

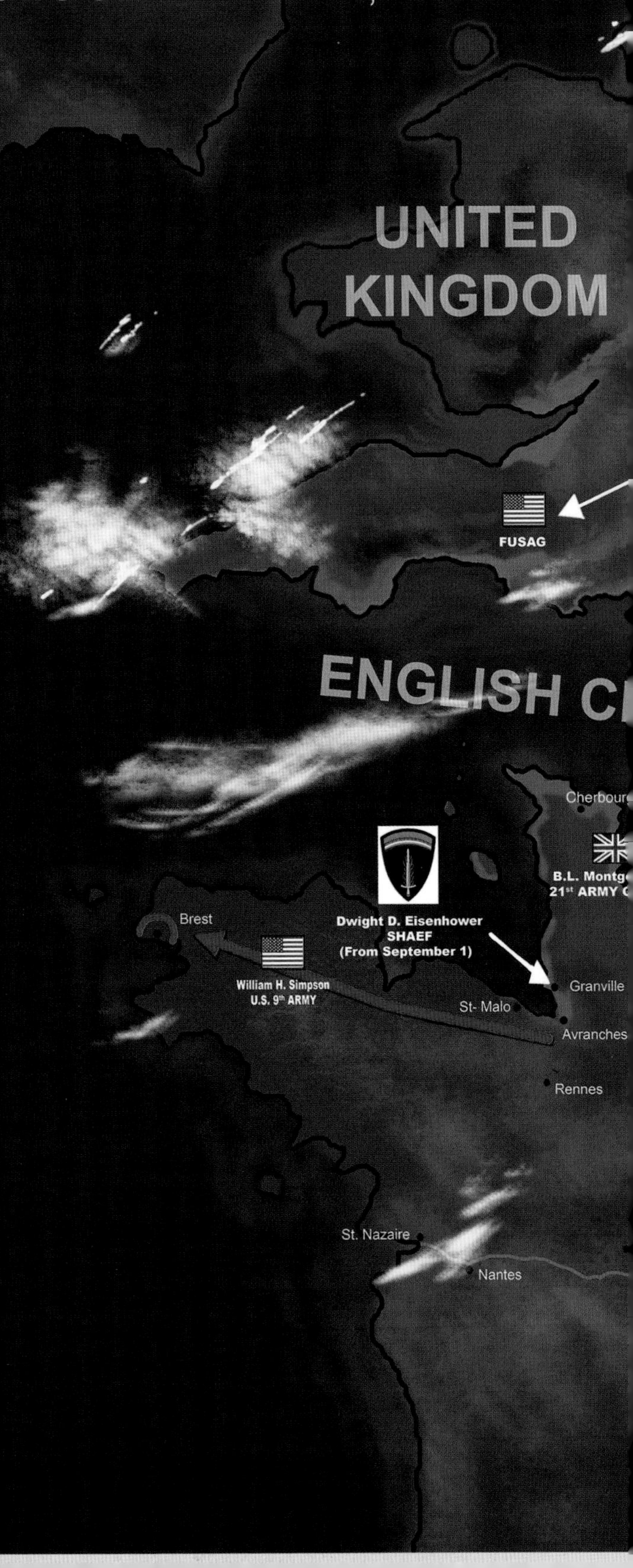

UNITED KINGDOM
FUSAG
Cherbour
B.L. Montg
21st ARMY
Dwight D. Eisenhower
SHAEF
(From September 1)
Brest
William H. Simpson
U.S. 9th ARMY
Granville
St- Malo
Avranches
Rennes
St. Nazaire
Nantes

THROUGHOUT THE DECISIVE SUCCESSES OF THE ALLIES AFTER THEIR LANDINGS IN NORMANDY, IT WAS LOGICAL TO ASSUME THAT THE GERMAN TROOPS WOULD RETREAT TOWARD THE NORTHEAST, THAT BEING THEIR ONLY ESCAPE ROUTE.

THE OPERATIONS AND BATTLES THAT TOOK PLACE BETWEEN JUNE AND SEPTEMBER OF 1944 LEFT THE WEHRMACHT ON THE EDGE OF COLLAPSE: OPERATION COBRA, OPERATION TOTALIZE, AND OPERATION ANVIL IN THE SOUTHEAST OF FRANCE. OPERATION ANVIL, RENAMED OPERATION DRAGOON, TOOK PLACE BETWEEN TOULON AND CANNES, FROM WHERE THE U.S. SEVENTH ARMY WAS TO HEAD UP NORTH. BUT AFTER THE FAILED SIEGE OF FALAISE IN AUGUST, BECAUSE OF THE STUBBORN GERMAN RESISTANCE AND THE IMPRISONMENT OF THE ALLIED FORCES IN CHAMBOIS, THERE WAS A GAP CREATED THROUGH WHICH APPROXIMATELY 100,000 MEN FROM THE GERMAN SEVENTH ARMY AND THE FIFTH PANZER ARMY ESCAPED. SOME HISTORIANS BLAME FIELD MARSHAL BERNARD MONTGOMERY, AND OTHERS CITE GEN. OMAR BRADLEY'S DECISION TO NOT CROSS THE ASSIGNED LINES.

THIS IS HOW THE CHASE BEGAN, IN VARIOUS DIRECTIONS, WHICH WOULD LEAVE THE FRONT STAGNANT AND STILL BLOCKED: GENERAL HARRY CRERAR AND LIEUTENANT GENERAL MILES DEMPSEY CARRIED ON NORTH, GEN. COURTNEY HODGES VEERED SLIGHTLY NORTHEAST, AND GEN. GEORGE PATTON MOVED EAST. EVEN THOUGH THEY FREED CITIES ON THEIR WAY, THE ENEMY'S RESISTANCE TURNED MORE FIERCE. FOR EXAMPLE, GENERAL BRIAN HORROCKS, IN COMMAND OF THE BRITISH XXX CORPS, HAD TO MAKE FULL USE OF THE MARSHLANDS OF BELGIUM, WHICH THE HITLERJUGEND HAD TURNED INTO TRAPS. HORROCKS WAS ABLE TO FREE BRUSSELS ON SEPTEMBER 3 AND ANTWERP ON SEPTEMBER 4, AFTER WHICH ANTWERP WOULD BE LEFT BOTTLED UP.

ON SEPTEMBER 4, GEN. DWIGHT D. EISENHOWER, NOW AT THE HEAD OF THE SUPREME HEADQUARTERS ALLIED EXPEDITIONARY FORCE (SHAEF), ACCEPTED THE PLAN OF "DOUBLE EFFORT" PLANNED BY MONTGOMERY, AND ON SEPTEMBER 10 OPERATION MARKET GARDEN WAS APPROVED.

THAT SAME AFTERNOON, THE ARMORED DIVISION OF THE IRISH GUARDS CAPTURED BRIDGE NO. 9, "JOE'S BRIDGE," OVER THE BOCHOLT-HERENTALS CANAL AT THE OUTSKIRTS OF NEERPELT, BELGIUM.

THE BATTLE FOR THE NETHERLANDS HAD BEGUN.

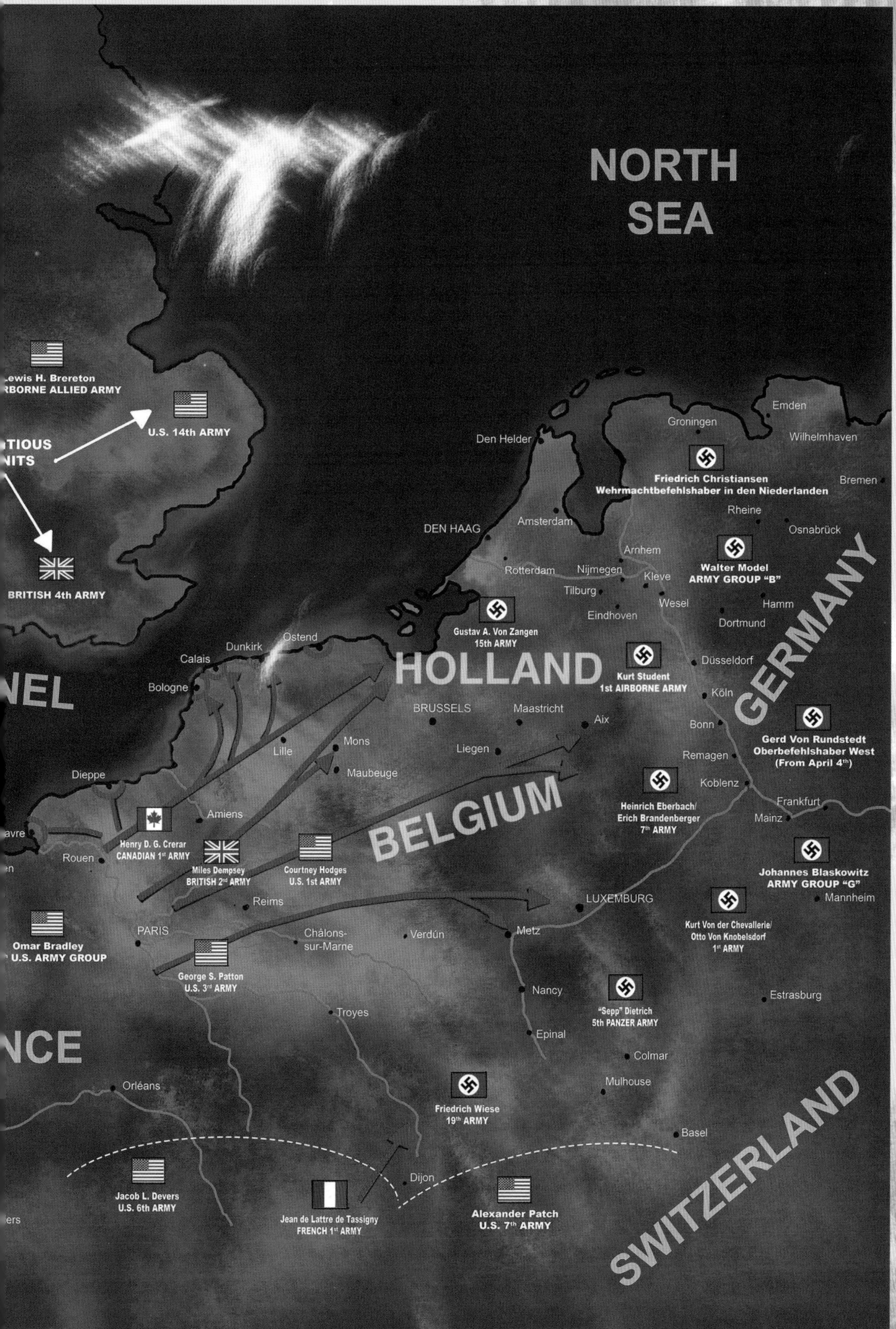
NORTH SEA
Lewis H. Brereton
RBORNE ALLIED ARMY
U.S. 14th ARMY
TIOUS
NITS
BRITISH 4th ARMY
Den Helder
Groningen
Emden
Wilhelmhaven
Friedrich Christiansen
Wehrmachtbefehlshaber in den Niederlanden
Bremen
Rheine
Osnabrück
DEN HAAG
Amsterdam
Arnhem
Walter Model
ARMY GROUP "B"
Rotterdam
Nijmegen
Kleve
Tilburg
Wesel
Hamm
Eindhoven
Dortmund
GERMANY
Gustav A. Von Zangen
15th ARMY
Dunkirk
Ostend
Calais
HOLLAND
Kurt Student
1st AIRBORNE ARMY
Düsseldorf
NEL
Bologne
Köln
BRUSSELS
Maastricht
Aix
Bonn
Gerd Von Rundstedt
Oberbefehlshaber West
(From April 4th)
Mons
Lille
Liegen
Remagen
Dieppe
Maubeuge
Koblenz
Heinrich Eberbach/
Erich Brandenberger
7th ARMY
Frankfurt
Amiens
BELGIUM
Mainz
avre
Henry D. G. Crerar
CANADIAN 1st ARMY
Rouen
Miles Dempsey
BRITISH 2nd ARMY
Courtney Hodges
U.S. 1st ARMY
Johannes Blaskowitz
ARMY GROUP "G"
Mannheim
Reims
LUXEMBURG
Kurt Von der Chevallerie/
Otto Von Knobelsdorf
1st ARMY
PARIS
Châlons-sur-Marne
Verdún
Metz
Omar Bradley
U.S. ARMY GROUP
George S. Patton
U.S. 3rd ARMY
Nancy
"Sepp" Dietrich
5th PANZER ARMY
Estrasburg
Troyes
Epinal
NCE
Colmar
Mulhouse
Orléans
Friedrich Wiese
19th ARMY
SWITZERLAND
Basel
Dijon
Jacob L. Devers
U.S. 6th ARMY
Jean de Lattre de Tassigny
FRENCH 1st ARMY
Alexander Patch
U.S. 7th ARMY

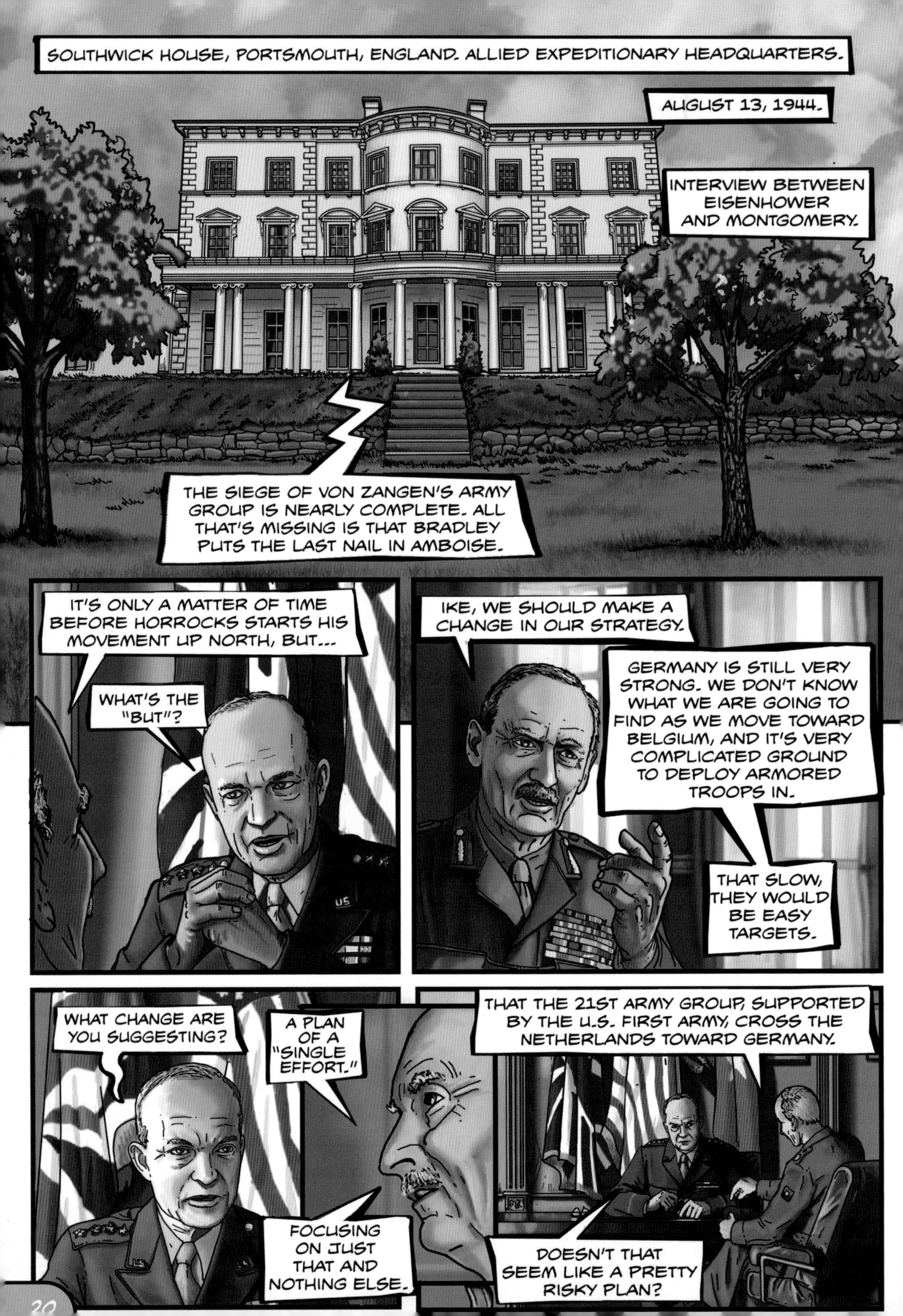
SOUTHWICK HOUSE, PORTSMOUTH, ENGLAND. ALLIED EXPEDITIONARY HEADQUARTERS.
AUGUST 13, 1944.
INTERVIEW BETWEEN EISENHOWER AND MONTGOMERY.
THE SIEGE OF VON ZANGEN'S ARMY GROUP IS NEARLY COMPLETE. ALL THAT'S MISSING IS THAT BRADLEY PUTS THE LAST NAIL IN AMBOISE.
IT'S ONLY A MATTER OF TIME BEFORE HORROCKS STARTS HIS MOVEMENT UP NORTH, BUT...
WHAT'S THE "BUT"?
IKE, WE SHOULD MAKE A CHANGE IN OUR STRATEGY.
GERMANY IS STILL VERY STRONG. WE DON'T KNOW WHAT WE ARE GOING TO FIND AS WE MOVE TOWARD BELGIUM, AND IT'S VERY COMPLICATED GROUND TO DEPLOY ARMORED TROOPS IN.
THAT SLOW, THEY WOULD BE EASY TARGETS.
WHAT CHANGE ARE YOU SUGGESTING?
A PLAN OF A "SINGLE EFFORT."
FOCUSING ON JUST THAT AND NOTHING ELSE.
THAT THE 21ST ARMY GROUP, SUPPORTED BY THE U.S. FIRST ARMY, CROSS THE NETHERLANDS TOWARD GERMANY.
DOESN'T THAT SEEM LIKE A PRETTY RISKY PLAN?

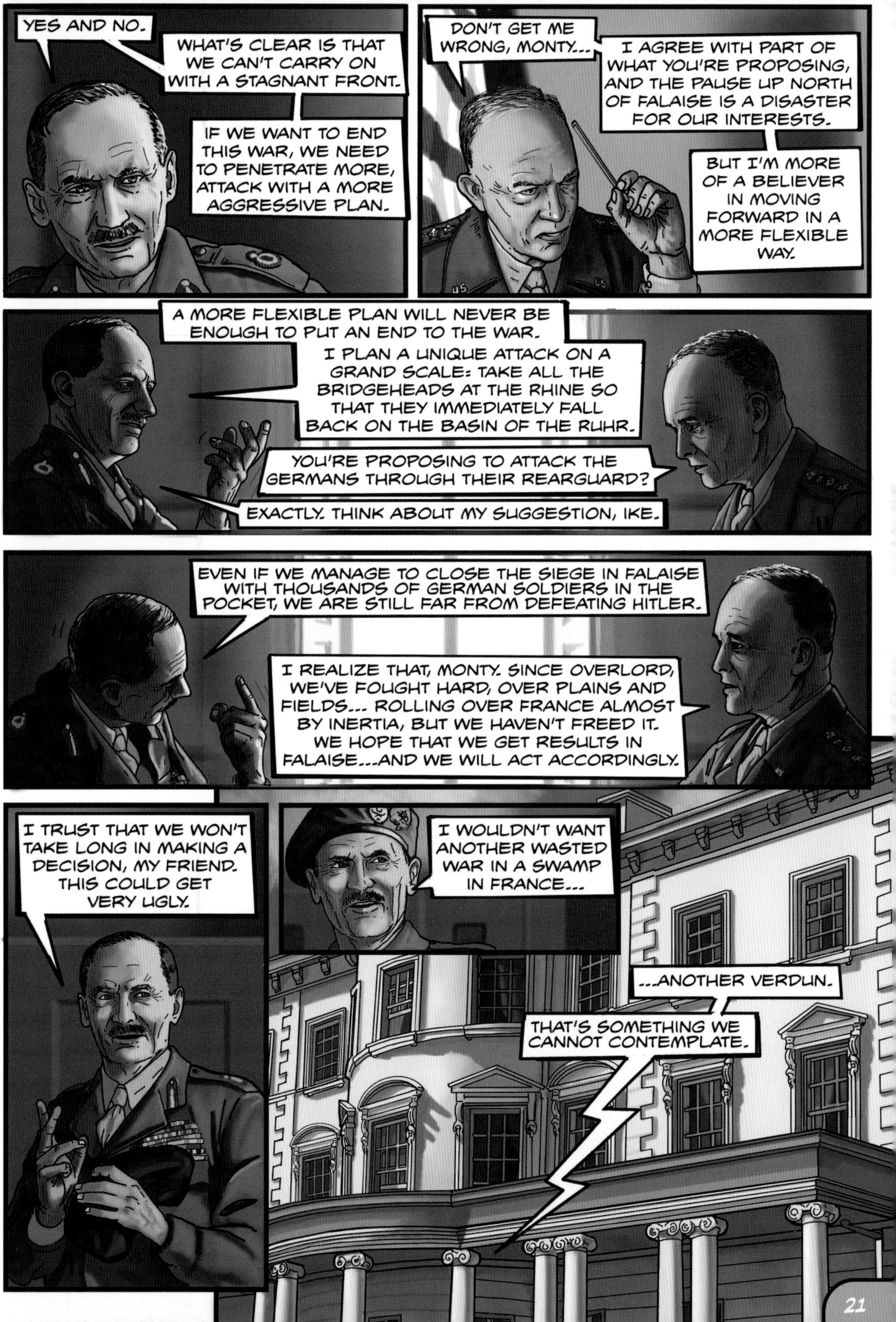
YES AND NO.
WHAT'S CLEAR IS THAT WE CAN'T CARRY ON WITH A STAGNANT FRONT.
IF WE WANT TO END THIS WAR, WE NEED TO PENETRATE MORE, ATTACK WITH A MORE AGGRESSIVE PLAN.
DON'T GET ME WRONG, MONTY...
I AGREE WITH PART OF WHAT YOU'RE PROPOSING, AND THE PAUSE UP NORTH OF FALAISE IS A DISASTER FOR OUR INTERESTS.
BUT I'M MORE OF A BELIEVER IN MOVING FORWARD IN A MORE FLEXIBLE WAY.
A MORE FLEXIBLE PLAN WILL NEVER BE ENOUGH TO PUT AN END TO THE WAR.
I PLAN A UNIQUE ATTACK ON A GRAND SCALE: TAKE ALL THE BRIDGEHEADS AT THE RHINE SO THAT THEY IMMEDIATELY FALL BACK ON THE BASIN OF THE RUHR.
YOU'RE PROPOSING TO ATTACK THE GERMANS THROUGH THEIR REARGUARD?
EXACTLY. THINK ABOUT MY SUGGESTION, IKE.
EVEN IF WE MANAGE TO CLOSE THE SIEGE IN FALAISE WITH THOUSANDS OF GERMAN SOLDIERS IN THE POCKET, WE ARE STILL FAR FROM DEFEATING HITLER.
I REALIZE THAT, MONTY. SINCE OVERLORD, WE'VE FOUGHT HARD, OVER PLAINS AND FIELDS... ROLLING OVER FRANCE ALMOST BY INERTIA, BUT WE HAVEN'T FREED IT. WE HOPE THAT WE GET RESULTS IN FALAISE...AND WE WILL ACT ACCORDINGLY.
I TRUST THAT WE WON'T TAKE LONG IN MAKING A DECISION, MY FRIEND. THIS COULD GET VERY UGLY.
I WOULDN'T WANT ANOTHER WASTED WAR IN A SWAMP IN FRANCE...
...ANOTHER VERDUN.
THAT'S SOMETHING WE CANNOT CONTEMPLATE.

I DON'T WANT TO THINK ABOUT THAT EITHER.

ANYWAY, ROOSEVELT, MARSHALL, AND THE MILITARY STAFF WON'T LET ME BREATHE. AND AS FOR DE GAULLE...

THAT DAMN GENERAL WANTS TO BE THE LIBERATOR OF FRANCE, TO ENTER IT LIKE THE REINCARNATION OF NAPOLEON, LIKE THE GRAND VICTOR OF THE WAR. AS IF BEING PROCLAIMED THE COMMANDER OF FREE FRANCE HAS GIVEN HIM A LITTLE TASTE OF GLORY, AND NOW HE WANTS MORE.

MONTY...

YOUR PLANS ARE NOT THE ONLY ONES THAT HAVE BEEN PROPOSED TO ME.

THE BRITISH HAVE THEIR IDEAS, AS DO THE AMERICANS.

THAT'S HOW THE RACE FOR POWER GOES.

THOSE BRIDGEHEADS IN HOLLAND ARE OUR BEST CHANCE, BELIEVE ME.

YES, BUT I HAVE DOUBTS.

UNTIL I RECEIVE SUPREME CONTROL OF THE ALLIED FORCES, I DON'T DARE CHANGE WHAT'S PLANNED FOR...

...A SUGGESTION.

EVEN SO, MONTY, WE'LL STUDY IT THOROUGHLY. WE STILL DON'T KNOW WHAT TYPES OF ENEMY TROOPS COULD BE WAITING FOR US, NOT ONLY IN HOLLAND...

...BUT BEYOND, ON THE MILES STILL LEFT TO CONQUER.

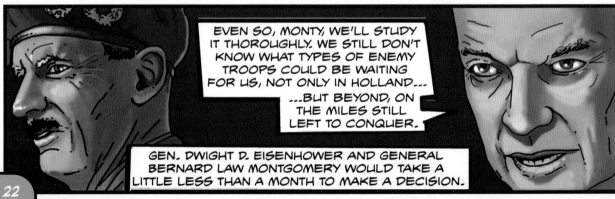

GEN. DWIGHT D. EISENHOWER AND GENERAL BERNARD LAW MONTGOMERY WOULD TAKE A LITTLE LESS THAN A MONTH TO MAKE A DECISION.

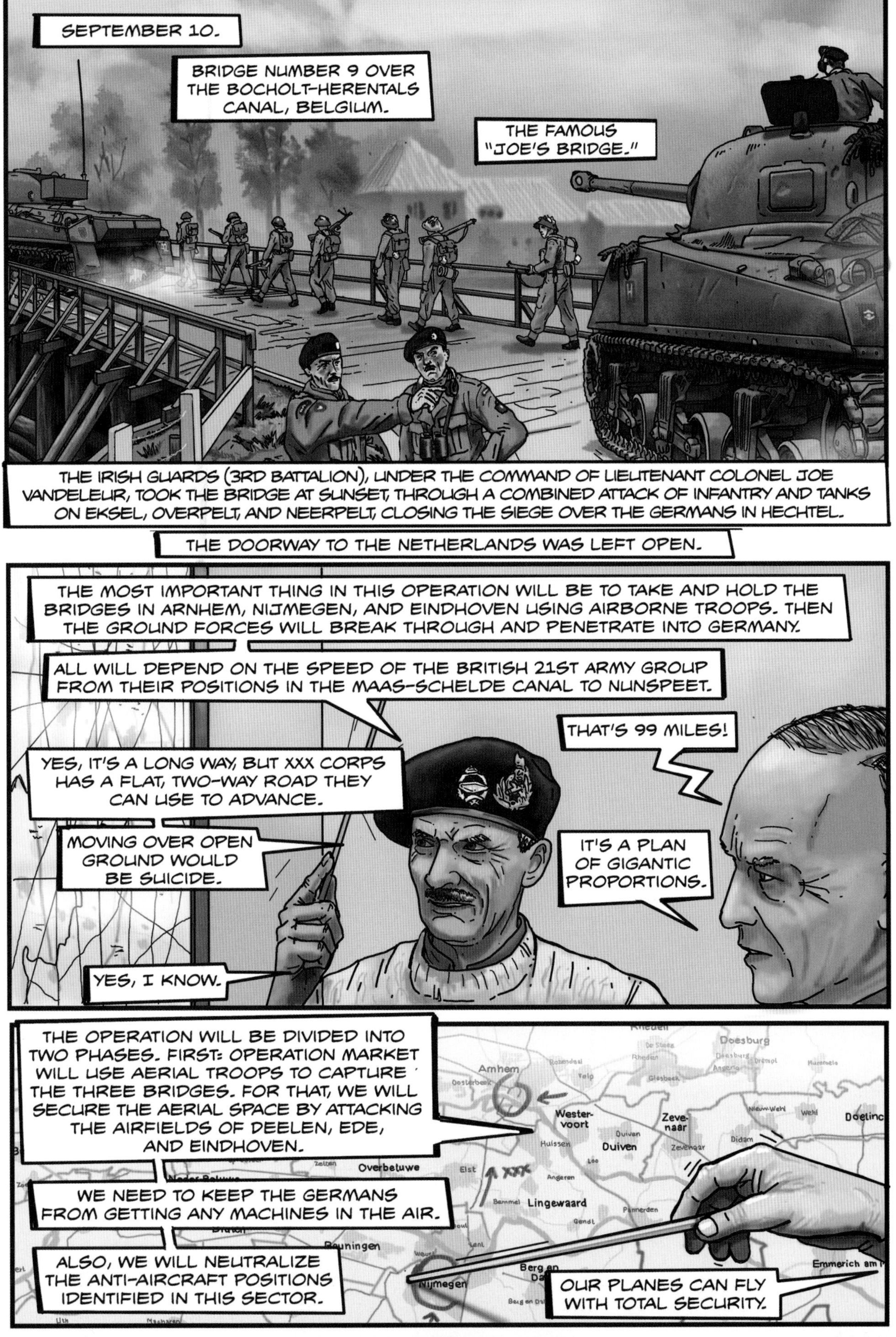
SEPTEMBER 10.
BRIDGE NUMBER 9 OVER THE BOCHOLT-HERENTALS CANAL, BELGIUM.
THE FAMOUS "JOE'S BRIDGE."
THE IRISH GUARDS (3RD BATTALION), UNDER THE COMMAND OF LIEUTENANT COLONEL JOE VANDELEUR, TOOK THE BRIDGE AT SUNSET, THROUGH A COMBINED ATTACK OF INFANTRY AND TANKS ON EKSEL, OVERPELT, AND NEERPELT, CLOSING THE SIEGE OVER THE GERMANS IN HECHTEL.
THE DOORWAY TO THE NETHERLANDS WAS LEFT OPEN.
THE MOST IMPORTANT THING IN THIS OPERATION WILL BE TO TAKE AND HOLD THE BRIDGES IN ARNHEM, NIJMEGEN, AND EINDHOVEN USING AIRBORNE TROOPS. THEN THE GROUND FORCES WILL BREAK THROUGH AND PENETRATE INTO GERMANY.
ALL WILL DEPEND ON THE SPEED OF THE BRITISH 21ST ARMY GROUP FROM THEIR POSITIONS IN THE MAAS-SCHELDE CANAL TO NUNSPEET.
THAT'S 99 MILES!
YES, IT'S A LONG WAY, BUT XXX CORPS HAS A FLAT, TWO-WAY ROAD THEY CAN USE TO ADVANCE.
MOVING OVER OPEN GROUND WOULD BE SUICIDE.
IT'S A PLAN OF GIGANTIC PROPORTIONS.
YES, I KNOW.
THE OPERATION WILL BE DIVIDED INTO TWO PHASES. FIRST: OPERATION MARKET WILL USE AERIAL TROOPS TO CAPTURE THE THREE BRIDGES. FOR THAT, WE WILL SECURE THE AERIAL SPACE BY ATTACKING THE AIRFIELDS OF DEELEN, EDE, AND EINDHOVEN.
WE NEED TO KEEP THE GERMANS FROM GETTING ANY MACHINES IN THE AIR.
ALSO, WE WILL NEUTRALIZE THE ANTI-AIRCRAFT POSITIONS IDENTIFIED IN THIS SECTOR.
OUR PLANES CAN FLY WITH TOTAL SECURITY.
Doesburg
Arnhem
Westervoort
Zevenaar
Duiven
Overbetuwe
XXX
Lingewaard
Nijmegen

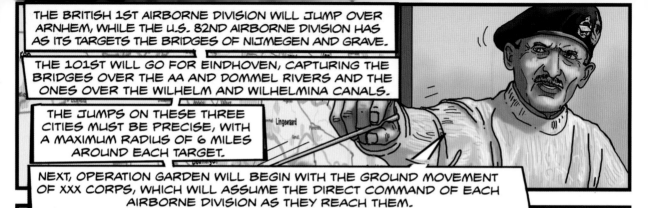

THE BRITISH 1ST AIRBORNE DIVISION WILL JUMP OVER ARNHEM, WHILE THE U.S. 82ND AIRBORNE DIVISION HAS AS ITS TARGETS THE BRIDGES OF NIJMEGEN AND GRAVE.

THE 101ST WILL GO FOR EINDHOVEN, CAPTURING THE BRIDGES OVER THE AA AND DOMMEL RIVERS AND THE ONES OVER THE WILHELM AND WILHELMINA CANALS.

THE JUMPS ON THESE THREE CITIES MUST BE PRECISE, WITH A MAXIMUM RADIUS OF 6 MILES AROUND EACH TARGET.

NEXT, OPERATION GARDEN WILL BEGIN WITH THE GROUND MOVEMENT OF XXX CORPS, WHICH WILL ASSUME THE DIRECT COMMAND OF EACH AIRBORNE DIVISION AS THEY REACH THEM.

WELL, BUT EACH DIVISION SHOULD GATHER A WIDE PERIMETER AND HOLD IT, WAITING FOR REINFORCEMENTS THAT WILL COME DOWN THAT ROAD...

... ALSO, WE KNOW THAT THE REPORTS ABOUT GERMAN TROOPS IN THAT SECTOR AREN'T AS OPTIMISTIC.

THAT NARROW ROAD COULD TURN INTO A GATEWAY TO HELL FOR XXX CORPS. COULD BE TERRIBLE.

IKE, IT'S A QUESTION OF WHETHER WE WANT TO SHORTEN THIS WAR OR NOT... WHAT IS OUR GOAL?

EVERYTHING WILL DEPEND ON THE PRECISION OF THE BOMBERS AND THE AIRBORNE JUMPS. ALSO ON THE DIVISIONS' DEPLOYMENT SPEED.

AND, OF COURSE, ON THE MANEUVERING SPEED OF THE GROUND FORCES.

THEN THERE IS NOTHING ELSE TO DISCUSS.

I WILL GIVE THE ORDERS SO THE RAF AND THE EIGHTH AIR FORCE ARE READY FOR THE ATTACK. BROWNING WILL TAKE CHARGE OF PREPARING THE I AIRBORNE CORPS.

I'M NOT VERY CONVINCED, AND A LOT OF GENERALS WON'T BE EITHER. BUT IF WE CAN END THE WAR WITH THIS OPERATION, LET'S DO IT.

THE GUYS ARE EXHAUSTED.

WE HAVE UNITS THAT HAVEN'T STOPPED SINCE JUNE, AND WE CAN'T AFFORD MORE CASUALTIES IF THERE ISN'T A PLAN THAT RESULTS IN VICTORY.

IT'S A BIG EFFORT THAT WILL REQUIRE A LOT OF COORDINATION, FROM THE FIRST PHASE TO THE LAST.

GOD HELP US.

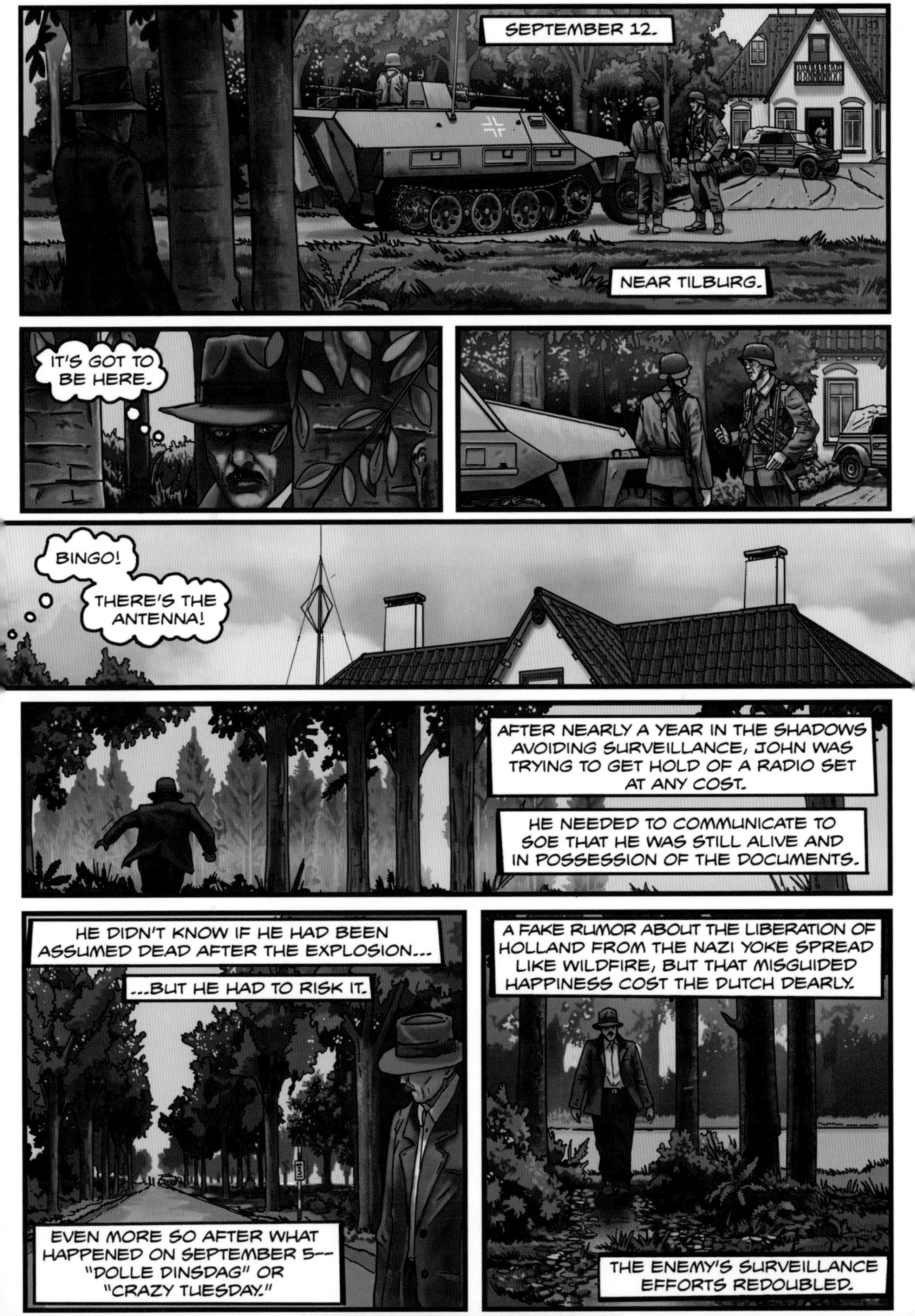
SEPTEMBER 12.
NEAR TILBURG.
IT'S GOT TO BE HERE.
BINGO!
THERE'S THE ANTENNA!
AFTER NEARLY A YEAR IN THE SHADOWS AVOIDING SURVEILLANCE, JOHN WAS TRYING TO GET HOLD OF A RADIO SET AT ANY COST.
HE NEEDED TO COMMUNICATE TO SOE THAT HE WAS STILL ALIVE AND IN POSSESSION OF THE DOCUMENTS.
HE DIDN'T KNOW IF HE HAD BEEN ASSUMED DEAD AFTER THE EXPLOSION...
...BUT HE HAD TO RISK IT.
EVEN MORE SO AFTER WHAT HAPPENED ON SEPTEMBER 5--"DOLLE DINSDAG" OR "CRAZY TUESDAY."
A FAKE RUMOR ABOUT THE LIBERATION OF HOLLAND FROM THE NAZI YOKE SPREAD LIKE WILDFIRE, BUT THAT MISGUIDED HAPPINESS COST THE DUTCH DEARLY.
THE ENEMY'S SURVEILLANCE EFFORTS REDOUBLED.

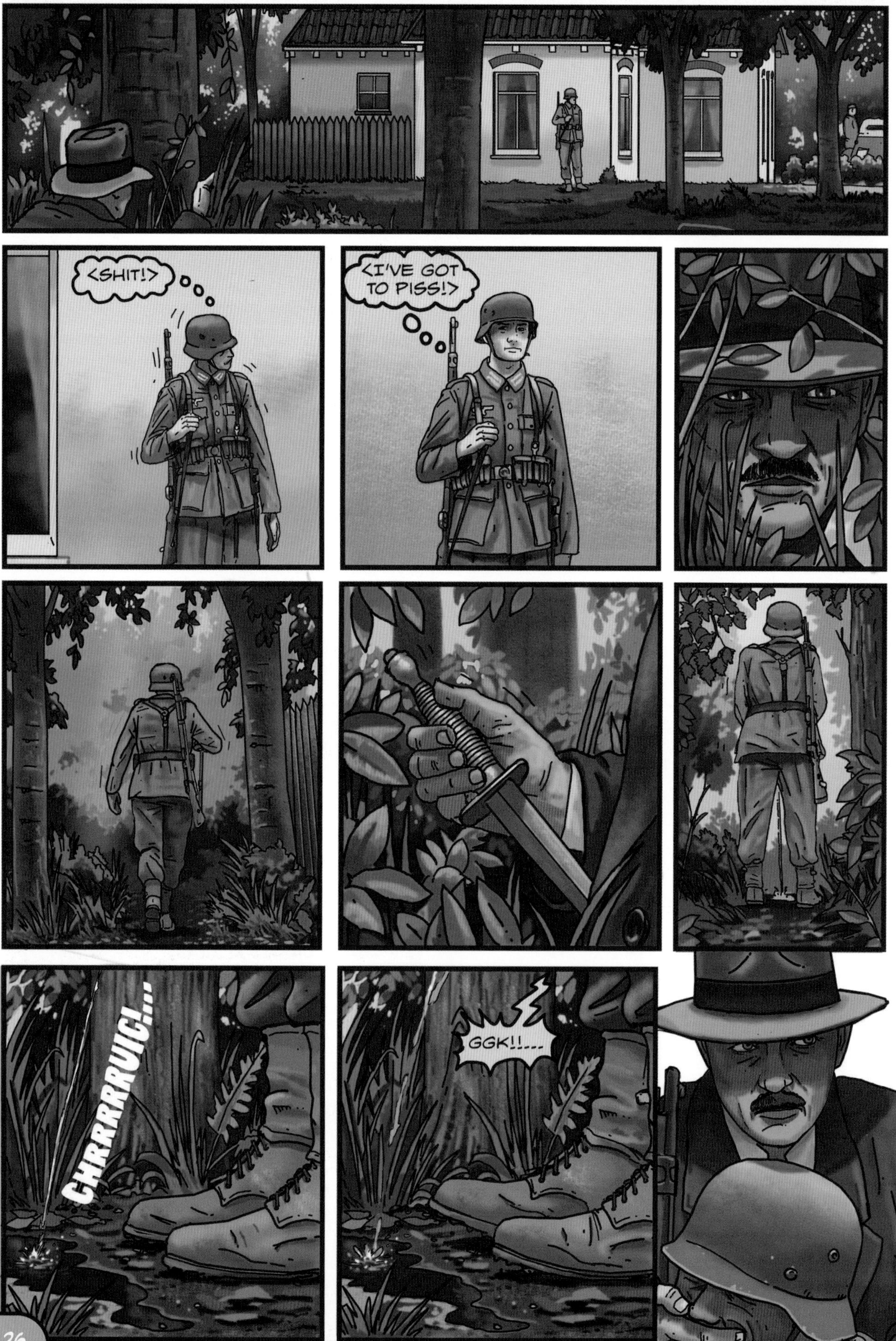
<SHIT!>
<I'VE GOT TO PISS!>
CHRRRRUIC!...
GGK!!....

BBZZZZZZ!!
PPPP-PPP...

<WHERE WAS THIS GUY?>

PPPPPPZZZZZ!!!
PPPP!!! PPP!!!

<LET'S GO, FELDWEBEL. I'M IN A HURRY!>

<YES, MY OBERST!>

VROM-ROOOOOOOOORR!!

THANKS, HERR COLONEL.

AND NOW... LET'S DO IT.

CRACK!
CRACHC!

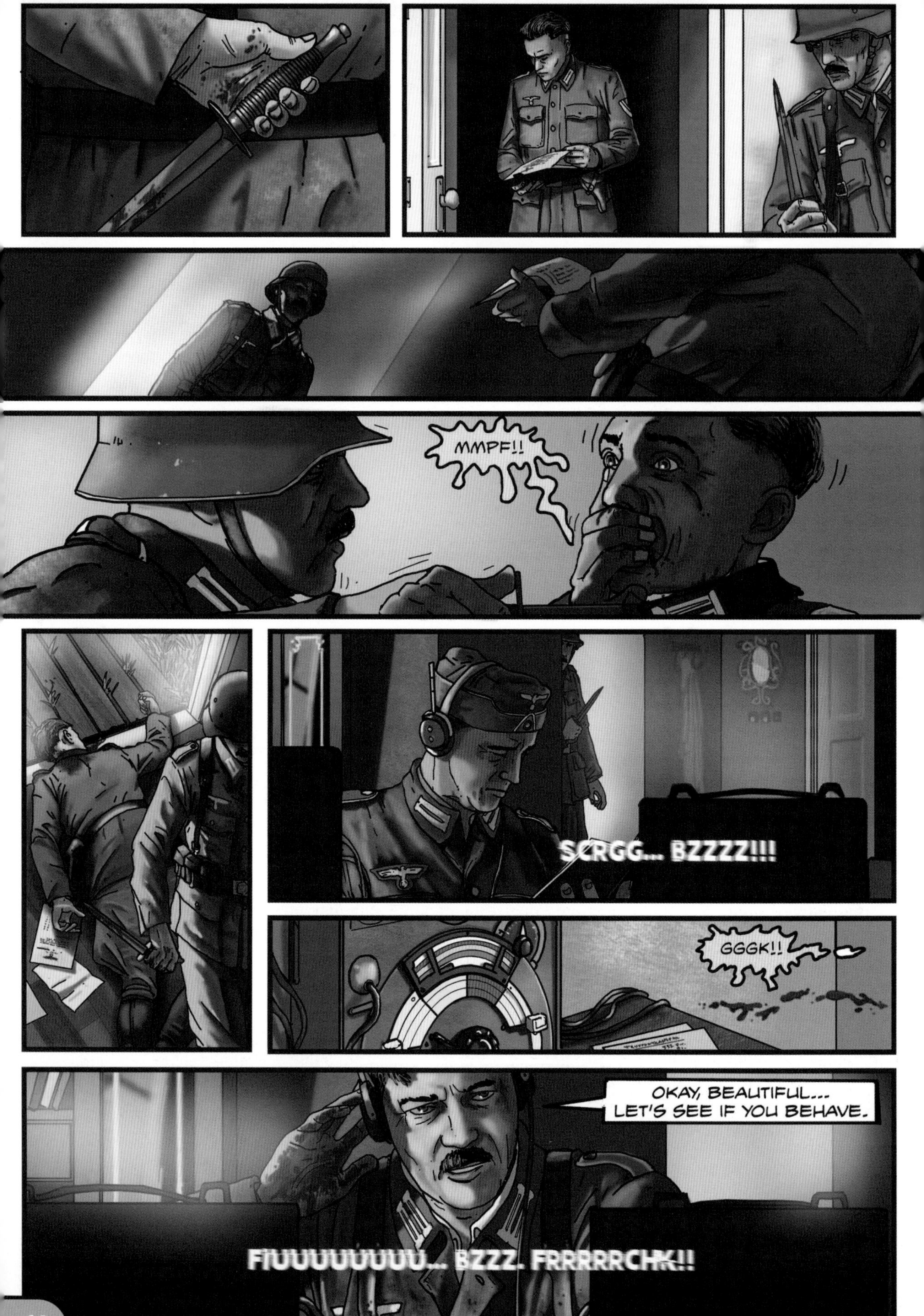
MMPF!!
SCRGG... BZZZZ!!!
GGGK!!
OKAY, BEAUTIFUL...
LET'S SEE IF YOU BEHAVE.
FIUUUUUUUU... BZZZ. FRRRRRCHK!!

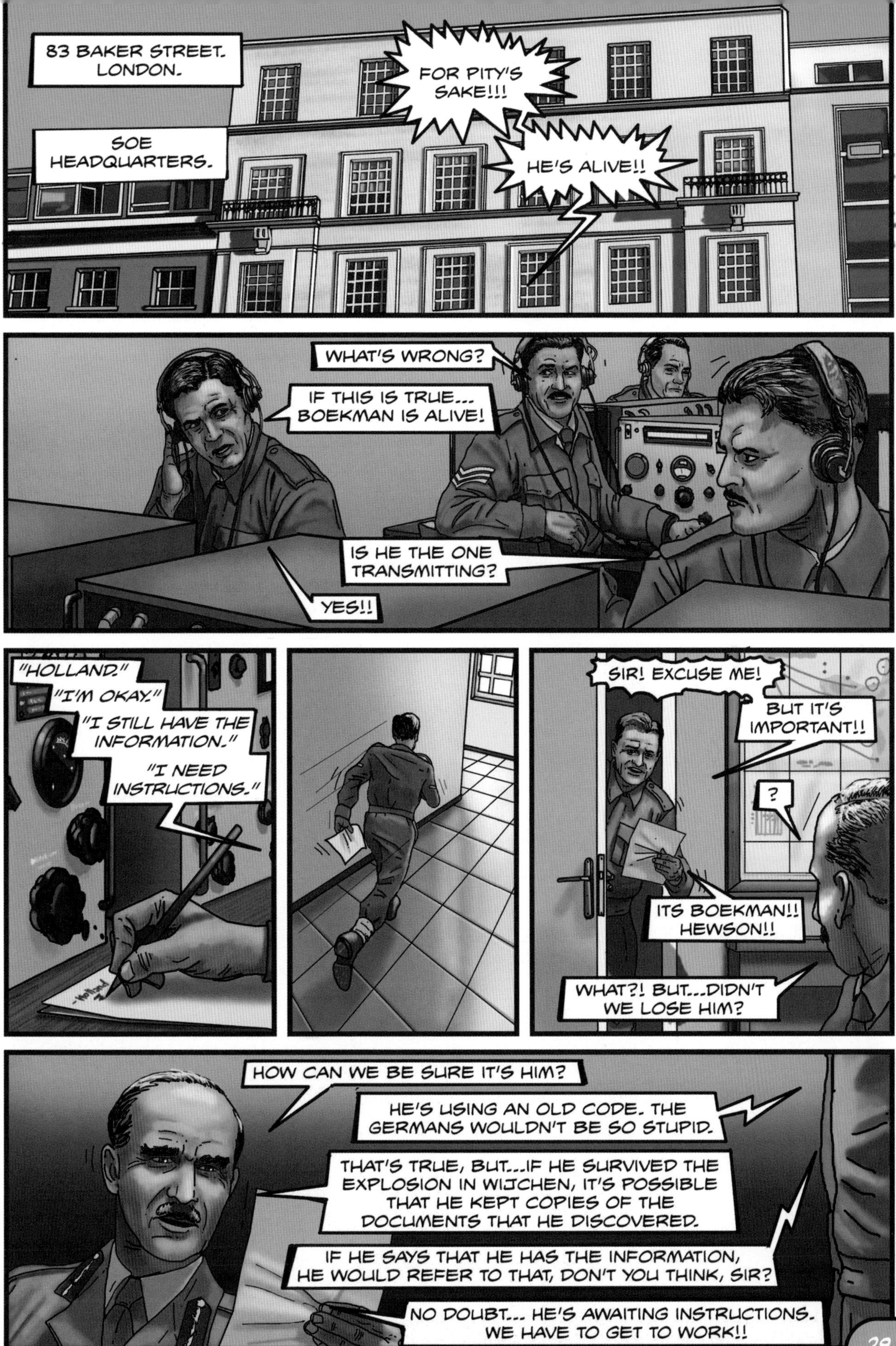
83 BAKER STREET. LONDON.
SOE HEADQUARTERS.
FOR PITY'S SAKE!!!
HE'S ALIVE!!
WHAT'S WRONG?
IF THIS IS TRUE... BOEKMAN IS ALIVE!
IS HE THE ONE TRANSMITTING?
YES!!
"HOLLAND."
"I'M OKAY."
"I STILL HAVE THE INFORMATION."
"I NEED INSTRUCTIONS."
SIR! EXCUSE ME!
BUT IT'S IMPORTANT!!
?
ITS BOEKMAN!! HEWSON!!
WHAT?! BUT...DIDN'T WE LOSE HIM?
HOW CAN WE BE SURE IT'S HIM?
HE'S USING AN OLD CODE. THE GERMANS WOULDN'T BE SO STUPID.
THAT'S TRUE, BUT...IF HE SURVIVED THE EXPLOSION IN WIJCHEN, IT'S POSSIBLE THAT HE KEPT COPIES OF THE DOCUMENTS THAT HE DISCOVERED.
IF HE SAYS THAT HE HAS THE INFORMATION, HE WOULD REFER TO THAT, DON'T YOU THINK, SIR?
NO DOUBT... HE'S AWAITING INSTRUCTIONS. WE HAVE TO GET TO WORK!!

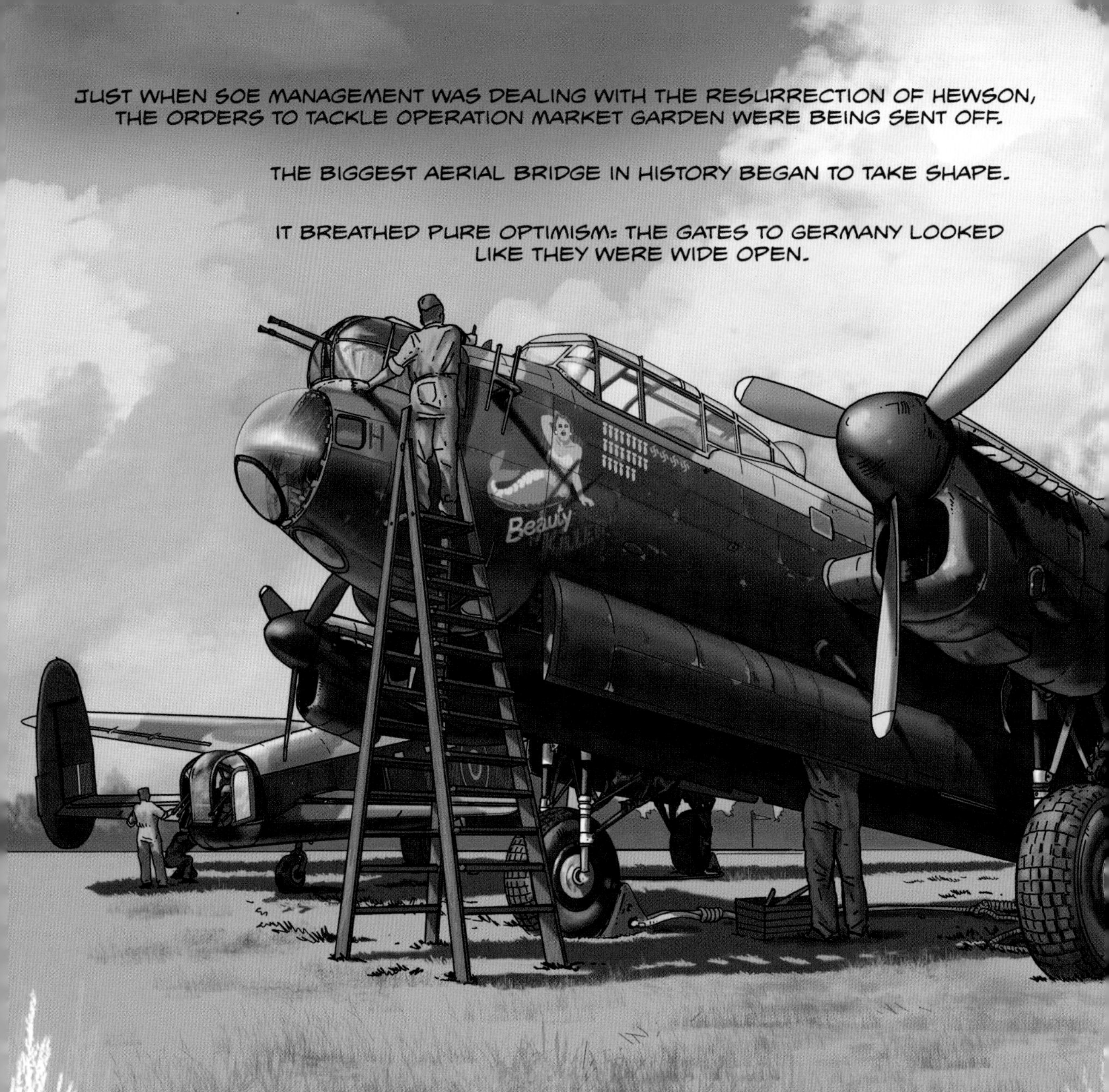
JUST WHEN SOE MANAGEMENT WAS DEALING WITH THE RESURRECTION OF HEWSON, THE ORDERS TO TACKLE OPERATION MARKET GARDEN WERE BEING SENT OFF.
THE BIGGEST AERIAL BRIDGE IN HISTORY BEGAN TO TAKE SHAPE.
IT BREATHED PURE OPTIMISM: THE GATES TO GERMANY LOOKED LIKE THEY WERE WIDE OPEN.
Beauty

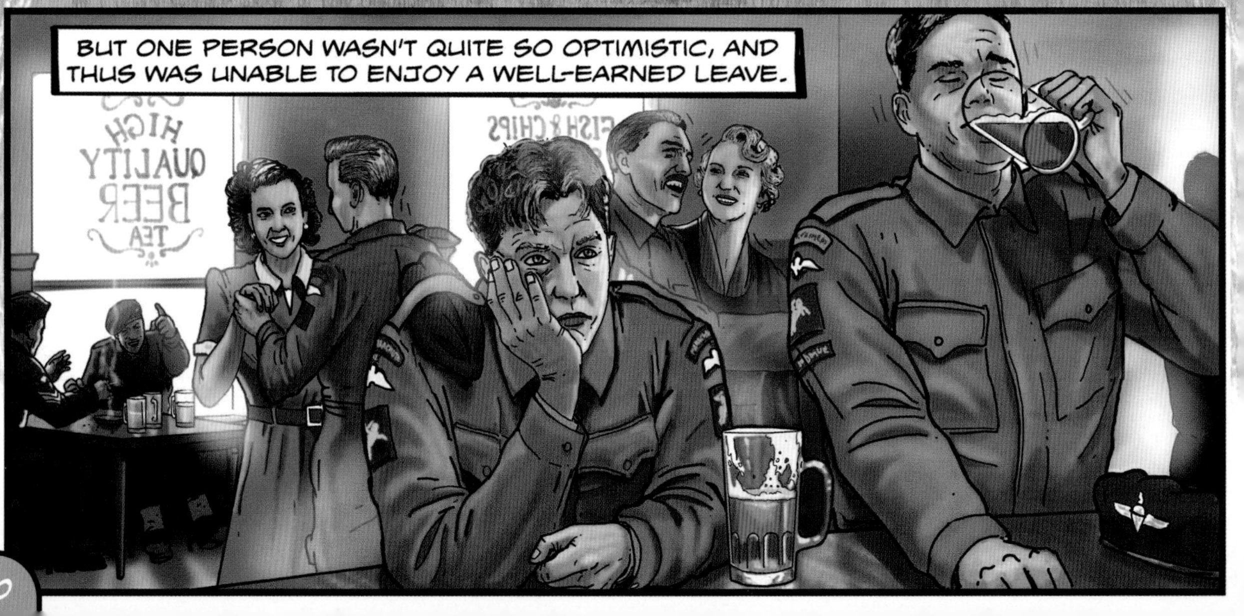
BUT ONE PERSON WASN'T QUITE SO OPTIMISTIC, AND THUS WAS UNABLE TO ENJOY A WELL-EARNED LEAVE.
HIGH QUALITY BEER TEA
FISH & CHIPS

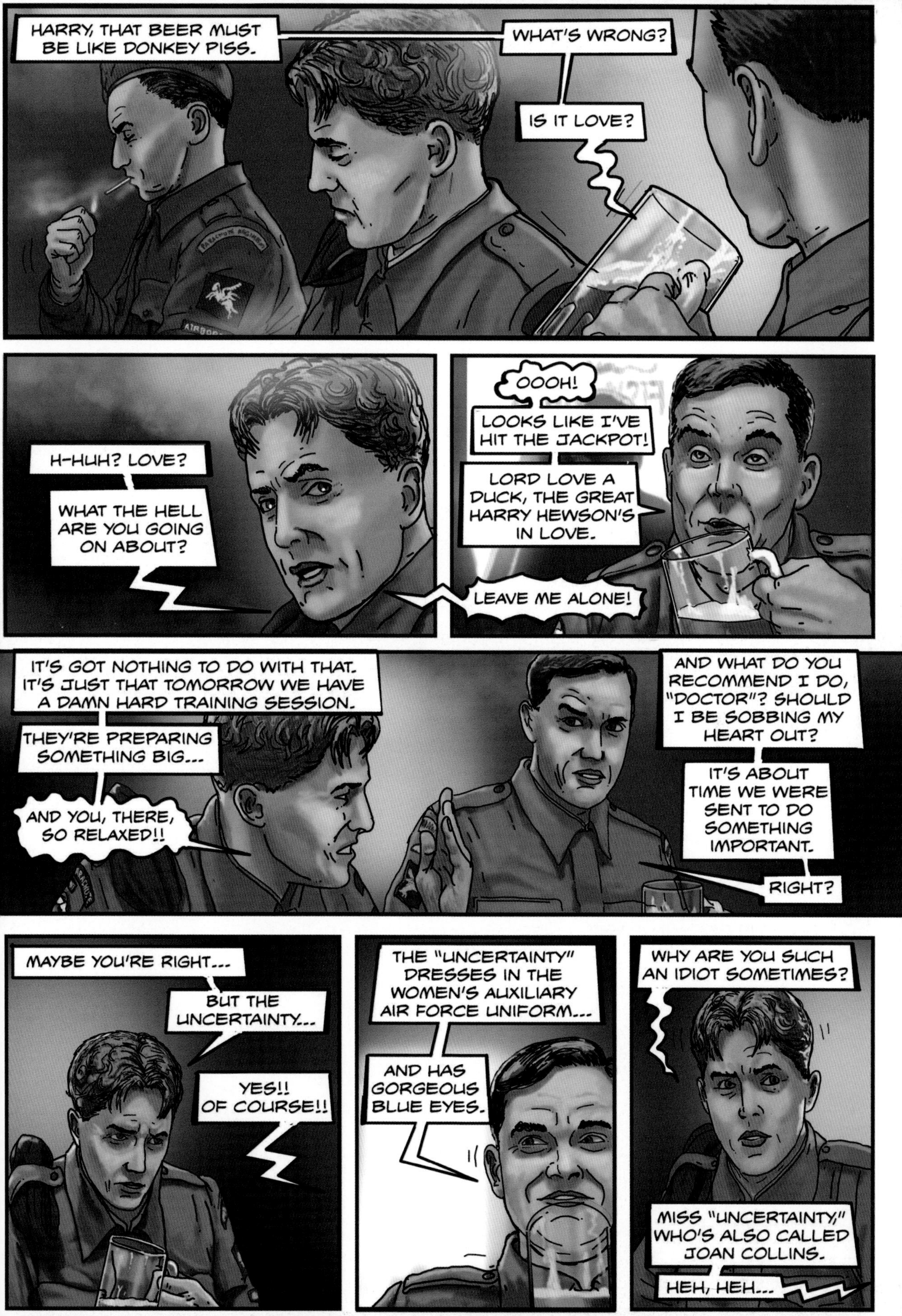
HARRY, THAT BEER MUST BE LIKE DONKEY PISS.
WHAT'S WRONG?
IS IT LOVE?
H-HUH? LOVE?
WHAT THE HELL ARE YOU GOING ON ABOUT?
OOOH!
LOOKS LIKE I'VE HIT THE JACKPOT!
LORD LOVE A DUCK, THE GREAT HARRY HEWSON'S IN LOVE.
LEAVE ME ALONE!
IT'S GOT NOTHING TO DO WITH THAT. IT'S JUST THAT TOMORROW WE HAVE A DAMN HARD TRAINING SESSION.
THEY'RE PREPARING SOMETHING BIG...
AND YOU, THERE, SO RELAXED!!
AND WHAT DO YOU RECOMMEND I DO, "DOCTOR"? SHOULD I BE SOBBING MY HEART OUT?
IT'S ABOUT TIME WE WERE SENT TO DO SOMETHING IMPORTANT.
RIGHT?
MAYBE YOU'RE RIGHT...
BUT THE UNCERTAINTY...
YES!! OF COURSE!!
THE "UNCERTAINTY" DRESSES IN THE WOMEN'S AUXILIARY AIR FORCE UNIFORM...
AND HAS GORGEOUS BLUE EYES.
WHY ARE YOU SUCH AN IDIOT SOMETIMES?
MISS "UNCERTAINTY," WHO'S ALSO CALLED JOAN COLLINS.
HEH, HEH...

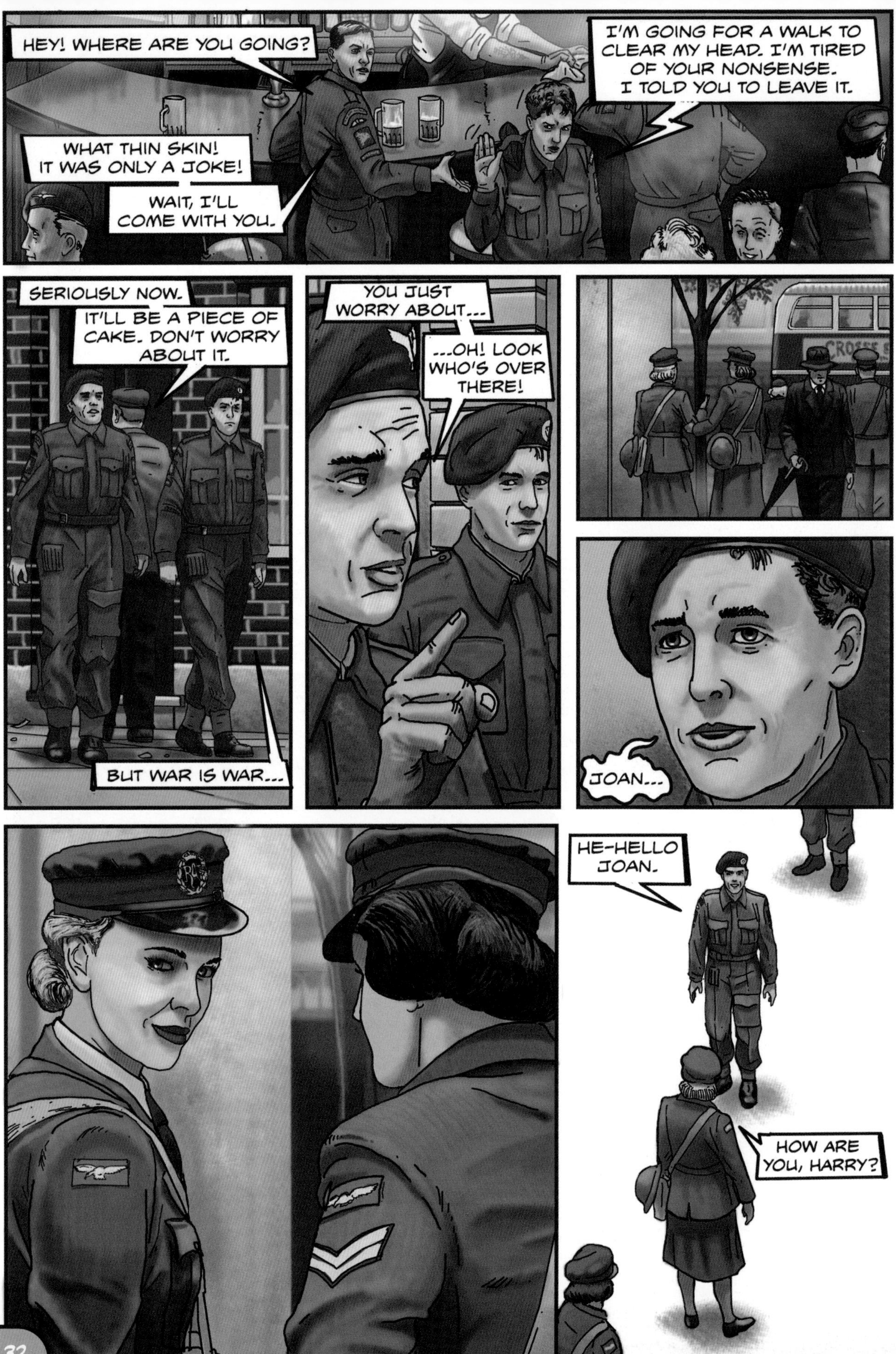
HEY! WHERE ARE YOU GOING?
I'M GOING FOR A WALK TO CLEAR MY HEAD. I'M TIRED OF YOUR NONSENSE. I TOLD YOU TO LEAVE IT.
WHAT THIN SKIN! IT WAS ONLY A JOKE!
WAIT, I'LL COME WITH YOU.
SERIOUSLY NOW.
IT'LL BE A PIECE OF CAKE. DON'T WORRY ABOUT IT.
BUT WAR IS WAR...
YOU JUST WORRY ABOUT...
...OH! LOOK WHO'S OVER THERE!
JOAN...
HE-HELLO JOAN.
HOW ARE YOU, HARRY?

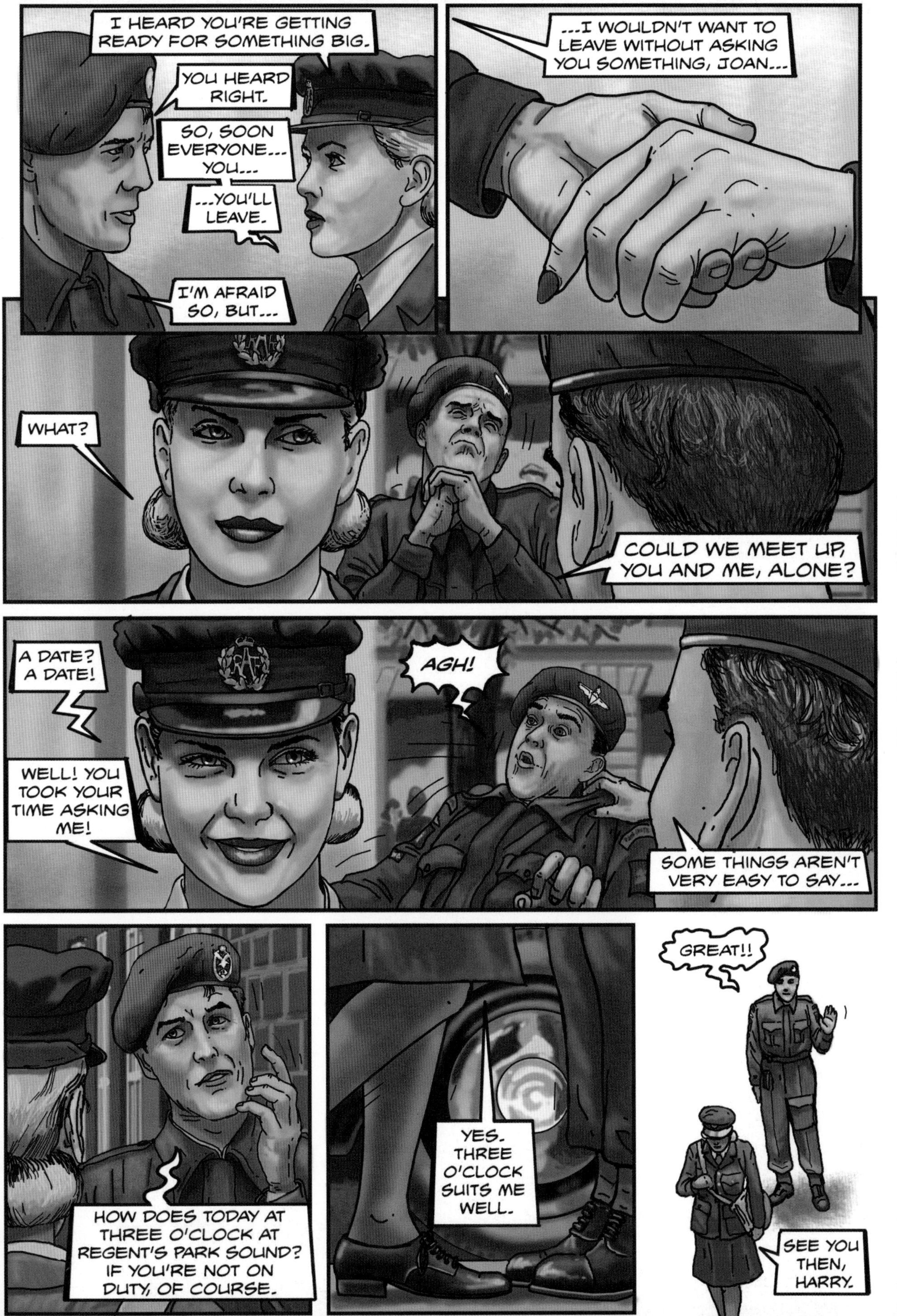

I HEARD YOU'RE GETTING READY FOR SOMETHING BIG.
YOU HEARD RIGHT.
SO, SOON EVERYONE... YOU...
...YOU'LL LEAVE.
I'M AFRAID SO, BUT...
...I WOULDN'T WANT TO LEAVE WITHOUT ASKING YOU SOMETHING, JOAN...
WHAT?
COULD WE MEET UP, YOU AND ME, ALONE?
A DATE? A DATE!
AGH!
WELL! YOU TOOK YOUR TIME ASKING ME!
SOME THINGS AREN'T VERY EASY TO SAY...
HOW DOES TODAY AT THREE O'CLOCK AT REGENT'S PARK SOUND? IF YOU'RE NOT ON DUTY, OF COURSE.
YES. THREE O'CLOCK SUITS ME WELL.
GREAT!!
SEE YOU THEN, HARRY.

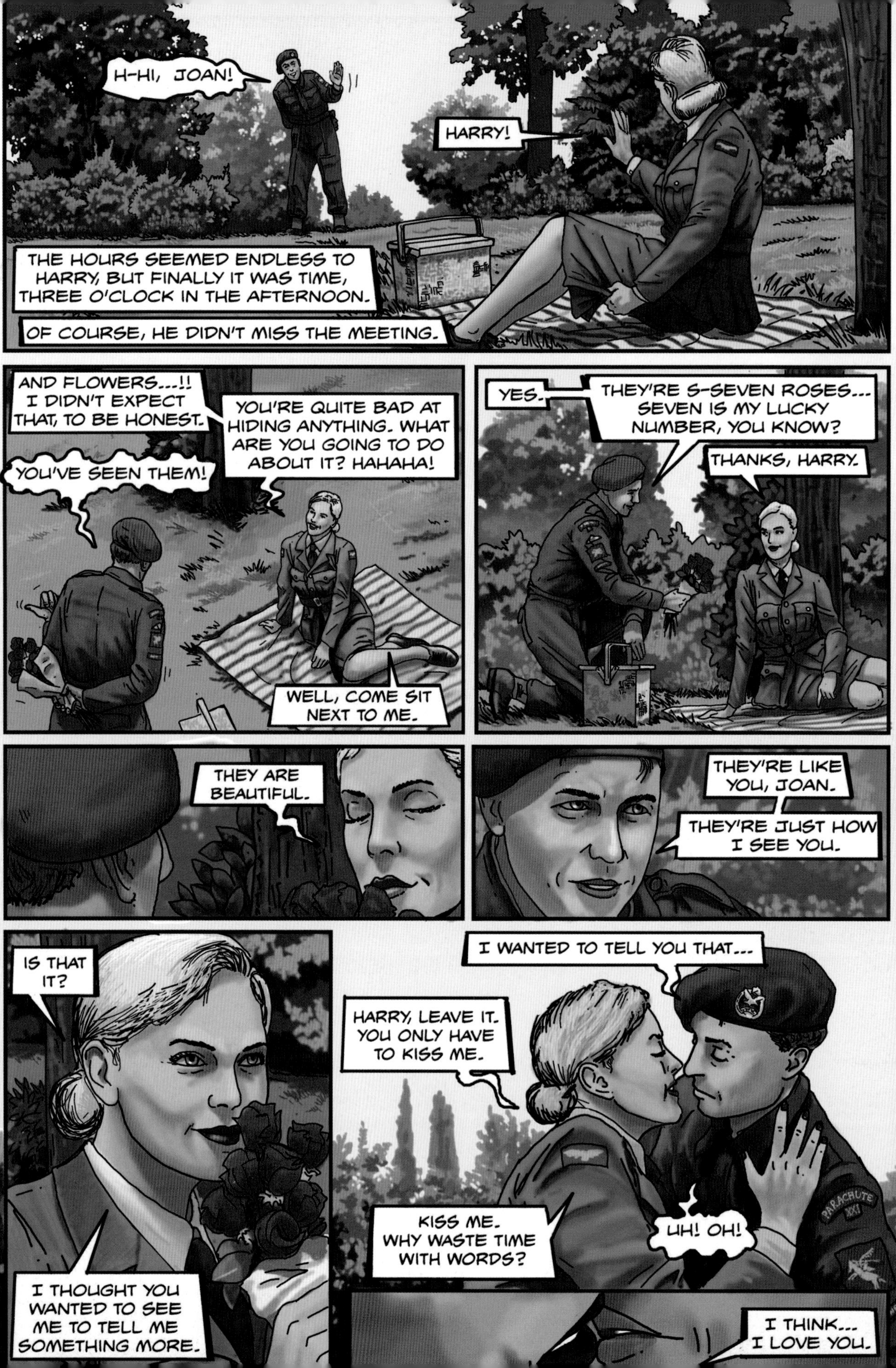
H-HI, JOAN!
HARRY!
THE HOURS SEEMED ENDLESS TO HARRY, BUT FINALLY IT WAS TIME, THREE O'CLOCK IN THE AFTERNOON.
OF COURSE, HE DIDN'T MISS THE MEETING.
AND FLOWERS...!! I DIDN'T EXPECT THAT, TO BE HONEST.
YOU'VE SEEN THEM!
YOU'RE QUITE BAD AT HIDING ANYTHING. WHAT ARE YOU GOING TO DO ABOUT IT? HAHAHA!
WELL, COME SIT NEXT TO ME.
YES.
THEY'RE S-SEVEN ROSES... SEVEN IS MY LUCKY NUMBER, YOU KNOW?
THANKS, HARRY.
THEY ARE BEAUTIFUL.
THEY'RE LIKE YOU, JOAN.
THEY'RE JUST HOW I SEE YOU.
IS THAT IT?
I THOUGHT YOU WANTED TO SEE ME TO TELL ME SOMETHING MORE.
I WANTED TO TELL YOU THAT...
HARRY, LEAVE IT. YOU ONLY HAVE TO KISS ME.
KISS ME. WHY WASTE TIME WITH WORDS?
UH! OH!
PARACHUTE XXI
I THINK... I LOVE YOU.

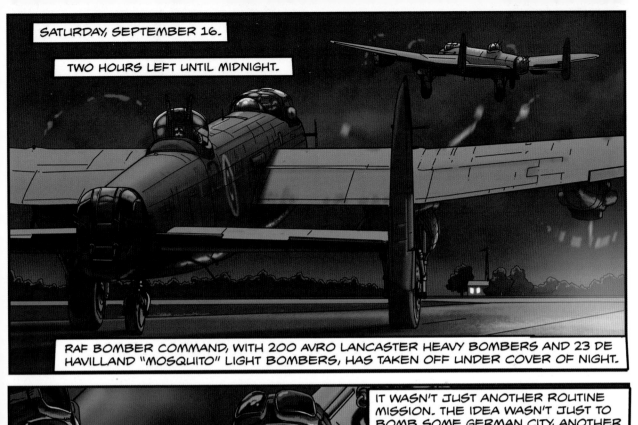

SATURDAY, SEPTEMBER 16.

TWO HOURS LEFT UNTIL MIDNIGHT.

RAF BOMBER COMMAND, WITH 200 AVRO LANCASTER HEAVY BOMBERS AND 23 DE HAVILLAND "MOSQUITO" LIGHT BOMBERS, HAS TAKEN OFF UNDER COVER OF NIGHT.

IT WASN'T JUST ANOTHER ROUTINE MISSION. THE IDEA WASN'T JUST TO BOMB SOME GERMAN CITY, ANOTHER SPOT ON THE MAP THAT WOULD START TO BURN AT EVERY CORNER.

THAT NIGHT THEY PLANNED TO NEUTRALIZE THE ENEMY'S POSITIONS IN HOLLAND, FROM THEIR AIRFIELDS AND THEIR ANTI-AIRCRAFT ARTILLERY TO THEIR GENERAL QUARTERS AND DEPOTS.

A DULL MURMUR, GENERATED BY NEARLY A THOUSAND ROLLS ROYCE MERLIN MOTORS, BROKE THE SILENCE OVER THE ENGLISH CHANNEL.

ROOOOOOOOOOOOOOOOOOOOOOOOOOOOOOOOARRR!!!!

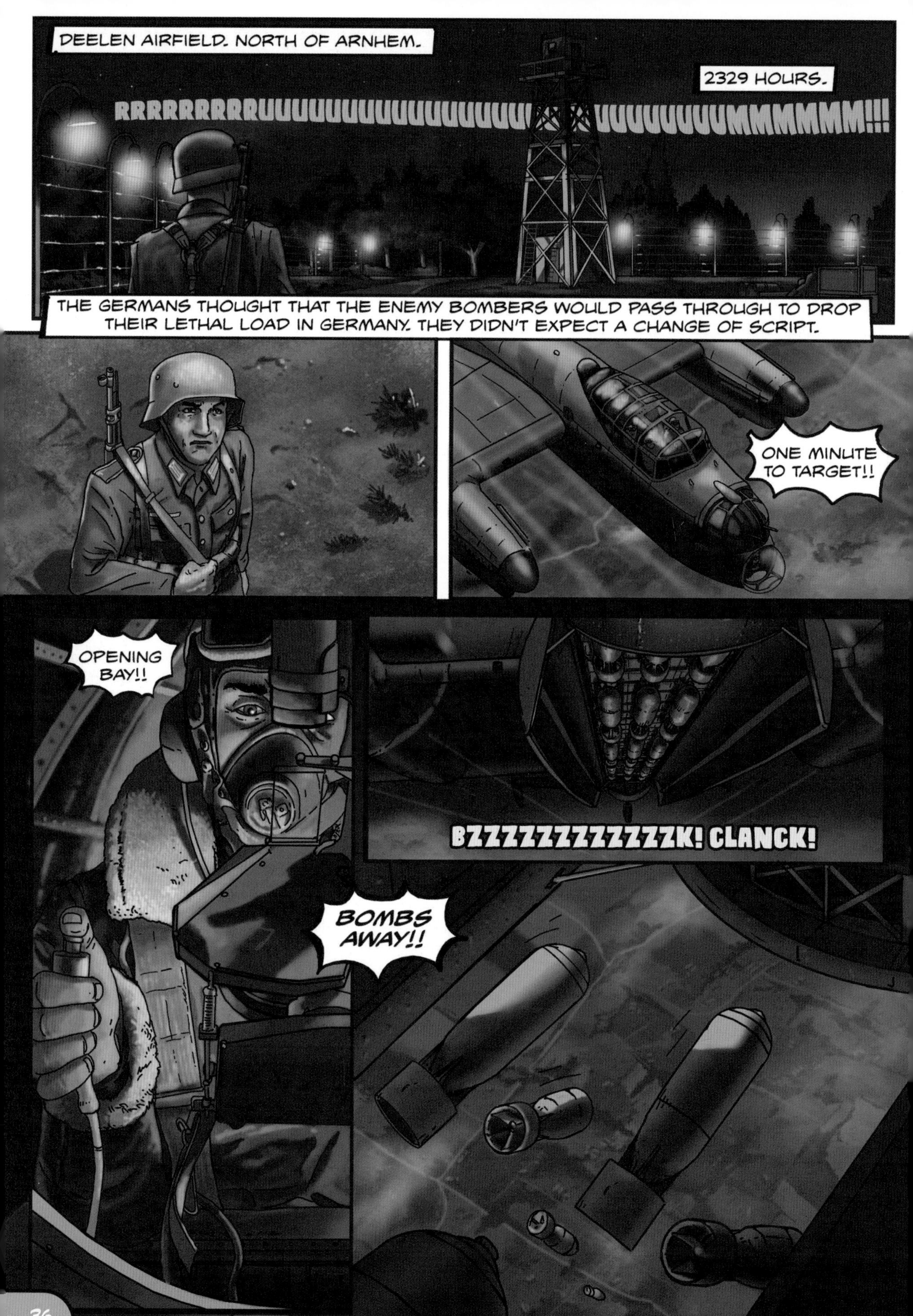
DEELEN AIRFIELD. NORTH OF ARNHEM.
2329 HOURS.
RRRRRRRRRUUUUUUUUUUUUUUUUUUUUUUUUUUUMMMMMM!!!
THE GERMANS THOUGHT THAT THE ENEMY BOMBERS WOULD PASS THROUGH TO DROP THEIR LETHAL LOAD IN GERMANY. THEY DIDN'T EXPECT A CHANGE OF SCRIPT.
ONE MINUTE TO TARGET!!
OPENING BAY!!
BZZZZZZZZZZZZZK! CLANCK!
BOMBS AWAY!!

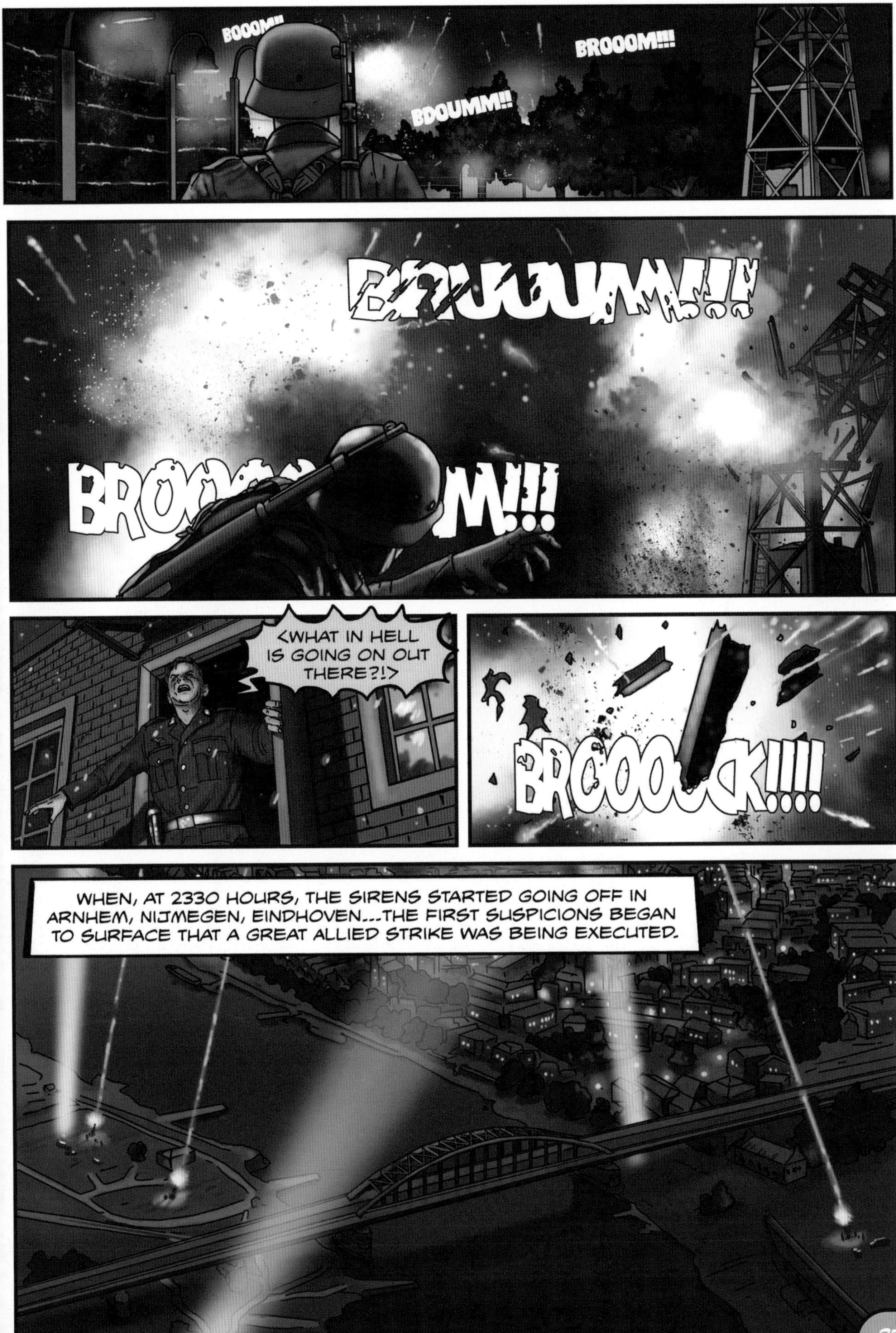
BOOOM!!
BROOOM!!!
BDOUMM!!
<WHAT IN HELL IS GOING ON OUT THERE?!>
WHEN, AT 2330 HOURS, THE SIRENS STARTED GOING OFF IN ARNHEM, NIJMEGEN, EINDHOVEN... THE FIRST SUSPICIONS BEGAN TO SURFACE THAT A GREAT ALLIED STRIKE WAS BEING EXECUTED.

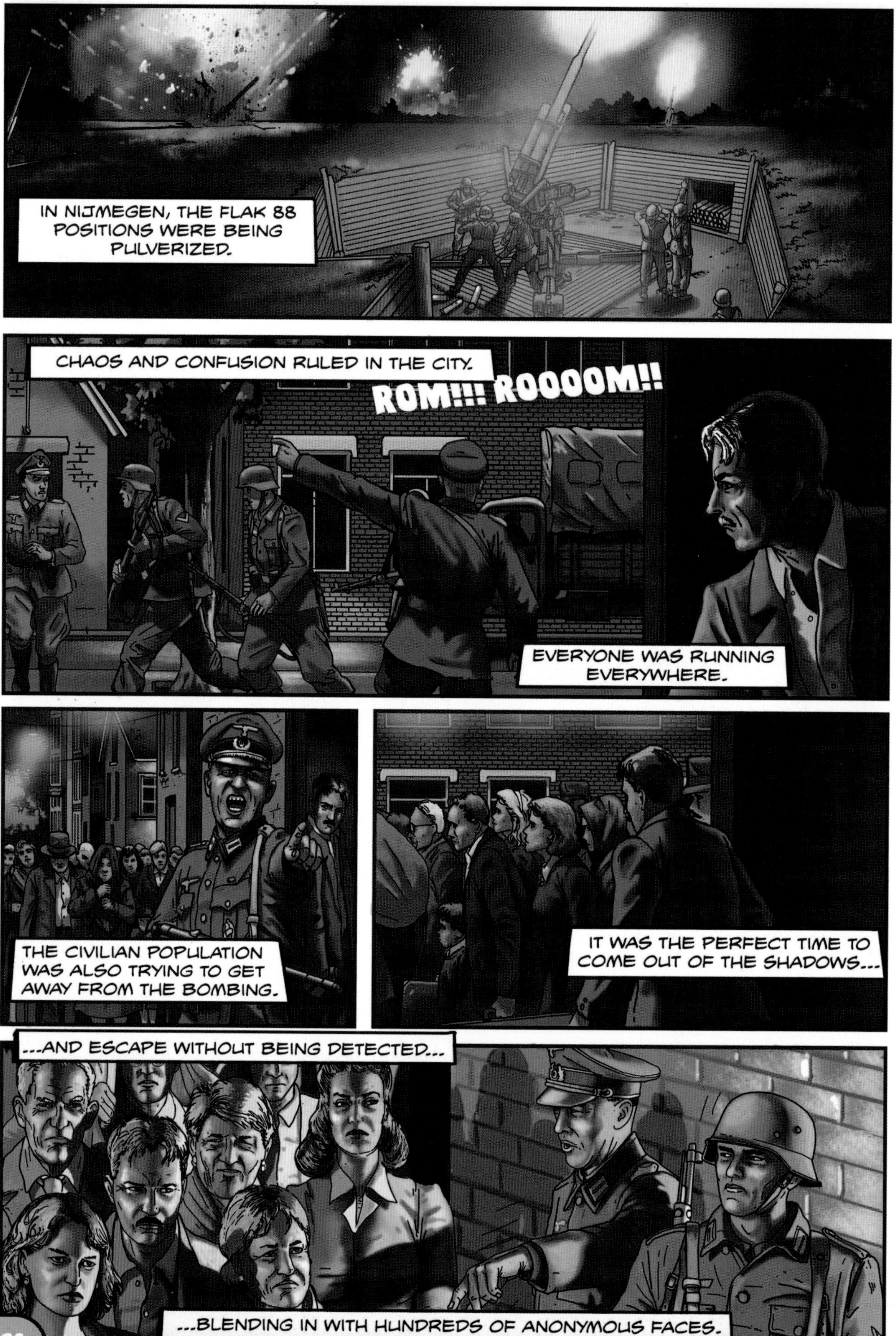
IN NIJMEGEN, THE FLAK 88 POSITIONS WERE BEING PULVERIZED.
CHAOS AND CONFUSION RULED IN THE CITY.
ROM!!! ROOOOM!!
EVERYONE WAS RUNNING EVERYWHERE.
THE CIVILIAN POPULATION WAS ALSO TRYING TO GET AWAY FROM THE BOMBING.
IT WAS THE PERFECT TIME TO COME OUT OF THE SHADOWS...
...AND ESCAPE WITHOUT BEING DETECTED...
...BLENDING IN WITH HUNDREDS OF ANONYMOUS FACES.

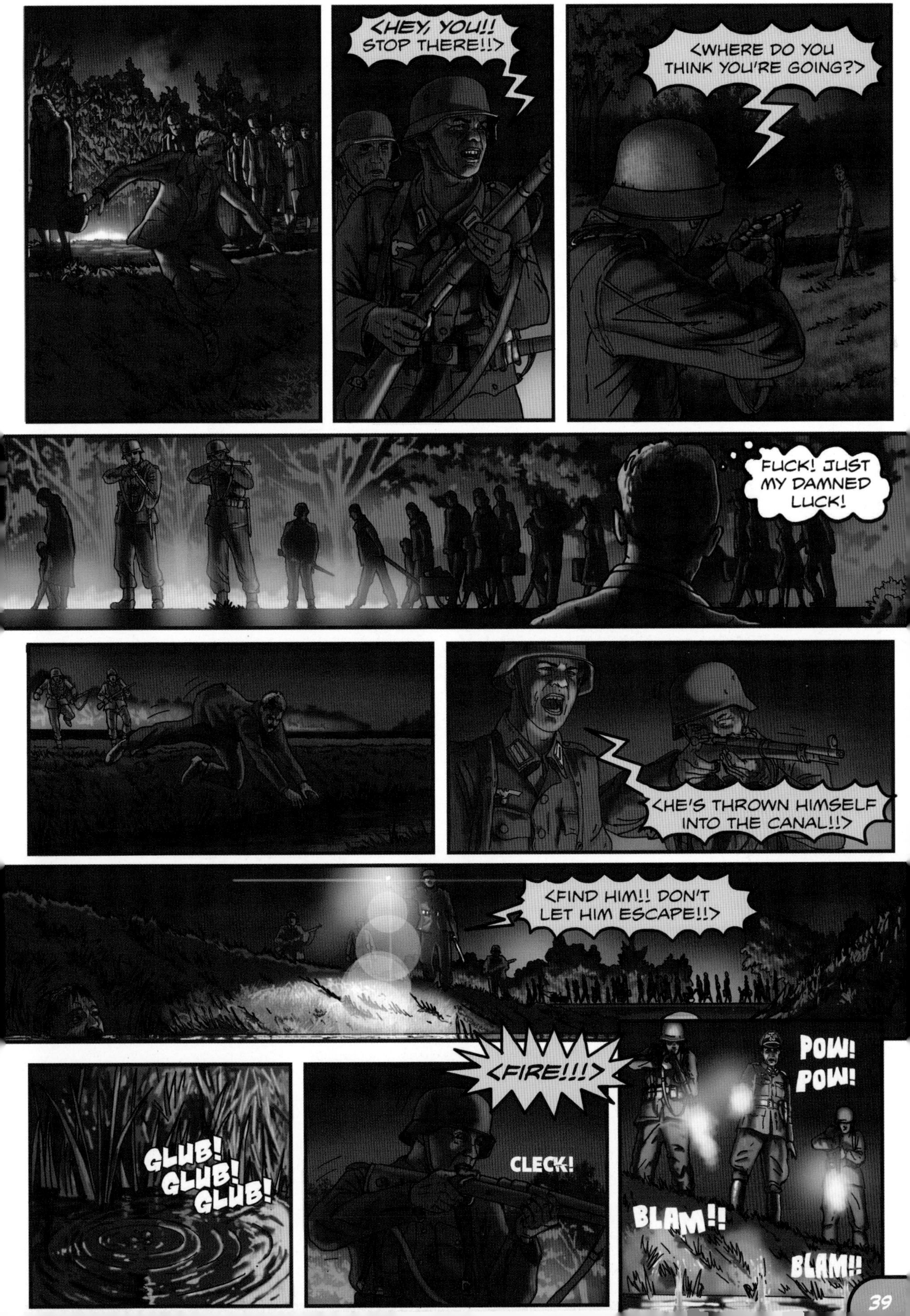
<HEY, YOU!! STOP THERE!!>
<WHERE DO YOU THINK YOU'RE GOING?>
FUCK! JUST MY DAMNED LUCK!
<HE'S THROWN HIMSELF INTO THE CANAL!!>
<FIND HIM!! DON'T LET HIM ESCAPE!!>
GLUB! GLUB! GLUB!
<FIRE!!!>
CLECK!
POW! POW!
BLAM!!
BLAM!!

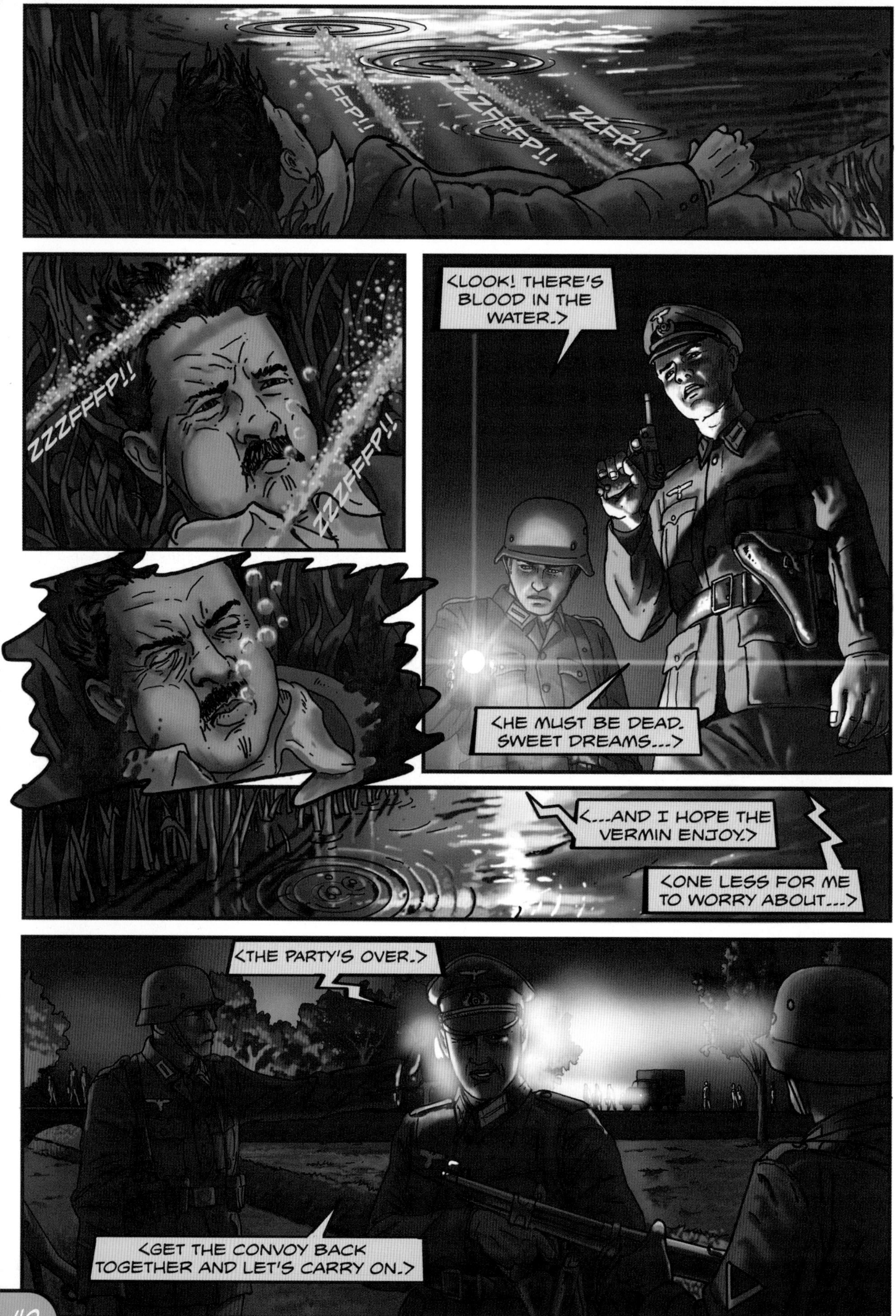
ZZFFP!!
ZZZFFFP!!
ZZFFP!!
ZZZFFFP!!
ZZZFFFP!!
<LOOK! THERE'S BLOOD IN THE WATER.>
<HE MUST BE DEAD. SWEET DREAMS...>
<...AND I HOPE THE VERMIN ENJOY.>
<ONE LESS FOR ME TO WORRY ABOUT...>
<THE PARTY'S OVER.>
<GET THE CONVOY BACK TOGETHER AND LET'S CARRY ON.>

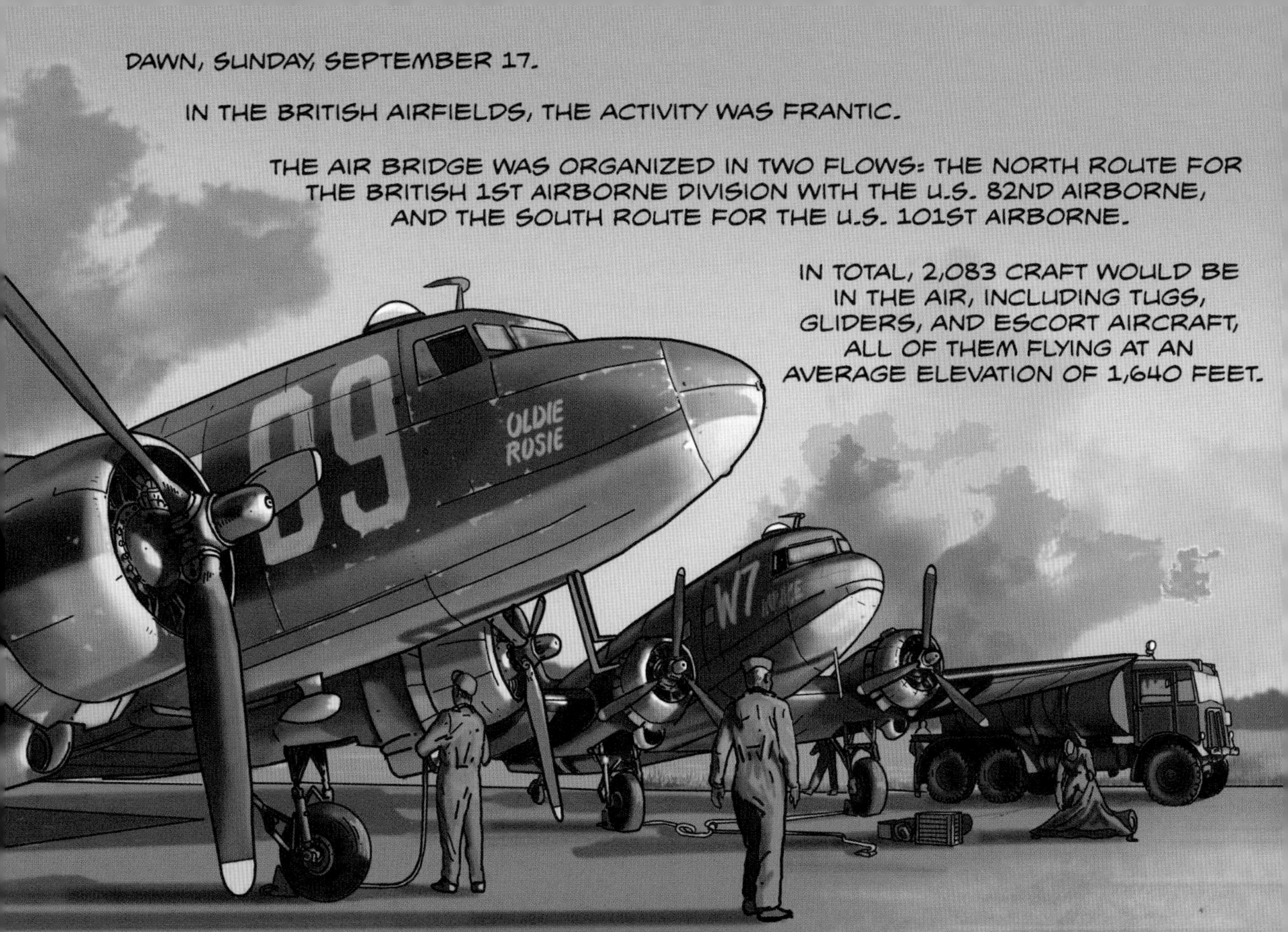
DAWN, SUNDAY, SEPTEMBER 17.
IN THE BRITISH AIRFIELDS, THE ACTIVITY WAS FRANTIC.
THE AIR BRIDGE WAS ORGANIZED IN TWO FLOWS: THE NORTH ROUTE FOR THE BRITISH 1ST AIRBORNE DIVISION WITH THE U.S. 82ND AIRBORNE, AND THE SOUTH ROUTE FOR THE U.S. 101ST AIRBORNE.
IN TOTAL, 2,083 CRAFT WOULD BE IN THE AIR, INCLUDING TUGS, GLIDERS, AND ESCORT AIRCRAFT, ALL OF THEM FLYING AT AN AVERAGE ELEVATION OF 1,640 FEET.
OLDIE ROSIE
W7

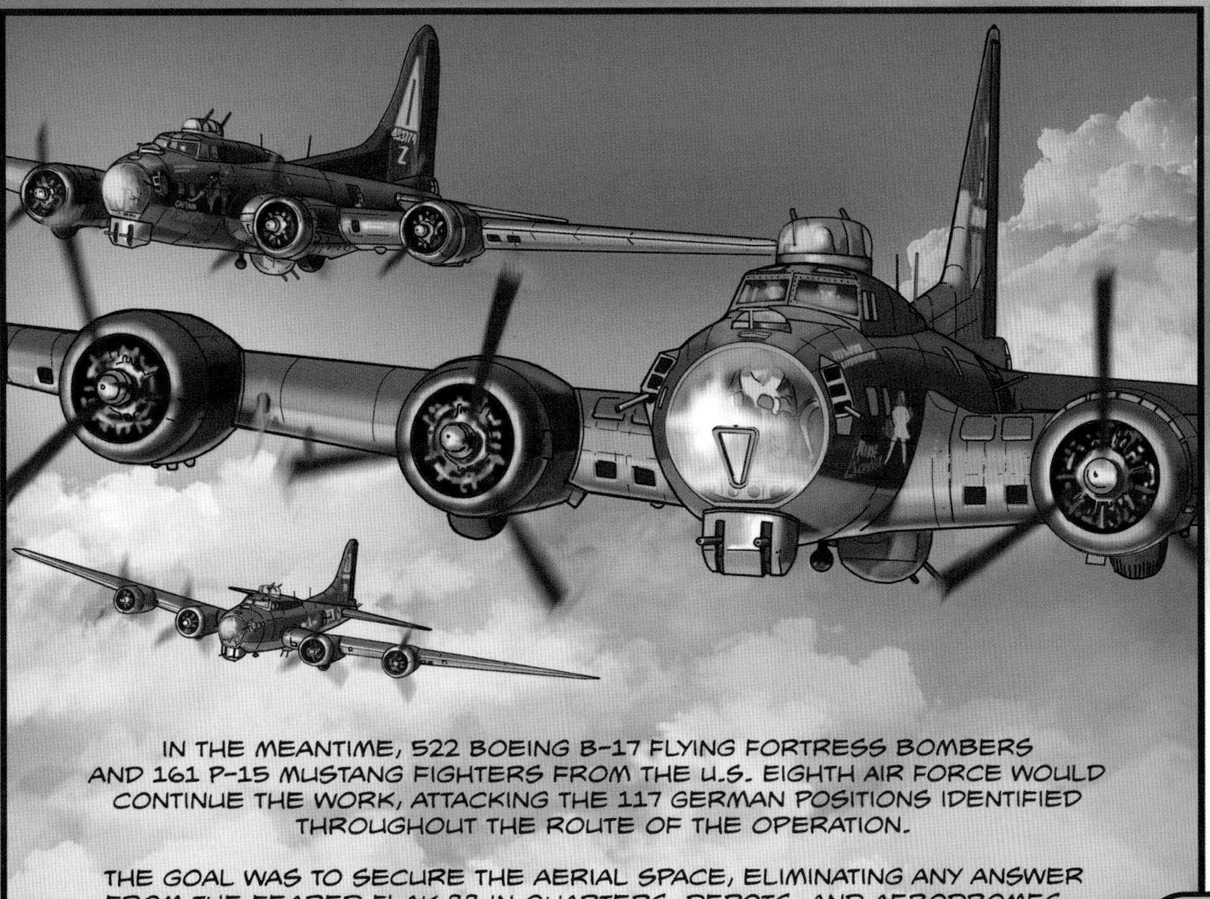
IN THE MEANTIME, 522 BOEING B-17 FLYING FORTRESS BOMBERS AND 161 P-15 MUSTANG FIGHTERS FROM THE U.S. EIGHTH AIR FORCE WOULD CONTINUE THE WORK, ATTACKING THE 117 GERMAN POSITIONS IDENTIFIED THROUGHOUT THE ROUTE OF THE OPERATION.
THE GOAL WAS TO SECURE THE AERIAL SPACE, ELIMINATING ANY ANSWER FROM THE FEARED FLAK 88 IN QUARTERS, DEPOTS, AND AERODROMES...

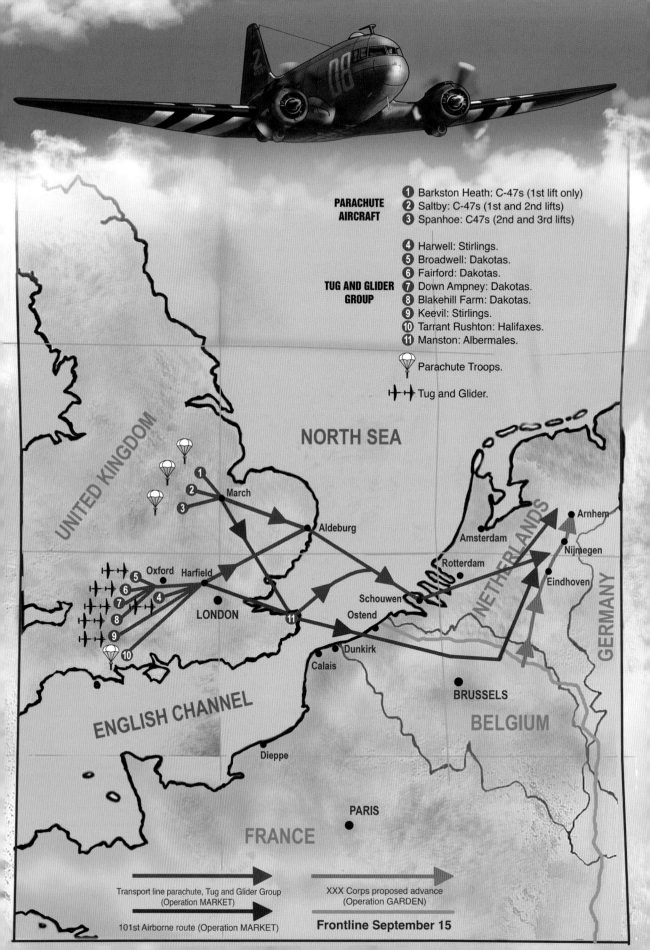

PARACHUTE AIRCRAFT

1 Barkston Heath: C-47s (1st lift only)
2 Saltby: C-47s (1st and 2nd lifts)
3 Spanhoe: C47s (2nd and 3rd lifts)

TUG AND GLIDER GROUP

4 Harwell: Stirlings.
5 Broadwell: Dakotas.
6 Fairford: Dakotas.
7 Down Ampney: Dakotas.
8 Blakehill Farm: Dakotas.
9 Keevil: Stirlings.
10 Tarrant Rushton: Halifaxes.
11 Manston: Albermales.

Parachute Troops.

Tug and Glider.

NORTH SEA

UNITED KINGDOM

March

Aldeburg

Amsterdam

Arnhem

Rotterdam

Nijmegen

NETHERLANDS

Eindhoven

GERMANY

Oxford   Harfield
5
6
7   4
8
9
10

LONDON

11

Schouwen

Ostend

Dunkirk

Calais

BRUSSELS

BELGIUM

ENGLISH CHANNEL

Dieppe

PARIS

FRANCE

Transport line parachute, Tug and Glider Group
(Operation MARKET)

XXX Corps proposed advance
(Operation GARDEN)

101st Airborne route (Operation MARKET)

Frontline September 15

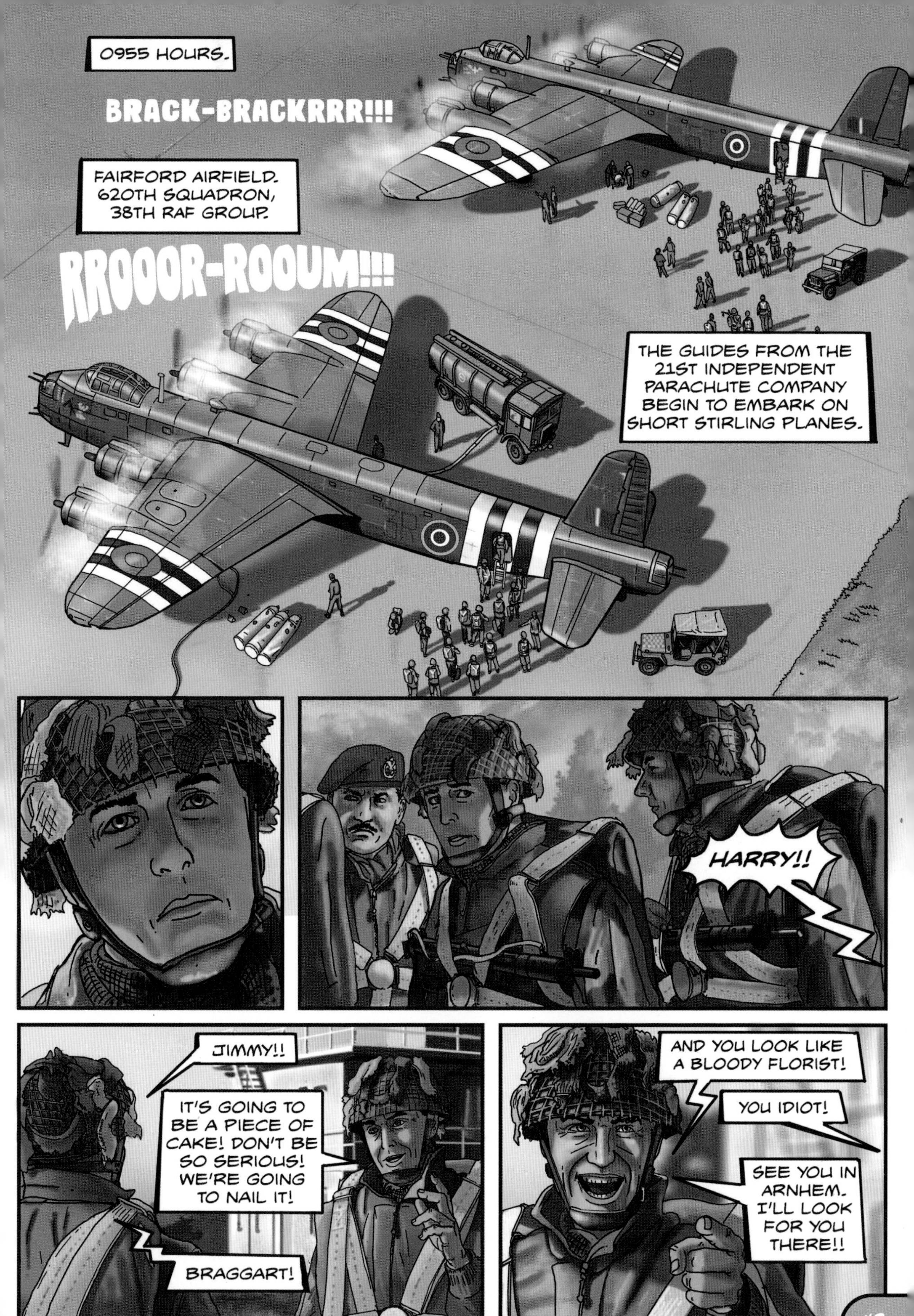

0955 HOURS.
BRACK-BRACKRRR!!!
FAIRFORD AIRFIELD. 620TH SQUADRON, 38TH RAF GROUP.
RROOOR-ROOUM!!!
THE GUIDES FROM THE 21ST INDEPENDENT PARACHUTE COMPANY BEGIN TO EMBARK ON SHORT STIRLING PLANES.
HARRY!!
JIMMY!!
IT'S GOING TO BE A PIECE OF CAKE! DON'T BE SO SERIOUS! WE'RE GOING TO NAIL IT!
BRAGGART!
AND YOU LOOK LIKE A BLOODY FLORIST!
YOU IDIOT!
SEE YOU IN ARNHEM. I'LL LOOK FOR YOU THERE!!

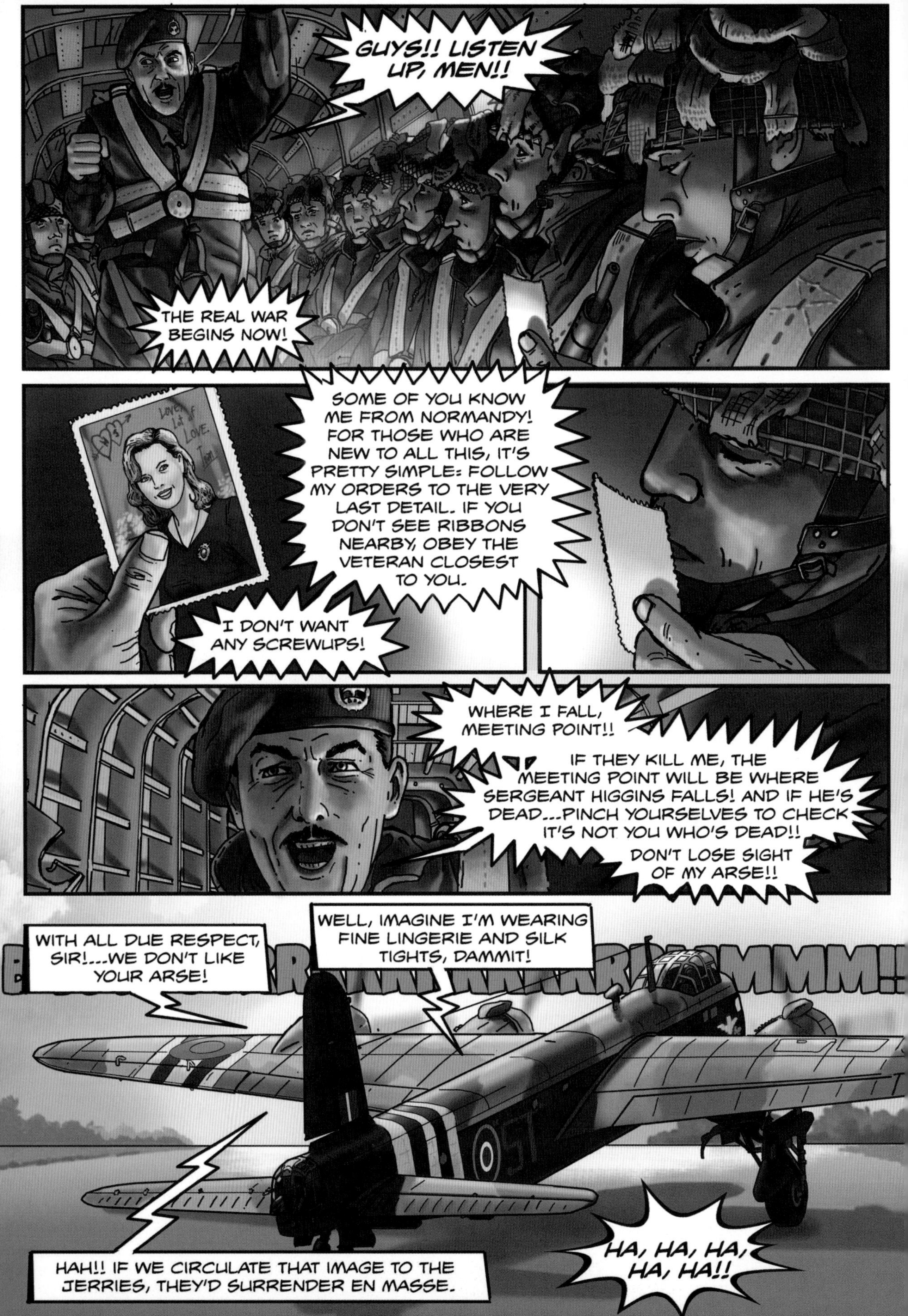
GUYS!! LISTEN UP, MEN!!
THE REAL WAR BEGINS NOW!
SOME OF YOU KNOW ME FROM NORMANDY! FOR THOSE WHO ARE NEW TO ALL THIS, IT'S PRETTY SIMPLE: FOLLOW MY ORDERS TO THE VERY LAST DETAIL. IF YOU DON'T SEE RIBBONS NEARBY, OBEY THE VETERAN CLOSEST TO YOU.
I DON'T WANT ANY SCREWUPS!
WHERE I FALL, MEETING POINT!!
IF THEY KILL ME, THE MEETING POINT WILL BE WHERE SERGEANT HIGGINS FALLS! AND IF HE'S DEAD...PINCH YOURSELVES TO CHECK IT'S NOT YOU WHO'S DEAD!!
DON'T LOSE SIGHT OF MY ARSE!!
WITH ALL DUE RESPECT, SIR!...WE DON'T LIKE YOUR ARSE!
WELL, IMAGINE I'M WEARING FINE LINGERIE AND SILK TIGHTS, DAMMIT!
HAH!! IF WE CIRCULATE THAT IMAGE TO THE JERRIES, THEY'D SURRENDER EN MASSE.
HA, HA, HA, HA, HA!!

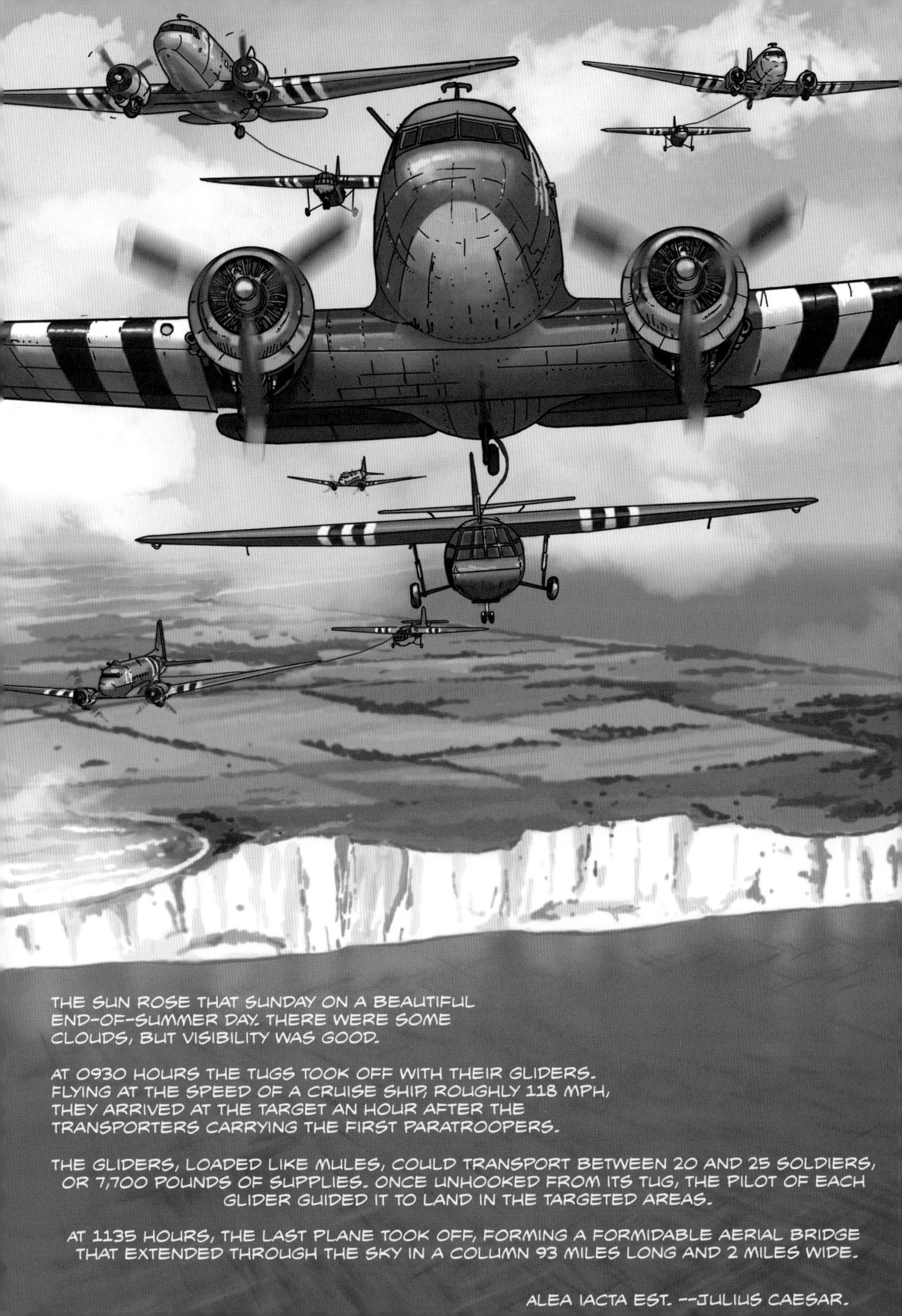
THE SUN ROSE THAT SUNDAY ON A BEAUTIFUL END-OF-SUMMER DAY. THERE WERE SOME CLOUDS, BUT VISIBILITY WAS GOOD.
AT 0930 HOURS THE TUGS TOOK OFF WITH THEIR GLIDERS. FLYING AT THE SPEED OF A CRUISE SHIP, ROUGHLY 118 MPH, THEY ARRIVED AT THE TARGET AN HOUR AFTER THE TRANSPORTERS CARRYING THE FIRST PARATROOPERS.
THE GLIDERS, LOADED LIKE MULES, COULD TRANSPORT BETWEEN 20 AND 25 SOLDIERS, OR 7,700 POUNDS OF SUPPLIES. ONCE UNHOOKED FROM ITS TUG, THE PILOT OF EACH GLIDER GUIDED IT TO LAND IN THE TARGETED AREAS.
AT 1135 HOURS, THE LAST PLANE TOOK OFF, FORMING A FORMIDABLE AERIAL BRIDGE THAT EXTENDED THROUGH THE SKY IN A COLUMN 93 MILES LONG AND 2 MILES WIDE.
ALEA IACTA EST. --JULIUS CAESAR.

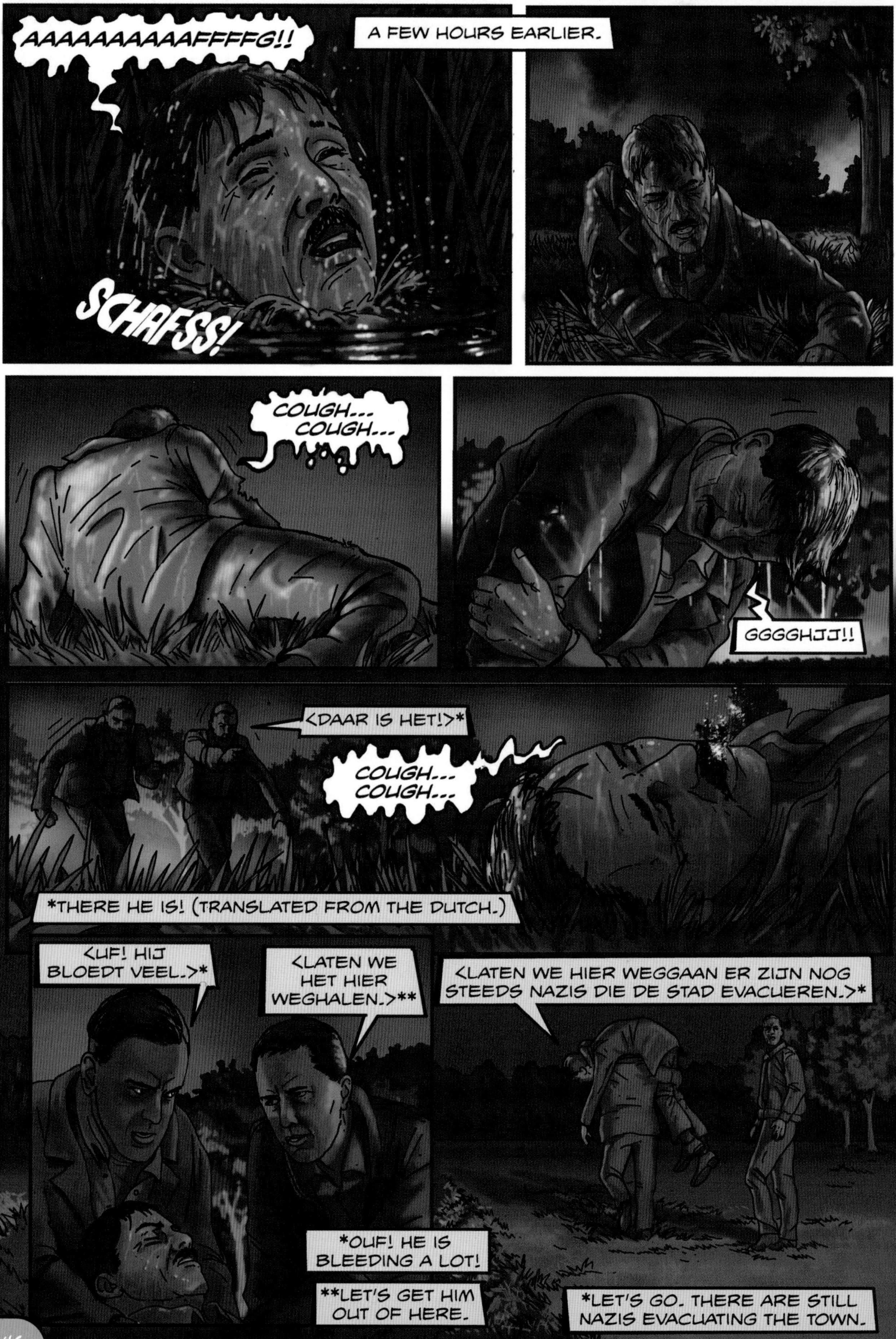
AAAAAAAAAAFFFFG!!
A FEW HOURS EARLIER.
SCHAFSS!
COUGH... COUGH...
GGGGHJJ!!
<DAAR IS HET!>*
COUGH... COUGH...
*THERE HE IS! (TRANSLATED FROM THE DUTCH.)
<UF! HIJ BLOEDT VEEL.>*
<LATEN WE HET HIER WEGHALEN.>**
<LATEN WE HIER WEGGAAN ER ZIJN NOG STEEDS NAZIS DIE DE STAD EVACUEREN.>*
*OUF! HE IS BLEEDING A LOT!
**LET'S GET HIM OUT OF HERE.
*LET'S GO. THERE ARE STILL NAZIS EVACUATING THE TOWN.

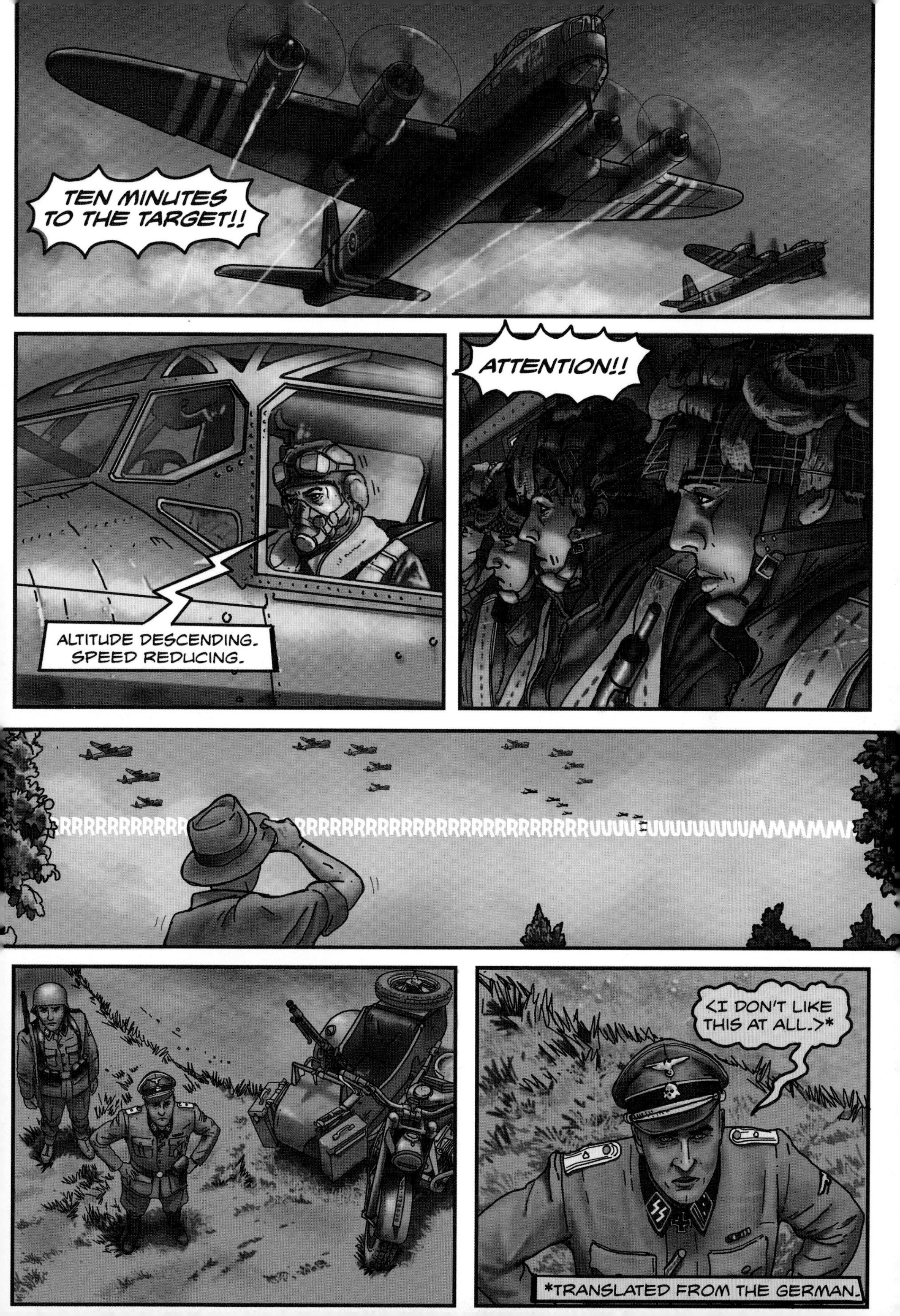
TEN MINUTES TO THE TARGET!!
ALTITUDE DESCENDING. SPEED REDUCING.
ATTENTION!!
RRRRRRRRRRRRRRRRRRRRRRRRRRRRRRRRRRRRRRRRRRRUUUUUUUUUUUUUUUUMMMMMM
<I DON'T LIKE THIS AT ALL.>*
*TRANSLATED FROM THE GERMAN.

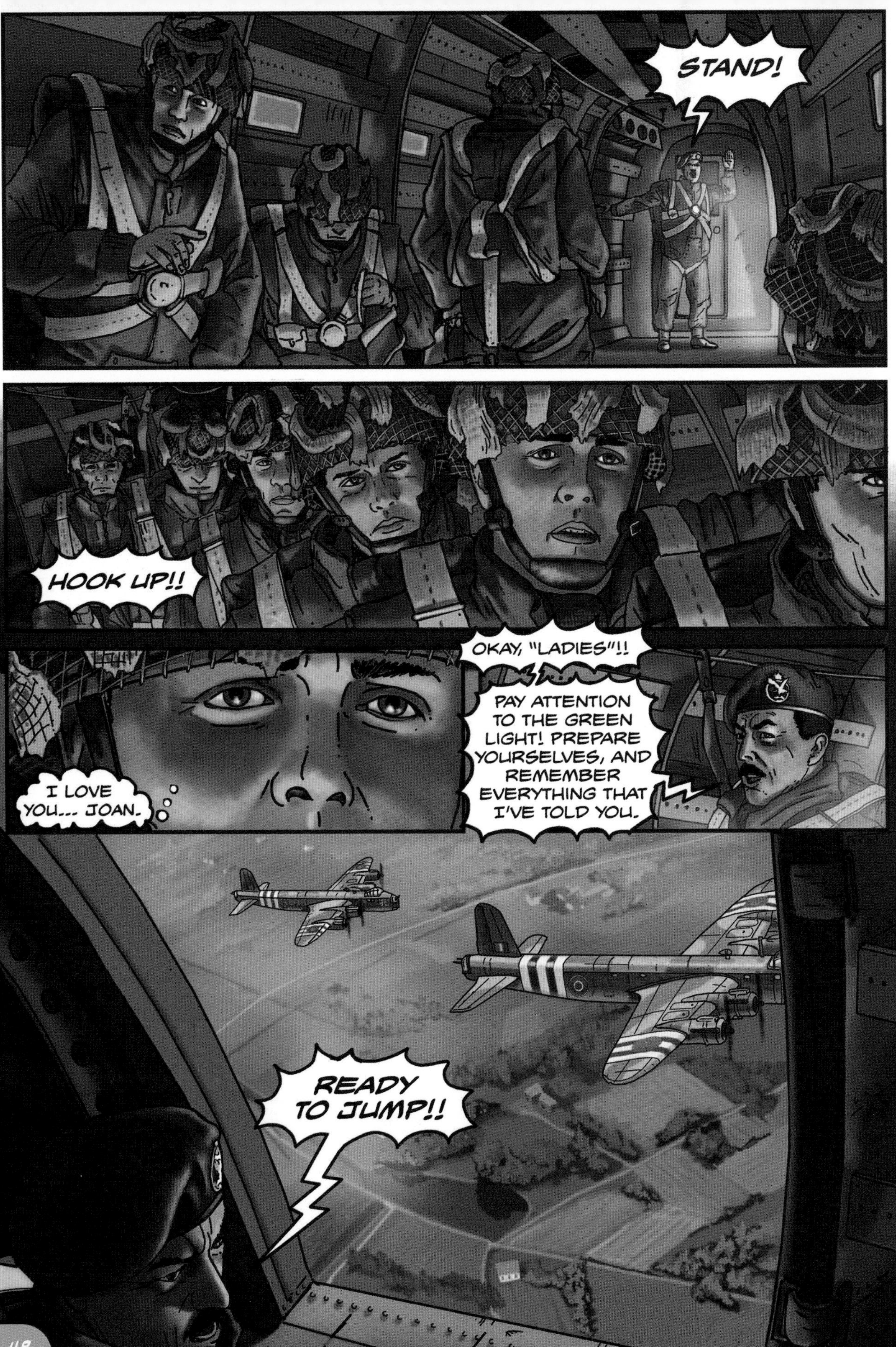
STAND!
HOOK UP!!
I LOVE YOU... JOAN.
OKAY, "LADIES"!!
PAY ATTENTION TO THE GREEN LIGHT! PREPARE YOURSELVES, AND REMEMBER EVERYTHING THAT I'VE TOLD YOU.
READY TO JUMP!!

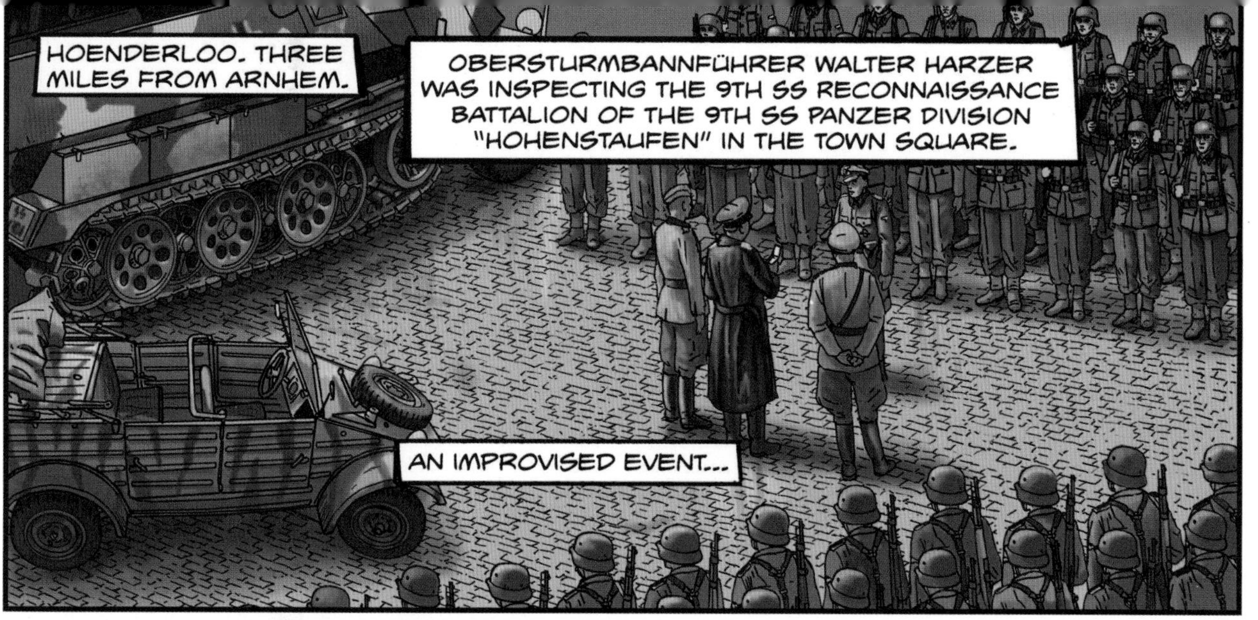
HOENDERLOO. THREE MILES FROM ARNHEM.
OBERSTURMBANNFÜHRER WALTER HARZER WAS INSPECTING THE 9TH SS RECONNAISSANCE BATTALION OF THE 9TH SS PANZER DIVISION "HOHENSTAUFEN" IN THE TOWN SQUARE.
AN IMPROVISED EVENT...

...IN WHICH THE CHIEF OF THE BATTALION, HAUPTSTURMFÜHRER VIKTOR GRABNER, RECEIVED THE KNIGHT'S CROSS AFTER A BRIEF SPEECH IN WHICH HARZER PRAISED THE UNIT.

BUT... AN UNEXPECTED BUZZ INTERRUPTED THE CEREMONY.

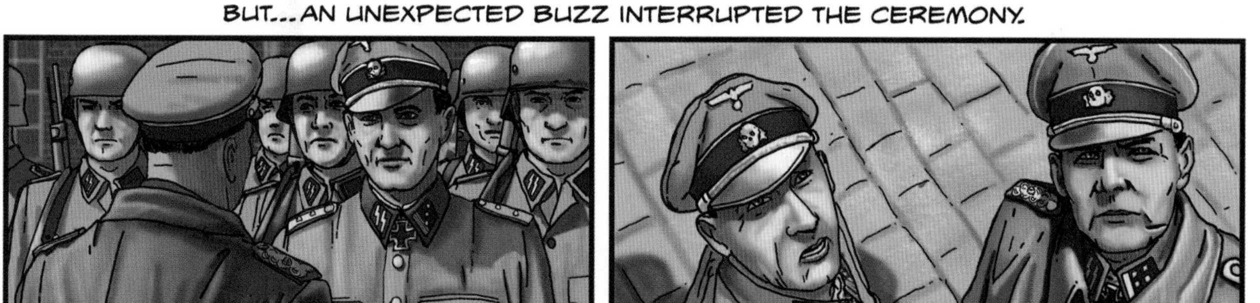

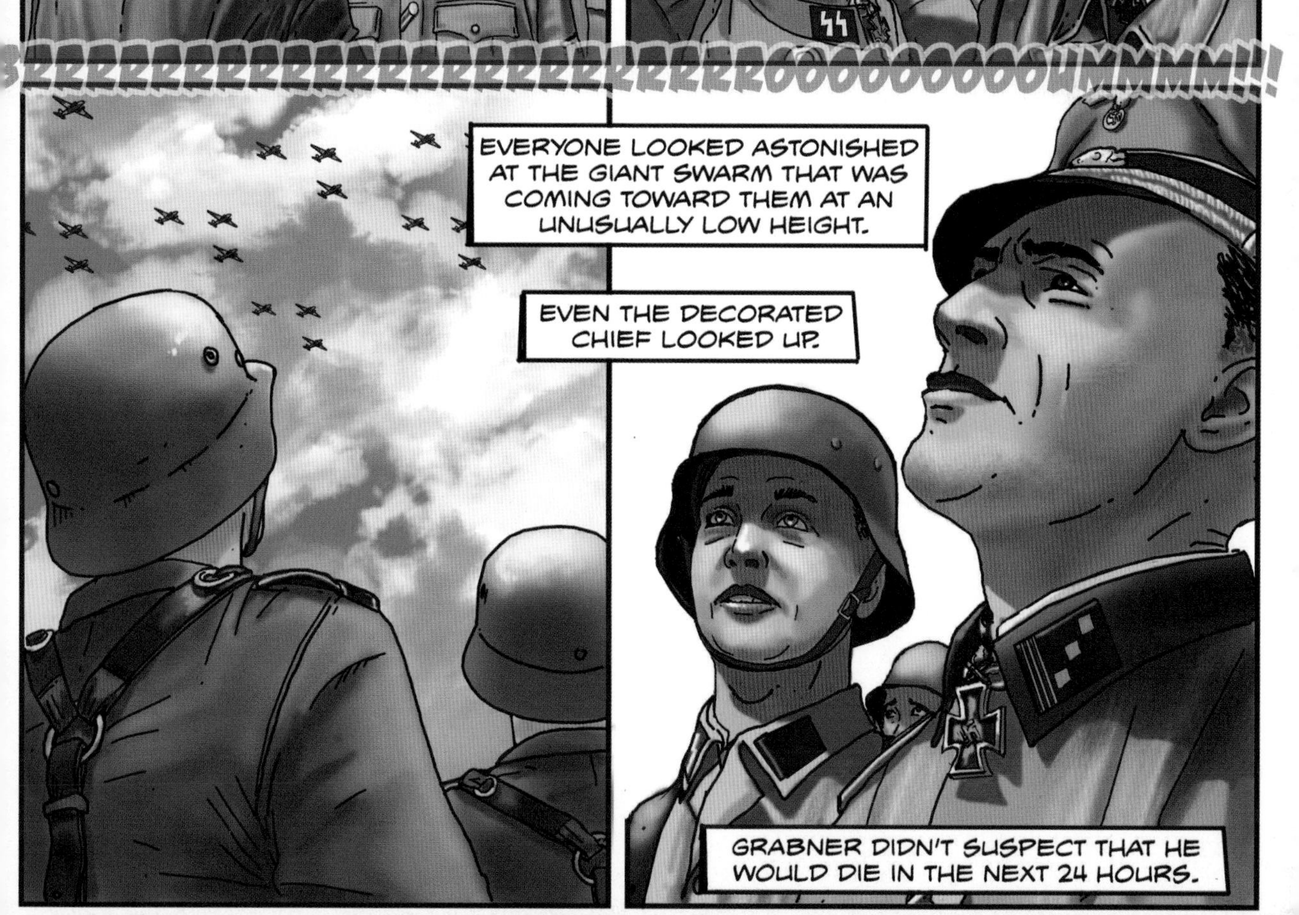
BRRRRRRRRRRRRRRRRRRRRRRRRRRRRRRRRROOOOOOOOOOOUMMMMM!!
EVERYONE LOOKED ASTONISHED AT THE GIANT SWARM THAT WAS COMING TOWARD THEM AT AN UNUSUALLY LOW HEIGHT.
EVEN THE DECORATED CHIEF LOOKED UP.
GRABNER DIDN'T SUSPECT THAT HE WOULD DIE IN THE NEXT 24 HOURS.

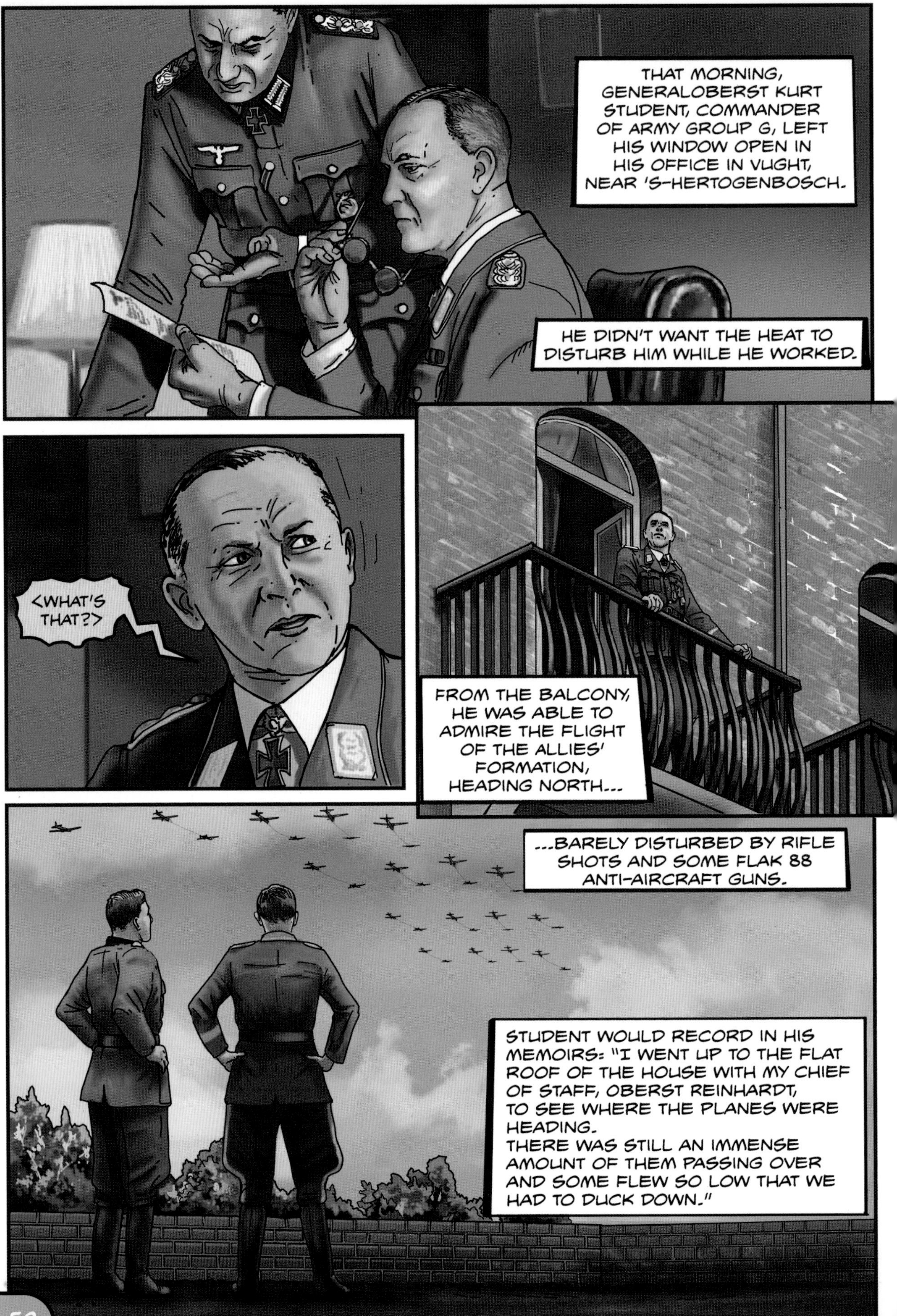
THAT MORNING, GENERALOBERST KURT STUDENT, COMMANDER OF ARMY GROUP G, LEFT HIS WINDOW OPEN IN HIS OFFICE IN VUGHT, NEAR 'S-HERTOGENBOSCH.
HE DIDN'T WANT THE HEAT TO DISTURB HIM WHILE HE WORKED.
<WHAT'S THAT?>
FROM THE BALCONY, HE WAS ABLE TO ADMIRE THE FLIGHT OF THE ALLIES' FORMATION, HEADING NORTH...
...BARELY DISTURBED BY RIFLE SHOTS AND SOME FLAK 88 ANTI-AIRCRAFT GUNS.
STUDENT WOULD RECORD IN HIS MEMOIRS: "I WENT UP TO THE FLAT ROOF OF THE HOUSE WITH MY CHIEF OF STAFF, OBERST REINHARDT, TO SEE WHERE THE PLANES WERE HEADING.
THERE WAS STILL AN IMMENSE AMOUNT OF THEM PASSING OVER AND SOME FLEW SO LOW THAT WE HAD TO DUCK DOWN."

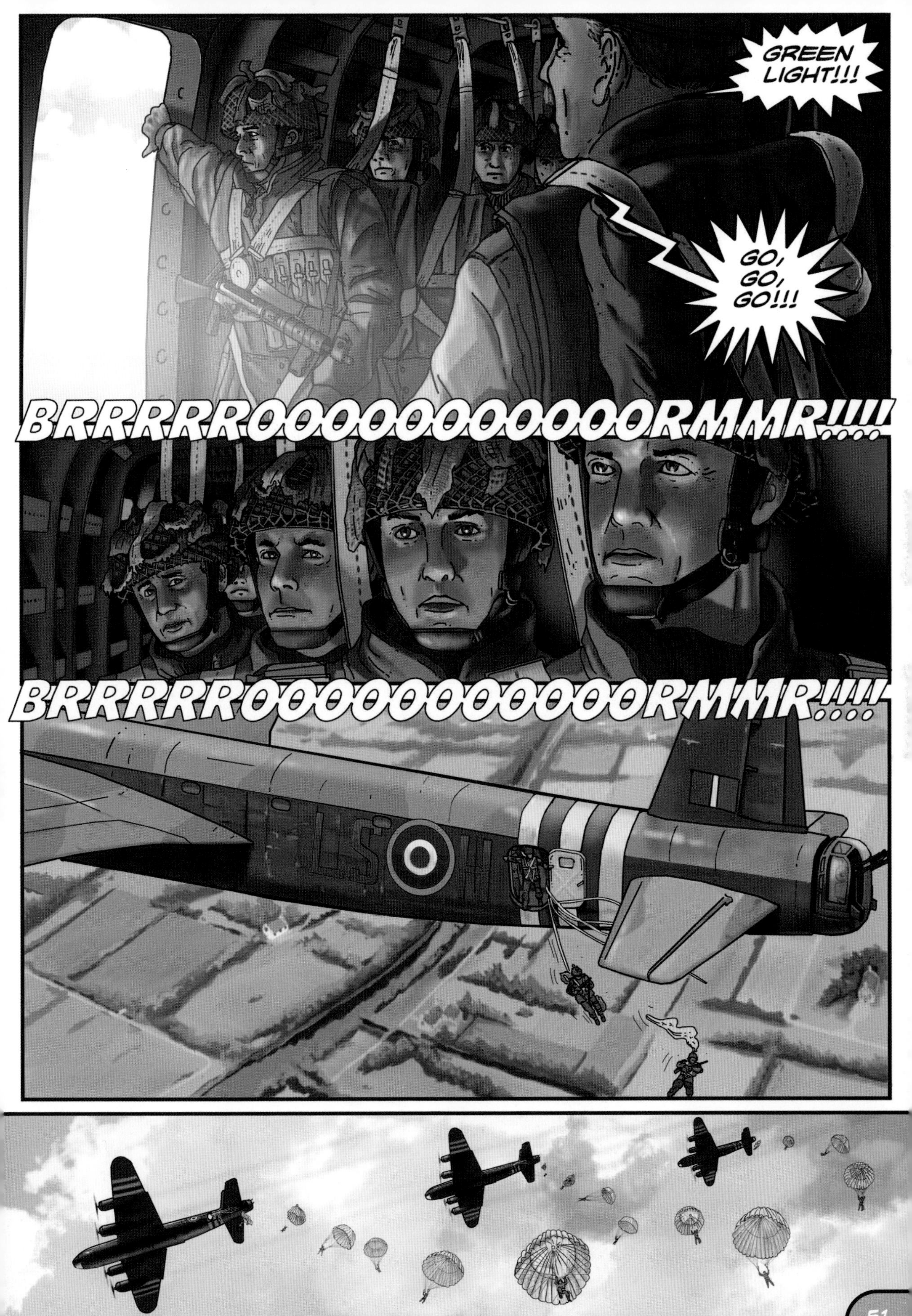
GREEN LIGHT!!!
GO, GO, GO!!!
BRRRRROOOOOOOOOOOORMMR!!!!
BRRRRROOOOOOOOOOOORMMR!!!!
LS H

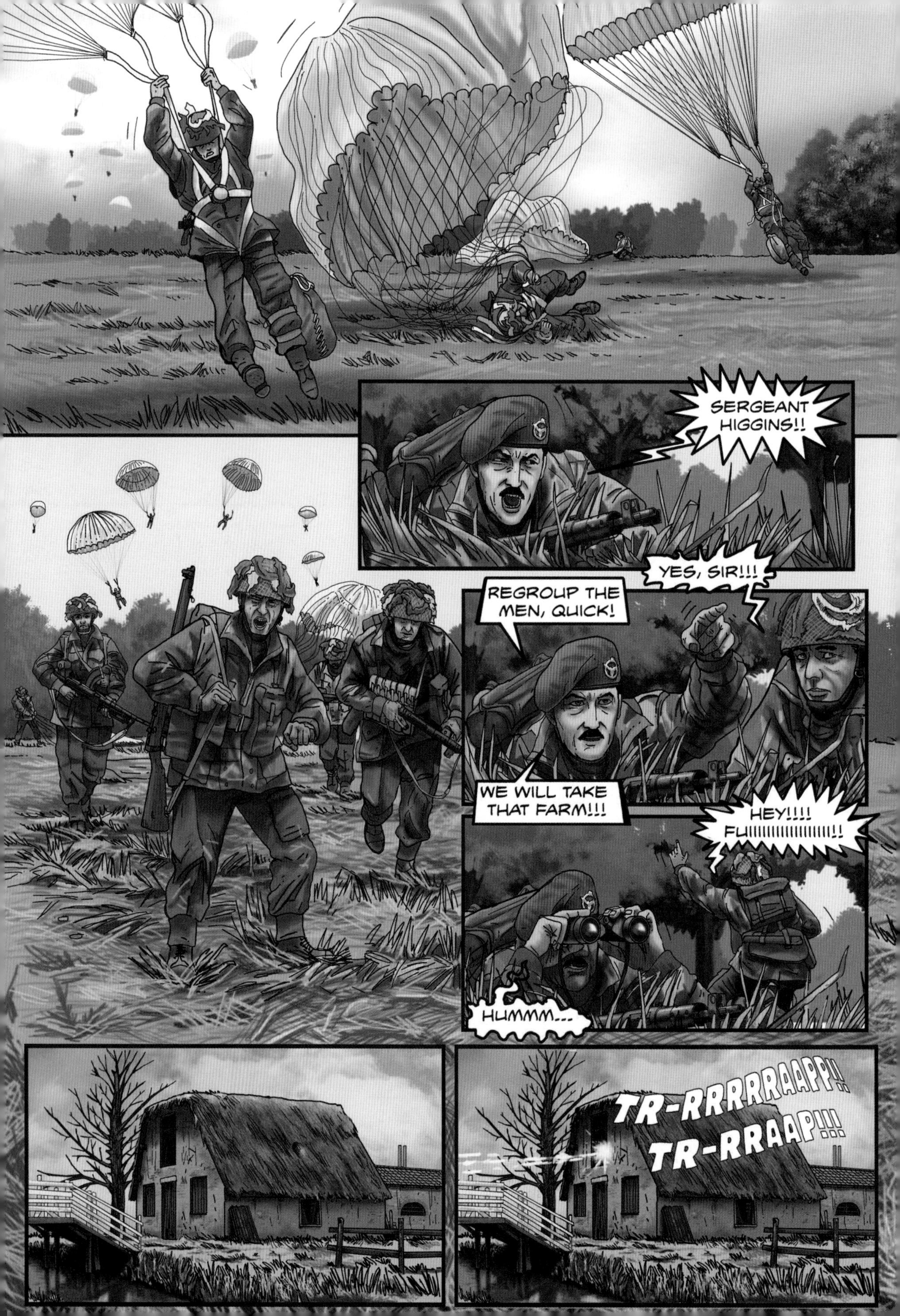
SERGEANT HIGGINS!!
YES, SIR!!!
REGROUP THE MEN, QUICK!
WE WILL TAKE THAT FARM!!!
HEY!!!! FUIIIIIIIIIIIIIIII!!
HUMMM...
TR-RRRRRAAPP!!
TR-RRAAP!!!

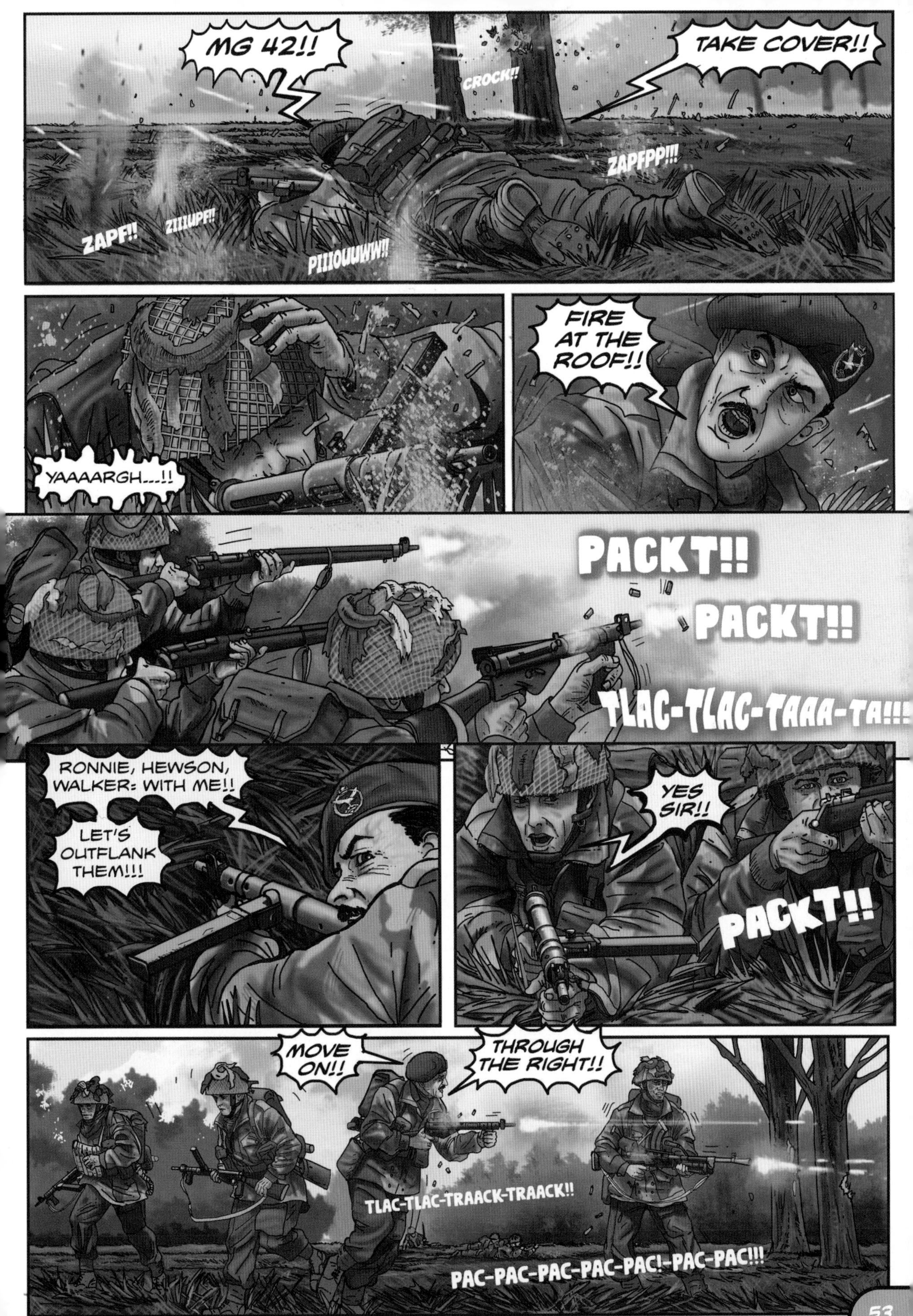
MG 42!!
CROCK!!
TAKE COVER!!
ZAPFPP!!!
ZAPF!!
ZIIIUPF!!
PIIIOUUWW!!
YAAAARGH...!!
FIRE AT THE ROOF!!
PACKT!!
PACKT!!
TLAC-TLAC-TAAA-TA!!!
RONNIE, HEWSON, WALKER: WITH ME!!
LET'S OUTFLANK THEM!!!
YES SIR!!
PACKT!!
MOVE ON!!
THROUGH THE RIGHT!!
TLAC-TLAC-TRAACK-TRAACK!!
PAC-PAC-PAC-PAC-PAC!-PAC-PAC!!!

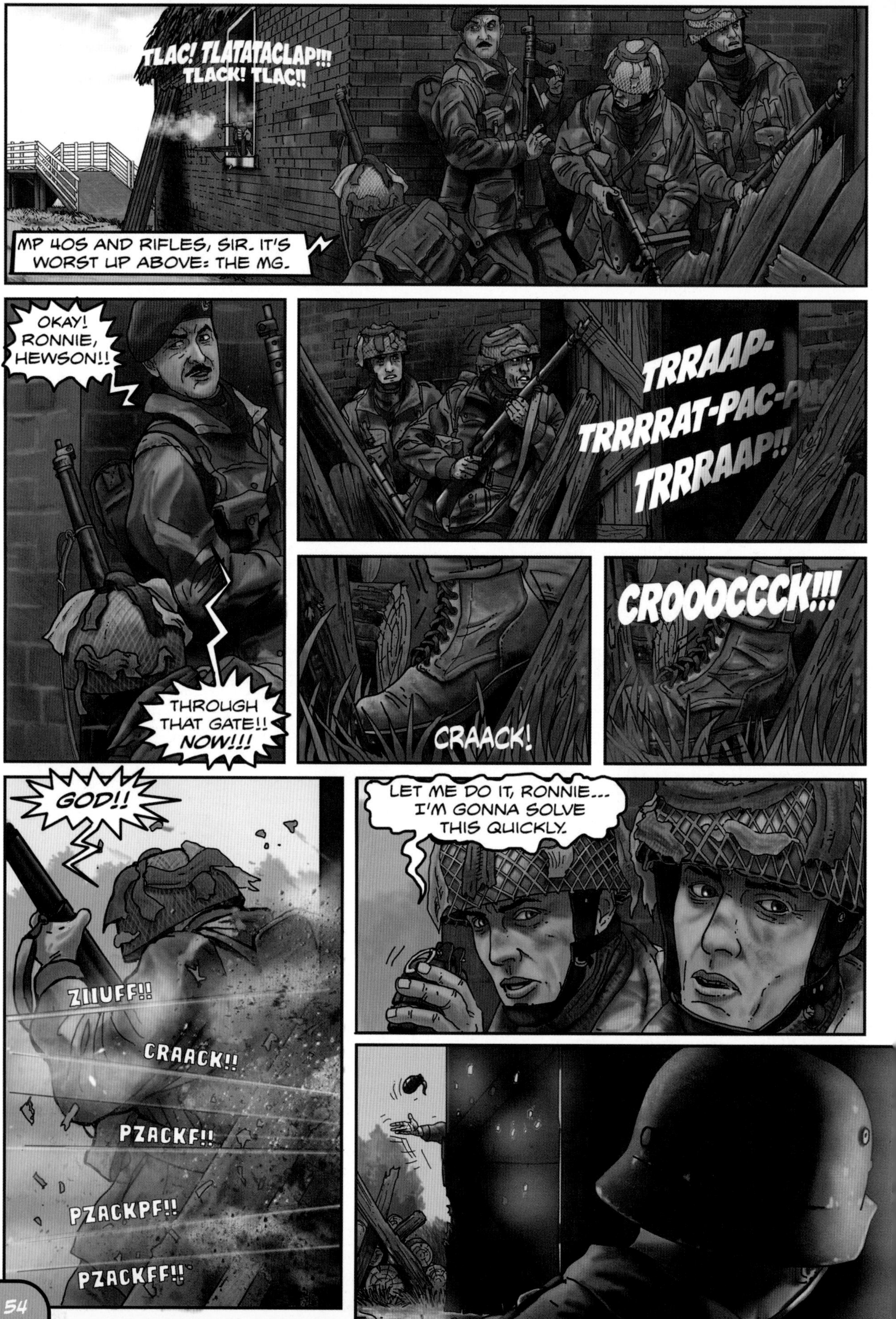

TLAC! TLATATACLAP!!!
TLACK! TLAC!!
MP 40S AND RIFLES, SIR. IT'S WORST UP ABOVE: THE MG.
OKAY! RONNIE, HEWSON!!
THROUGH THAT GATE!! NOW!!!
TRRAAP-
TRRRRAT-PAC-PA
TRRRAAP!!
CRAACK!
CROOOCCCK!!!
GOD!!
ZIIUFF!!
CRAACK!!
PZACKF!!
PZACKPF!!
PZACKFF!!
LET ME DO IT, RONNIE... I'M GONNA SOLVE THIS QUICKLY.

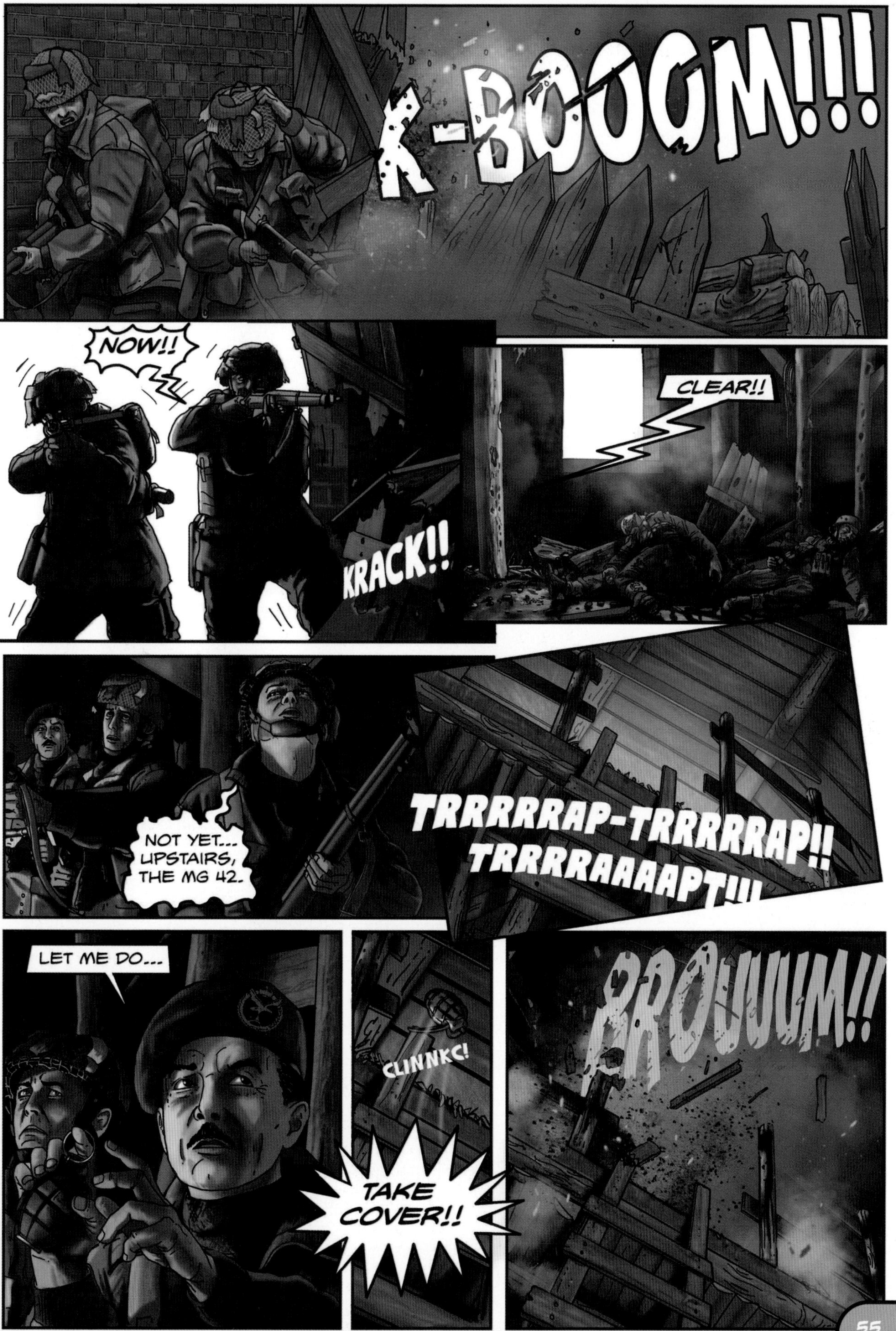
K-BOOOM!!!
NOW!!
KRACK!!
CLEAR!!
NOT YET... UPSTAIRS, THE MG 42.
TRRRRRAP-TRRRRRAP!! TRRRRAAAAPT!!!
LET ME DO...
TAKE COVER!!
CLINNKC!
BROUUUM!!

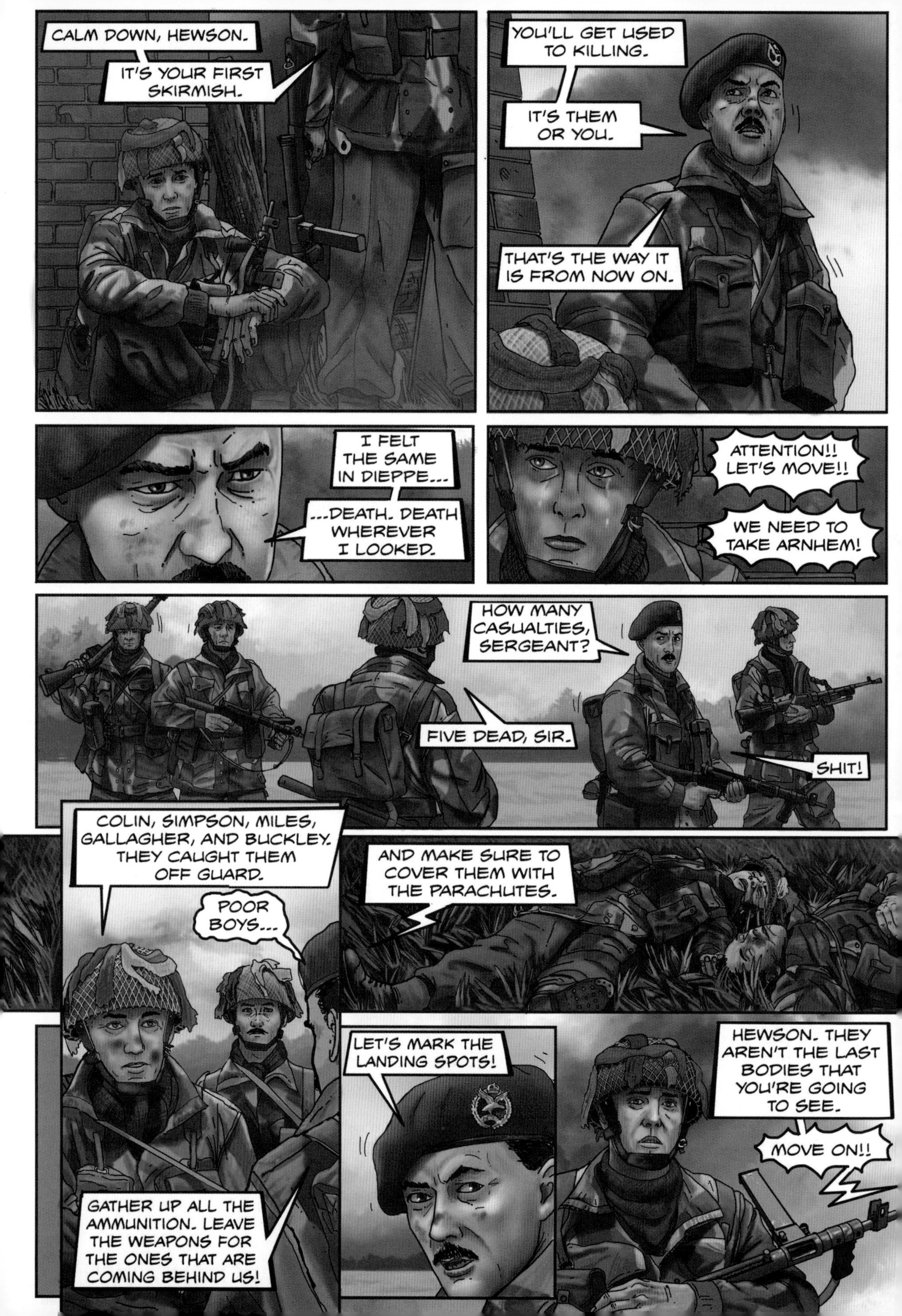
CALM DOWN, HEWSON.
IT'S YOUR FIRST SKIRMISH.
YOU'LL GET USED TO KILLING.
IT'S THEM OR YOU.
THAT'S THE WAY IT IS FROM NOW ON.
I FELT THE SAME IN DIEPPE...
...DEATH. DEATH WHEREVER I LOOKED.
ATTENTION!! LET'S MOVE!!
WE NEED TO TAKE ARNHEM!
HOW MANY CASUALTIES, SERGEANT?
FIVE DEAD, SIR.
SHIT!
COLIN, SIMPSON, MILES, GALLAGHER, AND BUCKLEY. THEY CAUGHT THEM OFF GUARD.
POOR BOYS...
AND MAKE SURE TO COVER THEM WITH THE PARACHUTES.
GATHER UP ALL THE AMMUNITION. LEAVE THE WEAPONS FOR THE ONES THAT ARE COMING BEHIND US!
LET'S MARK THE LANDING SPOTS!
HEWSON. THEY AREN'T THE LAST BODIES THAT YOU'RE GOING TO SEE.
MOVE ON!!

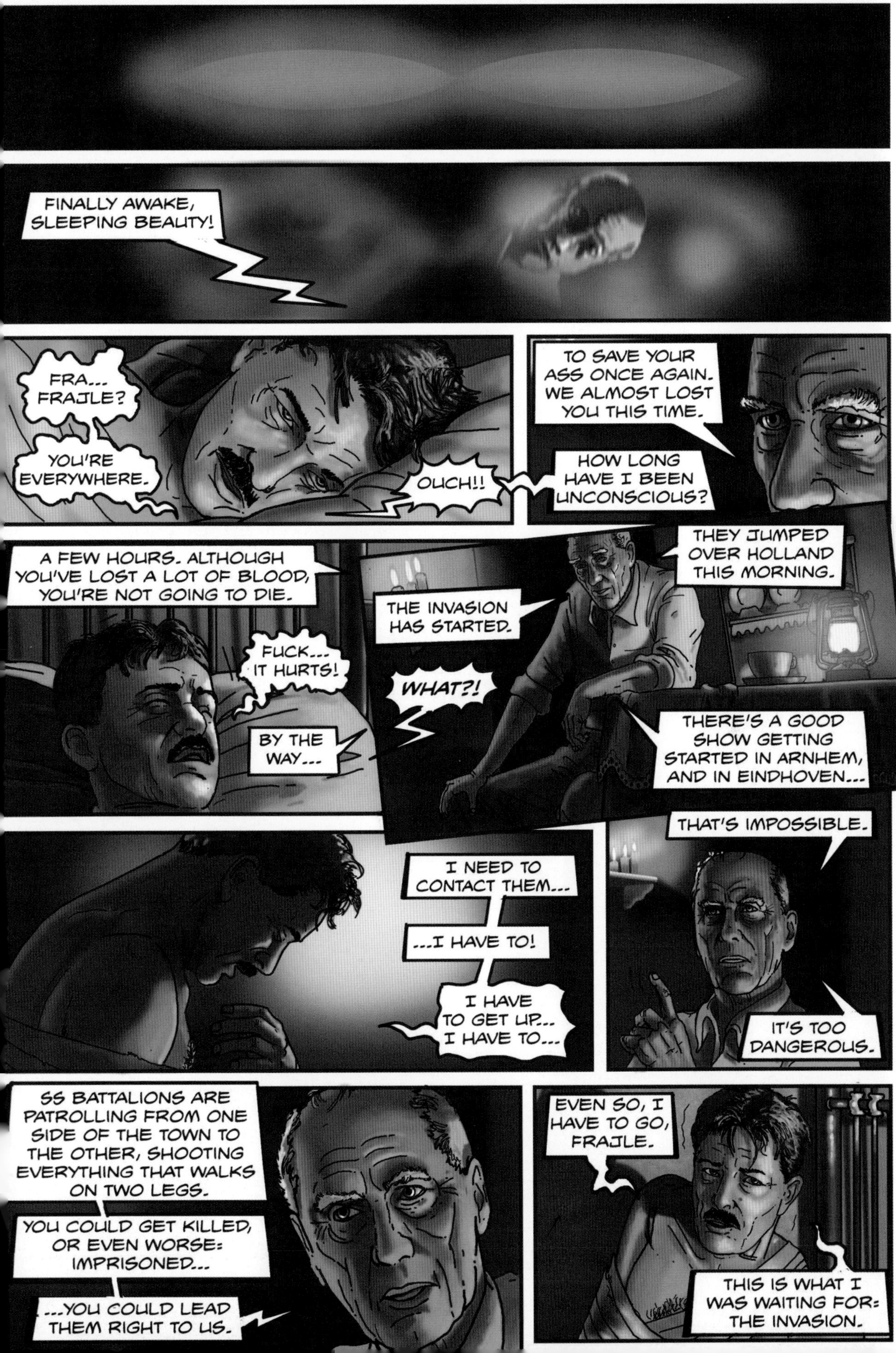
FINALLY AWAKE, SLEEPING BEAUTY!
FRA... FRAJLE?
YOU'RE EVERYWHERE.
OUCH!!
TO SAVE YOUR ASS ONCE AGAIN. WE ALMOST LOST YOU THIS TIME.
HOW LONG HAVE I BEEN UNCONSCIOUS?
A FEW HOURS. ALTHOUGH YOU'VE LOST A LOT OF BLOOD, YOU'RE NOT GOING TO DIE.
FUCK... IT HURTS!
BY THE WAY...
THE INVASION HAS STARTED.
THEY JUMPED OVER HOLLAND THIS MORNING.
WHAT?!
THERE'S A GOOD SHOW GETTING STARTED IN ARNHEM, AND IN EINDHOVEN...
I NEED TO CONTACT THEM...
...I HAVE TO!
I HAVE TO GET UP... I HAVE TO...
THAT'S IMPOSSIBLE.
IT'S TOO DANGEROUS.
SS BATTALIONS ARE PATROLLING FROM ONE SIDE OF THE TOWN TO THE OTHER, SHOOTING EVERYTHING THAT WALKS ON TWO LEGS.
YOU COULD GET KILLED, OR EVEN WORSE: IMPRISONED...
...YOU COULD LEAD THEM RIGHT TO US.
EVEN SO, I HAVE TO GO, FRAJLE.
THIS IS WHAT I WAS WAITING FOR: THE INVASION.

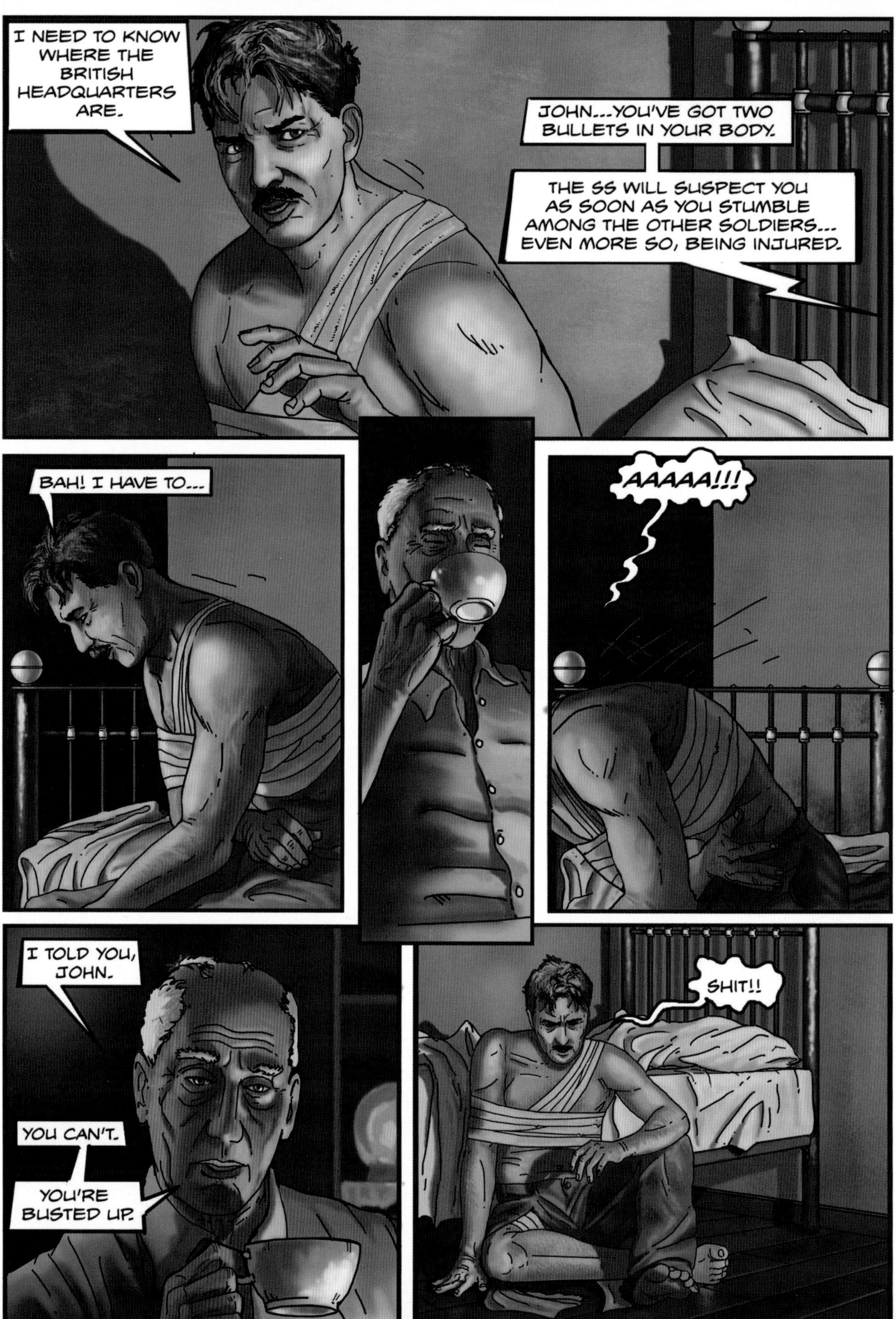
I NEED TO KNOW WHERE THE BRITISH HEADQUARTERS ARE.
JOHN...YOU'VE GOT TWO BULLETS IN YOUR BODY.
THE SS WILL SUSPECT YOU AS SOON AS YOU STUMBLE AMONG THE OTHER SOLDIERS... EVEN MORE SO, BEING INJURED.
BAH! I HAVE TO...
AAAAA!!!
I TOLD YOU, JOHN.
YOU CAN'T.
YOU'RE BUSTED UP.
SHIT!!

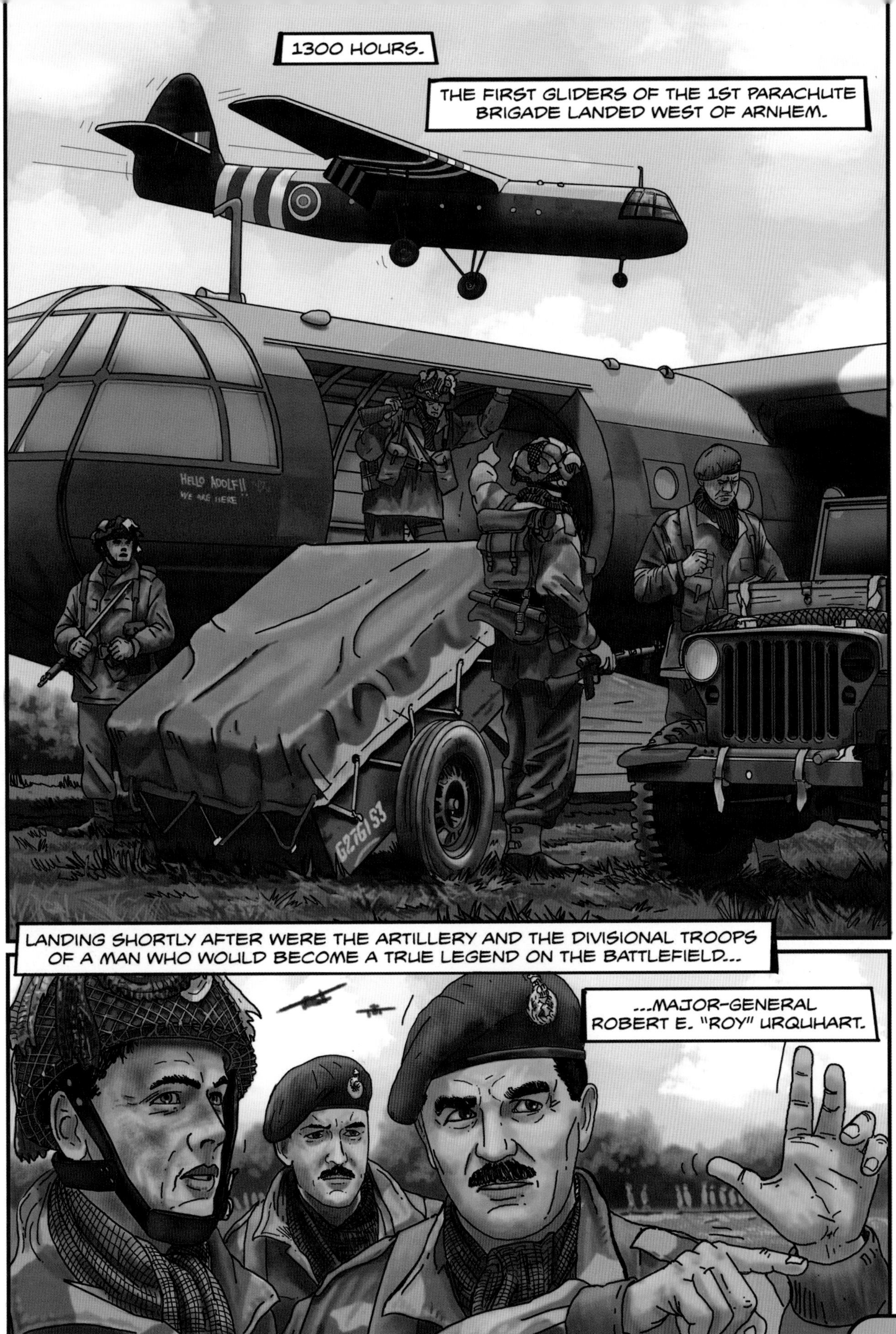
1300 HOURS.
THE FIRST GLIDERS OF THE 1ST PARACHUTE BRIGADE LANDED WEST OF ARNHEM.
HELLO ADOLF!!
WE ARE HERE
LANDING SHORTLY AFTER WERE THE ARTILLERY AND THE DIVISIONAL TROOPS OF A MAN WHO WOULD BECOME A TRUE LEGEND ON THE BATTLEFIELD...
...MAJOR-GENERAL ROBERT E. "ROY" URQUHART.

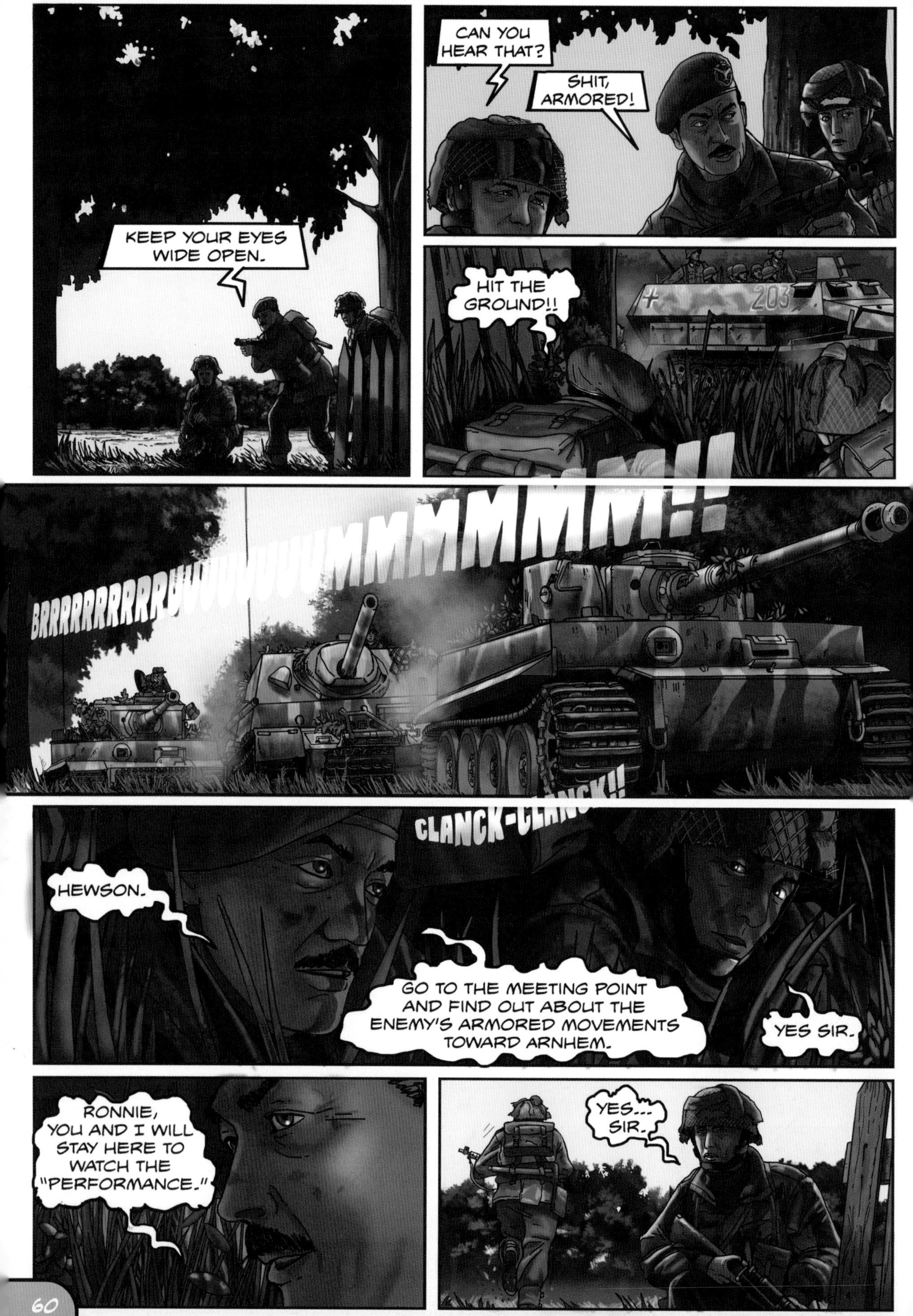
KEEP YOUR EYES WIDE OPEN.
CAN YOU HEAR THAT?
SHIT, ARMORED!
HIT THE GROUND!!
BRRRRRRRRRRRUUUUUUUUMMMMMMMM!!
CLANCK-CLANCK!!
HEWSON.
GO TO THE MEETING POINT AND FIND OUT ABOUT THE ENEMY'S ARMORED MOVEMENTS TOWARD ARNHEM.
YES SIR.
RONNIE, YOU AND I WILL STAY HERE TO WATCH THE "PERFORMANCE."
YES... SIR.

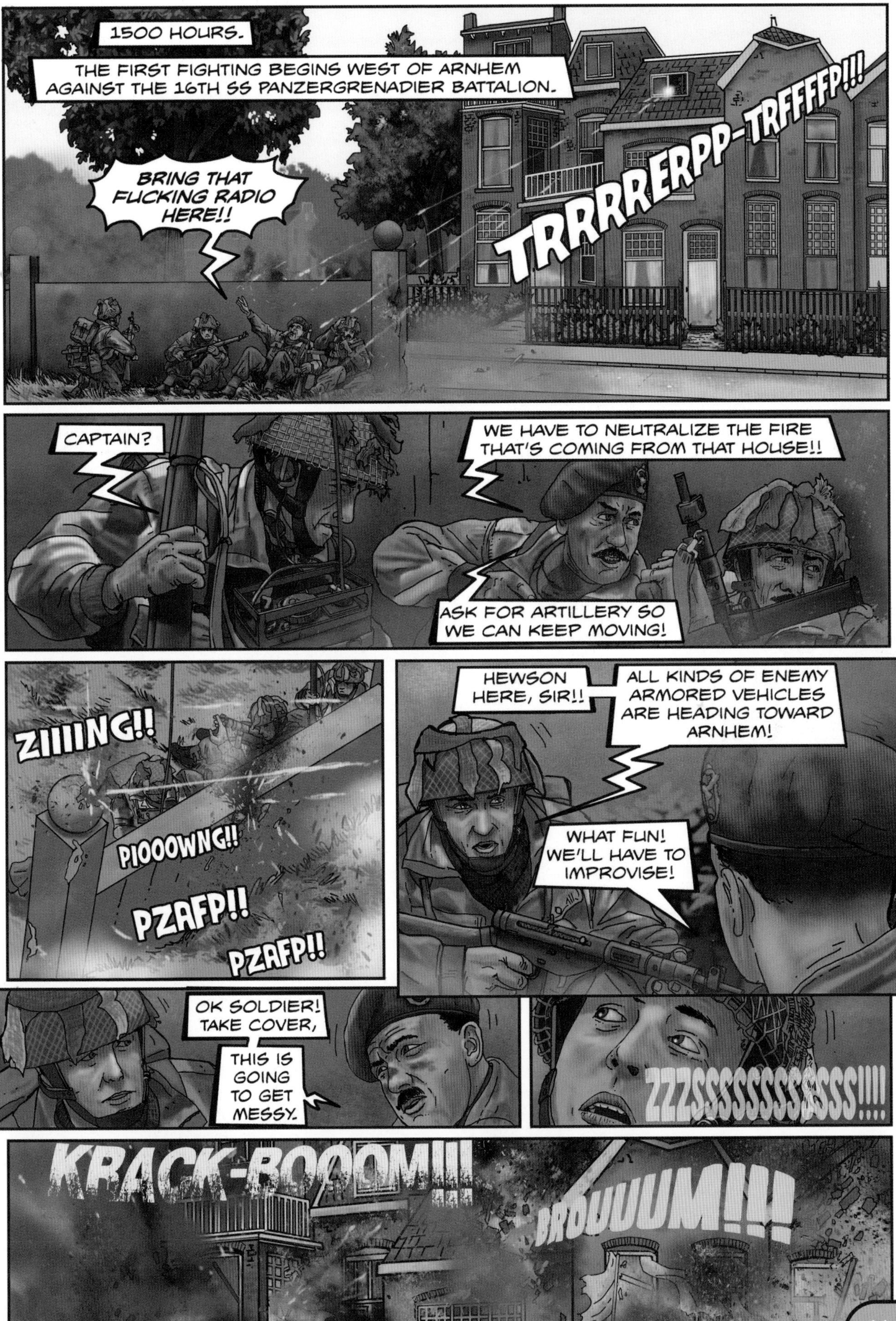
1500 HOURS.
THE FIRST FIGHTING BEGINS WEST OF ARNHEM AGAINST THE 16TH SS PANZERGRENADIER BATTALION.
BRING THAT FUCKING RADIO HERE!!
TRRRRERPP-TRFFFFP!!!
CAPTAIN?
WE HAVE TO NEUTRALIZE THE FIRE THAT'S COMING FROM THAT HOUSE!!
ASK FOR ARTILLERY SO WE CAN KEEP MOVING!
ZIIIING!!
PIOOOWNG!!
PZAFP!!
PZAFP!!
HEWSON HERE, SIR!!
ALL KINDS OF ENEMY ARMORED VEHICLES ARE HEADING TOWARD ARNHEM!
WHAT FUN! WE'LL HAVE TO IMPROVISE!
OK SOLDIER! TAKE COVER,
THIS IS GOING TO GET MESSY.
ZZZSSSSSSSSSSSS!!!!
KRACK-BOOOM!!!
BROUUUM!!!

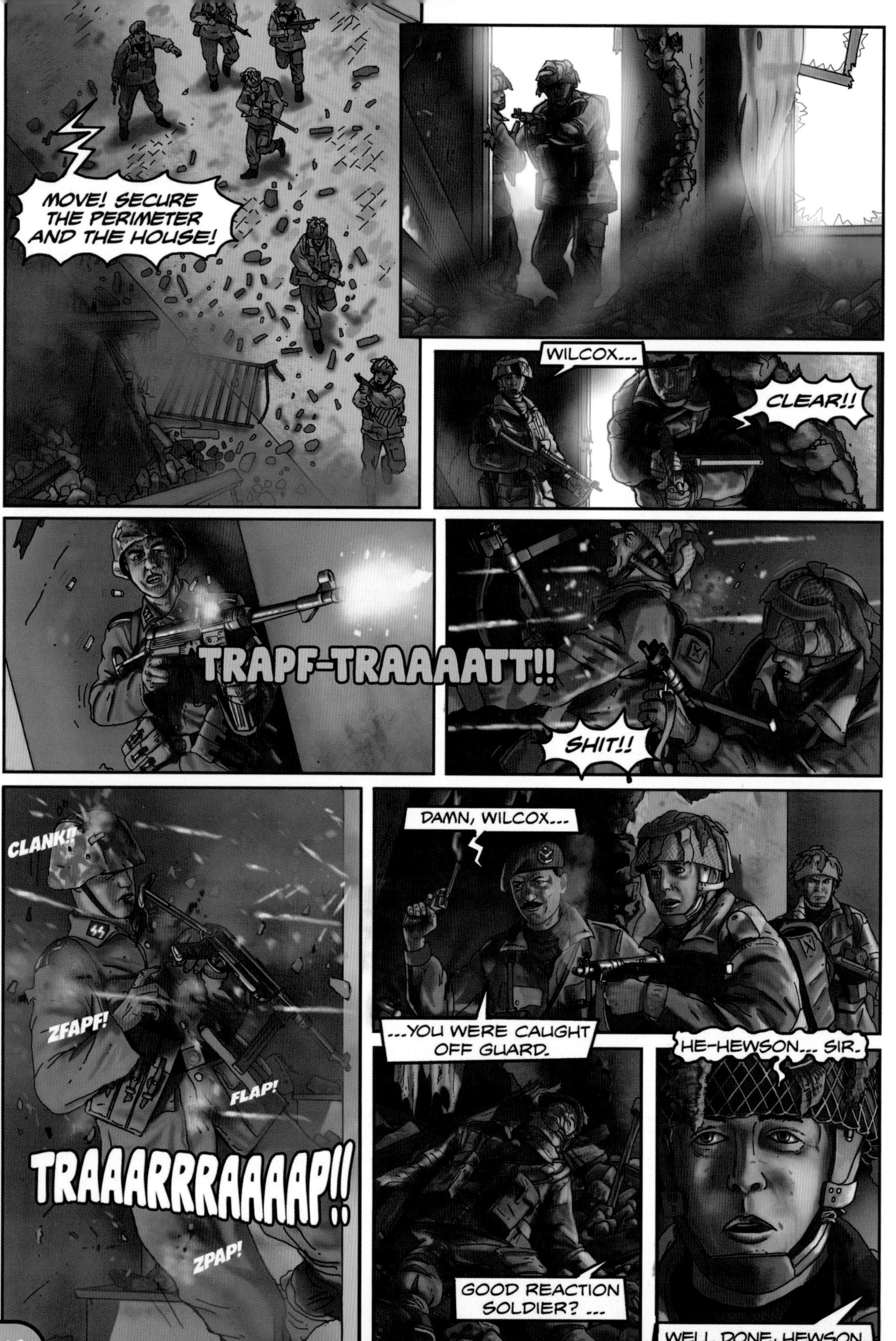
MOVE! SECURE THE PERIMETER AND THE HOUSE!
WILCOX...
CLEAR!!
TRAPF-TRAAAATT!!
SHIT!!
CLANK!!
ZFAPF!
FLAP!
TRAAARRRAAAAP!!
ZPAP!
DAMN, WILCOX...
...YOU WERE CAUGHT OFF GUARD.
GOOD REACTION SOLDIER? ...
HE-HEWSON... SIR.
WELL DONE, HEWSON.

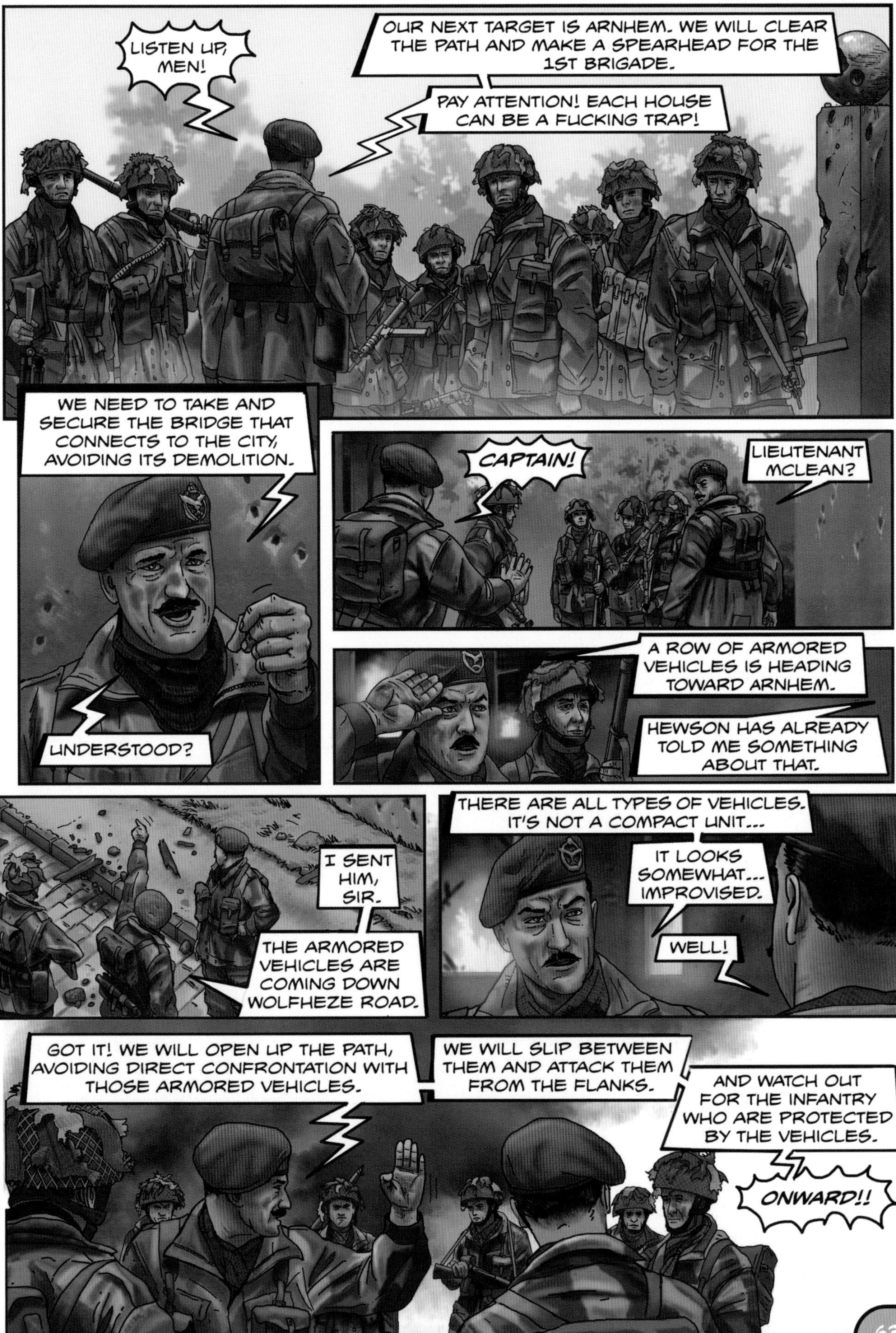
LISTEN UP, MEN!
OUR NEXT TARGET IS ARNHEM. WE WILL CLEAR THE PATH AND MAKE A SPEARHEAD FOR THE 1ST BRIGADE.
PAY ATTENTION! EACH HOUSE CAN BE A FUCKING TRAP!
WE NEED TO TAKE AND SECURE THE BRIDGE THAT CONNECTS TO THE CITY, AVOIDING ITS DEMOLITION.
UNDERSTOOD?
CAPTAIN!
LIEUTENANT MCLEAN?
A ROW OF ARMORED VEHICLES IS HEADING TOWARD ARNHEM.
HEWSON HAS ALREADY TOLD ME SOMETHING ABOUT THAT.
I SENT HIM, SIR.
THE ARMORED VEHICLES ARE COMING DOWN WOLFHEZE ROAD.
THERE ARE ALL TYPES OF VEHICLES. IT'S NOT A COMPACT UNIT...
IT LOOKS SOMEWHAT... IMPROVISED.
WELL!
GOT IT! WE WILL OPEN UP THE PATH, AVOIDING DIRECT CONFRONTATION WITH THOSE ARMORED VEHICLES.
WE WILL SLIP BETWEEN THEM AND ATTACK THEM FROM THE FLANKS.
AND WATCH OUT FOR THE INFANTRY WHO ARE PROTECTED BY THE VEHICLES.
ONWARD!!

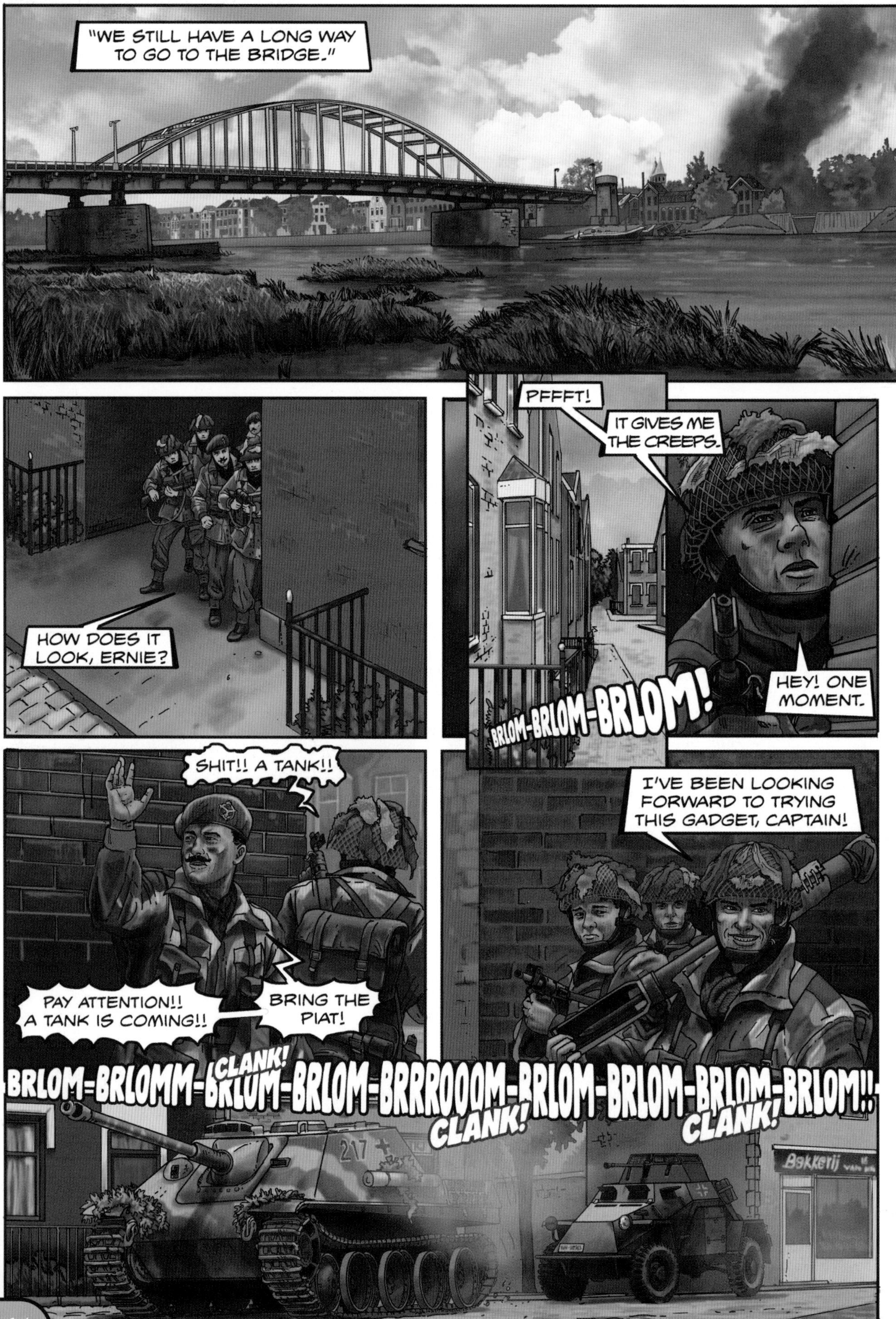

"WE STILL HAVE A LONG WAY TO GO TO THE BRIDGE."
HOW DOES IT LOOK, ERNIE?
PFFFT!
IT GIVES ME THE CREEPS.
HEY! ONE MOMENT.
BRLOM-BRLOM-BRLOM!
SHIT!! A TANK!!
PAY ATTENTION!! A TANK IS COMING!!
BRING THE PIAT!
I'VE BEEN LOOKING FORWARD TO TRYING THIS GADGET, CAPTAIN!
BRLOM=BRLOMM-BRLUM-BRLOM-BRRROOOM-BRLOM-BRLOM-BRLOM-BRLOM!!
CLANK!
CLANK!
CLANK!
217
Bakkerij

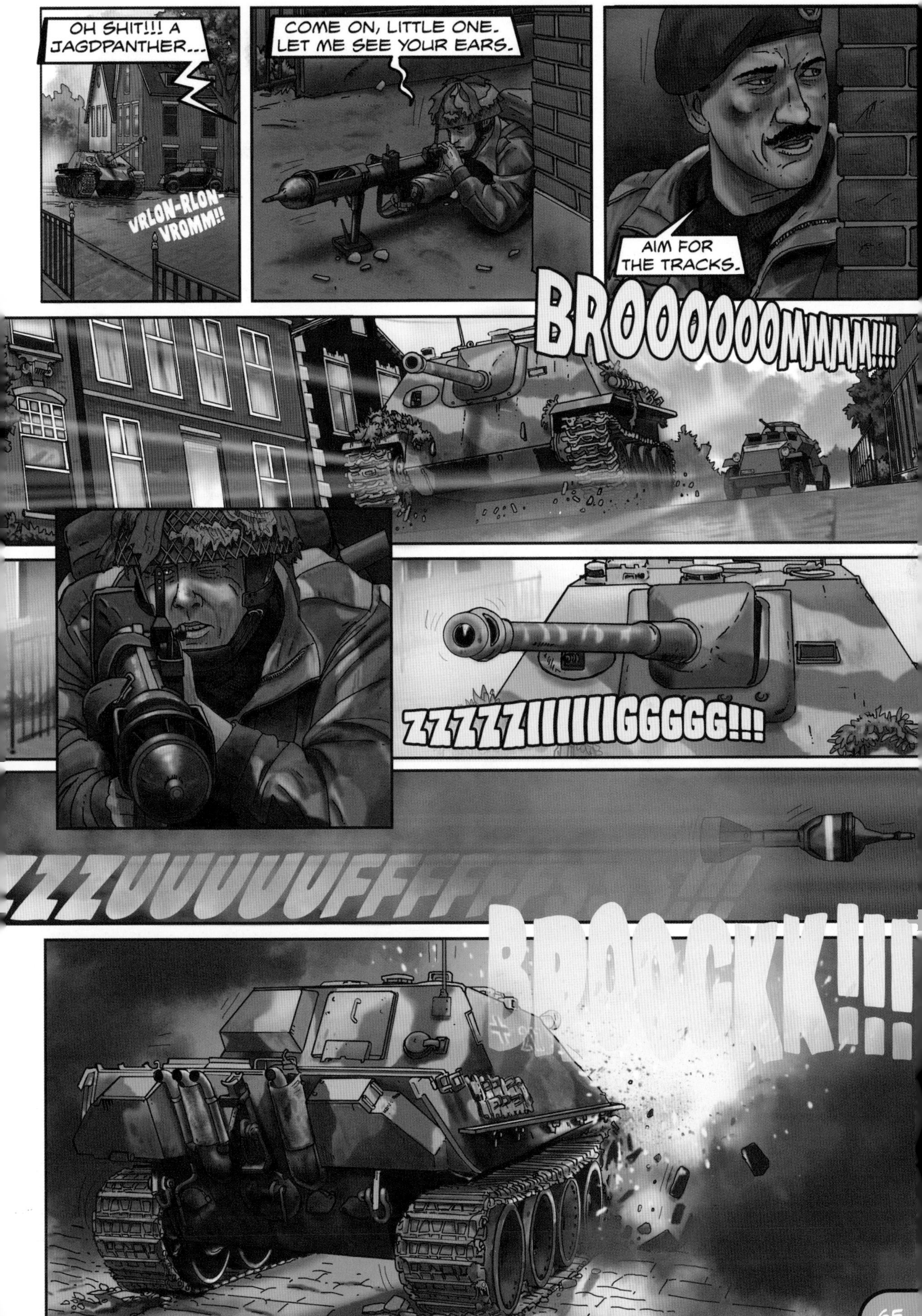

OH SHIT!!! A JAGDPANTHER...
VRLON-RLON-VROMM!!
COME ON, LITTLE ONE. LET ME SEE YOUR EARS.
AIM FOR THE TRACKS.
BROOOOOOMMMM!!!!
ZZZZZIIIIIIGGGGG!!!
ZZUUUUUUFFF
BROOCKK!!!

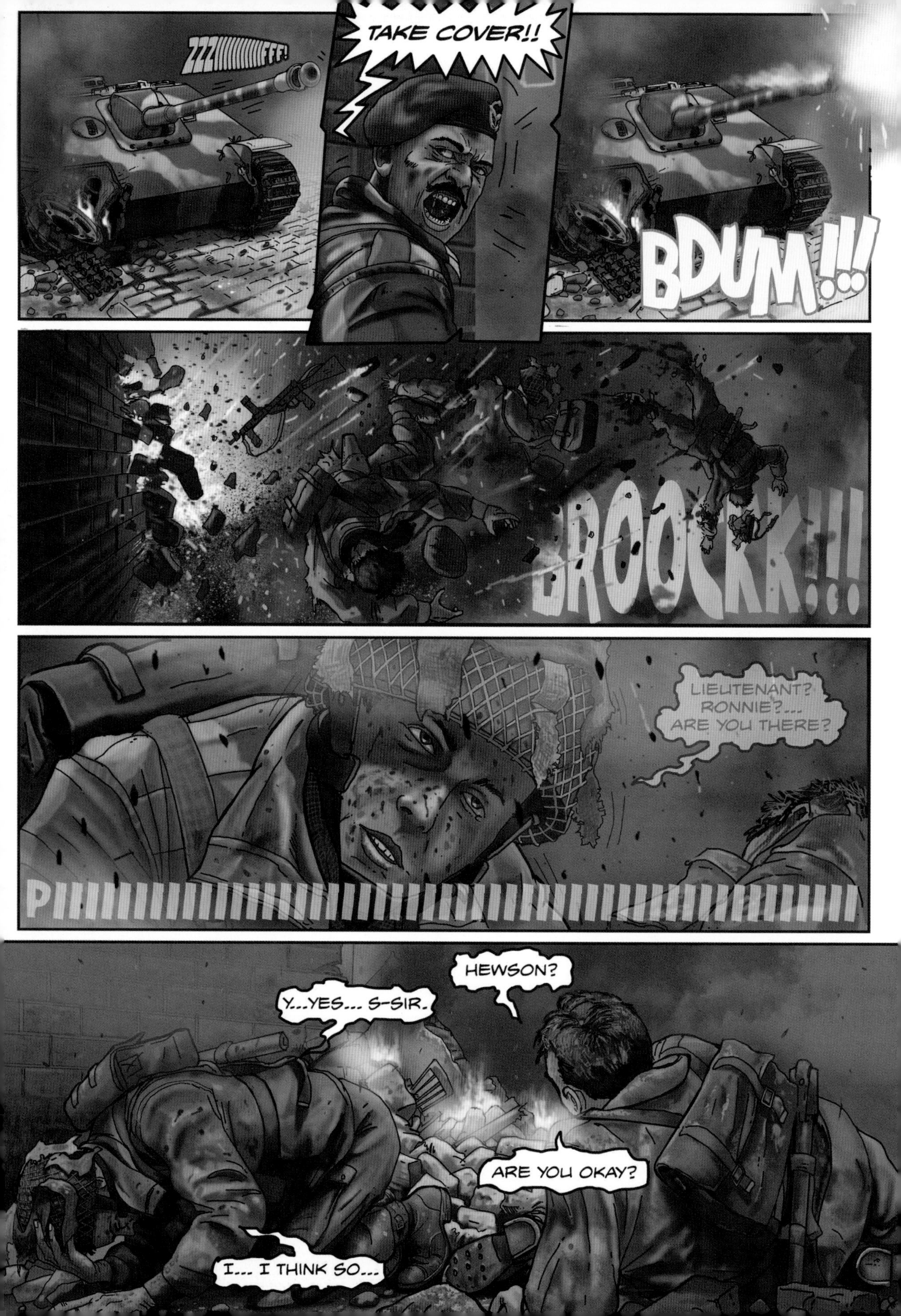
ZZZIIIIIIIIIIIFFF!
TAKE COVER!!
BDUM!!!
BROOCKK!!!
LIEUTENANT? RONNIE?... ARE YOU THERE?
PIIIIIIIIIIIIIIIIIIIIIIIIIIIIIIIIIIIIIIIIIIIIII
HEWSON?
Y...YES... S-SIR.
ARE YOU OKAY?
I... I THINK SO...

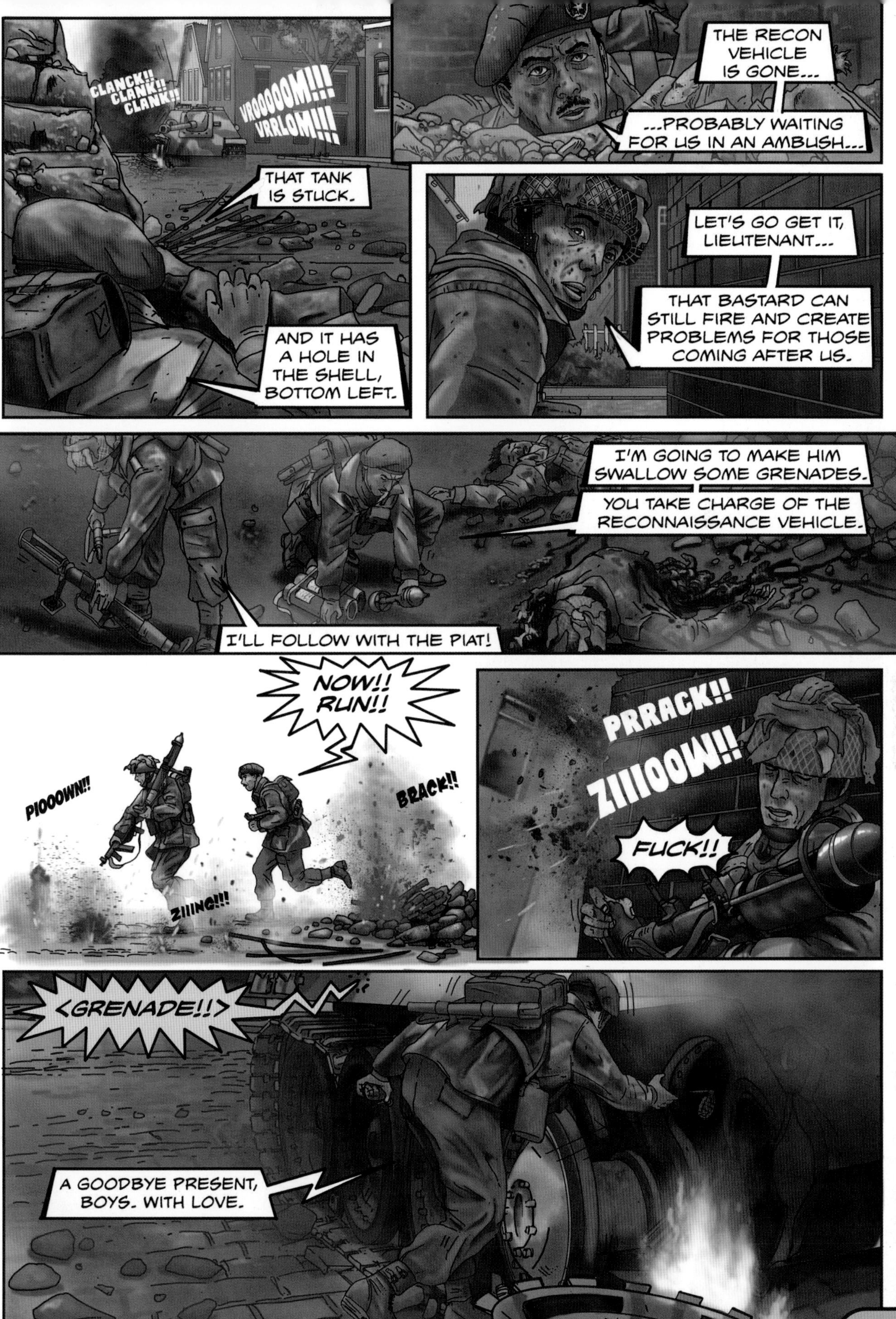
CLANCK!! CLANK!! CLANK!!
VROOOOOM!!! VRRLOM!!!
THAT TANK IS STUCK.
AND IT HAS A HOLE IN THE SHELL, BOTTOM LEFT.
THE RECON VEHICLE IS GONE...
...PROBABLY WAITING FOR US IN AN AMBUSH...
LET'S GO GET IT, LIEUTENANT...
THAT BASTARD CAN STILL FIRE AND CREATE PROBLEMS FOR THOSE COMING AFTER US.
I'M GOING TO MAKE HIM SWALLOW SOME GRENADES.
YOU TAKE CHARGE OF THE RECONNAISSANCE VEHICLE.
I'LL FOLLOW WITH THE PIAT!
NOW!! RUN!!
PIOOOWN!!
BRACK!!
ZIIING!!!
PRRACK!!
ZIIIOOW!!
FUCK!!
<GRENADE!!>
A GOODBYE PRESENT, BOYS. WITH LOVE.

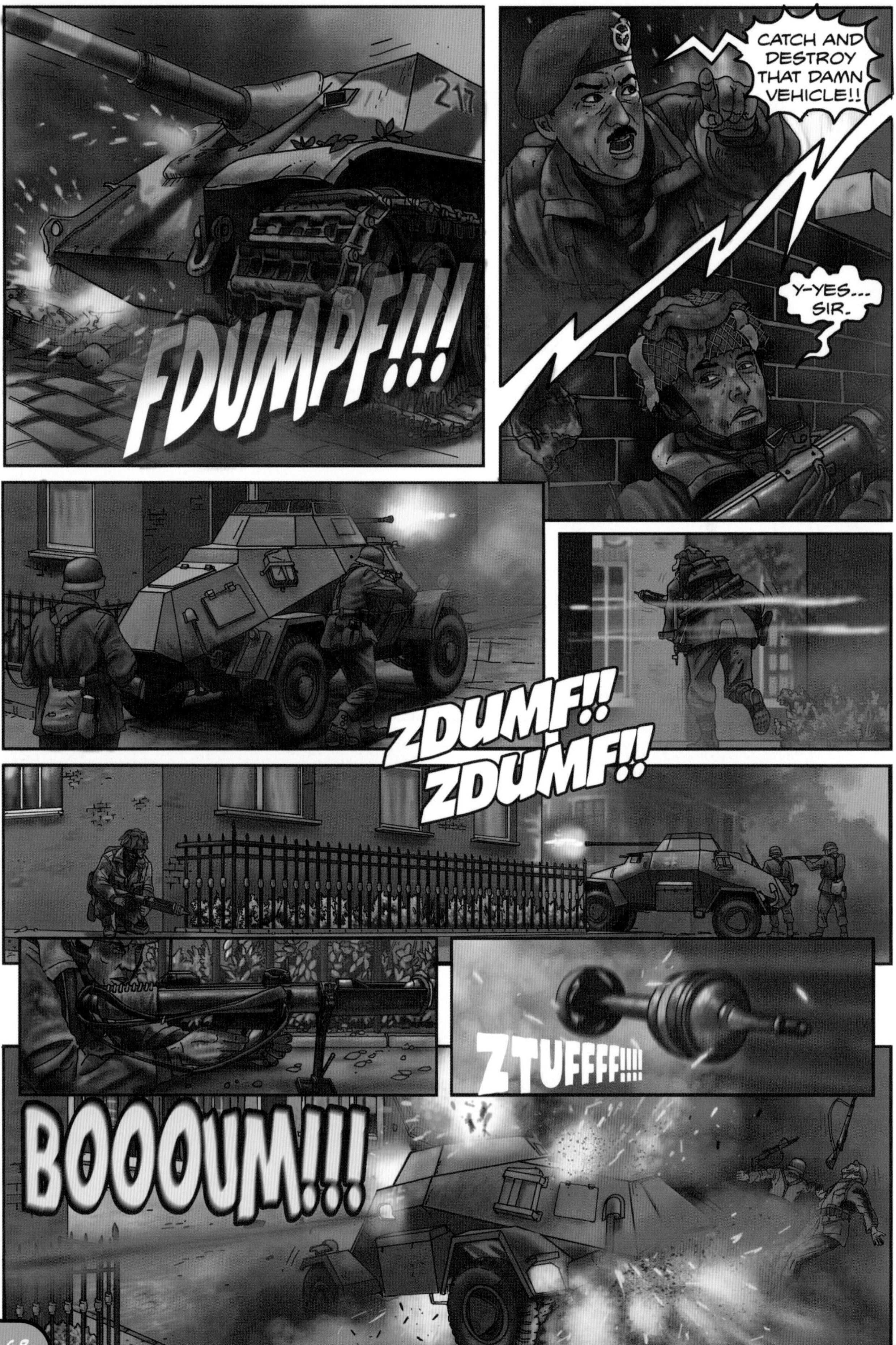

FDUMPF!!!
CATCH AND DESTROY THAT DAMN VEHICLE!!
Y-YES... SIR.
ZDUMF!!
ZDUMF!!
ZTUFFFF!!!!
BOOOUM!!!

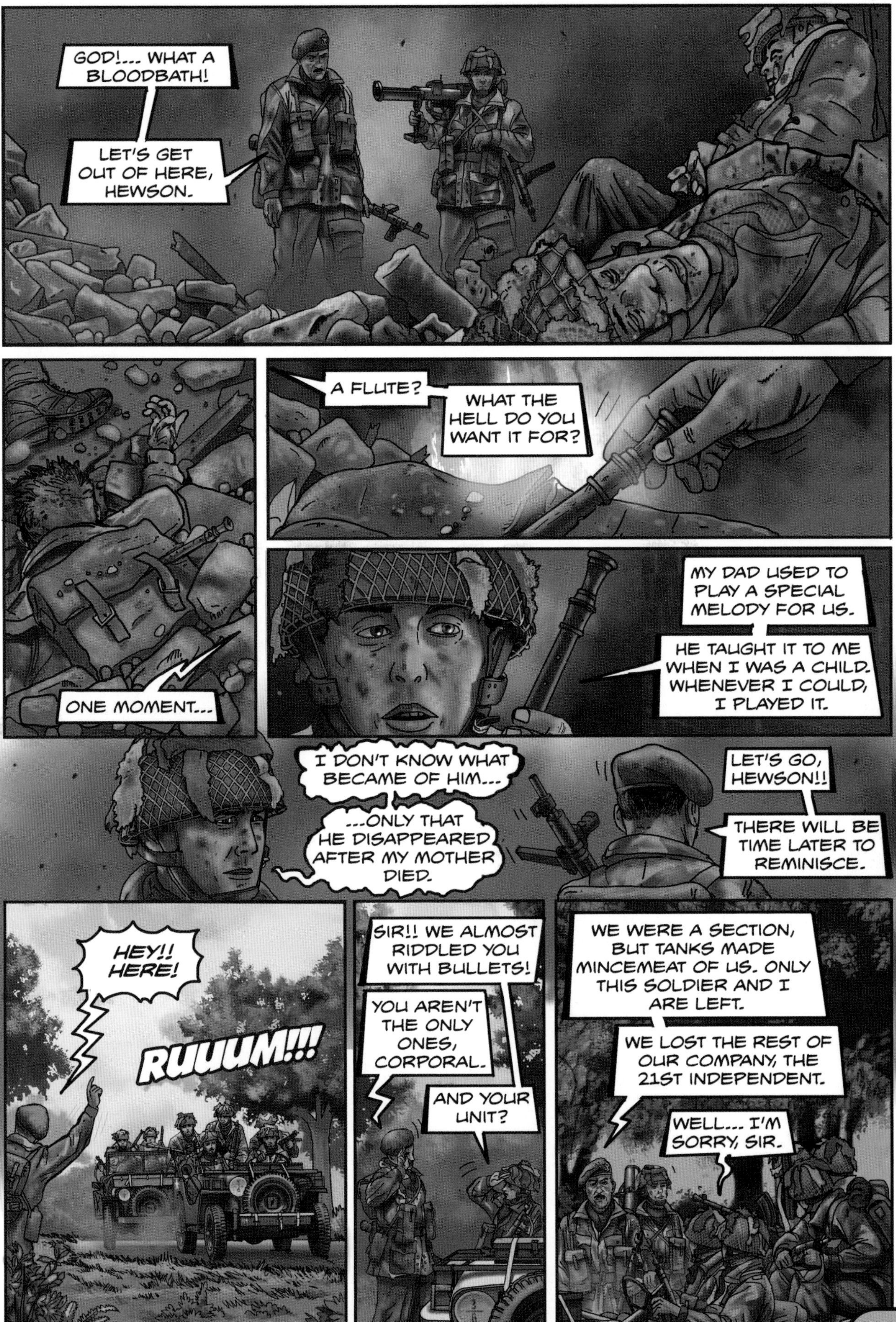
GOD!... WHAT A BLOODBATH!
LET'S GET OUT OF HERE, HEWSON.
A FLUTE?
WHAT THE HELL DO YOU WANT IT FOR?
ONE MOMENT...
MY DAD USED TO PLAY A SPECIAL MELODY FOR US.
HE TAUGHT IT TO ME WHEN I WAS A CHILD. WHENEVER I COULD, I PLAYED IT.
I DON'T KNOW WHAT BECAME OF HIM...
...ONLY THAT HE DISAPPEARED AFTER MY MOTHER DIED.
LET'S GO, HEWSON!!
THERE WILL BE TIME LATER TO REMINISCE.
HEY!! HERE!
RUUUM!!!
SIR!! WE ALMOST RIDDLED YOU WITH BULLETS!
YOU AREN'T THE ONLY ONES, CORPORAL.
AND YOUR UNIT?
WE WERE A SECTION, BUT TANKS MADE MINCEMEAT OF US. ONLY THIS SOLDIER AND I ARE LEFT.
WE LOST THE REST OF OUR COMPANY, THE 21ST INDEPENDENT.
WELL... I'M SORRY, SIR.

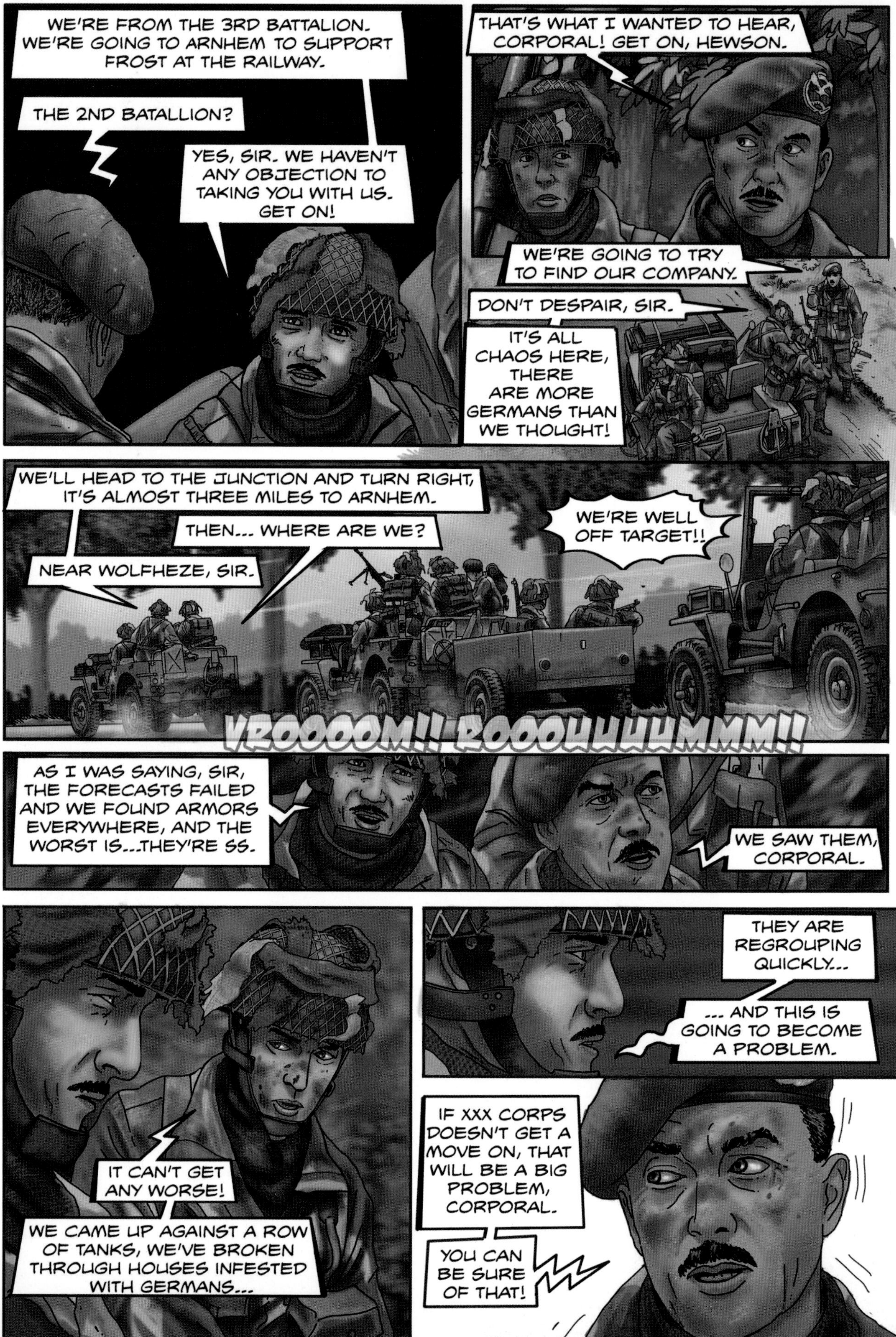
WE'RE FROM THE 3RD BATTALION. WE'RE GOING TO ARNHEM TO SUPPORT FROST AT THE RAILWAY.
THE 2ND BATALLION?
YES, SIR. WE HAVEN'T ANY OBJECTION TO TAKING YOU WITH US. GET ON!
THAT'S WHAT I WANTED TO HEAR, CORPORAL! GET ON, HEWSON.
WE'RE GOING TO TRY TO FIND OUR COMPANY.
DON'T DESPAIR, SIR.
IT'S ALL CHAOS HERE, THERE ARE MORE GERMANS THAN WE THOUGHT!
WE'LL HEAD TO THE JUNCTION AND TURN RIGHT, IT'S ALMOST THREE MILES TO ARNHEM.
THEN... WHERE ARE WE?
NEAR WOLFHEZE, SIR.
WE'RE WELL OFF TARGET!!
VROOOOOM!! ROOOUUUUUMMMM!!
AS I WAS SAYING, SIR, THE FORECASTS FAILED AND WE FOUND ARMORS EVERYWHERE, AND THE WORST IS...THEY'RE SS.
WE SAW THEM, CORPORAL.
IT CAN'T GET ANY WORSE!
WE CAME UP AGAINST A ROW OF TANKS, WE'VE BROKEN THROUGH HOUSES INFESTED WITH GERMANS...
THEY ARE REGROUPING QUICKLY...
... AND THIS IS GOING TO BECOME A PROBLEM.
IF XXX CORPS DOESN'T GET A MOVE ON, THAT WILL BE A BIG PROBLEM, CORPORAL.
YOU CAN BE SURE OF THAT!

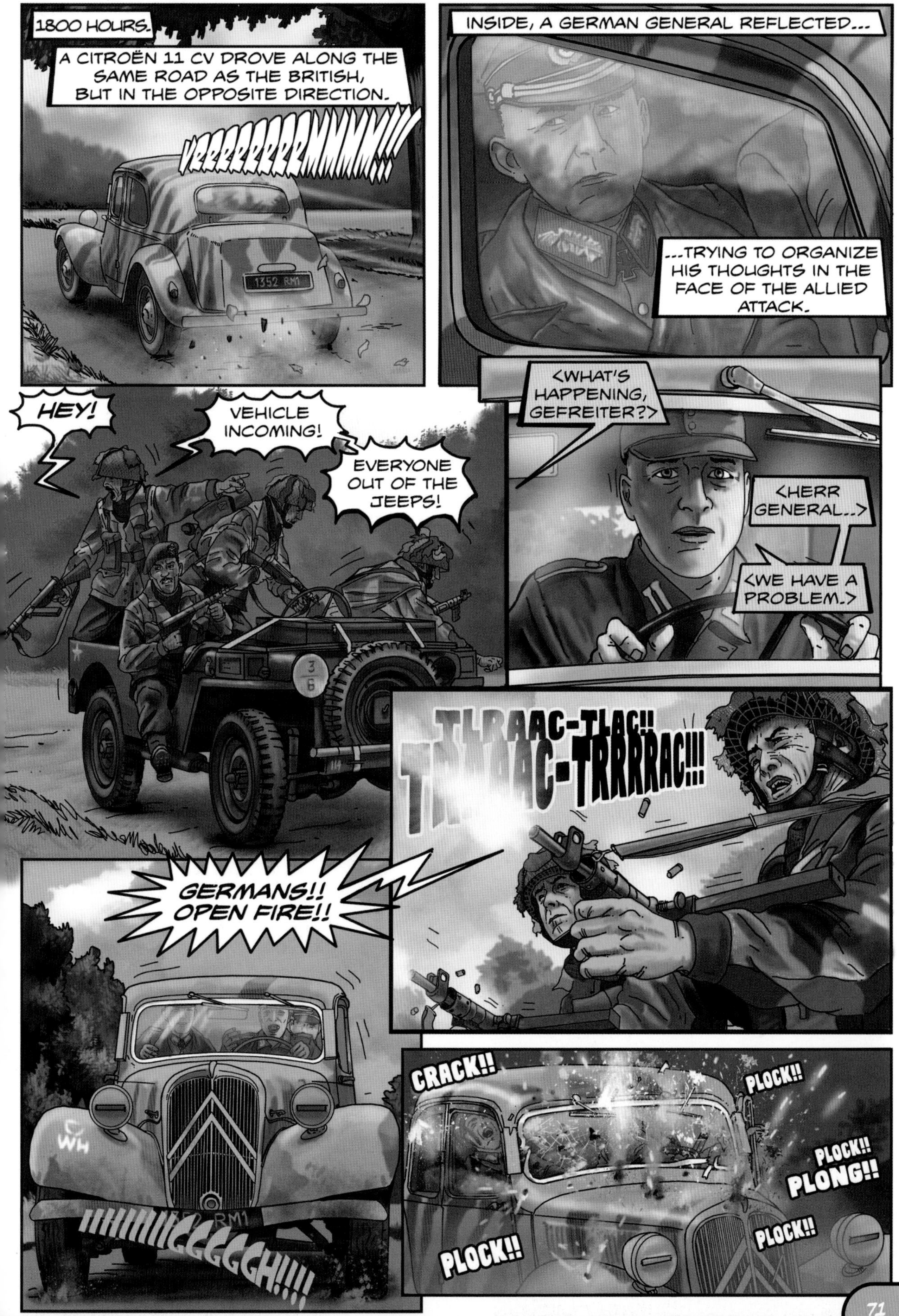
1800 HOURS.
A CITROËN 11 CV DROVE ALONG THE SAME ROAD AS THE BRITISH, BUT IN THE OPPOSITE DIRECTION.
VRRRRRRRRMMMM!!!
1352 RM1
INSIDE, A GERMAN GENERAL REFLECTED...
...TRYING TO ORGANIZE HIS THOUGHTS IN THE FACE OF THE ALLIED ATTACK.
HEY!
VEHICLE INCOMING!
EVERYONE OUT OF THE JEEPS!
<WHAT'S HAPPENING, GEFREITER?>
<HERR GENERAL..>
<WE HAVE A PROBLEM.>
GERMANS!! OPEN FIRE!!
WH
IIIIIIIIIGGGGGH!!!!
TLRAAC-TLAC!!
TRAAAC-TRRRRAC!!!
CRACK!!
PLOCK!!
PLOCK!!
PLONG!!
PLOCK!!
PLOCK!!

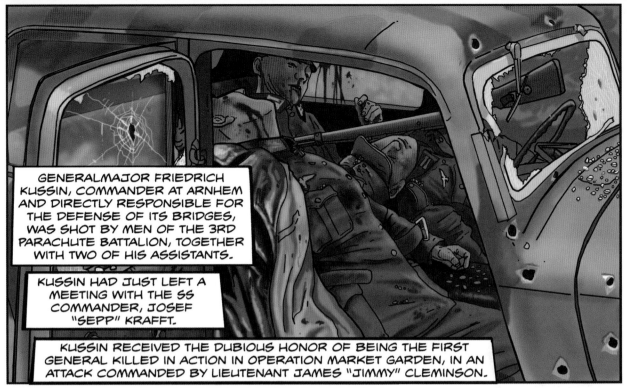

GENERALMAJOR FRIEDRICH KUSSIN, COMMANDER AT ARNHEM AND DIRECTLY RESPONSIBLE FOR THE DEFENSE OF ITS BRIDGES, WAS SHOT BY MEN OF THE 3RD PARACHUTE BATTALION, TOGETHER WITH TWO OF HIS ASSISTANTS.

KUSSIN HAD JUST LEFT A MEETING WITH THE SS COMMANDER, JOSEF "SEPP" KRAFFT.

KUSSIN RECEIVED THE DUBIOUS HONOR OF BEING THE FIRST GENERAL KILLED IN ACTION IN OPERATION MARKET GARDEN, IN AN ATTACK COMMANDED BY LIEUTENANT JAMES "JIMMY" CLEMINSON.

SHIT...LIEUTENANT, A REAL GENERAL.

BAH! LET'S GET BACK TO THE JEEPS.

LUCKY SHOT, LIEUTENANT!

YES, CORPORAL, BUT BETTER TO KILL A GENERAL THAN TO FIGHT AGAINST A WHOLE DIVISION.

I CERTAINLY AGREE, SIR!

ROOOOOM!!!

BETWEEN DEAFENING EXPLOSIONS AND BLASTS OF GUNFIRE...

...A GENTLE MELODY, COULD BE HEARD IN THAT HELL.

NIGHT WAS FALLING ON ARNHEM.

BANG!! BANG!! PAK!

RRRTAAATTT!!!

BDOUUM!!

SKIRMISHES BECAME FIERCER, AND THE BRITISH WERE TRYING TO TAKE POSITIONS.

PAK!

TRRRRRTTTATATA!

NIJMEGEN.

MONDAY, SEPTEMBER 18.

GO NOW, GET OUT!!

TOC-TOC!

COME IN...

JOHN?

HOW ARE YOU?

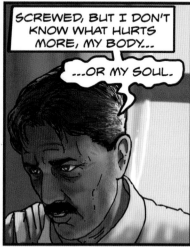

SCREWED, BUT I DON'T KNOW WHAT HURTS MORE, MY BODY...

...OR MY SOUL.

I UNDERSTAND, BUT YOU MUST STAY CALM, CENTERED.

ALL OF US HAVE MADE SACRIFICES OR LOST SOMEONE ALONG THE WAY.

YES FRAJLE, BUT...

...FIRST WAS THE DEATH OF MY WIFE, THEN I HAD TO GIVE UP MY SON, HARRY, MY BOY... ALL TO SERVE MY COUNTRY.

AND NOW, LUCI...

IT'S HARD, I KNOW.

BY THE WAY, THE BRITISH COMMAND IS IN ARNHEM.

ARNHEM? SO...I HAVE TO GO THERE! FIND ME A WAY, OR THINK UP A PLAN.

I CAN'T STAY LIKE THIS HERE, DOING NOTHING.

I'VE BEEN ENTRUSTED WITH A MISSION, AND I MUST COMPLETE IT.

THERE'S NO WAY THAT YOU'LL CHANGE YOUR MIND, IS THERE?

WE'LL THINK OF SOMETHING, BUT YOU MUST KNOW THAT THE ENTIRE AREA HAS NOW BECOME A LIVING HELL.

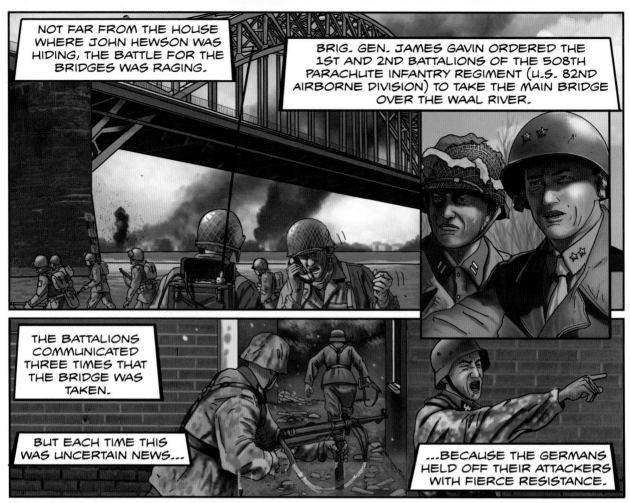

NOT FAR FROM THE HOUSE WHERE JOHN HEWSON WAS HIDING, THE BATTLE FOR THE BRIDGES WAS RAGING.

BRIG. GEN. JAMES GAVIN ORDERED THE 1ST AND 2ND BATTALIONS OF THE 508TH PARACHUTE INFANTRY REGIMENT (U.S. 82ND AIRBORNE DIVISION) TO TAKE THE MAIN BRIDGE OVER THE WAAL RIVER.

THE BATTALIONS COMMUNICATED THREE TIMES THAT THE BRIDGE WAS TAKEN.

BUT EACH TIME THIS WAS UNCERTAIN NEWS...

...BECAUSE THE GERMANS HELD OFF THEIR ATTACKERS WITH FIERCE RESISTANCE.

IN THE MIDST OF THIS MESS, IT MIGHT BE EASY TO SNEAK OUT...

I DON'T KNOW, JOHN. IT LOOKS COMPLICATED TO ME.

I MAY YET TRY IT. MY HOPE IS TO MEET WITH A BRITISH GENERAL AT THE COMMAND.

ACCORDING TO MY SOURCES, THERE'S ONE CALLED...

...URQUHART.

URQUHART?! I KNOW HIM WELL!!

WE APPLIED TO SANDHURST TOGETHER. HE GOT IN... I WASN'T QUITE SO LUCKY.

THAT'S GOOD NEWS FOR ME.

FOR YOU, YES. WE DON'T CARE.

NOBODY WILL COMPENSATE US FOR WHAT HAS HAPPENED THESE PAST FEW YEARS.

LET'S RETREAT BEFORE ANY SOLDIERS GET HERE.

ONE MOMENT...!

WAIT... ARMORED, SHIT!!

RUUUUUMMMMMMMM!!!

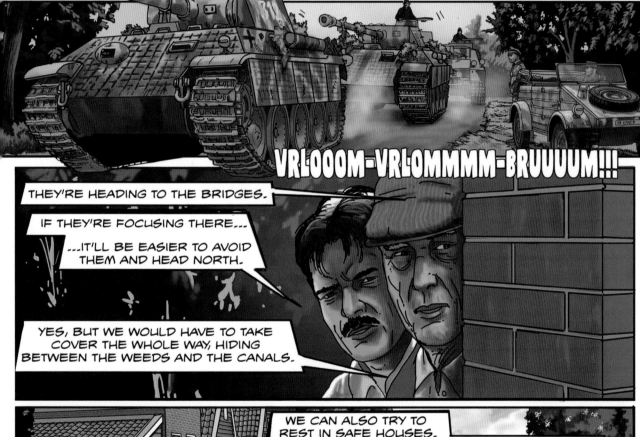

VRLOOOM-VRLOMMMM-BRUUUUM!!!

THEY'RE HEADING TO THE BRIDGES.

IF THEY'RE FOCUSING THERE...

...IT'LL BE EASIER TO AVOID THEM AND HEAD NORTH.

YES, BUT WE WOULD HAVE TO TAKE COVER THE WHOLE WAY; HIDING BETWEEN THE WEEDS AND THE CANALS.

WE CAN ALSO TRY TO REST IN SAFE HOUSES.

THAT WILL TAKE LONGER...

...BUT IT'S LESS RISKY.

THE GERMANS CONTROL THE ROADS. THERE MAY BE SOME IN THE FARMS...

...BUT IT WILL BE EASIER TO DETECT THOSE. WE JUST NEED A LITTLE LUCK, AND WE NEED TO BE AS INVISIBLE AS POSSIBLE.

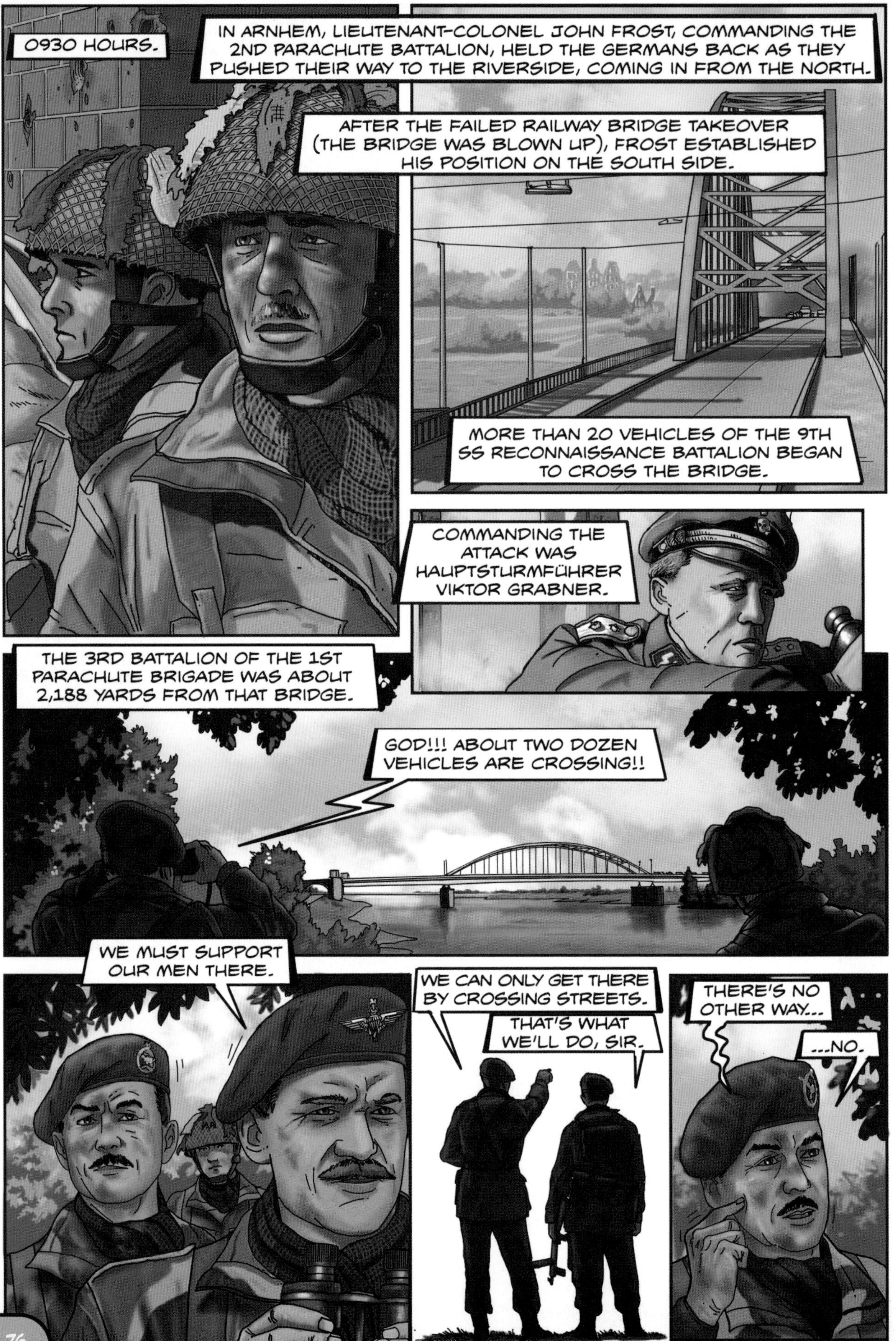

0930 HOURS.
IN ARNHEM, LIEUTENANT-COLONEL JOHN FROST, COMMANDING THE 2ND PARACHUTE BATTALION, HELD THE GERMANS BACK AS THEY PUSHED THEIR WAY TO THE RIVERSIDE, COMING IN FROM THE NORTH.
AFTER THE FAILED RAILWAY BRIDGE TAKEOVER (THE BRIDGE WAS BLOWN UP), FROST ESTABLISHED HIS POSITION ON THE SOUTH SIDE.
MORE THAN 20 VEHICLES OF THE 9TH SS RECONNAISSANCE BATTALION BEGAN TO CROSS THE BRIDGE.
COMMANDING THE ATTACK WAS HAUPTSTURMFÜHRER VIKTOR GRABNER.
THE 3RD BATTALION OF THE 1ST PARACHUTE BRIGADE WAS ABOUT 2,188 YARDS FROM THAT BRIDGE.
GOD!!! ABOUT TWO DOZEN VEHICLES ARE CROSSING!!
WE MUST SUPPORT OUR MEN THERE.
WE CAN ONLY GET THERE BY CROSSING STREETS.
THAT'S WHAT WE'LL DO, SIR.
THERE'S NO OTHER WAY...
...NO.

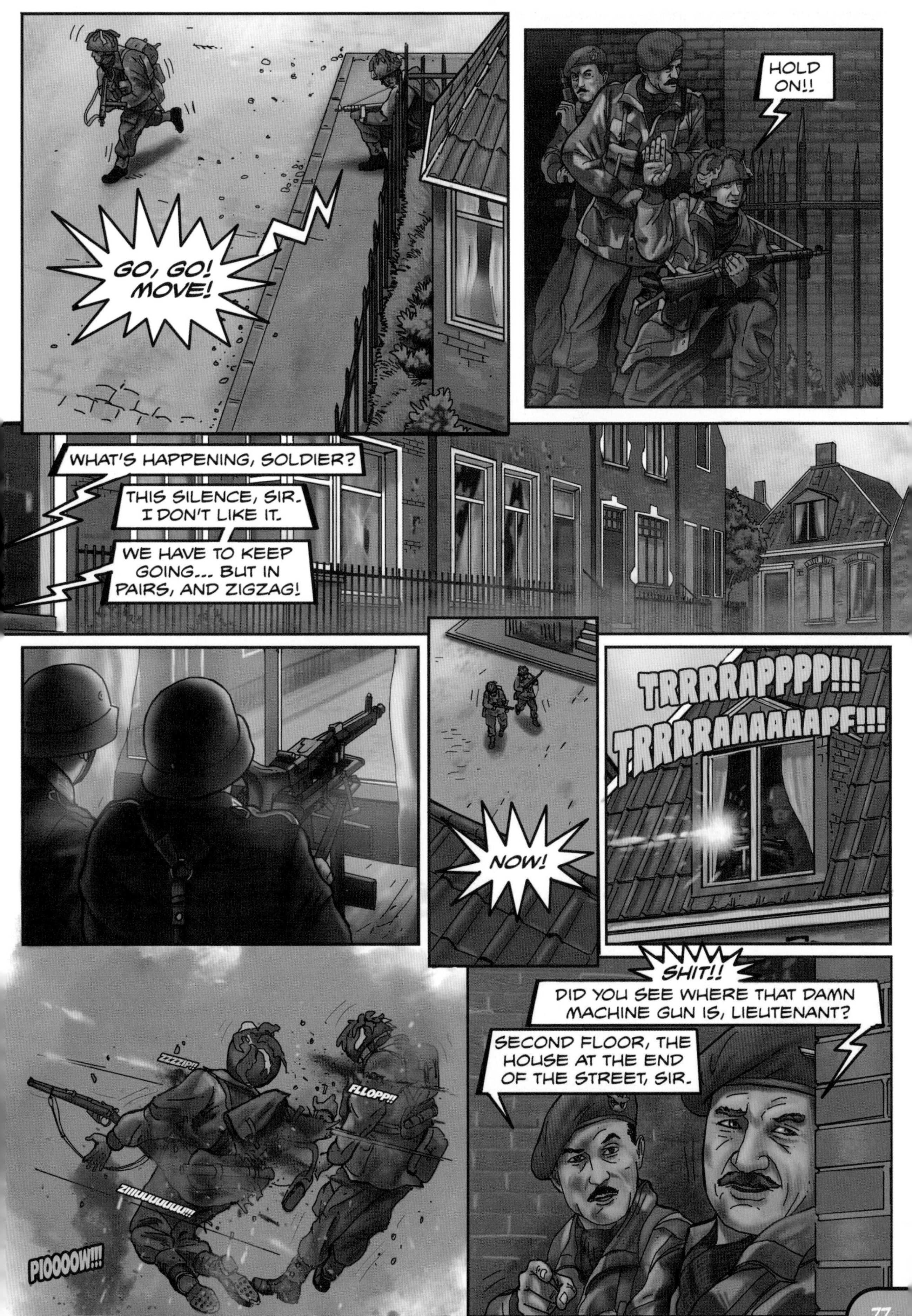
GO, GO! MOVE!
HOLD ON!!
WHAT'S HAPPENING, SOLDIER?
THIS SILENCE, SIR. I DON'T LIKE IT.
WE HAVE TO KEEP GOING... BUT IN PAIRS, AND ZIGZAG!
NOW!
TRRRRAPPPP!!!
TRRRRAAAAAAPF!!!
ZZZZIP!!
FLLOPP!!
PIOOOOW!!!
SHIT!!
DID YOU SEE WHERE THAT DAMN MACHINE GUN IS, LIEUTENANT?
SECOND FLOOR, THE HOUSE AT THE END OF THE STREET, SIR.

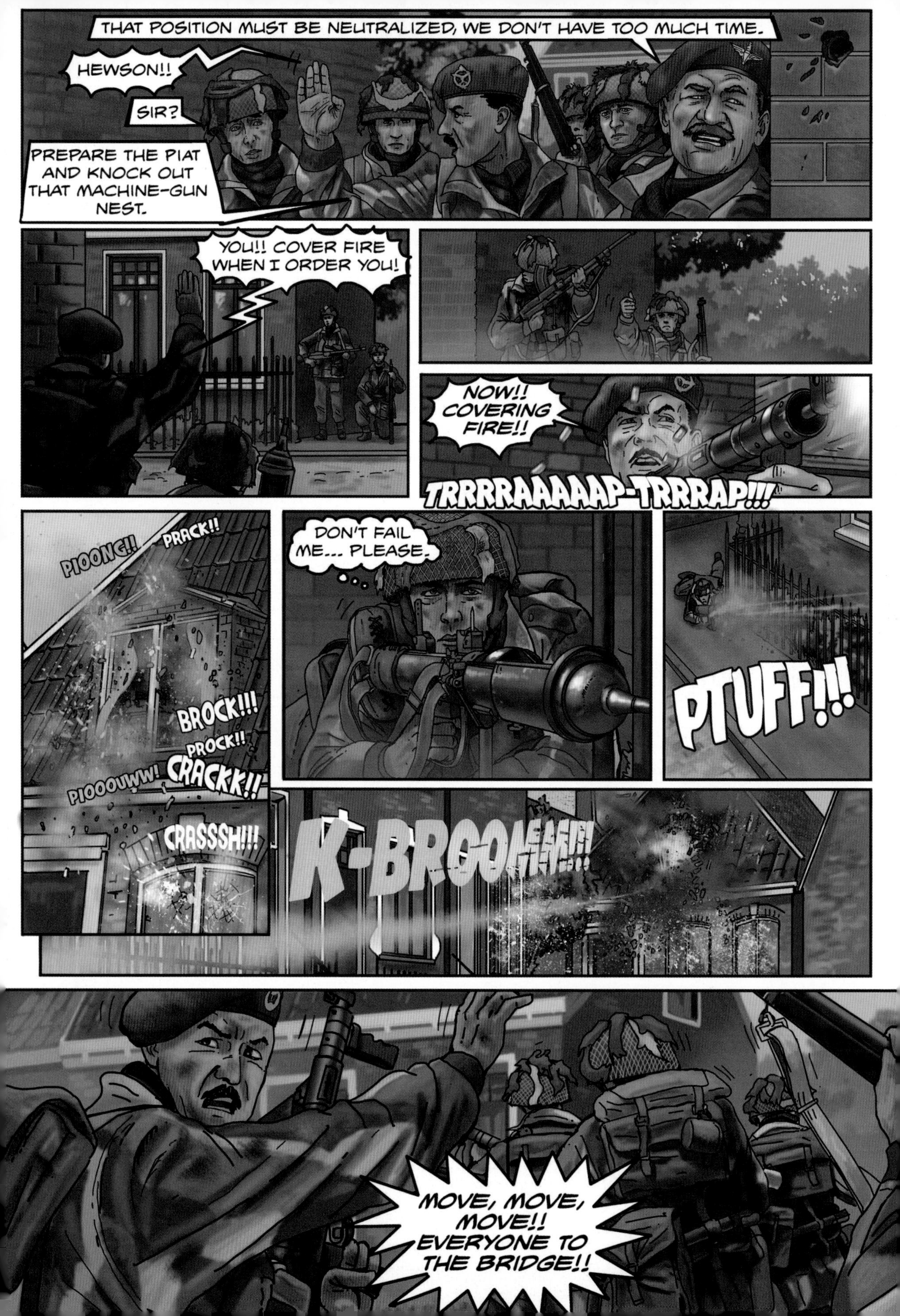
THAT POSITION MUST BE NEUTRALIZED, WE DON'T HAVE TOO MUCH TIME.
HEWSON!!
SIR?
PREPARE THE PIAT AND KNOCK OUT THAT MACHINE-GUN NEST.
YOU!! COVER FIRE WHEN I ORDER YOU!
NOW!! COVERING FIRE!!
TRRRRAAAAAP-TRRRAP!!!
PIOONG!!
PRACK!!
BROCK!!!
PROCK!!
PIOOOUWW!
CRACKK!!
CRASSSH!!!
DON'T FAIL ME... PLEASE.
PTUFF!!!
K-BROOMM!!!
MOVE, MOVE, MOVE!! EVERYONE TO THE BRIDGE!!

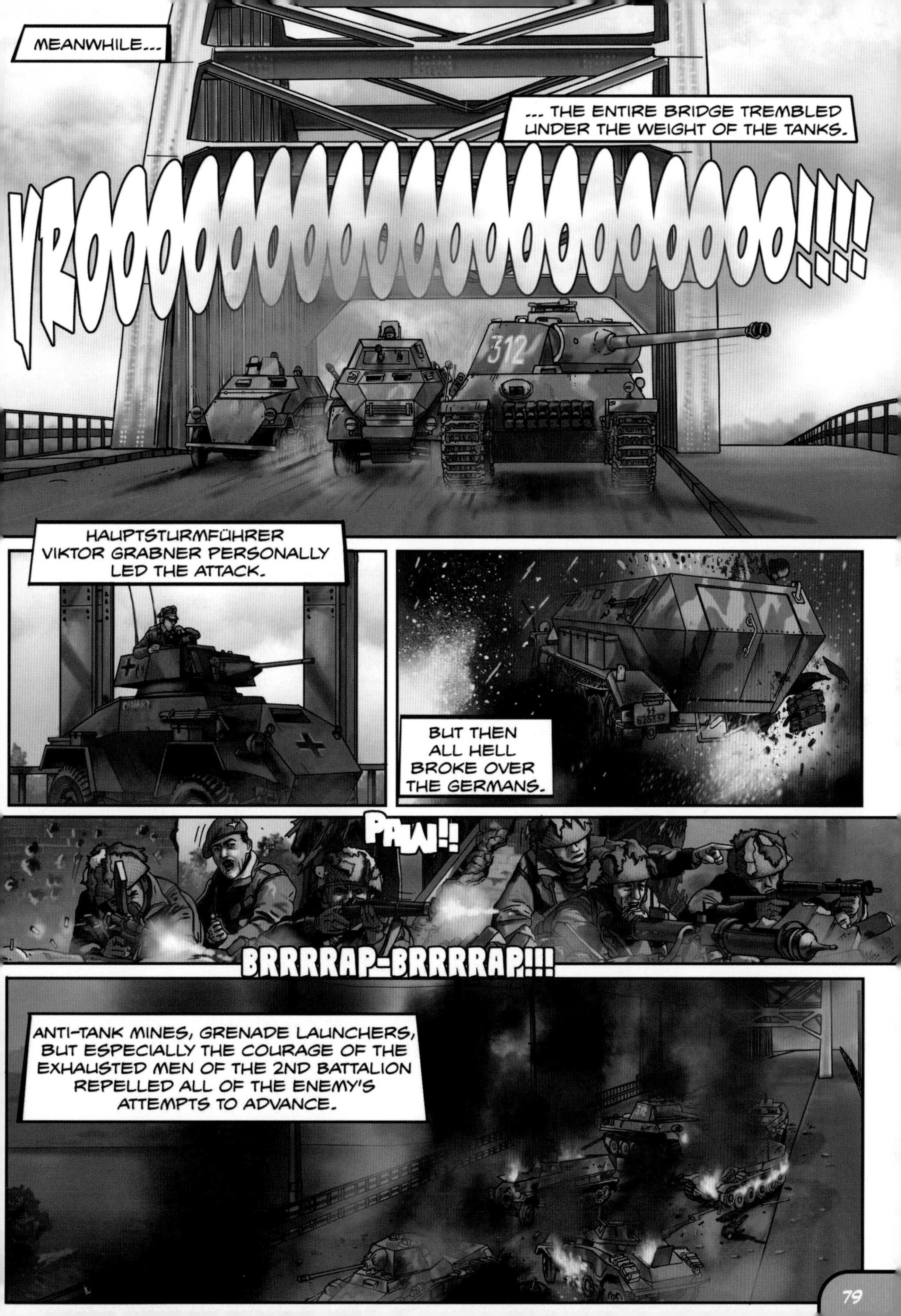
MEANWHILE...
... THE ENTIRE BRIDGE TREMBLED UNDER THE WEIGHT OF THE TANKS.
VROOOOOOOOOOOOOOOOOOO!!!!
HAUPTSTURMFÜHRER VIKTOR GRABNER PERSONALLY LED THE ATTACK.
BUT THEN ALL HELL BROKE OVER THE GERMANS.
PAW!!
BRRRRAP-BRRRRAP!!!
ANTI-TANK MINES, GRENADE LAUNCHERS, BUT ESPECIALLY THE COURAGE OF THE EXHAUSTED MEN OF THE 2ND BATTALION REPELLED ALL OF THE ENEMY'S ATTEMPTS TO ADVANCE.

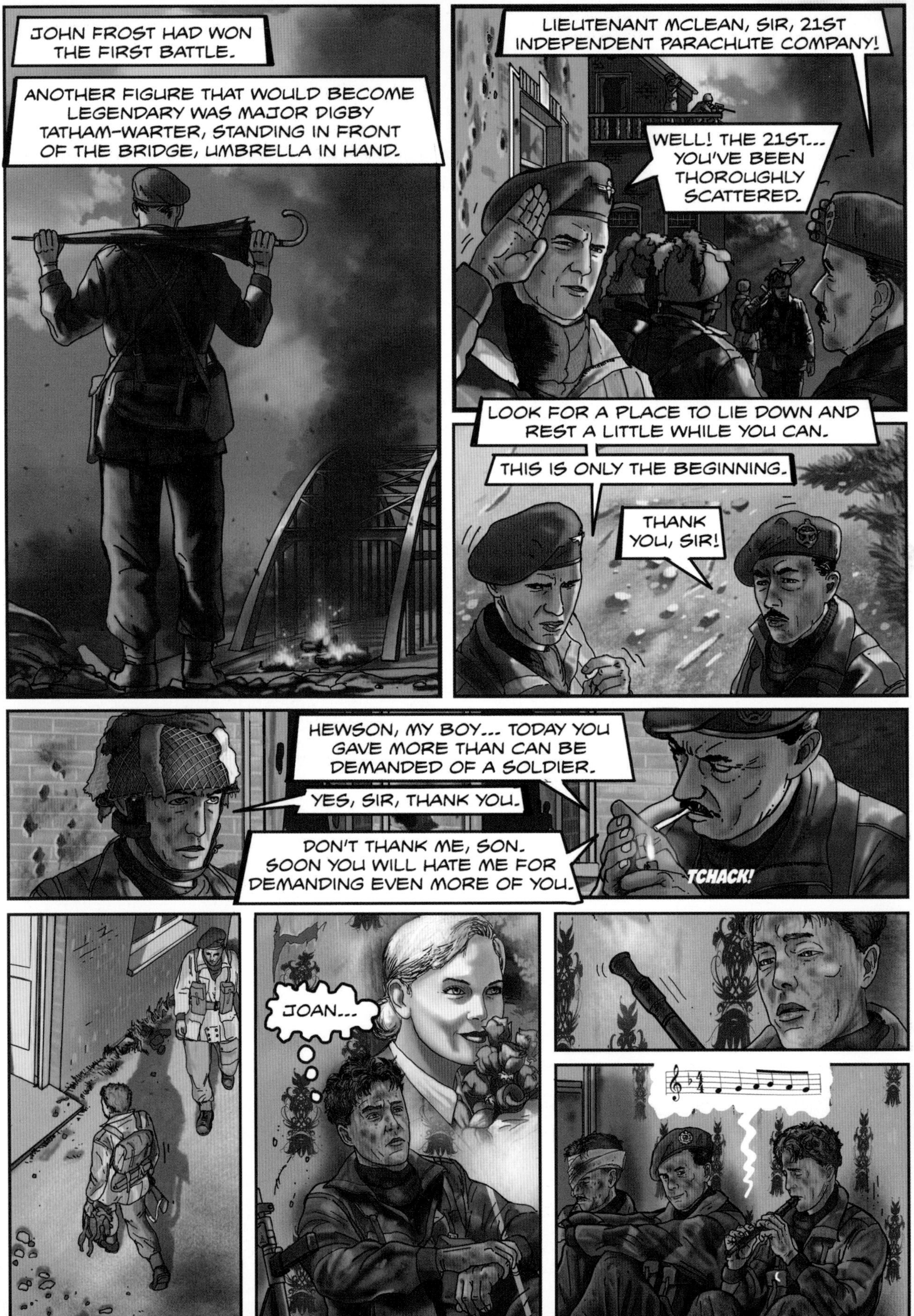
JOHN FROST HAD WON THE FIRST BATTLE.
ANOTHER FIGURE THAT WOULD BECOME LEGENDARY WAS MAJOR DIGBY TATHAM-WARTER, STANDING IN FRONT OF THE BRIDGE, UMBRELLA IN HAND.
LIEUTENANT MCLEAN, SIR, 21ST INDEPENDENT PARACHUTE COMPANY!
WELL! THE 21ST... YOU'VE BEEN THOROUGHLY SCATTERED.
LOOK FOR A PLACE TO LIE DOWN AND REST A LITTLE WHILE YOU CAN.
THIS IS ONLY THE BEGINNING.
THANK YOU, SIR!
HEWSON, MY BOY... TODAY YOU GAVE MORE THAN CAN BE DEMANDED OF A SOLDIER.
YES, SIR, THANK YOU.
DON'T THANK ME, SON. SOON YOU WILL HATE ME FOR DEMANDING EVEN MORE OF YOU.
TCHACK!
JOAN...

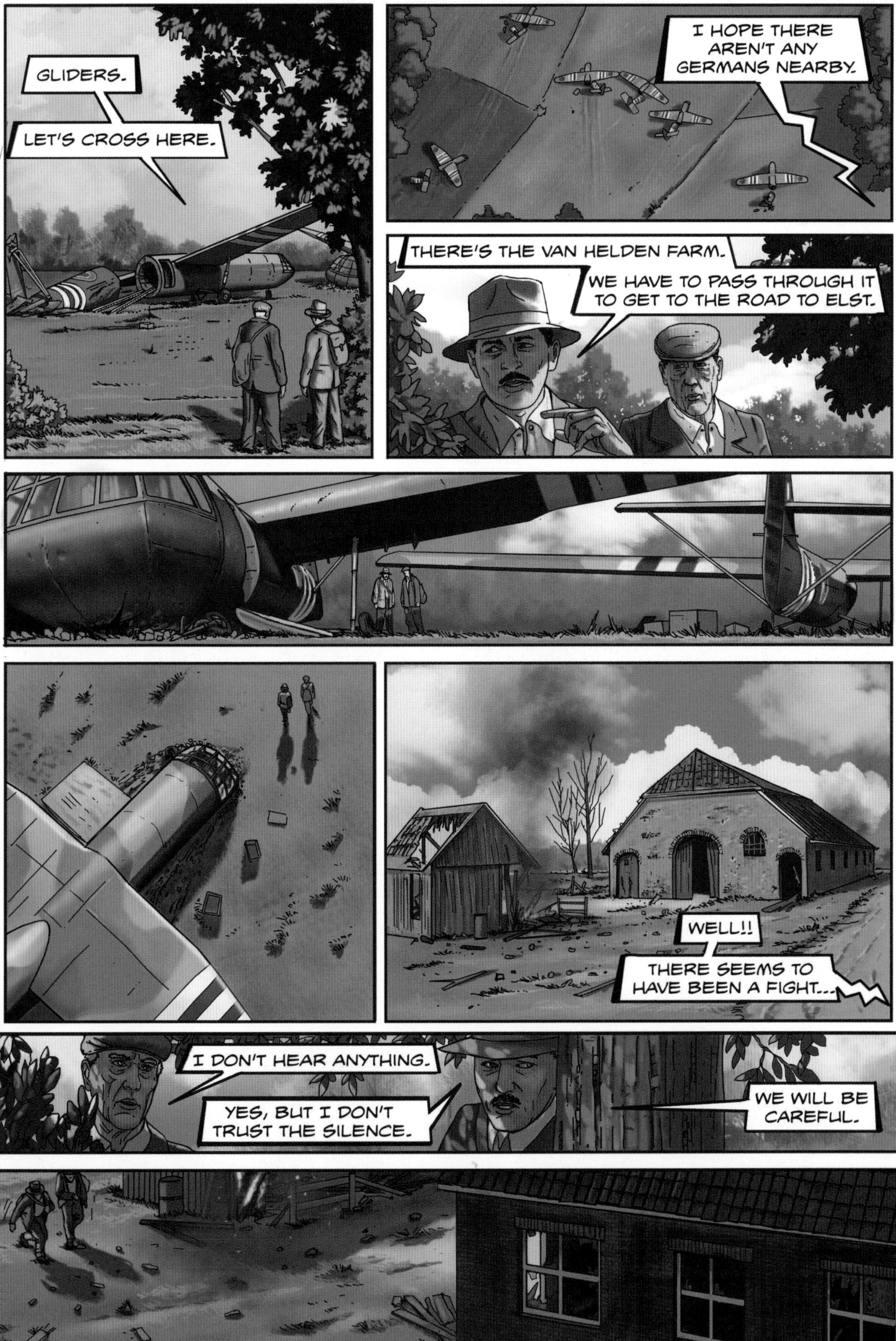
GLIDERS.
LET'S CROSS HERE.
I HOPE THERE AREN'T ANY GERMANS NEARBY.
THERE'S THE VAN HELDEN FARM.
WE HAVE TO PASS THROUGH IT TO GET TO THE ROAD TO ELST.
WELL!!
THERE SEEMS TO HAVE BEEN A FIGHT...
I DON'T HEAR ANYTHING.
YES, BUT I DON'T TRUST THE SILENCE.
WE WILL BE CAREFUL.

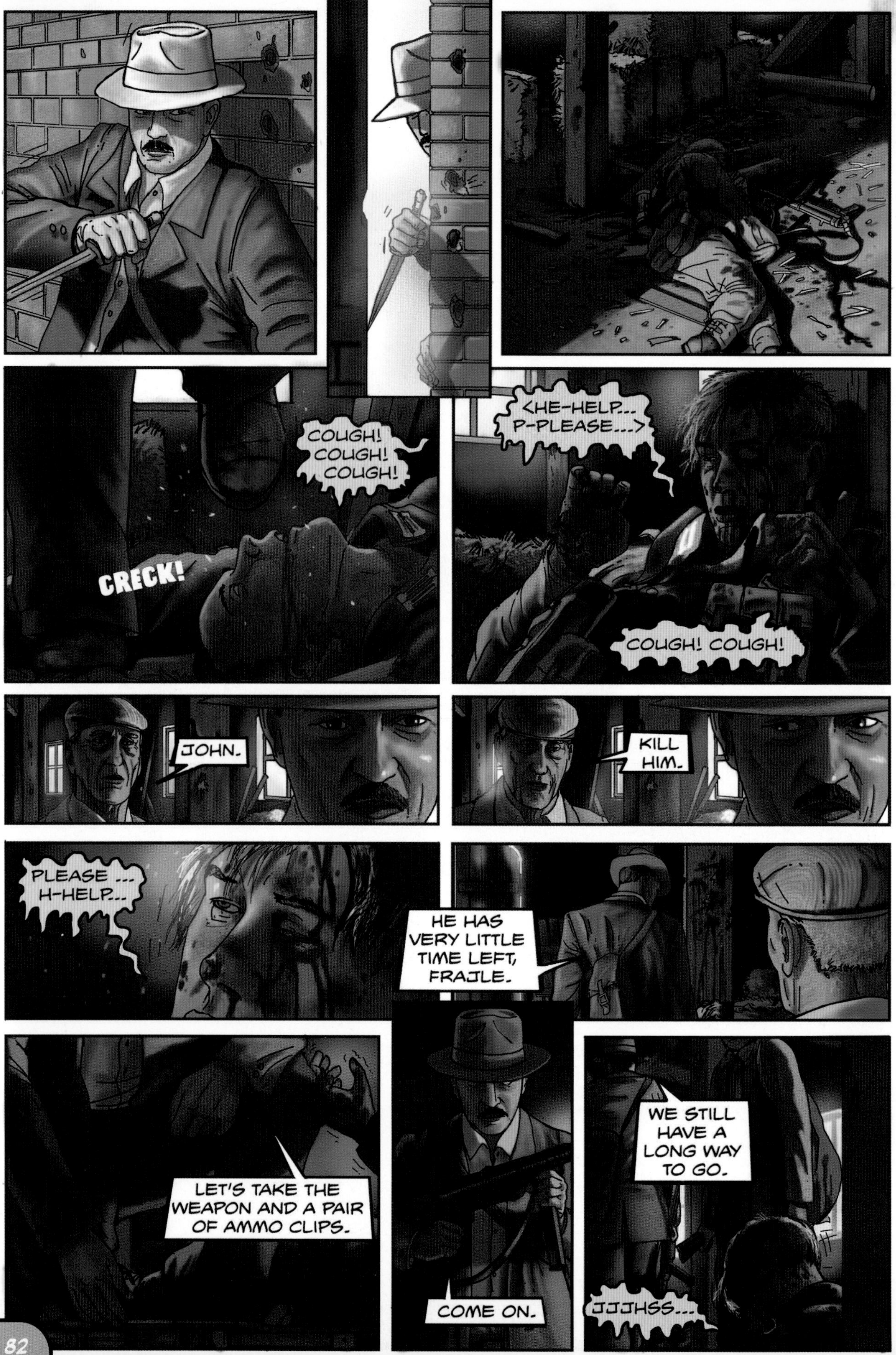
COUGH! COUGH! COUGH!
CRECK!
<HE-HELP... P-PLEASE...>
COUGH! COUGH!
JOHN.
KILL HIM.
PLEASE ... H-HELP...
HE HAS VERY LITTLE TIME LEFT, FRAJLE.
LET'S TAKE THE WEAPON AND A PAIR OF AMMO CLIPS.
COME ON.
WE STILL HAVE A LONG WAY TO GO.
JJJHSS...

1100 HOURS.

A DENSE AND OILY SMOKE ROSE FROM THE BRIDGE AS A RESULT OF THE STRONG RESISTANCE PUT UP BY FROST AND HIS MEN.

BUT THE GERMAN COMMAND REFUSED TO GIVE UP THE AREA.

HEWSON!

PUT DOWN THAT DAMN FLUTE AND FOLLOW ME!

WE'RE GOING ON A TRIP TO OOSTERBEEK.

ARE OUR MEN THERE?

I DON'T KNOW.

DON'T LOAD THE PIAT, IT WILL BE NEEDED MORE HERE.

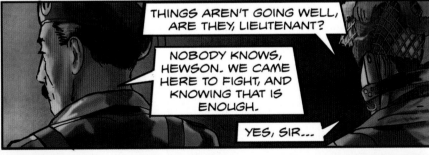

THINGS AREN'T GOING WELL, ARE THEY, LIEUTENANT?

NOBODY KNOWS, HEWSON. WE CAME HERE TO FIGHT, AND KNOWING THAT IS ENOUGH.

YES, SIR....

YES, SIR.

GET A MOVE ON, MEN! WE DON'T HAVE ALL DAY!

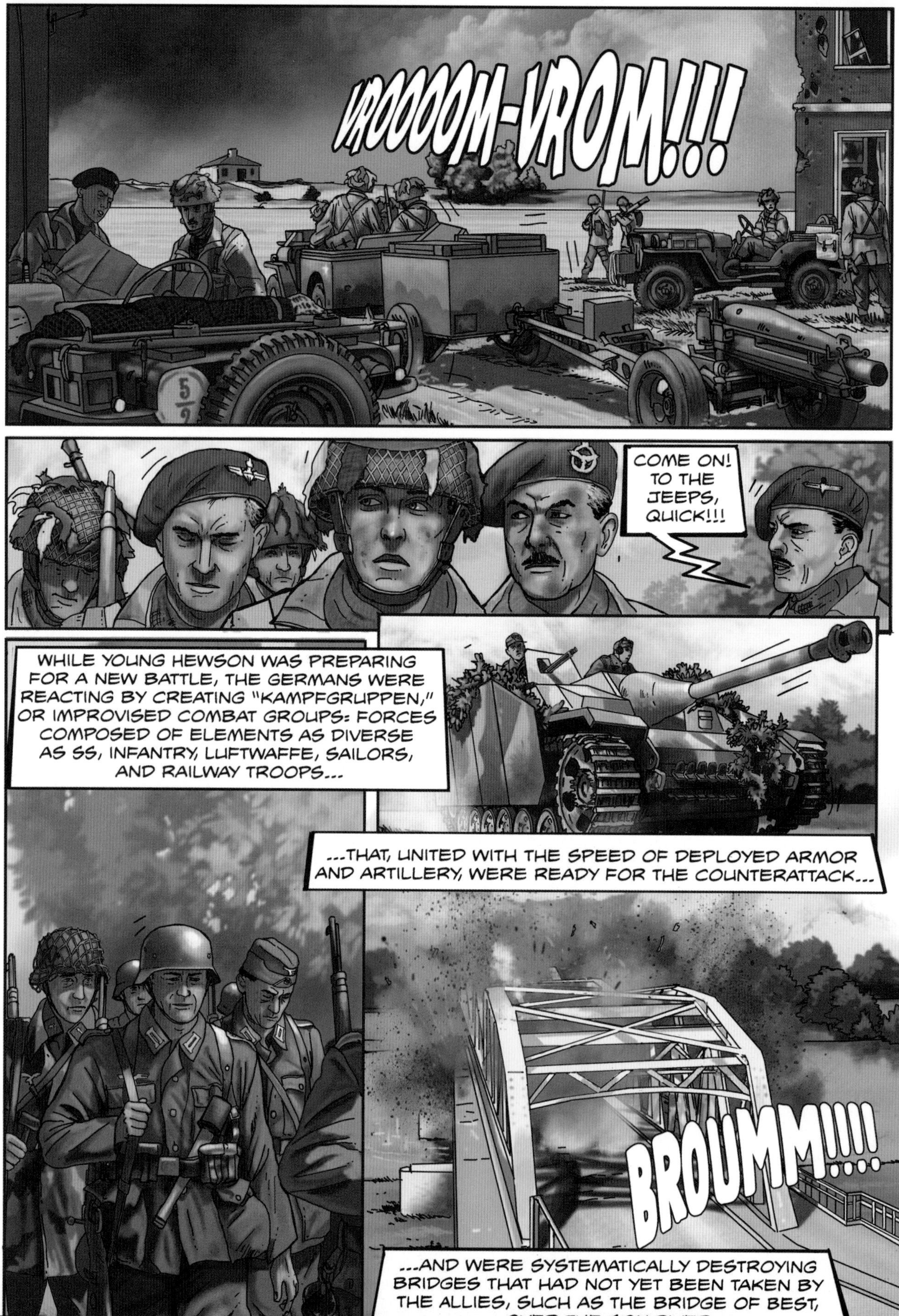

VROOOOM-VROM!!!
COME ON! TO THE JEEPS, QUICK!!!
WHILE YOUNG HEWSON WAS PREPARING FOR A NEW BATTLE, THE GERMANS WERE REACTING BY CREATING "KAMPFGRUPPEN," OR IMPROVISED COMBAT GROUPS: FORCES COMPOSED OF ELEMENTS AS DIVERSE AS SS, INFANTRY, LUFTWAFFE, SAILORS, AND RAILWAY TROOPS...
...THAT, UNITED WITH THE SPEED OF DEPLOYED ARMOR AND ARTILLERY, WERE READY FOR THE COUNTERATTACK...
BROUMM!!!!
...AND WERE SYSTEMATICALLY DESTROYING BRIDGES THAT HAD NOT YET BEEN TAKEN BY THE ALLIES, SUCH AS THE BRIDGE OF BEST, OVER THE SON RIVER.

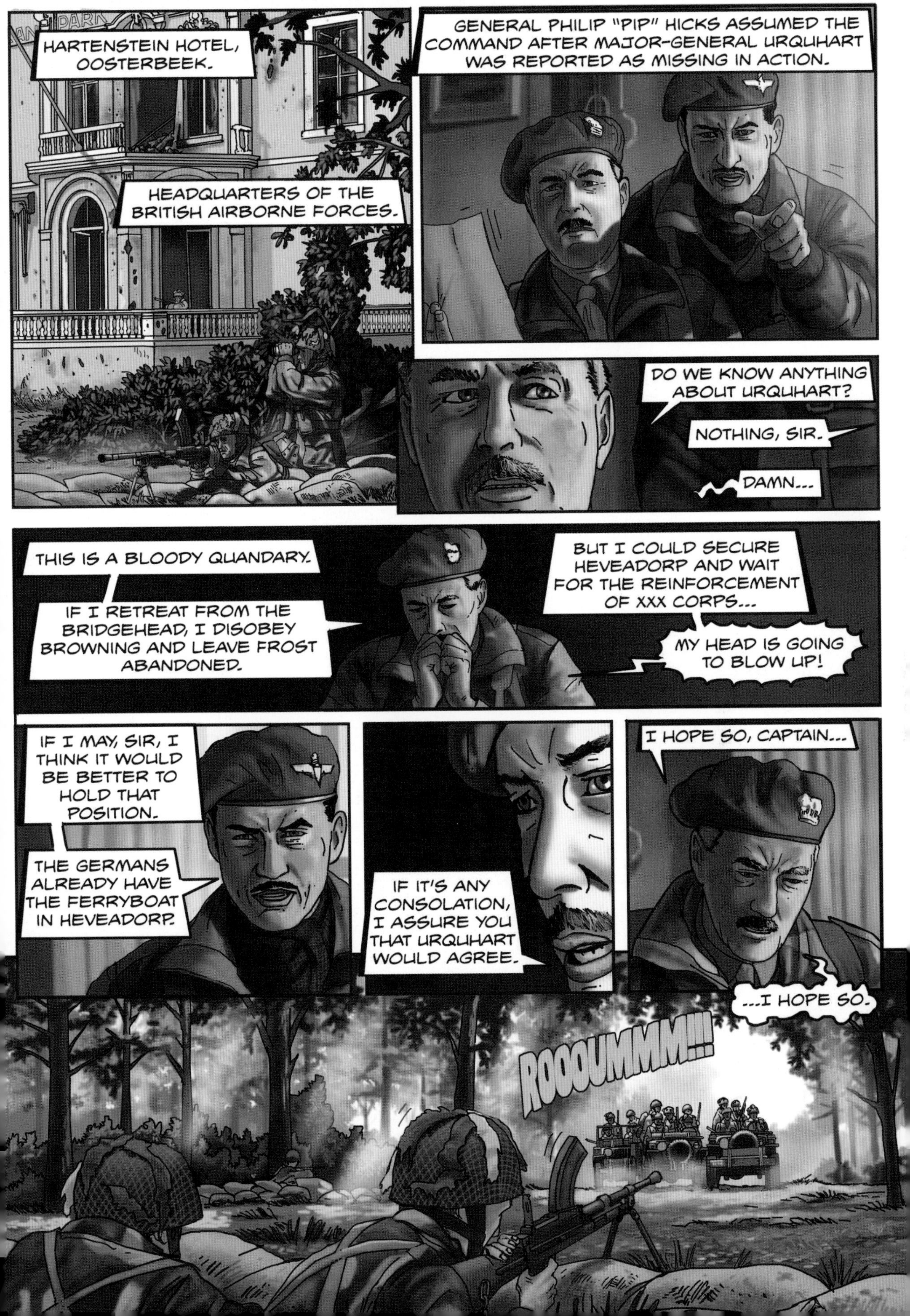

HARTENSTEIN HOTEL, OOSTERBEEK.
HEADQUARTERS OF THE BRITISH AIRBORNE FORCES.
GENERAL PHILIP "PIP" HICKS ASSUMED THE COMMAND AFTER MAJOR-GENERAL URQUHART WAS REPORTED AS MISSING IN ACTION.
DO WE KNOW ANYTHING ABOUT URQUHART?
NOTHING, SIR.
DAMN...
THIS IS A BLOODY QUANDARY.
IF I RETREAT FROM THE BRIDGEHEAD, I DISOBEY BROWNING AND LEAVE FROST ABANDONED.
BUT I COULD SECURE HEVEADORP AND WAIT FOR THE REINFORCEMENT OF XXX CORPS...
MY HEAD IS GOING TO BLOW UP!
IF I MAY, SIR, I THINK IT WOULD BE BETTER TO HOLD THAT POSITION.
THE GERMANS ALREADY HAVE THE FERRYBOAT IN HEVEADORP.
IF IT'S ANY CONSOLATION, I ASSURE YOU THAT URQUHART WOULD AGREE.
I HOPE SO, CAPTAIN...
...I HOPE SO.
ROOOUMMM!!!

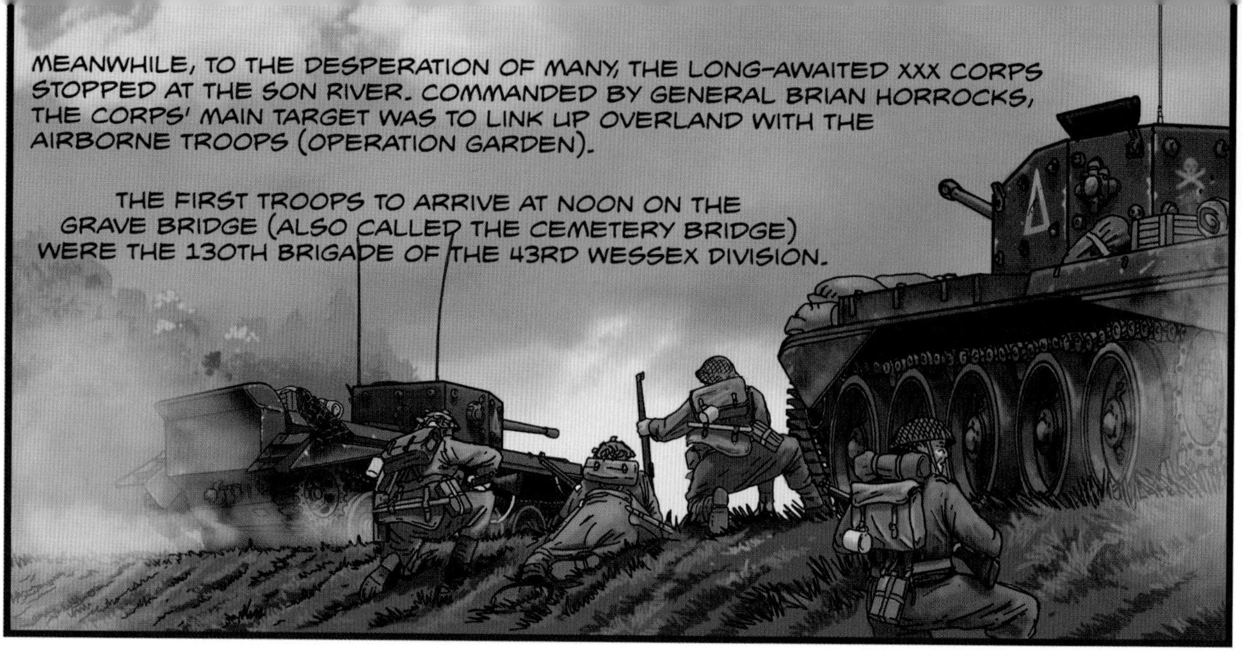
MEANWHILE, TO THE DESPERATION OF MANY, THE LONG-AWAITED XXX CORPS STOPPED AT THE SON RIVER. COMMANDED BY GENERAL BRIAN HORROCKS, THE CORPS' MAIN TARGET WAS TO LINK UP OVERLAND WITH THE AIRBORNE TROOPS (OPERATION GARDEN).
THE FIRST TROOPS TO ARRIVE AT NOON ON THE GRAVE BRIDGE (ALSO CALLED THE CEMETERY BRIDGE) WERE THE 130TH BRIGADE OF THE 43RD WESSEX DIVISION.

MANY CURSED THE SLOWNESS OF A SICK GENERAL HORROCKS.

ALTHOUGH THE BRITISH FOUGHT WITH TENACITY, THE GERMANS DID NOT SHOW ANY INTENTION OF YIELDING GROUND.

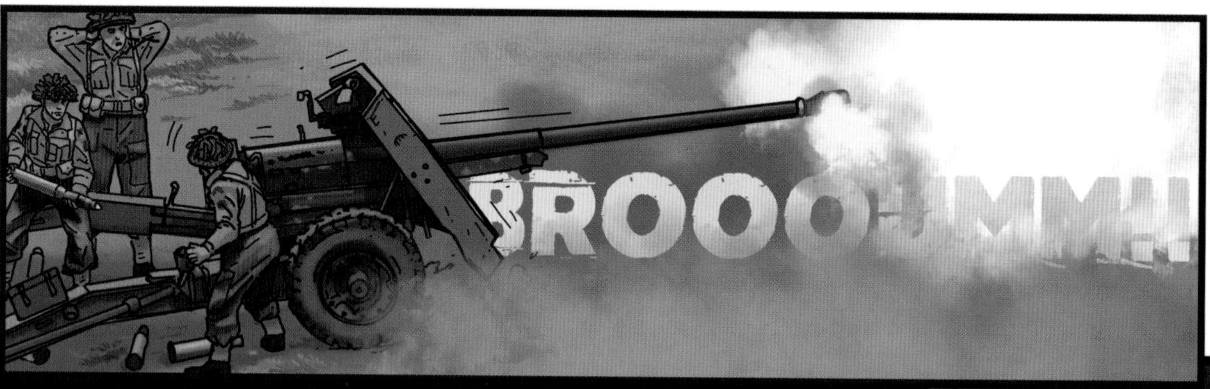
BROOOMMM

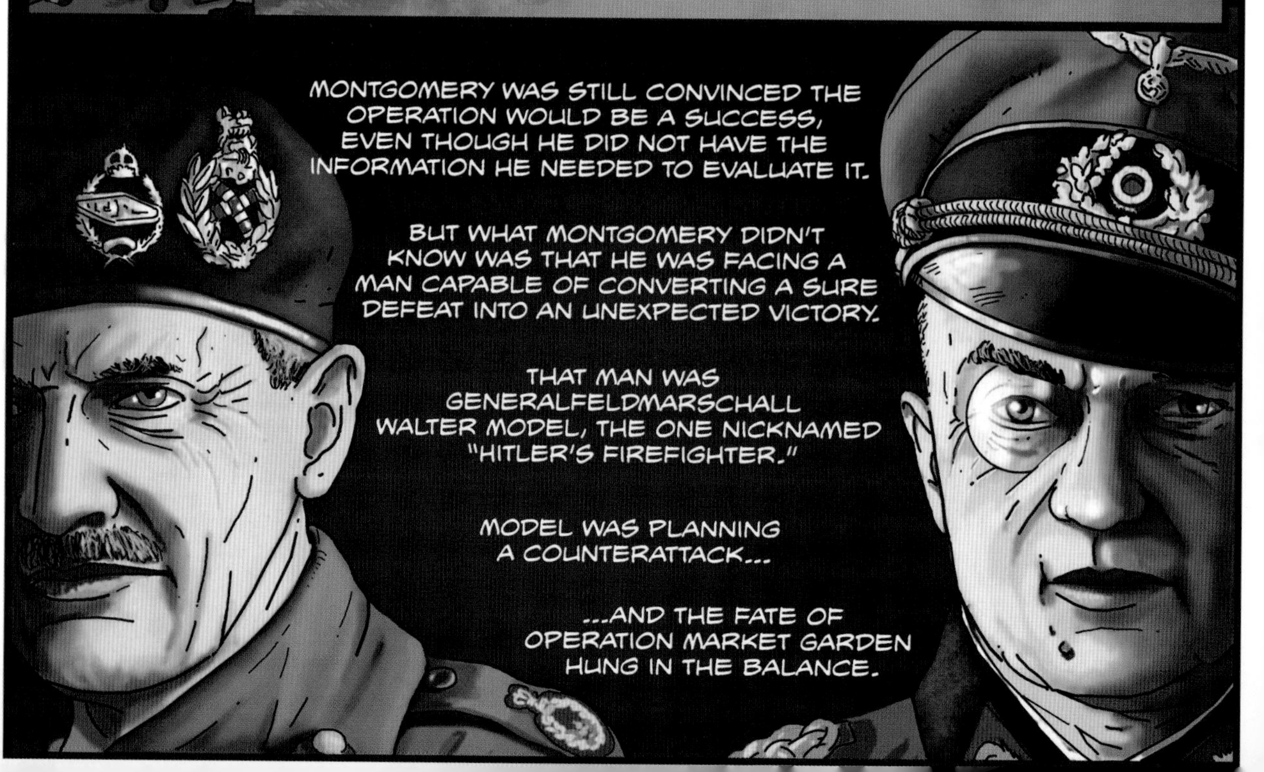
MONTGOMERY WAS STILL CONVINCED THE OPERATION WOULD BE A SUCCESS, EVEN THOUGH HE DID NOT HAVE THE INFORMATION HE NEEDED TO EVALUATE IT.
BUT WHAT MONTGOMERY DIDN'T KNOW WAS THAT HE WAS FACING A MAN CAPABLE OF CONVERTING A SURE DEFEAT INTO AN UNEXPECTED VICTORY.
THAT MAN WAS GENERALFELDMARSCHALL WALTER MODEL, THE ONE NICKNAMED "HITLER'S FIREFIGHTER."
MODEL WAS PLANNING A COUNTERATTACK...
...AND THE FATE OF OPERATION MARKET GARDEN HUNG IN THE BALANCE.

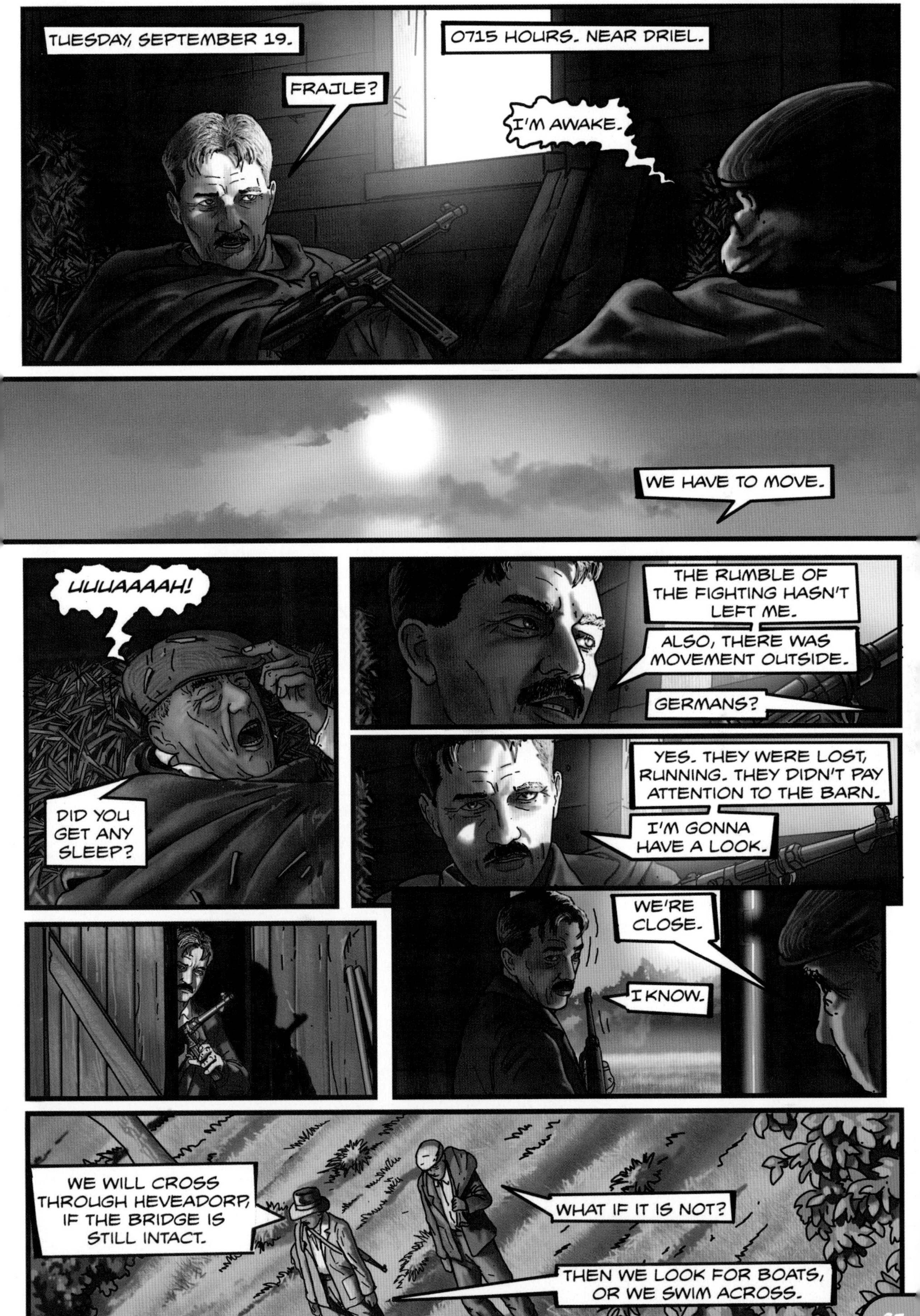

TUESDAY, SEPTEMBER 19.
0715 HOURS. NEAR DRIEL.
FRAJLE?
I'M AWAKE.
WE HAVE TO MOVE.
UUUAAAAH!
DID YOU GET ANY SLEEP?
THE RUMBLE OF THE FIGHTING HASN'T LEFT ME.
ALSO, THERE WAS MOVEMENT OUTSIDE.
GERMANS?
YES. THEY WERE LOST, RUNNING. THEY DIDN'T PAY ATTENTION TO THE BARN.
I'M GONNA HAVE A LOOK.
WE'RE CLOSE.
I KNOW.
WE WILL CROSS THROUGH HEVEADORP, IF THE BRIDGE IS STILL INTACT.
WHAT IF IT IS NOT?
THEN WE LOOK FOR BOATS, OR WE SWIM ACROSS.

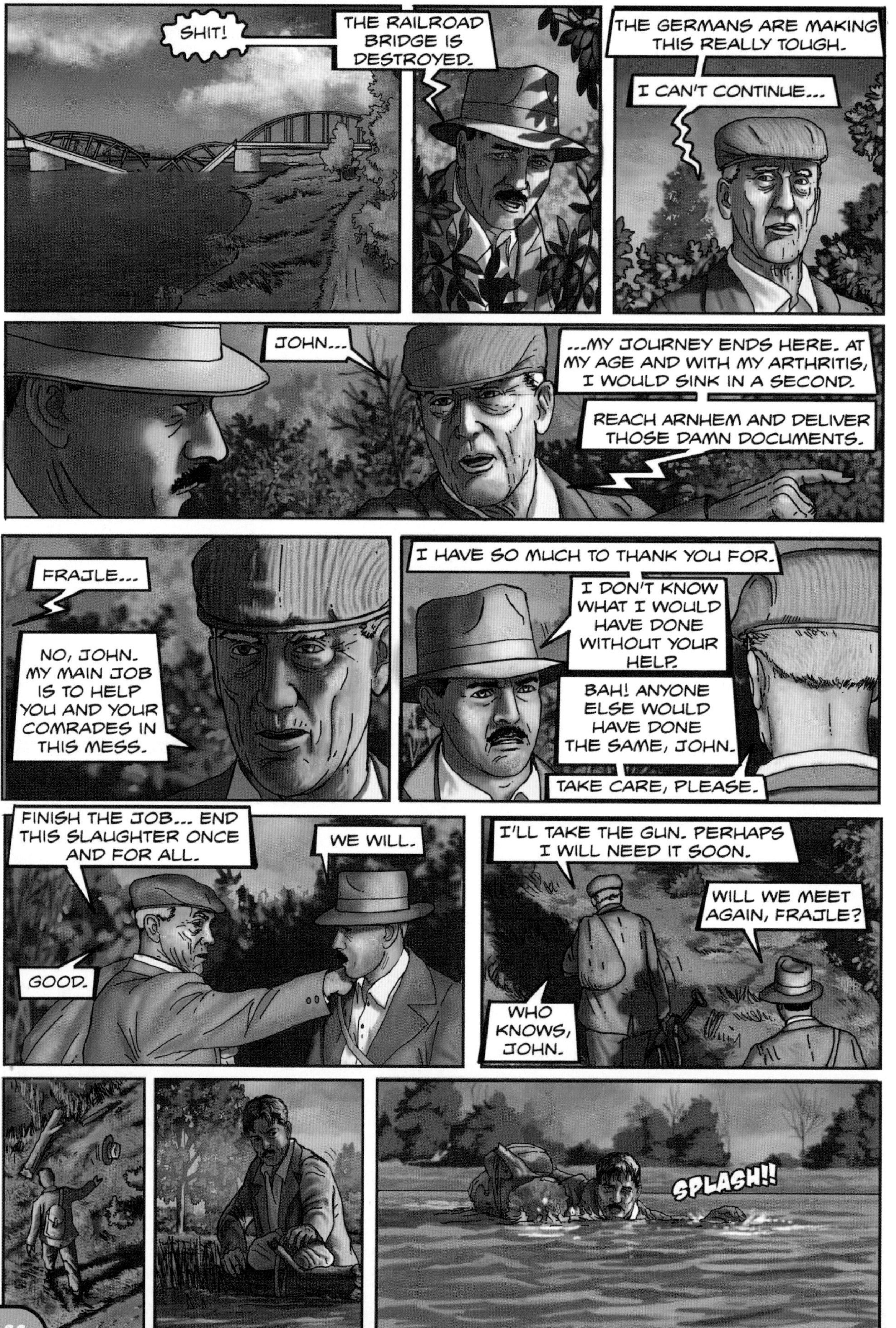
SHIT!
THE RAILROAD BRIDGE IS DESTROYED.
THE GERMANS ARE MAKING THIS REALLY TOUGH.
I CAN'T CONTINUE...
JOHN...
...MY JOURNEY ENDS HERE. AT MY AGE AND WITH MY ARTHRITIS, I WOULD SINK IN A SECOND.
REACH ARNHEM AND DELIVER THOSE DAMN DOCUMENTS.
FRAJLE...
NO, JOHN. MY MAIN JOB IS TO HELP YOU AND YOUR COMRADES IN THIS MESS.
I HAVE SO MUCH TO THANK YOU FOR.
I DON'T KNOW WHAT I WOULD HAVE DONE WITHOUT YOUR HELP.
BAH! ANYONE ELSE WOULD HAVE DONE THE SAME, JOHN.
TAKE CARE, PLEASE.
FINISH THE JOB... END THIS SLAUGHTER ONCE AND FOR ALL.
WE WILL.
GOOD.
I'LL TAKE THE GUN. PERHAPS I WILL NEED IT SOON.
WILL WE MEET AGAIN, FRAJLE?
WHO KNOWS, JOHN.
SPLASH!!

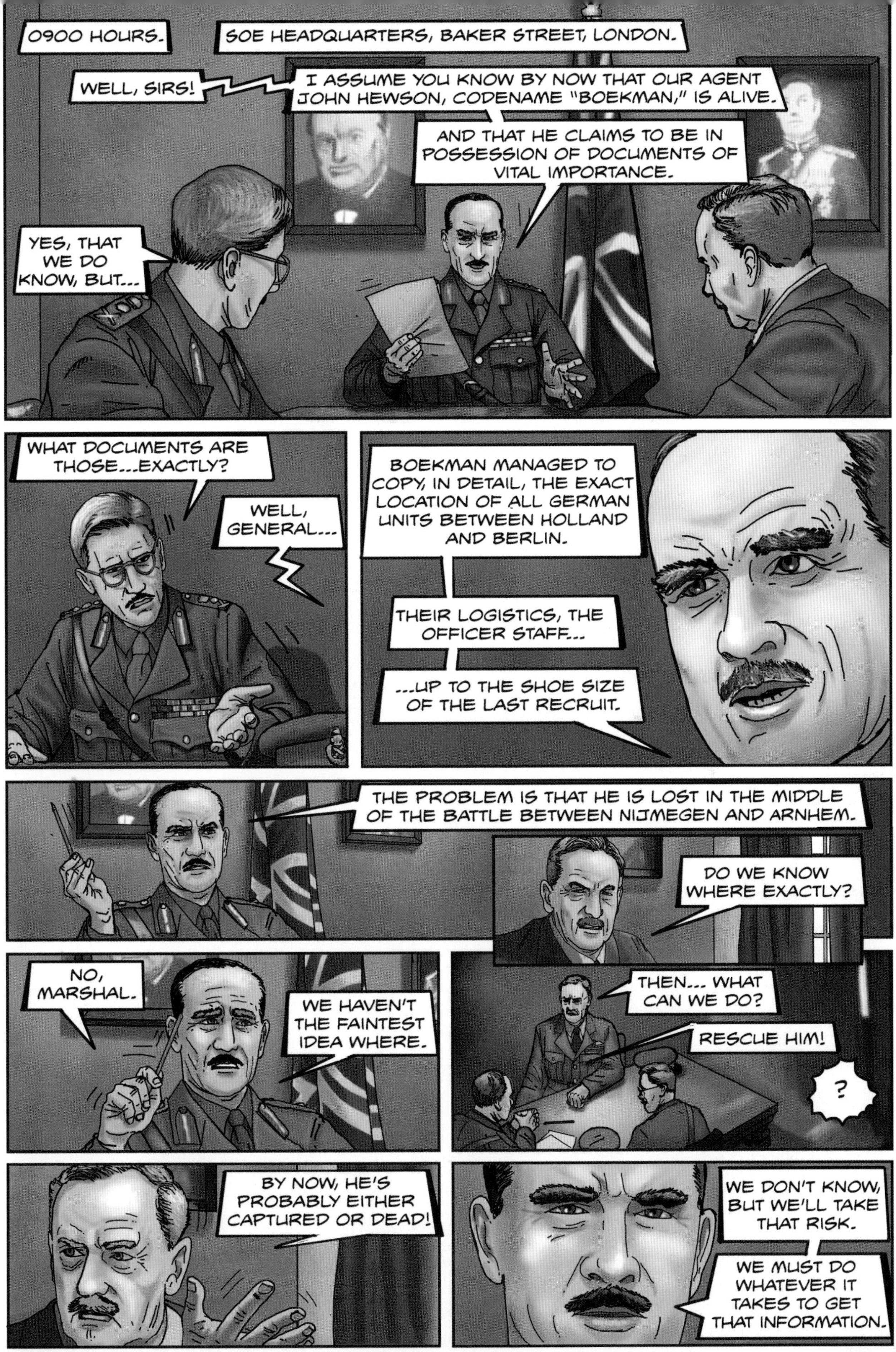
0900 HOURS.
SOE HEADQUARTERS, BAKER STREET, LONDON.
WELL, SIRS!
I ASSUME YOU KNOW BY NOW THAT OUR AGENT JOHN HEWSON, CODENAME "BOEKMAN," IS ALIVE.
AND THAT HE CLAIMS TO BE IN POSSESSION OF DOCUMENTS OF VITAL IMPORTANCE.
YES, THAT WE DO KNOW, BUT...
WHAT DOCUMENTS ARE THOSE...EXACTLY?
WELL, GENERAL...
BOEKMAN MANAGED TO COPY, IN DETAIL, THE EXACT LOCATION OF ALL GERMAN UNITS BETWEEN HOLLAND AND BERLIN.
THEIR LOGISTICS, THE OFFICER STAFF...
...UP TO THE SHOE SIZE OF THE LAST RECRUIT.
THE PROBLEM IS THAT HE IS LOST IN THE MIDDLE OF THE BATTLE BETWEEN NIJMEGEN AND ARNHEM.
DO WE KNOW WHERE EXACTLY?
NO, MARSHAL.
WE HAVEN'T THE FAINTEST IDEA WHERE.
THEN... WHAT CAN WE DO?
RESCUE HIM!
?
BY NOW, HE'S PROBABLY EITHER CAPTURED OR DEAD!
WE DON'T KNOW, BUT WE'LL TAKE THAT RISK.
WE MUST DO WHATEVER IT TAKES TO GET THAT INFORMATION.

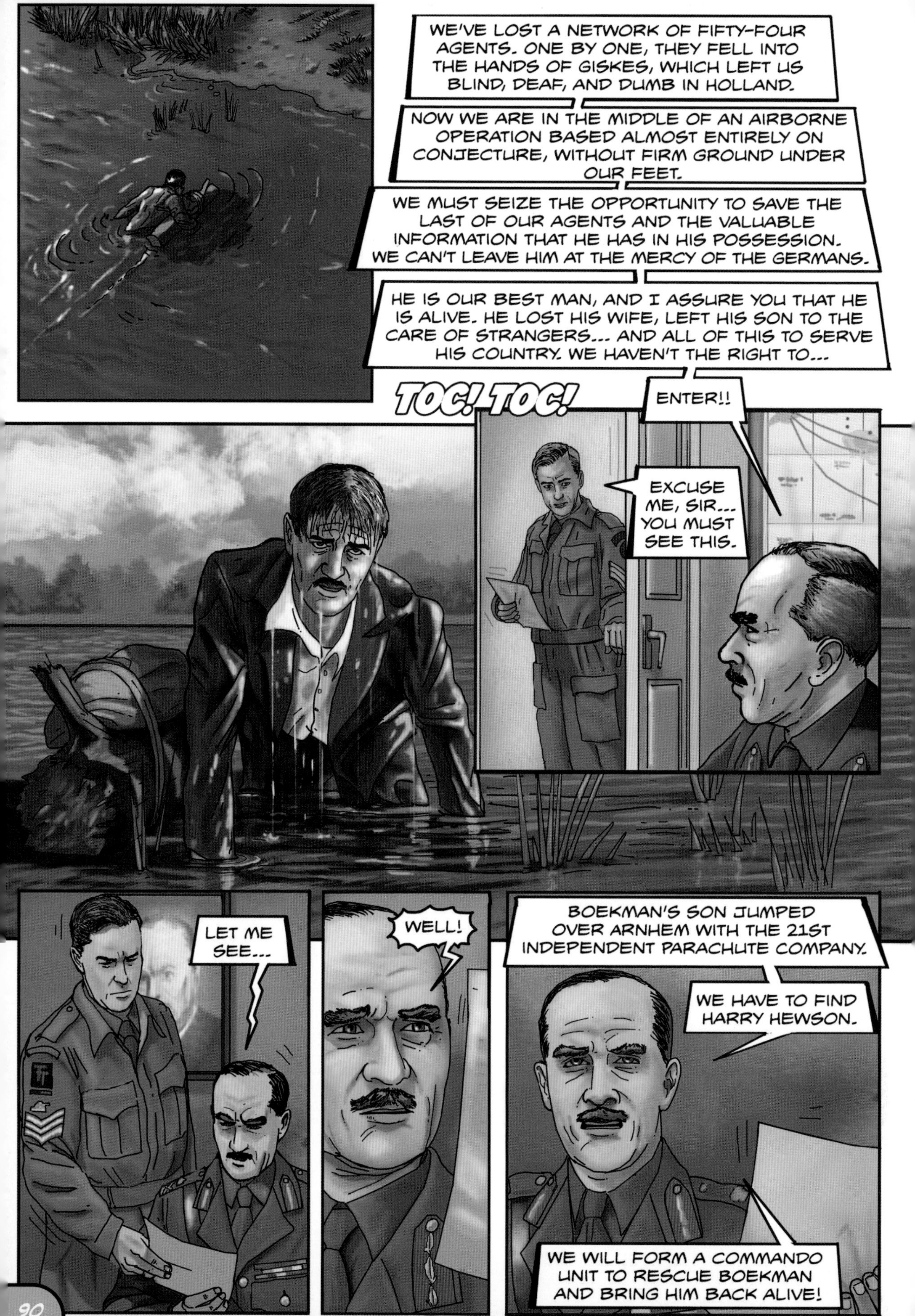
WE'VE LOST A NETWORK OF FIFTY-FOUR AGENTS. ONE BY ONE, THEY FELL INTO THE HANDS OF GISKES, WHICH LEFT US BLIND, DEAF, AND DUMB IN HOLLAND.
NOW WE ARE IN THE MIDDLE OF AN AIRBORNE OPERATION BASED ALMOST ENTIRELY ON CONJECTURE, WITHOUT FIRM GROUND UNDER OUR FEET.
WE MUST SEIZE THE OPPORTUNITY TO SAVE THE LAST OF OUR AGENTS AND THE VALUABLE INFORMATION THAT HE HAS IN HIS POSSESSION. WE CAN'T LEAVE HIM AT THE MERCY OF THE GERMANS.
HE IS OUR BEST MAN, AND I ASSURE YOU THAT HE IS ALIVE. HE LOST HIS WIFE, LEFT HIS SON TO THE CARE OF STRANGERS... AND ALL OF THIS TO SERVE HIS COUNTRY. WE HAVEN'T THE RIGHT TO...
TOC! TOC!
ENTER!!
EXCUSE ME, SIR... YOU MUST SEE THIS.
LET ME SEE...
WELL!
BOEKMAN'S SON JUMPED OVER ARNHEM WITH THE 21ST INDEPENDENT PARACHUTE COMPANY.
WE HAVE TO FIND HARRY HEWSON.
WE WILL FORM A COMMANDO UNIT TO RESCUE BOEKMAN AND BRING HIM BACK ALIVE!

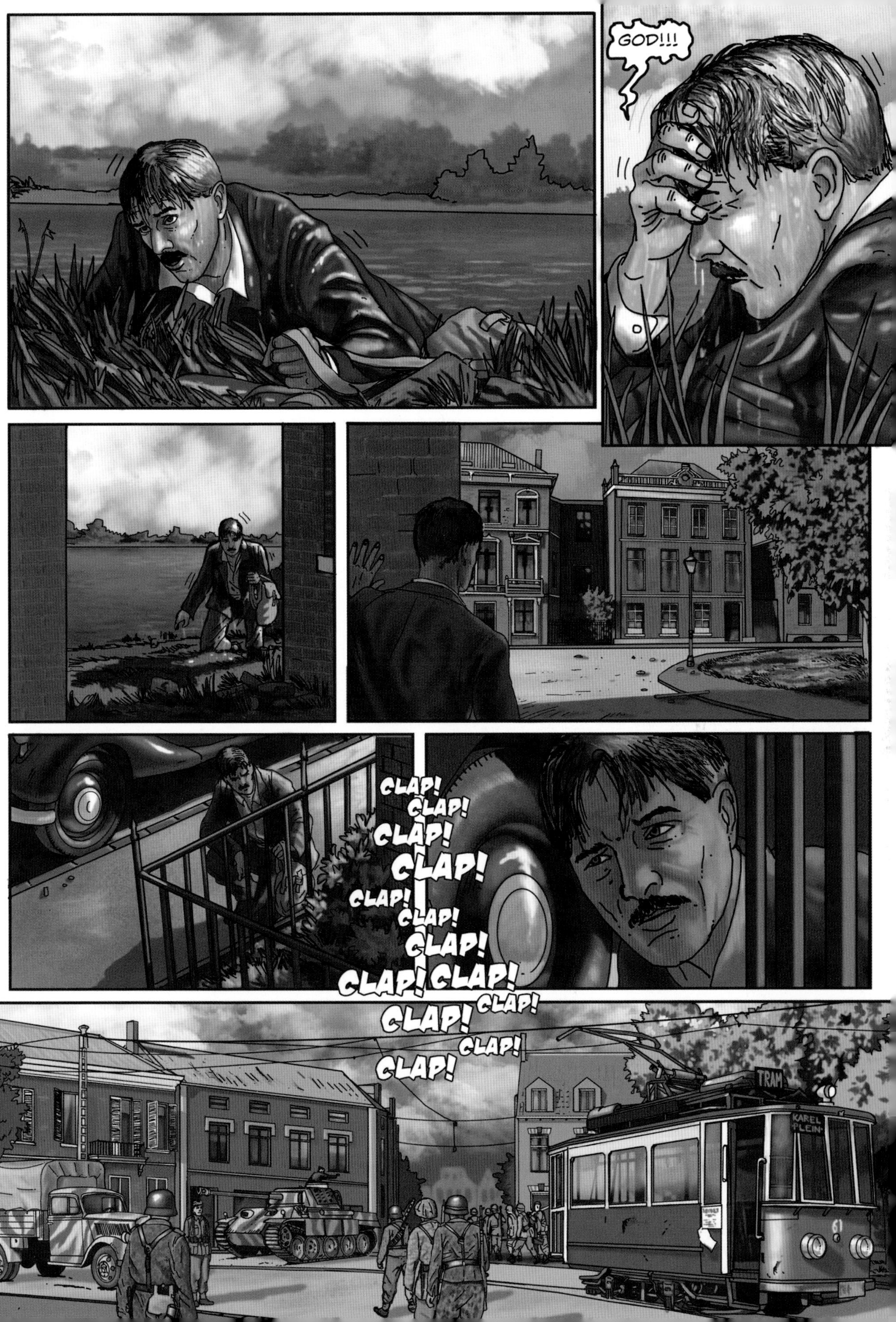
GOD!!!
CLAP!
CLAP!
CLAP!
CLAP!
CLAP!
CLAP!
CLAP!
CLAP! CLAP!
CLAP!
CLAP!
CLAP!
CLAP!
TRAM
KAREL PLEIN
61

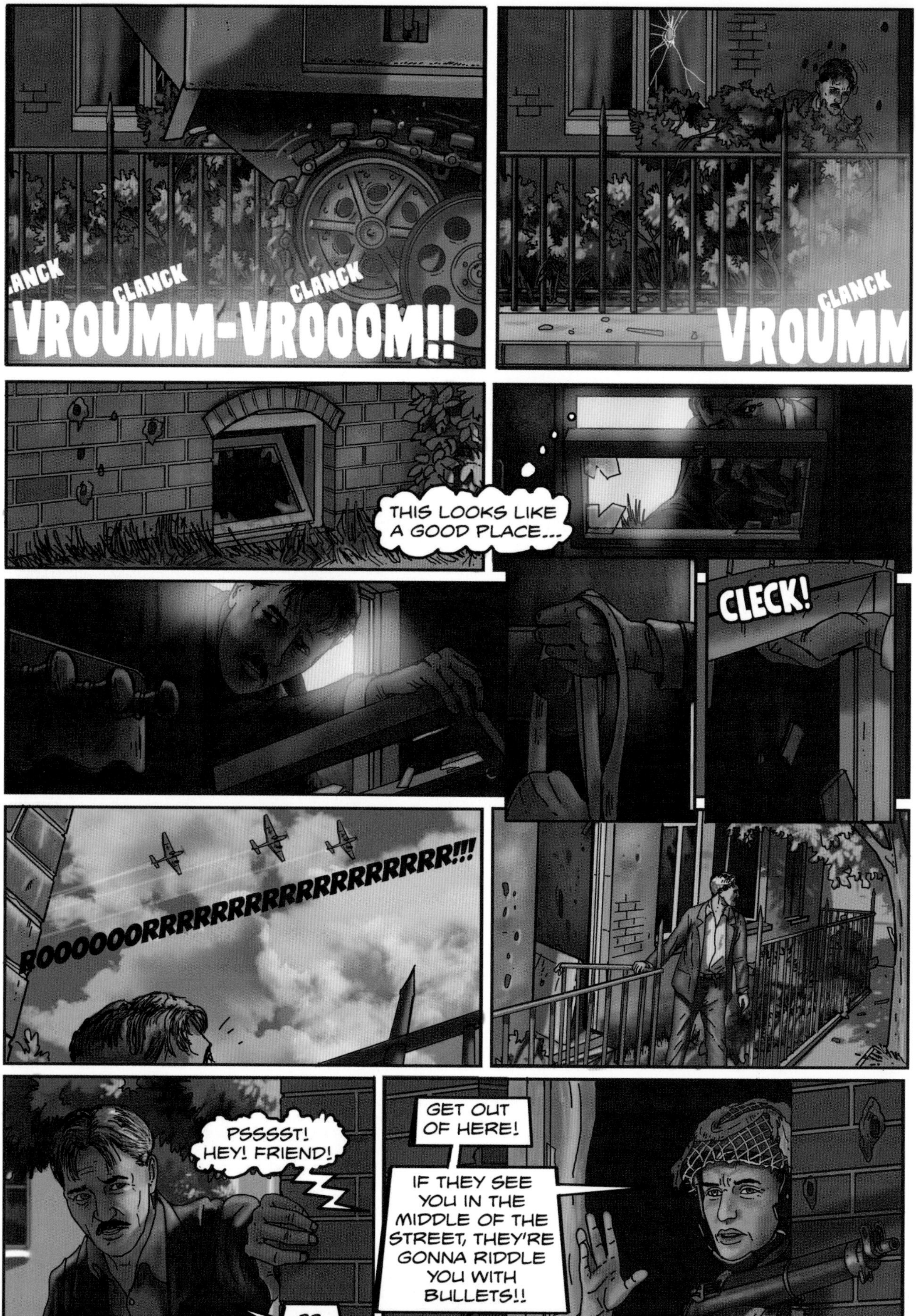

LANCK
CLANCK
CLANCK
VROUMM-VROOOM!!
CLANCK
VROUMM
THIS LOOKS LIKE A GOOD PLACE...
CLECK!
ROOOOOOORRRRRRRRRRRRRRRRRR!!!
PSSSST! HEY! FRIEND!
??
GET OUT OF HERE!
IF THEY SEE YOU IN THE MIDDLE OF THE STREET, THEY'RE GONNA RIDDLE YOU WITH BULLETS!!

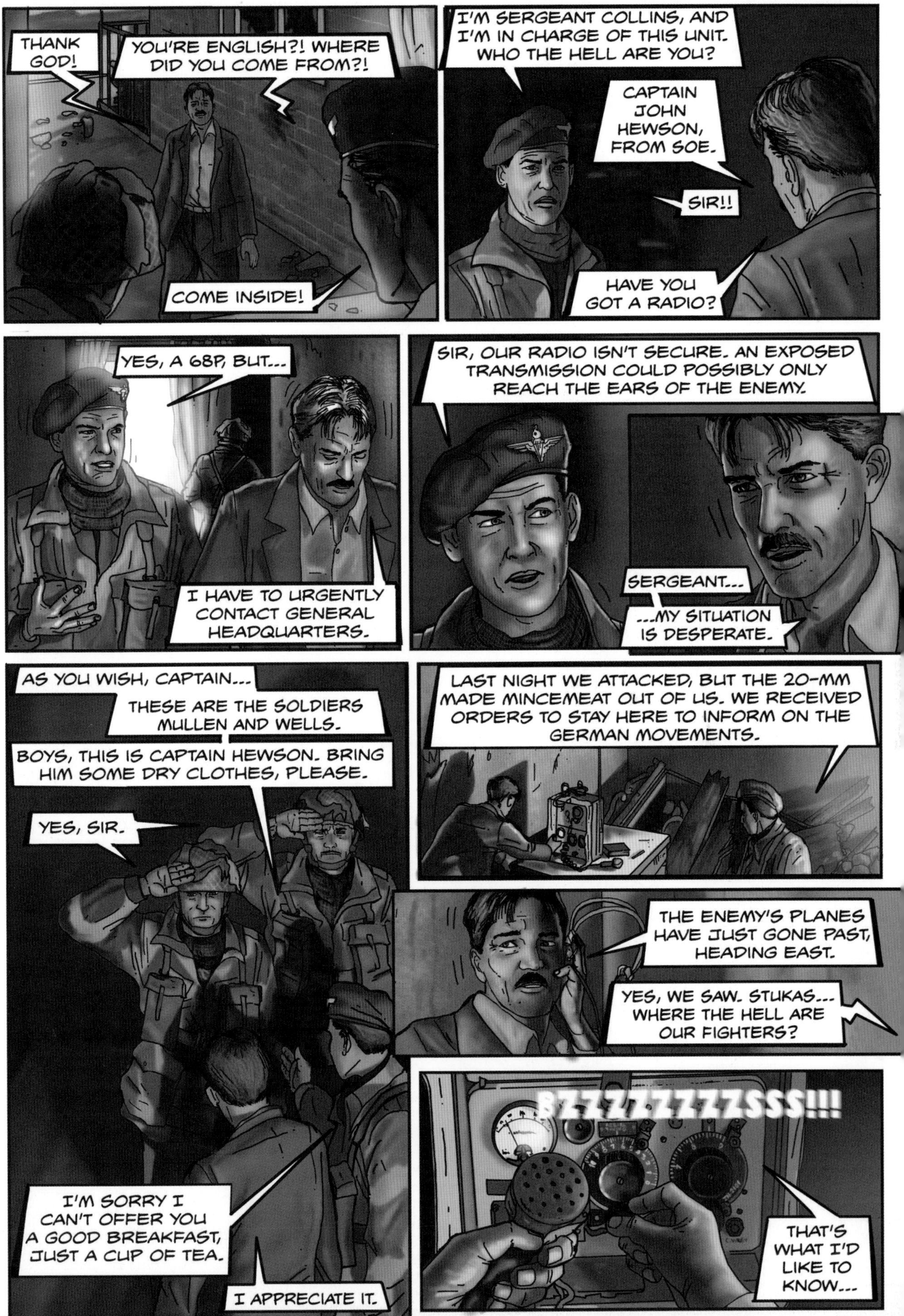
THANK GOD!
YOU'RE ENGLISH?! WHERE DID YOU COME FROM?!
COME INSIDE!
I'M SERGEANT COLLINS, AND I'M IN CHARGE OF THIS UNIT. WHO THE HELL ARE YOU?
CAPTAIN JOHN HEWSON, FROM SOE.
SIR!!
HAVE YOU GOT A RADIO?
YES, A 68P, BUT...
I HAVE TO URGENTLY CONTACT GENERAL HEADQUARTERS.
SIR, OUR RADIO ISN'T SECURE. AN EXPOSED TRANSMISSION COULD POSSIBLY ONLY REACH THE EARS OF THE ENEMY.
SERGEANT...
...MY SITUATION IS DESPERATE.
AS YOU WISH, CAPTAIN...
THESE ARE THE SOLDIERS MULLEN AND WELLS.
BOYS, THIS IS CAPTAIN HEWSON. BRING HIM SOME DRY CLOTHES, PLEASE.
YES, SIR.
I'M SORRY I CAN'T OFFER YOU A GOOD BREAKFAST, JUST A CUP OF TEA.
I APPRECIATE IT.
LAST NIGHT WE ATTACKED, BUT THE 20-MM MADE MINCEMEAT OUT OF US. WE RECEIVED ORDERS TO STAY HERE TO INFORM ON THE GERMAN MOVEMENTS.
THE ENEMY'S PLANES HAVE JUST GONE PAST, HEADING EAST.
YES, WE SAW. STUKAS... WHERE THE HELL ARE OUR FIGHTERS?
BZZZZZZZZZSSS!!!
THAT'S WHAT I'D LIKE TO KNOW...

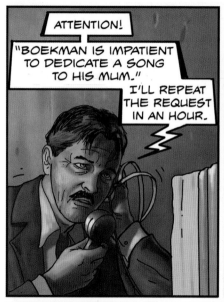

ATTENTION!

"BOEKMAN IS IMPATIENT TO DEDICATE A SONG TO HIS MUM."

I'LL REPEAT THE REQUEST IN AN HOUR.

WE HAVE HIM!!

WE MUST NOTIFY URQUHART AND LONDON!

<HE SPEAKS IN CODE.>

<YES, WE HAVE HIM.>

<LOOK FOR THE SOURCE OF THAT TRANSMISSION.>

<YES, HAUPTSTURMFÜHRER!>

WE HAVE TO WAIT FOR AN HOUR.

DAMN... THEN WE WILL WAIT...

IF YOU HAVE FINISHED FOR THE TIME BEING, CAPTAIN...

...WE SHOULD LEAVE THE POSITION SOON. THE NAZIS HAVE ALREADY SMELLED US.

UNDERSTOOD.

PAY ATTENTION, MEN!! WE NEED TO GO TONIGHT!!

THERE WILL BE DANCING SOON!!

YES SIR!!

TELL ME SOMETHING: WHAT SENSE IS THERE IN THE SOE BEING IN THIS DUMP?

A LOT.

MY PRESENCE HERE IS MORE IMPORTANT THAN YOU CAN IMAGINE...

WE WILL CHANGE OUR POSITION, SERGEANT, BUT I CAN'T GO FAR FROM HERE.

WILL YOU GIVE A REASON?

IT'S NOT THE TIME OR PLACE FOR EXPLANATIONS. JUST DO AS I SAY.

I'M IN CHARGE NOW.

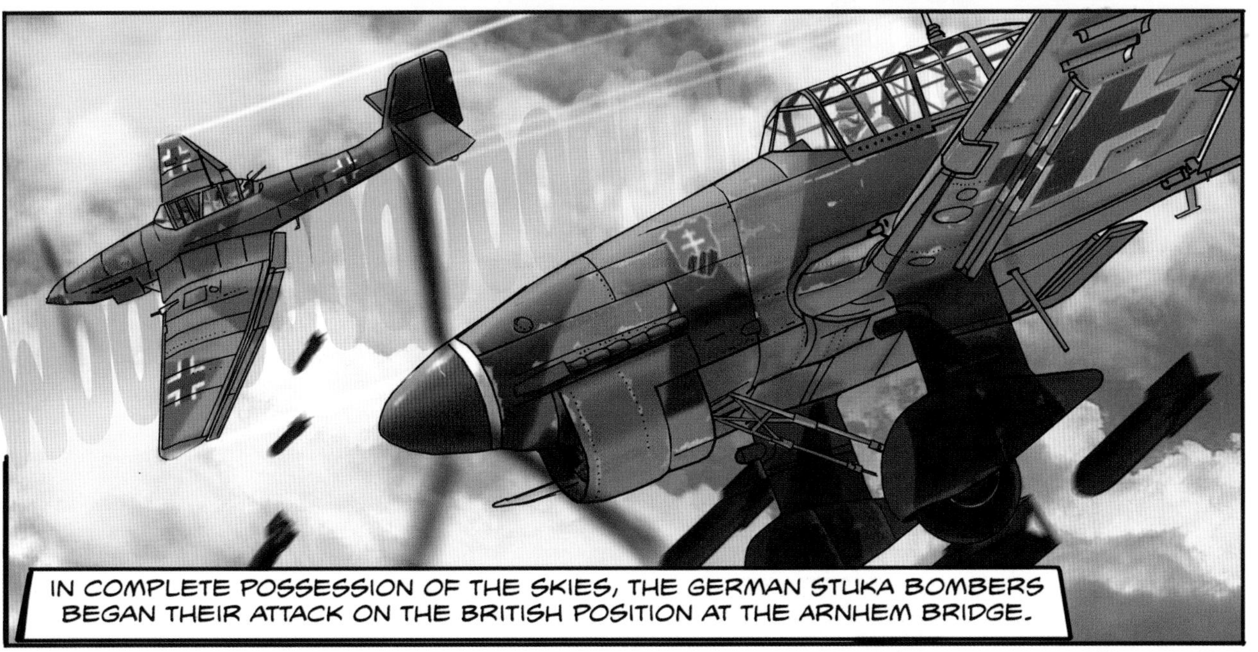
IN COMPLETE POSSESSION OF THE SKIES, THE GERMAN STUKA BOMBERS BEGAN THEIR ATTACK ON THE BRITISH POSITION AT THE ARNHEM BRIDGE.

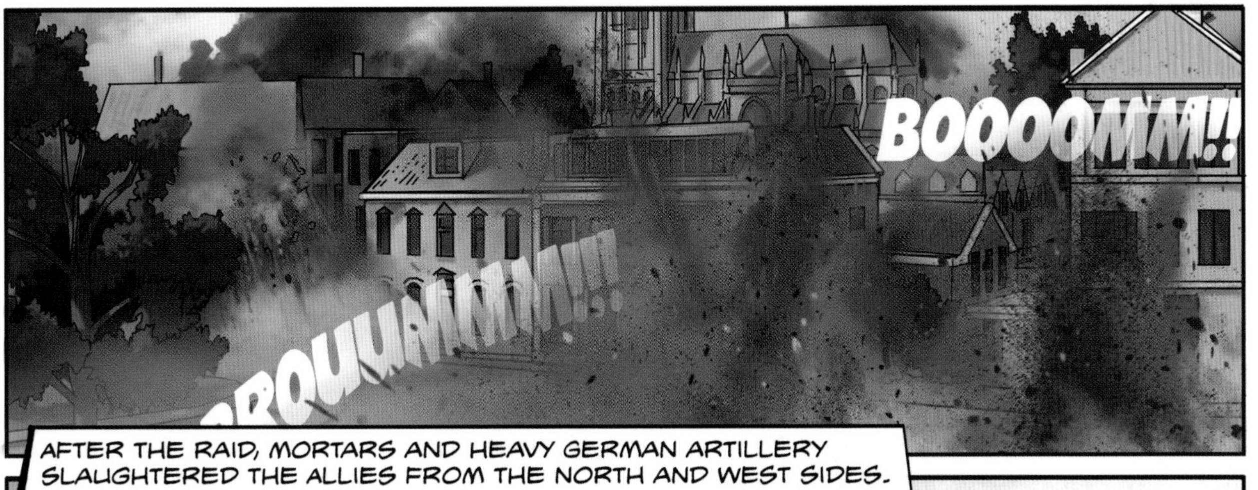
BOOOOMM!!
AFTER THE RAID, MORTARS AND HEAVY GERMAN ARTILLERY SLAUGHTERED THE ALLIES FROM THE NORTH AND WEST SIDES.

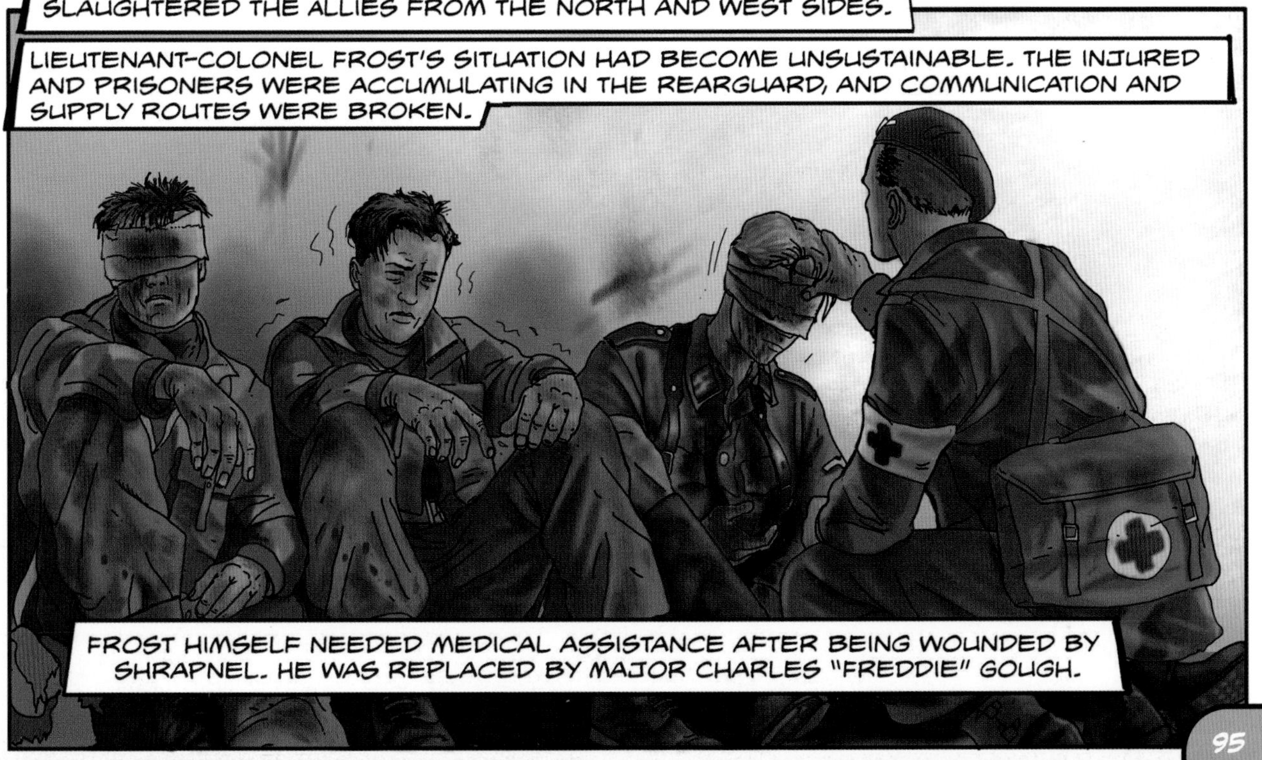
LIEUTENANT-COLONEL FROST'S SITUATION HAD BECOME UNSUSTAINABLE. THE INJURED AND PRISONERS WERE ACCUMULATING IN THE REARGUARD, AND COMMUNICATION AND SUPPLY ROUTES WERE BROKEN.
FROST HIMSELF NEEDED MEDICAL ASSISTANCE AFTER BEING WOUNDED BY SHRAPNEL. HE WAS REPLACED BY MAJOR CHARLES "FREDDIE" GOUGH.

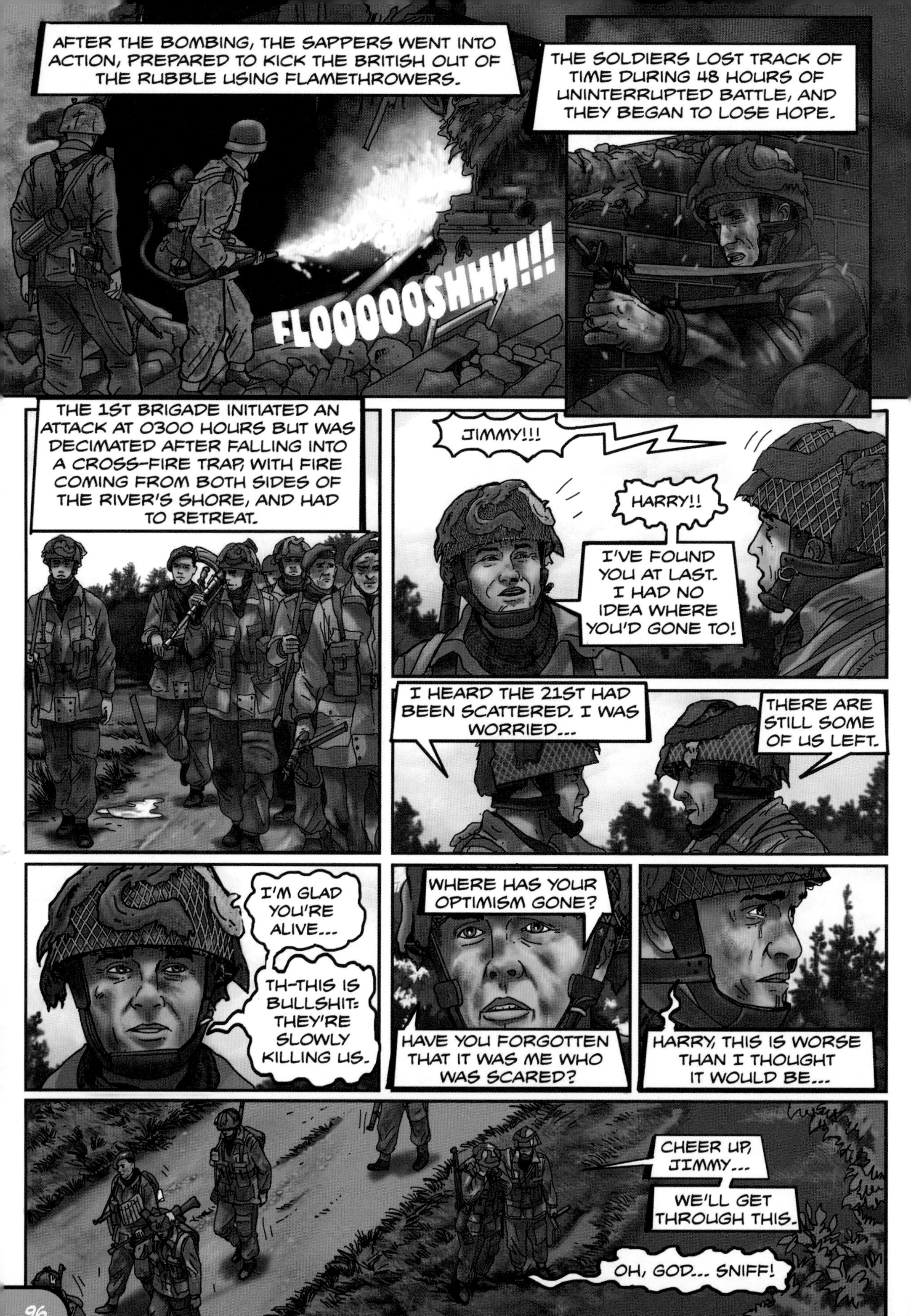
AFTER THE BOMBING, THE SAPPERS WENT INTO ACTION, PREPARED TO KICK THE BRITISH OUT OF THE RUBBLE USING FLAMETHROWERS.
FLOOOOOOSHHH!!!
THE SOLDIERS LOST TRACK OF TIME DURING 48 HOURS OF UNINTERRUPTED BATTLE, AND THEY BEGAN TO LOSE HOPE.
THE 1ST BRIGADE INITIATED AN ATTACK AT 0300 HOURS BUT WAS DECIMATED AFTER FALLING INTO A CROSS-FIRE TRAP, WITH FIRE COMING FROM BOTH SIDES OF THE RIVER'S SHORE, AND HAD TO RETREAT.
JIMMY!!!
HARRY!!
I'VE FOUND YOU AT LAST. I HAD NO IDEA WHERE YOU'D GONE TO!
I HEARD THE 21ST HAD BEEN SCATTERED. I WAS WORRIED...
THERE ARE STILL SOME OF US LEFT.
I'M GLAD YOU'RE ALIVE...
TH-THIS IS BULLSHIT: THEY'RE SLOWLY KILLING US.
WHERE HAS YOUR OPTIMISM GONE?
HAVE YOU FORGOTTEN THAT IT WAS ME WHO WAS SCARED?
HARRY, THIS IS WORSE THAN I THOUGHT IT WOULD BE...
CHEER UP, JIMMY...
WE'LL GET THROUGH THIS.
OH, GOD... SNIFF!

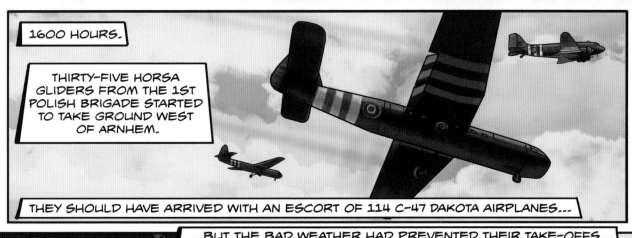

1600 HOURS.

THIRTY-FIVE HORSA GLIDERS FROM THE 1ST POLISH BRIGADE STARTED TO TAKE GROUND WEST OF ARNHEM.

THEY SHOULD HAVE ARRIVED WITH AN ESCORT OF 114 C-47 DAKOTA AIRPLANES...

...BUT THE BAD WEATHER HAD PREVENTED THEIR TAKE-OFFS...

...ANOTHER DAY HAD BEEN LOST.

ZIIDDFFF!!!!

SZYBKO, SZYBKO, WYSKAKIWAĆ!*

*GO, GO, EVERYBODY DOWN!! (TRANSLATED FROM THE POLISH.)

THE HORSA GLIDERS HAD LANDED IN THE MIDDLE OF THE CROSS FIRE.

NA ZIEMIE!!*

*DOWN!!

BRRRRTTTAAAP!!!! BRRAP!!!

NA LITOŚĆ BOSKA ZNAJDŹCIE JAKAŚ OSŁONĘ, CHOĆBY ZA SZYBOWCAMI!!!!*

*FOR GOD'S SAKE!! LOOK FOR COVER, EVEN IF IT'S BEHIND THE GLIDERS!!

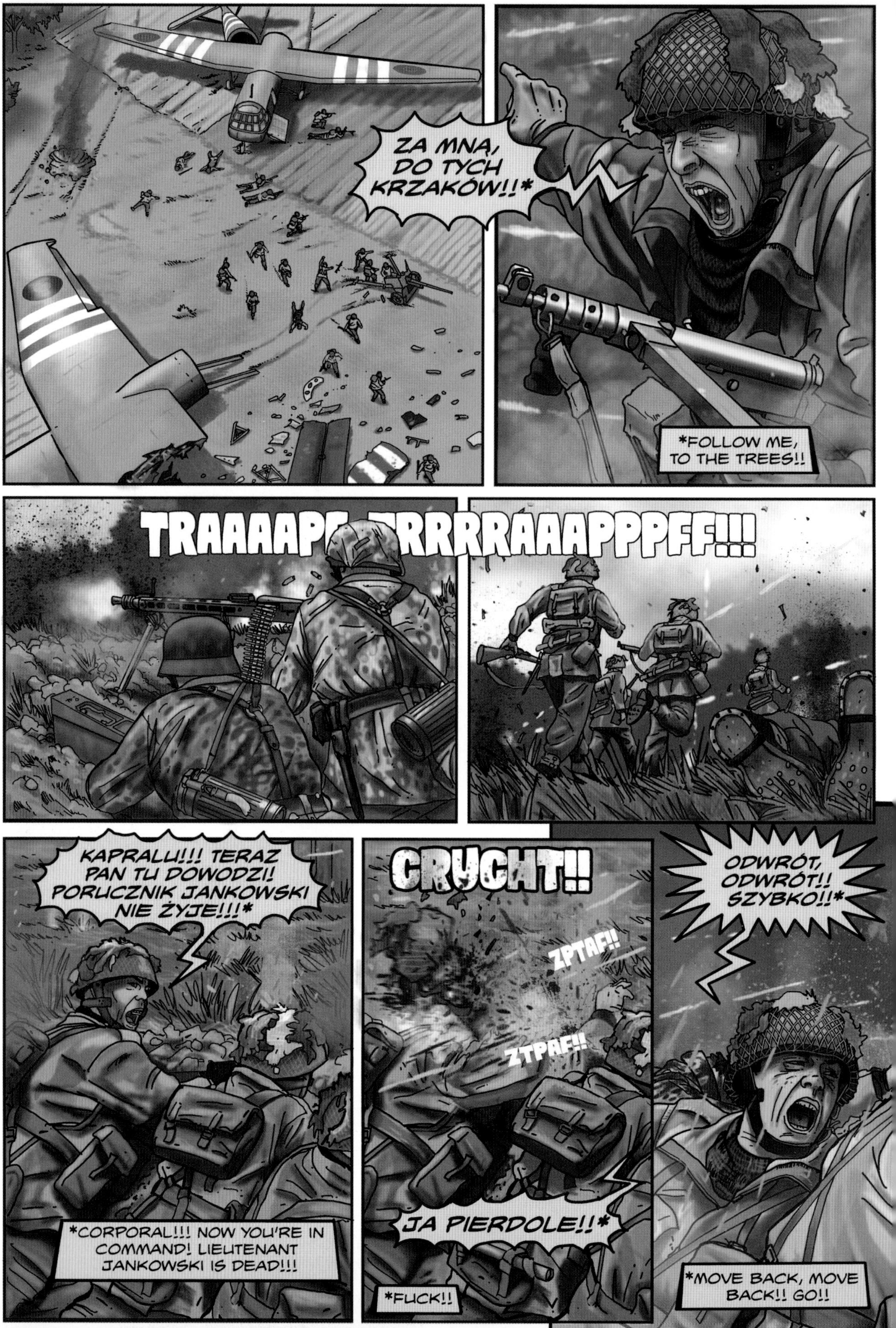
ZA MNĄ, DO TYCH KRZAKÓW!!*
*FOLLOW ME, TO THE TREES!!
TRAAAAPF TRRRRAAAPPPFF!!!
KAPRALU!!! TERAZ PAN TU DOWODZI! PORUCZNIK JANKOWSKI NIE ŻYJE!!!*
*CORPORAL!!! NOW YOU'RE IN COMMAND! LIEUTENANT JANKOWSKI IS DEAD!!!
CRUCHT!!
ZPTAF!!
ZTPAF!!
JA PIERDOLE!!*
*FUCK!!
ODWRÓT, ODWRÓT!! SZYBKO!!*
*MOVE BACK, MOVE BACK!! GO!!

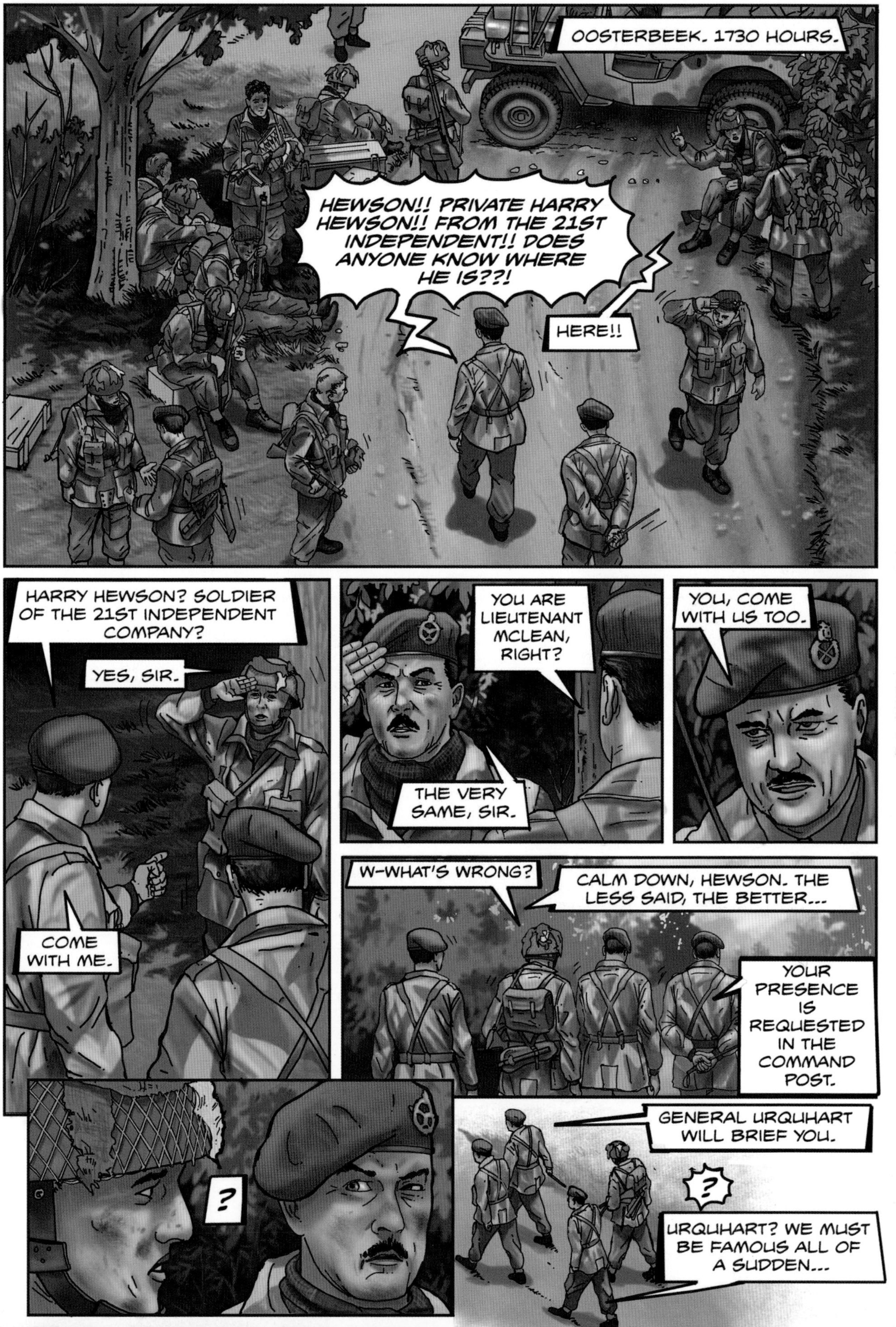
OOSTERBEEK. 1730 HOURS.
HEWSON!! PRIVATE HARRY HEWSON!! FROM THE 21ST INDEPENDENT!! DOES ANYONE KNOW WHERE HE IS??!
HERE!!
HARRY HEWSON? SOLDIER OF THE 21ST INDEPENDENT COMPANY?
YES, SIR.
COME WITH ME.
YOU ARE LIEUTENANT MCLEAN, RIGHT?
THE VERY SAME, SIR.
YOU, COME WITH US TOO.
W-WHAT'S WRONG?
CALM DOWN, HEWSON. THE LESS SAID, THE BETTER...
YOUR PRESENCE IS REQUESTED IN THE COMMAND POST.
?
GENERAL URQUHART WILL BRIEF YOU.
?
URQUHART? WE MUST BE FAMOUS ALL OF A SUDDEN...

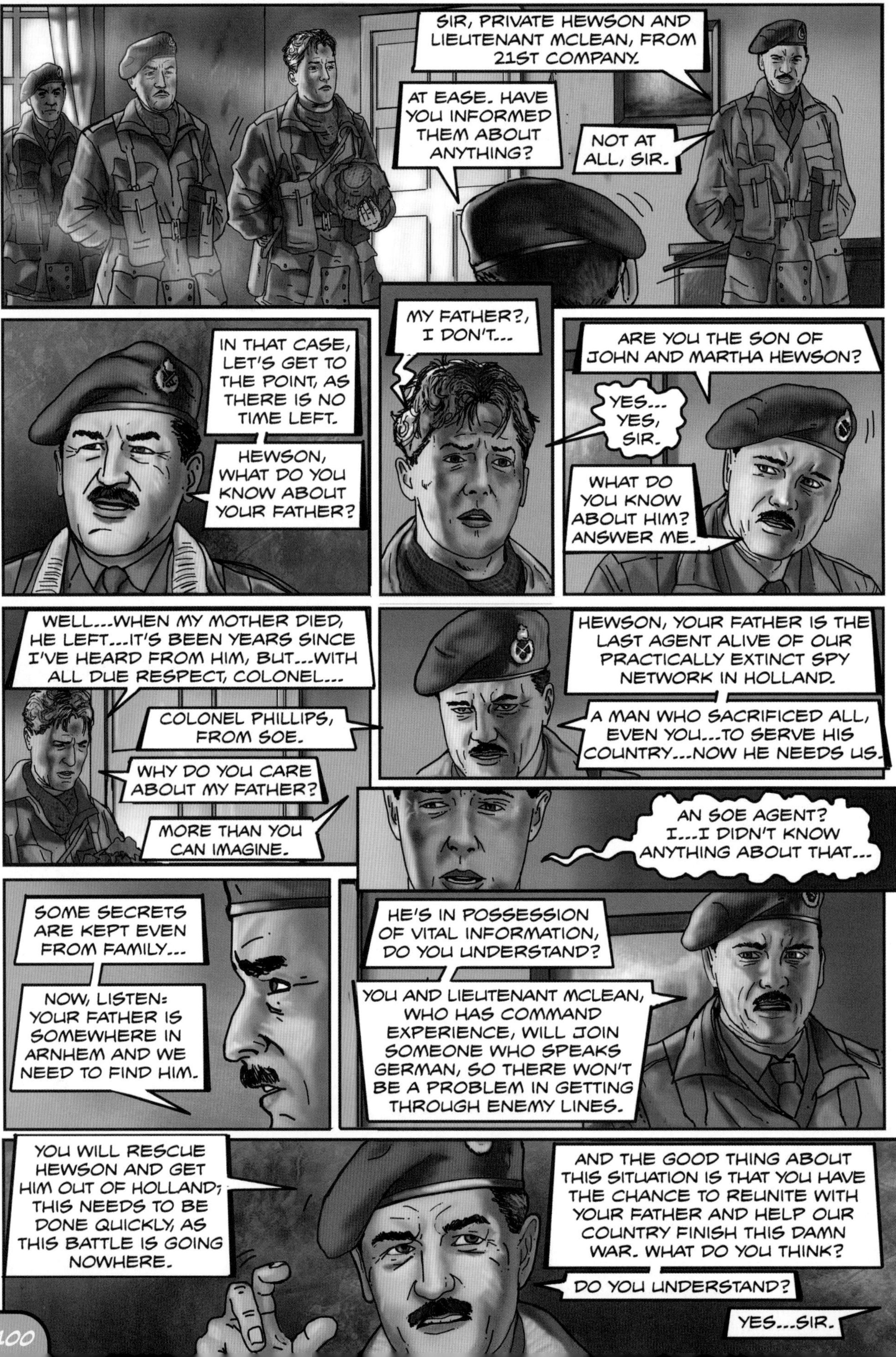
SIR, PRIVATE HEWSON AND LIEUTENANT MCLEAN, FROM 21ST COMPANY.
AT EASE. HAVE YOU INFORMED THEM ABOUT ANYTHING?
NOT AT ALL, SIR.
IN THAT CASE, LET'S GET TO THE POINT, AS THERE IS NO TIME LEFT.
HEWSON, WHAT DO YOU KNOW ABOUT YOUR FATHER?
MY FATHER?, I DON'T...
ARE YOU THE SON OF JOHN AND MARTHA HEWSON?
YES... YES, SIR.
WHAT DO YOU KNOW ABOUT HIM? ANSWER ME.
WELL...WHEN MY MOTHER DIED, HE LEFT...IT'S BEEN YEARS SINCE I'VE HEARD FROM HIM, BUT...WITH ALL DUE RESPECT, COLONEL...
COLONEL PHILLIPS, FROM SOE.
WHY DO YOU CARE ABOUT MY FATHER?
MORE THAN YOU CAN IMAGINE.
HEWSON, YOUR FATHER IS THE LAST AGENT ALIVE OF OUR PRACTICALLY EXTINCT SPY NETWORK IN HOLLAND.
A MAN WHO SACRIFICED ALL, EVEN YOU...TO SERVE HIS COUNTRY...NOW HE NEEDS US.
AN SOE AGENT? I...I DIDN'T KNOW ANYTHING ABOUT THAT...
SOME SECRETS ARE KEPT EVEN FROM FAMILY...
NOW, LISTEN: YOUR FATHER IS SOMEWHERE IN ARNHEM AND WE NEED TO FIND HIM.
HE'S IN POSSESSION OF VITAL INFORMATION, DO YOU UNDERSTAND?
YOU AND LIEUTENANT MCLEAN, WHO HAS COMMAND EXPERIENCE, WILL JOIN SOMEONE WHO SPEAKS GERMAN, SO THERE WON'T BE A PROBLEM IN GETTING THROUGH ENEMY LINES.
YOU WILL RESCUE HEWSON AND GET HIM OUT OF HOLLAND; THIS NEEDS TO BE DONE QUICKLY, AS THIS BATTLE IS GOING NOWHERE.
AND THE GOOD THING ABOUT THIS SITUATION IS THAT YOU HAVE THE CHANCE TO REUNITE WITH YOUR FATHER AND HELP OUR COUNTRY FINISH THIS DAMN WAR. WHAT DO YOU THINK?
DO YOU UNDERSTAND?
YES...SIR.

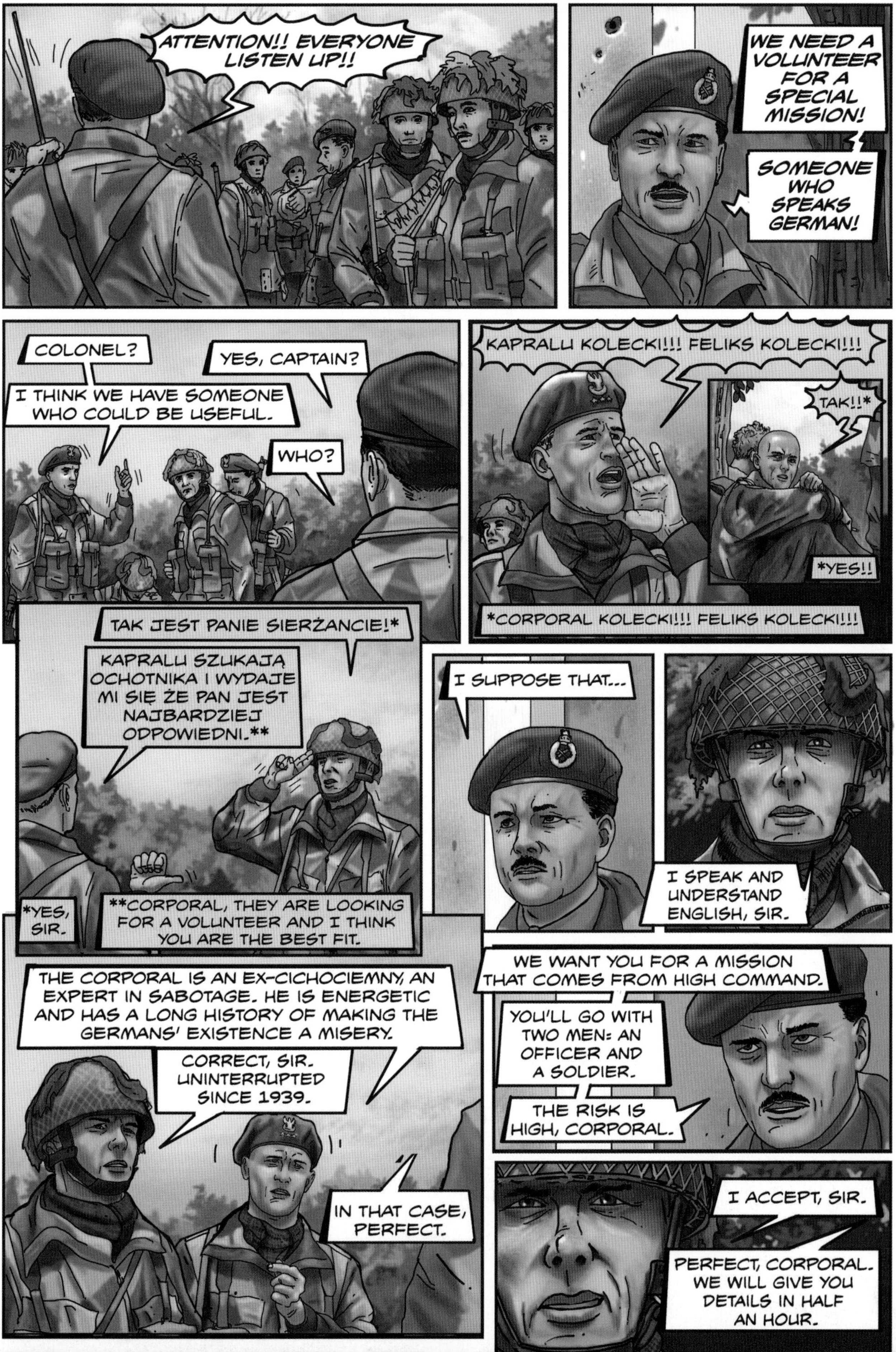
ATTENTION!! EVERYONE LISTEN UP!!
WE NEED A VOLUNTEER FOR A SPECIAL MISSION!
SOMEONE WHO SPEAKS GERMAN!
COLONEL?
YES, CAPTAIN?
I THINK WE HAVE SOMEONE WHO COULD BE USEFUL.
WHO?
KAPRALU KOLECKI!!! FELIKS KOLECKI!!!
TAK!!*
*YES!!
*CORPORAL KOLECKI!!! FELIKS KOLECKI!!!
TAK JEST PANIE SIERŻANCIE!*
KAPRALU SZUKAJĄ OCHOTNIKA I WYDAJE MI SIĘ ŻE PAN JEST NAJBARDZIEJ ODPOWIEDNI.**
*YES, SIR.
**CORPORAL, THEY ARE LOOKING FOR A VOLUNTEER AND I THINK YOU ARE THE BEST FIT.
I SUPPOSE THAT...
I SPEAK AND UNDERSTAND ENGLISH, SIR.
THE CORPORAL IS AN EX-CICHOCIEMNY, AN EXPERT IN SABOTAGE. HE IS ENERGETIC AND HAS A LONG HISTORY OF MAKING THE GERMANS' EXISTENCE A MISERY.
CORRECT, SIR. UNINTERRUPTED SINCE 1939.
IN THAT CASE, PERFECT.
WE WANT YOU FOR A MISSION THAT COMES FROM HIGH COMMAND.
YOU'LL GO WITH TWO MEN: AN OFFICER AND A SOLDIER.
THE RISK IS HIGH, CORPORAL.
I ACCEPT, SIR.
PERFECT, CORPORAL. WE WILL GIVE YOU DETAILS IN HALF AN HOUR.

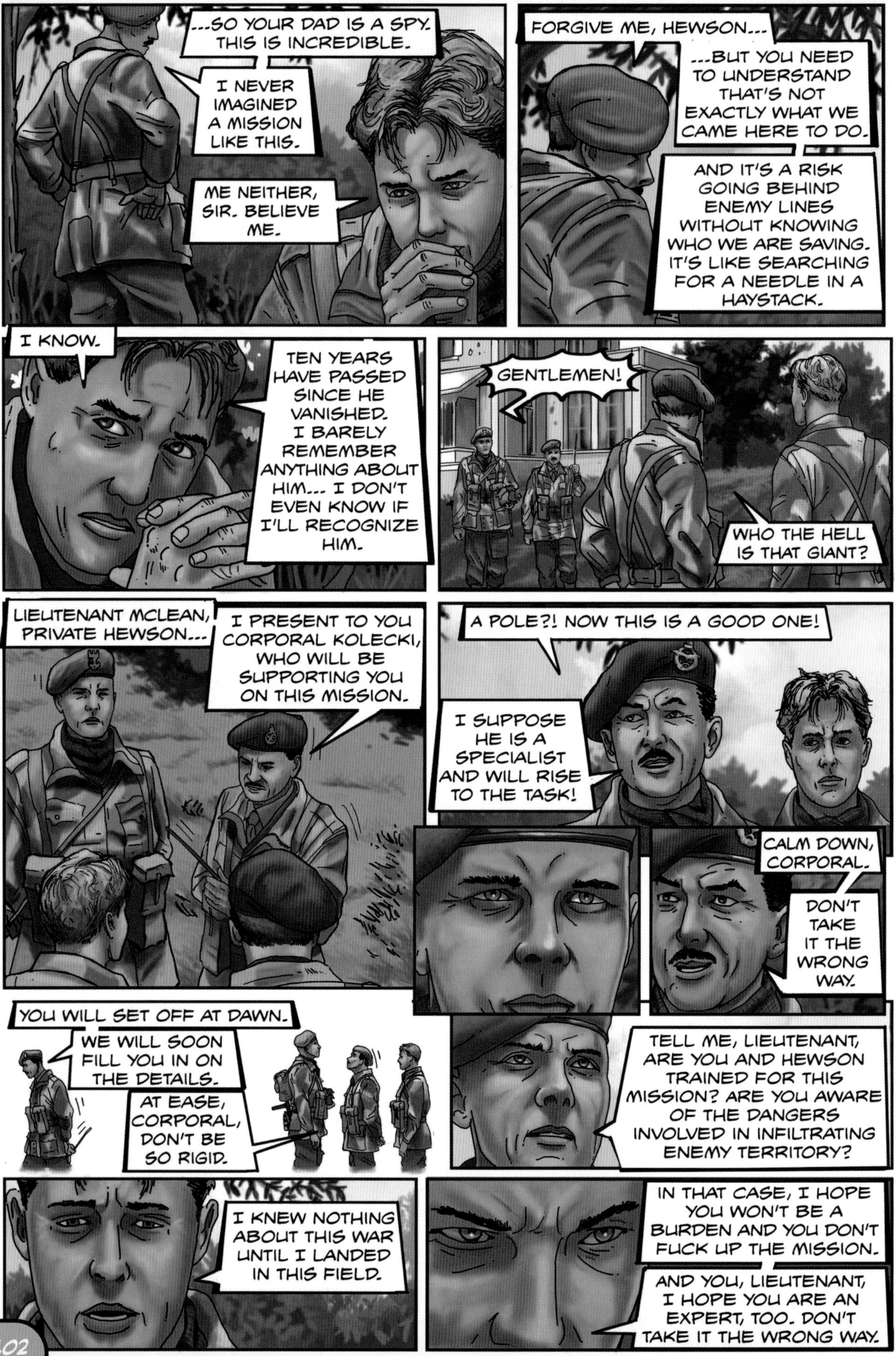
...SO YOUR DAD IS A SPY. THIS IS INCREDIBLE.
I NEVER IMAGINED A MISSION LIKE THIS.
ME NEITHER, SIR. BELIEVE ME.
FORGIVE ME, HEWSON...
...BUT YOU NEED TO UNDERSTAND THAT'S NOT EXACTLY WHAT WE CAME HERE TO DO.
AND IT'S A RISK GOING BEHIND ENEMY LINES WITHOUT KNOWING WHO WE ARE SAVING. IT'S LIKE SEARCHING FOR A NEEDLE IN A HAYSTACK.
I KNOW.
TEN YEARS HAVE PASSED SINCE HE VANISHED. I BARELY REMEMBER ANYTHING ABOUT HIM... I DON'T EVEN KNOW IF I'LL RECOGNIZE HIM.
GENTLEMEN!
WHO THE HELL IS THAT GIANT?
LIEUTENANT MCLEAN, PRIVATE HEWSON...
I PRESENT TO YOU CORPORAL KOLECKI, WHO WILL BE SUPPORTING YOU ON THIS MISSION.
A POLE?! NOW THIS IS A GOOD ONE!
I SUPPOSE HE IS A SPECIALIST AND WILL RISE TO THE TASK!
CALM DOWN, CORPORAL.
DON'T TAKE IT THE WRONG WAY.
YOU WILL SET OFF AT DAWN.
WE WILL SOON FILL YOU IN ON THE DETAILS.
AT EASE, CORPORAL, DON'T BE SO RIGID.
TELL ME, LIEUTENANT, ARE YOU AND HEWSON TRAINED FOR THIS MISSION? ARE YOU AWARE OF THE DANGERS INVOLVED IN INFILTRATING ENEMY TERRITORY?
I KNEW NOTHING ABOUT THIS WAR UNTIL I LANDED IN THIS FIELD.
IN THAT CASE, I HOPE YOU WON'T BE A BURDEN AND YOU DON'T FUCK UP THE MISSION.
AND YOU, LIEUTENANT, I HOPE YOU ARE AN EXPERT, TOO. DON'T TAKE IT THE WRONG WAY.

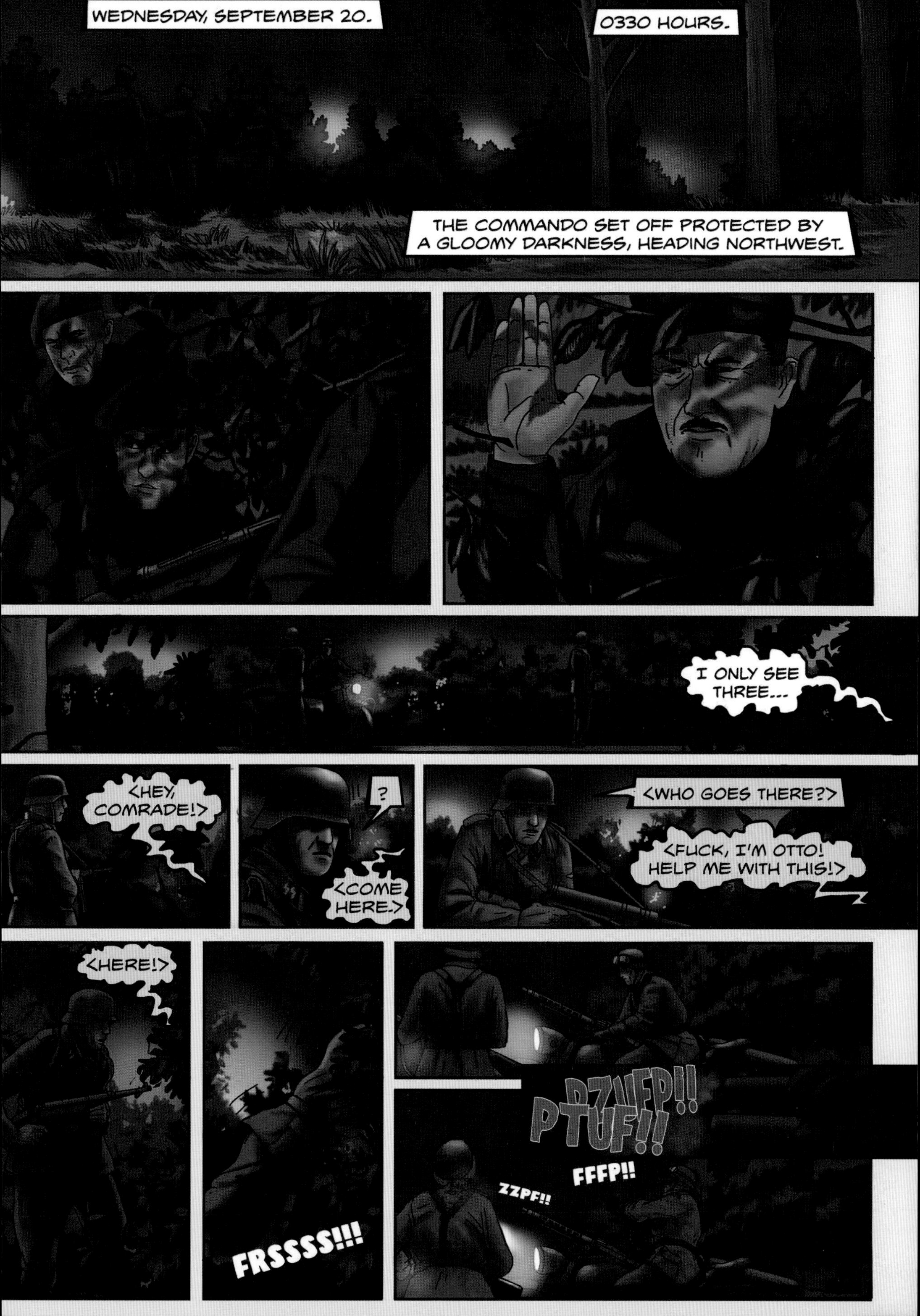
WEDNESDAY, SEPTEMBER 20.
0330 HOURS.
THE COMMANDO SET OFF PROTECTED BY A GLOOMY DARKNESS, HEADING NORTHWEST.
I ONLY SEE THREE...
<HEY, COMRADE!>
?
<COME HERE.>
<WHO GOES THERE?>
<FUCK, I'M OTTO! HELP ME WITH THIS!>
<HERE!>
FRSSSS!!!
DZUFP!!
PTUF!!
FFFP!!
ZZPF!!

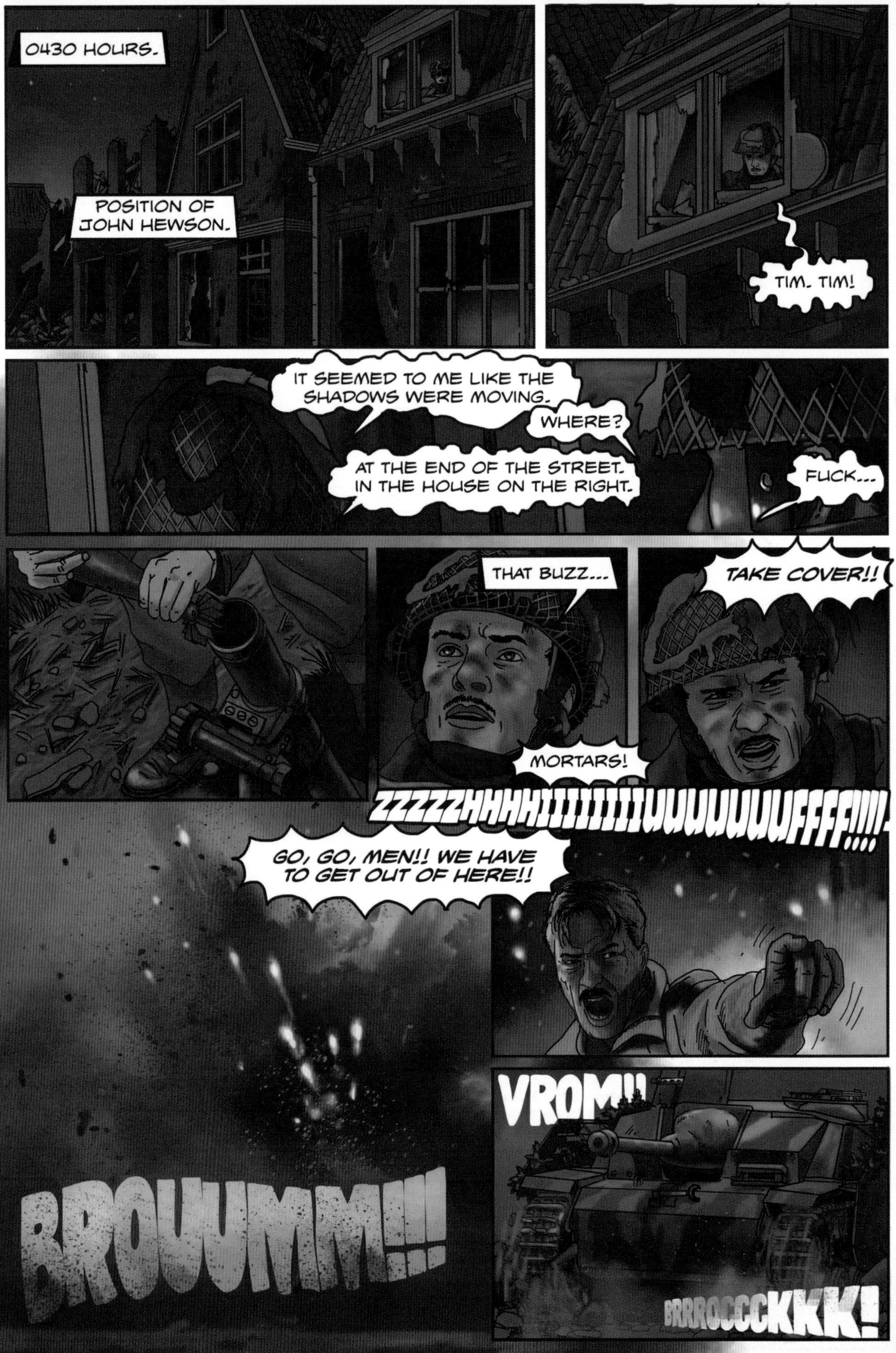
0430 HOURS.
POSITION OF JOHN HEWSON.
TIM. TIM!
IT SEEMED TO ME LIKE THE SHADOWS WERE MOVING.
WHERE?
AT THE END OF THE STREET. IN THE HOUSE ON THE RIGHT.
FUCK...
THAT BUZZ...
MORTARS!
TAKE COVER!!
ZZZZZHHHHIIIIIIIIIUUUUUUUUFFFF!!!!...
GO, GO, MEN!! WE HAVE TO GET OUT OF HERE!!
BROUUMM!!!
VROM!!
BRRROCCCKKK!

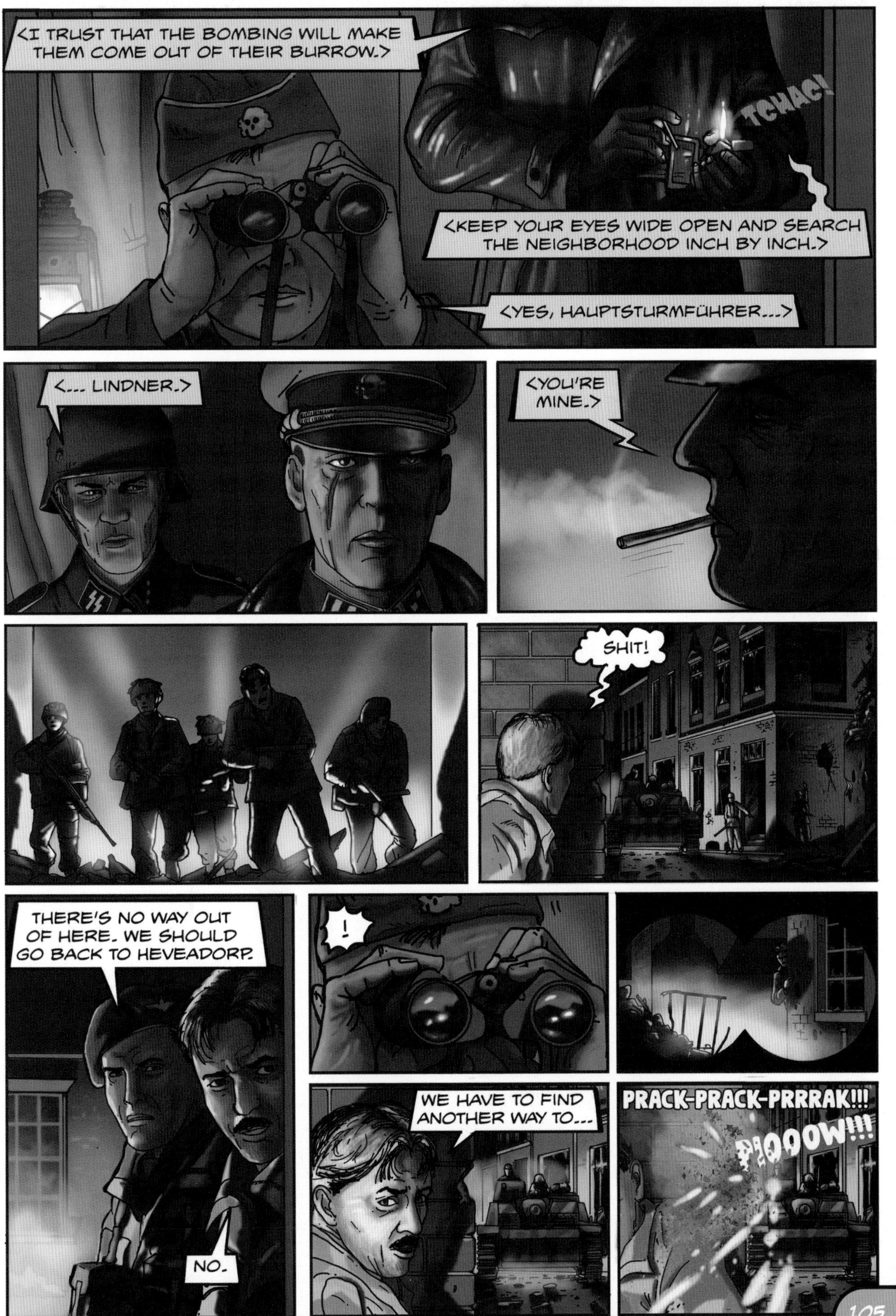

<I TRUST THAT THE BOMBING WILL MAKE THEM COME OUT OF THEIR BURROW.>
TCHAC!
<KEEP YOUR EYES WIDE OPEN AND SEARCH THE NEIGHBORHOOD INCH BY INCH.>
<YES, HAUPTSTURMFÜHRER...>
<... LINDNER.>
<YOU'RE MINE.>
SHIT!
THERE'S NO WAY OUT OF HERE. WE SHOULD GO BACK TO HEVEADORP.
NO.
!
WE HAVE TO FIND ANOTHER WAY TO...
PRACK-PRACK-PRRRAK!!!
PIOOOW!!!

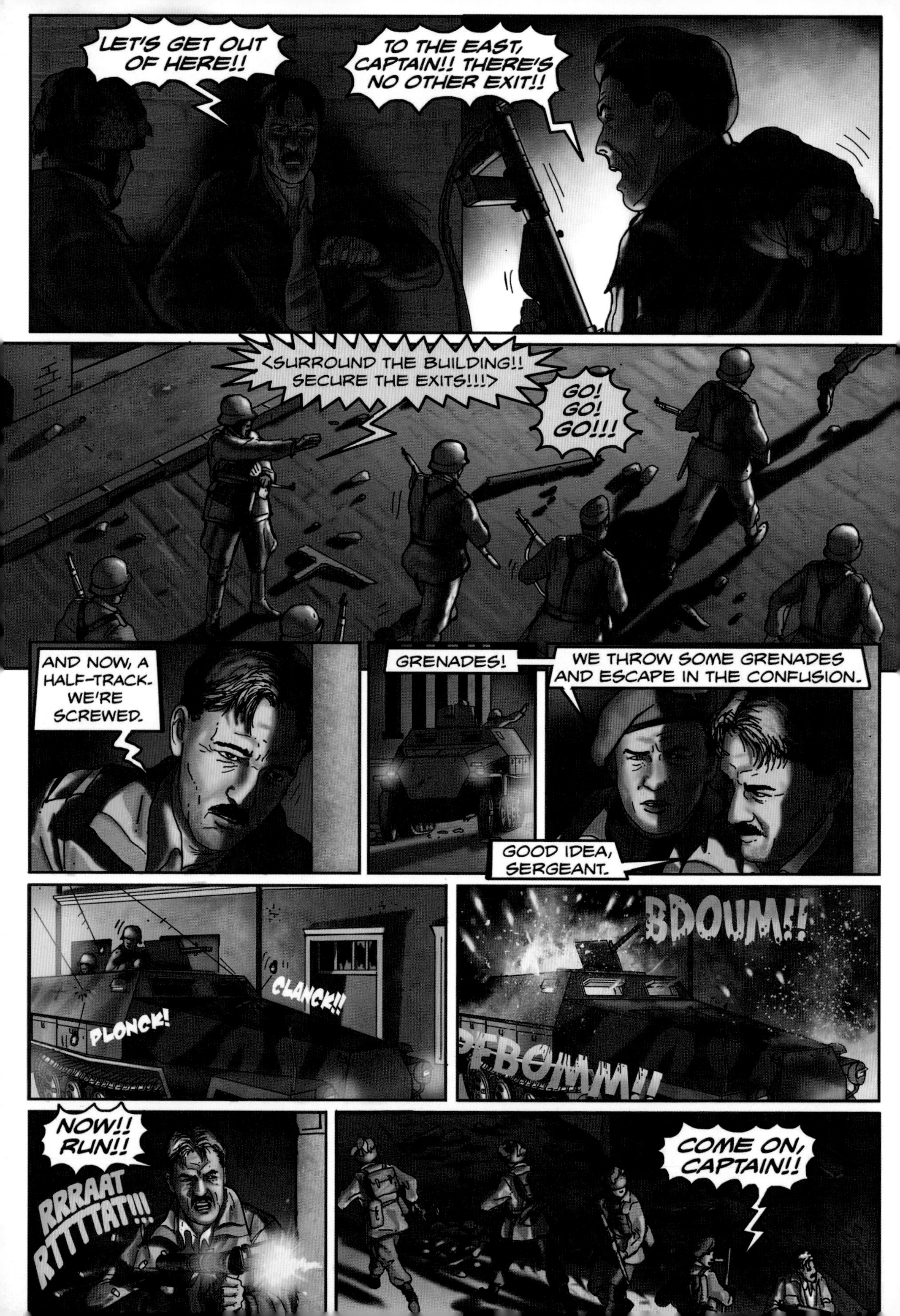
LET'S GET OUT OF HERE!!
TO THE EAST, CAPTAIN!! THERE'S NO OTHER EXIT!!
<SURROUND THE BUILDING!! SECURE THE EXITS!!!>
GO! GO! GO!!!
AND NOW, A HALF-TRACK. WE'RE SCREWED.
GRENADES!
WE THROW SOME GRENADES AND ESCAPE IN THE CONFUSION.
GOOD IDEA, SERGEANT.
PLONCK!
CLANCK!!
BDOUM!!
BOMM!!
NOW!! RUN!!
RRRAAT RTTTTAT!!!
COME ON, CAPTAIN!!

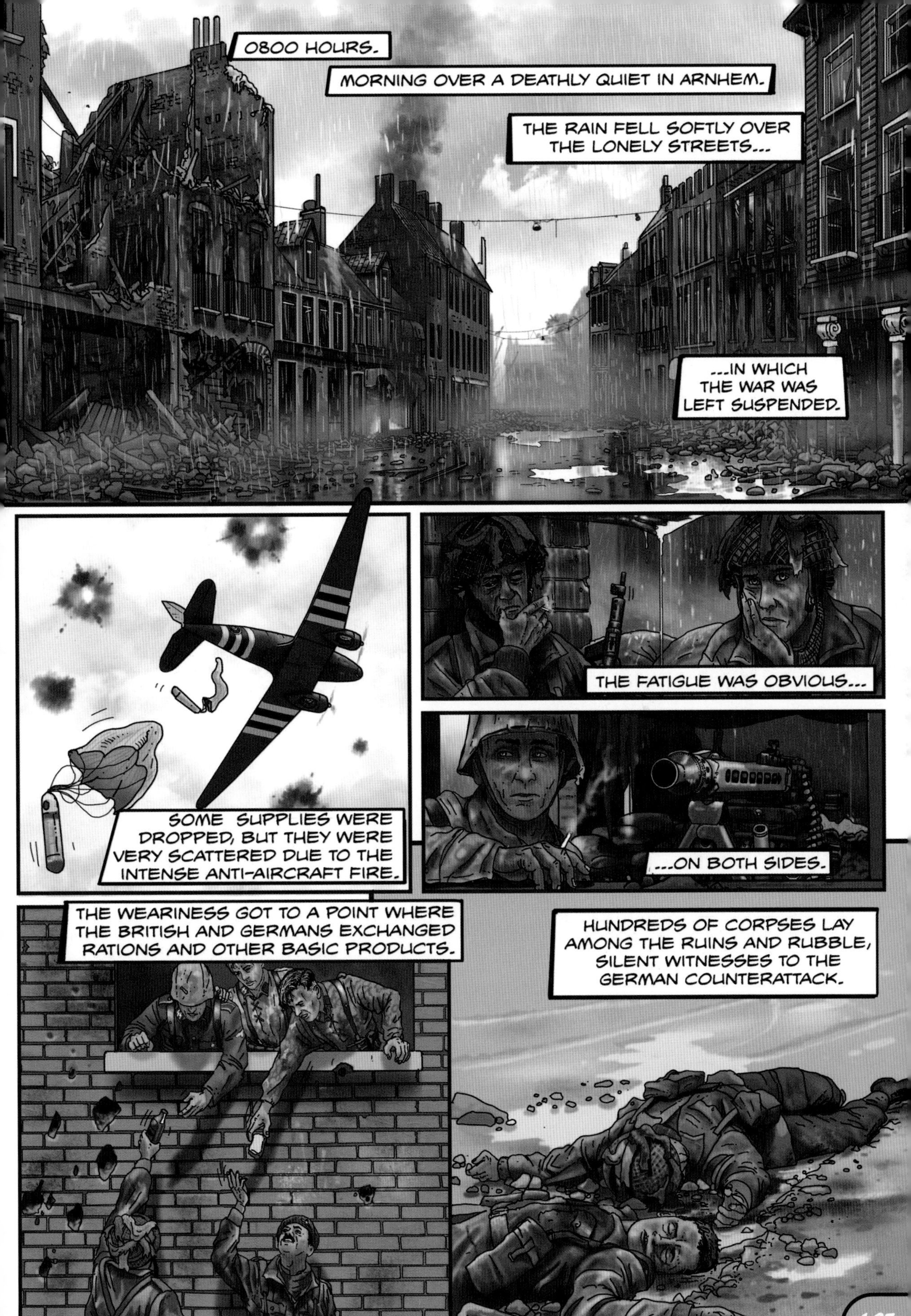
0800 HOURS.
MORNING OVER A DEATHLY QUIET IN ARNHEM.
THE RAIN FELL SOFTLY OVER THE LONELY STREETS...
...IN WHICH THE WAR WAS LEFT SUSPENDED.
SOME SUPPLIES WERE DROPPED, BUT THEY WERE VERY SCATTERED DUE TO THE INTENSE ANTI-AIRCRAFT FIRE.
THE FATIGUE WAS OBVIOUS...
...ON BOTH SIDES.
THE WEARINESS GOT TO A POINT WHERE THE BRITISH AND GERMANS EXCHANGED RATIONS AND OTHER BASIC PRODUCTS.
HUNDREDS OF CORPSES LAY AMONG THE RUINS AND RUBBLE, SILENT WITNESSES TO THE GERMAN COUNTERATTACK.

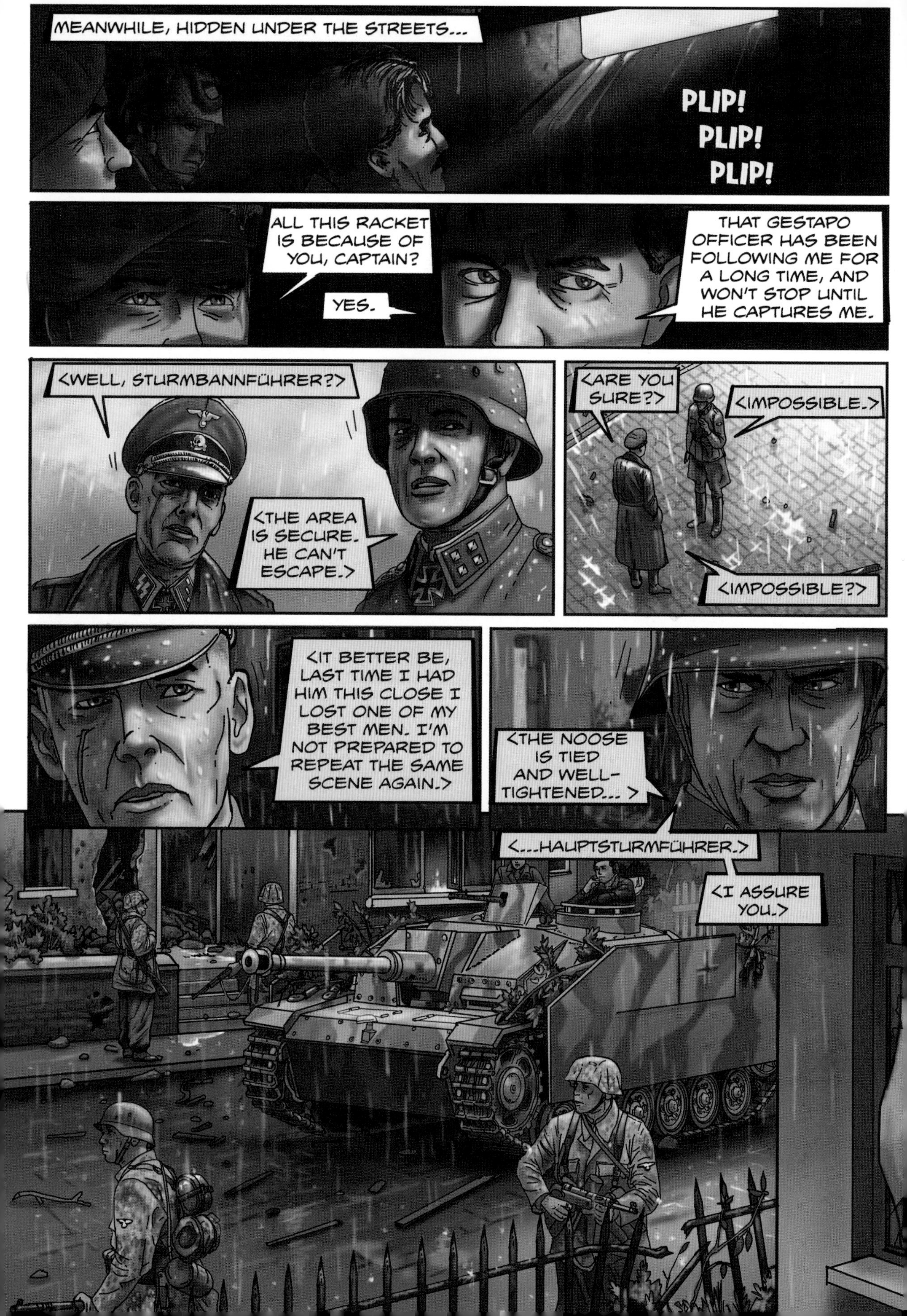
MEANWHILE, HIDDEN UNDER THE STREETS...
PLIP!
PLIP!
PLIP!
ALL THIS RACKET IS BECAUSE OF YOU, CAPTAIN?
YES.
THAT GESTAPO OFFICER HAS BEEN FOLLOWING ME FOR A LONG TIME, AND WON'T STOP UNTIL HE CAPTURES ME.
<WELL, STURMBANNFÜHRER?>
<THE AREA IS SECURE. HE CAN'T ESCAPE.>
<ARE YOU SURE?>
<IMPOSSIBLE.>
<IMPOSSIBLE?>
<IT BETTER BE, LAST TIME I HAD HIM THIS CLOSE I LOST ONE OF MY BEST MEN. I'M NOT PREPARED TO REPEAT THE SAME SCENE AGAIN.>
<THE NOOSE IS TIED AND WELL-TIGHTENED... >
<...HAUPTSTURMFÜHRER.>
<I ASSURE YOU.>

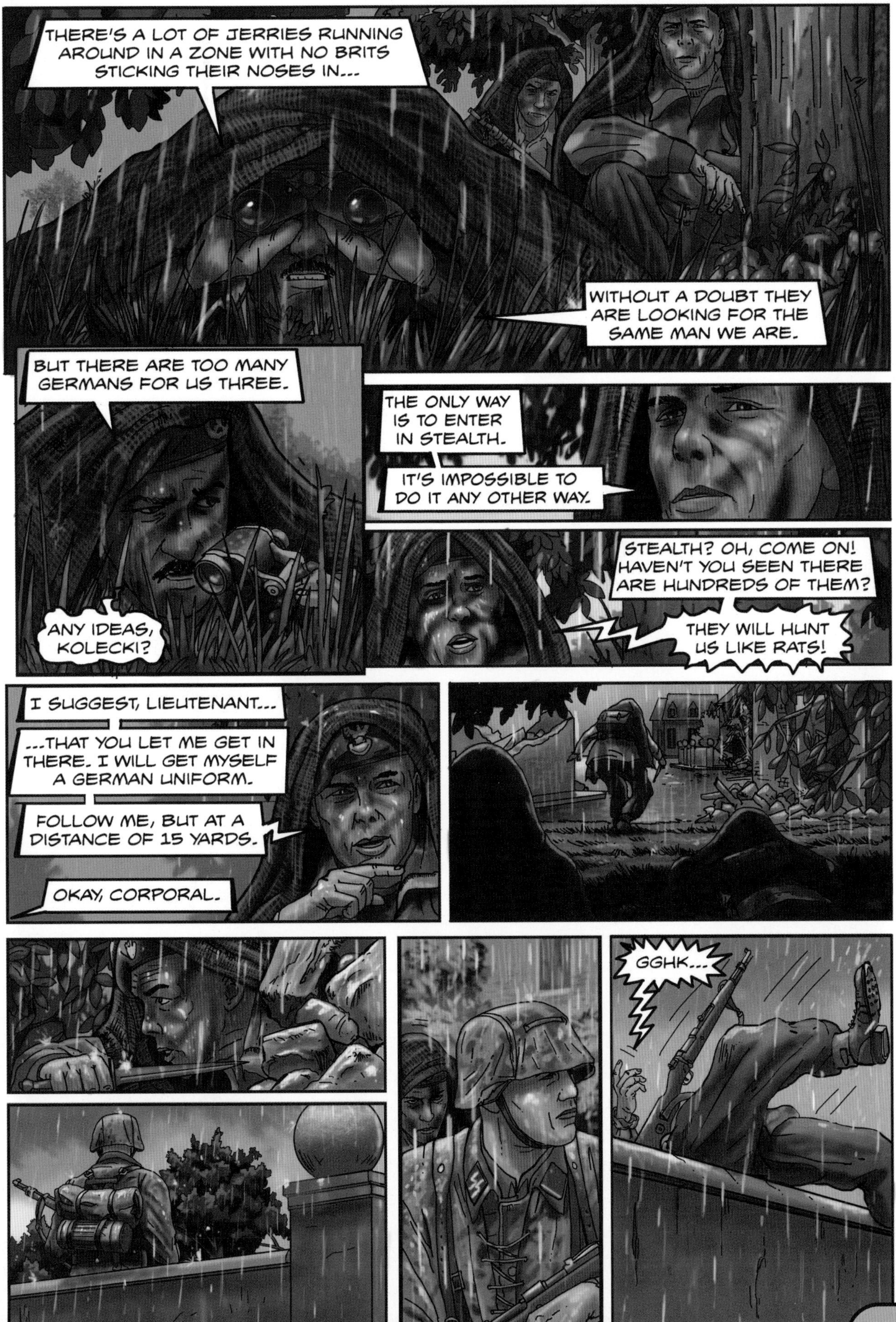
THERE'S A LOT OF JERRIES RUNNING AROUND IN A ZONE WITH NO BRITS STICKING THEIR NOSES IN...
WITHOUT A DOUBT THEY ARE LOOKING FOR THE SAME MAN WE ARE.
BUT THERE ARE TOO MANY GERMANS FOR US THREE.
ANY IDEAS, KOLECKI?
THE ONLY WAY IS TO ENTER IN STEALTH.
IT'S IMPOSSIBLE TO DO IT ANY OTHER WAY.
STEALTH? OH, COME ON! HAVEN'T YOU SEEN THERE ARE HUNDREDS OF THEM?
THEY WILL HUNT US LIKE RATS!
I SUGGEST, LIEUTENANT...
...THAT YOU LET ME GET IN THERE. I WILL GET MYSELF A GERMAN UNIFORM.
FOLLOW ME, BUT AT A DISTANCE OF 15 YARDS.
OKAY, CORPORAL.
GGHK...

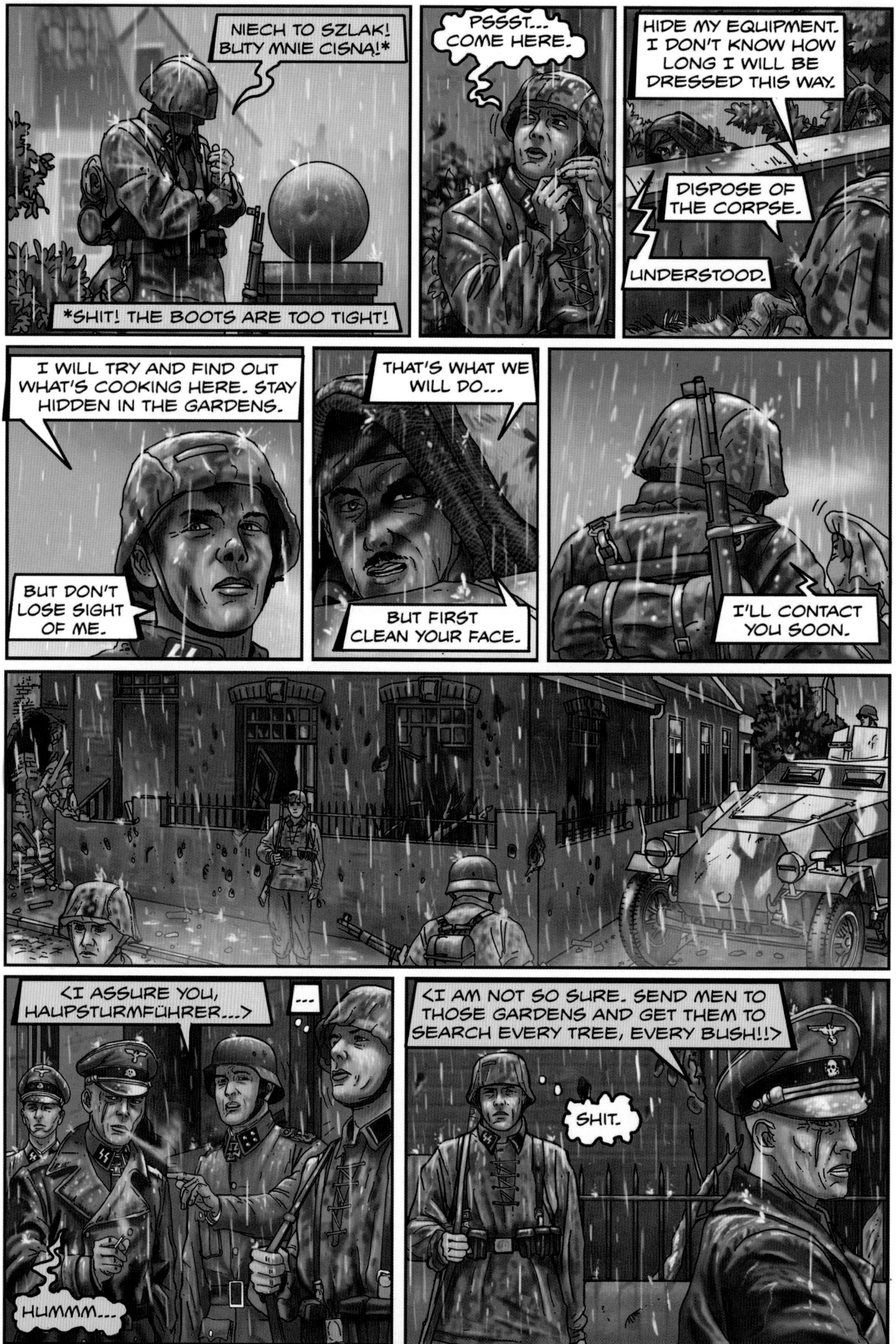

NIECH TO SZLAK! BUTY MNIE CISNĄ!*
*SHIT! THE BOOTS ARE TOO TIGHT!
PSSST... COME HERE.
HIDE MY EQUIPMENT. I DON'T KNOW HOW LONG I WILL BE DRESSED THIS WAY.
DISPOSE OF THE CORPSE.
UNDERSTOOD.
I WILL TRY AND FIND OUT WHAT'S COOKING HERE. STAY HIDDEN IN THE GARDENS.
BUT DON'T LOSE SIGHT OF ME.
THAT'S WHAT WE WILL DO...
BUT FIRST CLEAN YOUR FACE.
I'LL CONTACT YOU SOON.
<I ASSURE YOU, HAUPSTURMFÜHRER...>
...
HUMMM...
<I AM NOT SO SURE. SEND MEN TO THOSE GARDENS AND GET THEM TO SEARCH EVERY TREE, EVERY BUSH!!>
SHIT.

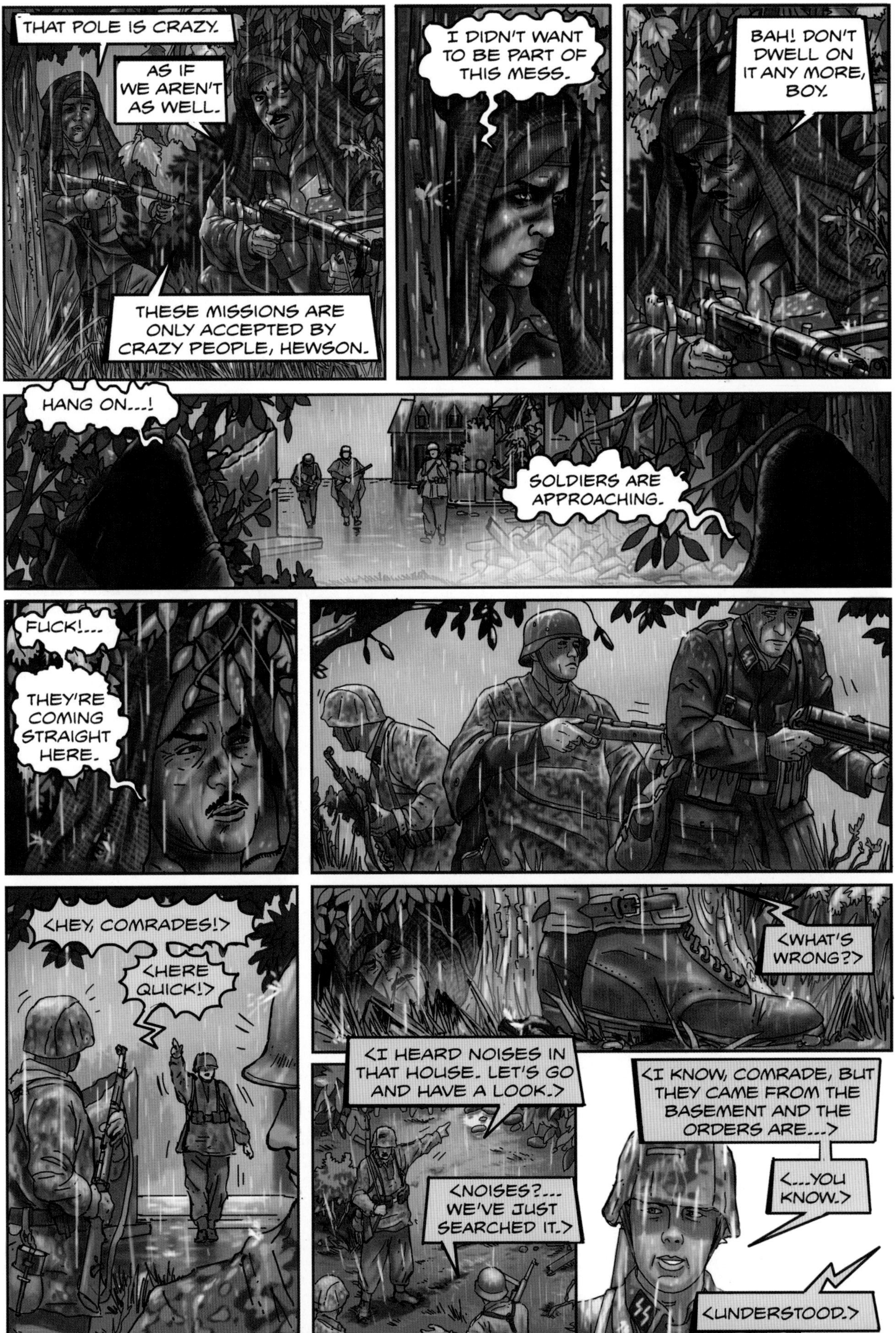
THAT POLE IS CRAZY.
AS IF WE AREN'T AS WELL.
THESE MISSIONS ARE ONLY ACCEPTED BY CRAZY PEOPLE, HEWSON.
I DIDN'T WANT TO BE PART OF THIS MESS.
BAH! DON'T DWELL ON IT ANY MORE, BOY.
HANG ON...!
SOLDIERS ARE APPROACHING.
FUCK!...
THEY'RE COMING STRAIGHT HERE.
<HEY, COMRADES!>
<HERE QUICK!>
<WHAT'S WRONG?>
<I HEARD NOISES IN THAT HOUSE. LET'S GO AND HAVE A LOOK.>
<NOISES?... WE'VE JUST SEARCHED IT.>
<I KNOW, COMRADE, BUT THEY CAME FROM THE BASEMENT AND THE ORDERS ARE...>
<...YOU KNOW.>
<UNDERSTOOD.>

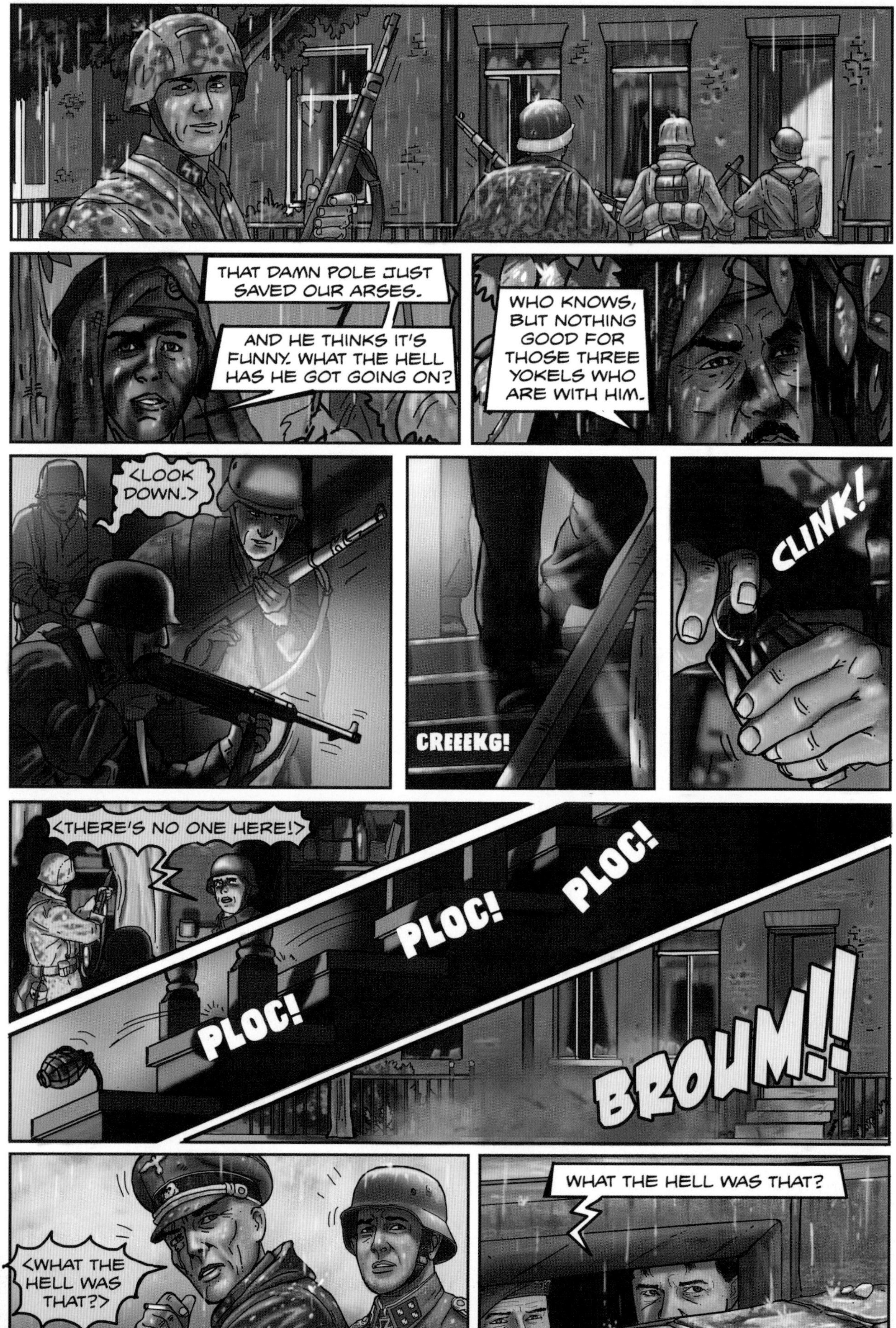

THAT DAMN POLE JUST SAVED OUR ARSES.
AND HE THINKS IT'S FUNNY. WHAT THE HELL HAS HE GOT GOING ON?
WHO KNOWS, BUT NOTHING GOOD FOR THOSE THREE YOKELS WHO ARE WITH HIM.
<LOOK DOWN.>
CREEEKG!
CLINK!
<THERE'S NO ONE HERE!>
PLOC!
PLOC!
PLOC!
PLOC!
BROUM!!
<WHAT THE HELL WAS THAT?>
WHAT THE HELL WAS THAT?

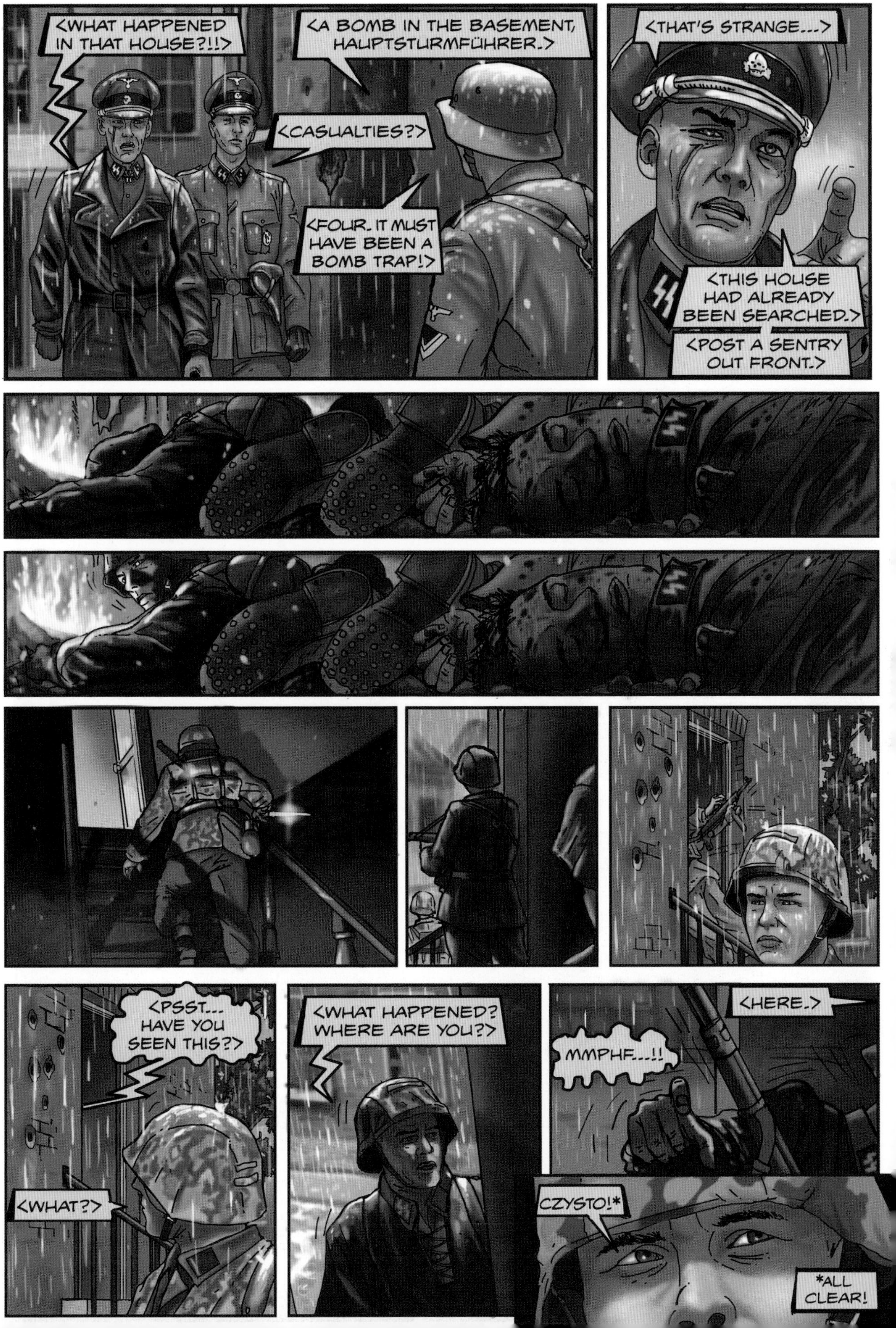
<WHAT HAPPENED IN THAT HOUSE?!!>
<A BOMB IN THE BASEMENT, HAUPTSTURMFÜHRER.>
<CASUALTIES?>
<FOUR. IT MUST HAVE BEEN A BOMB TRAP!>
<THAT'S STRANGE...>
<THIS HOUSE HAD ALREADY BEEN SEARCHED.>
<POST A SENTRY OUT FRONT.>
<PSST... HAVE YOU SEEN THIS?>
<WHAT?>
<WHAT HAPPENED? WHERE ARE YOU?>
<HERE.>
MMPHF...!!
CZYSTO!*
*ALL CLEAR!

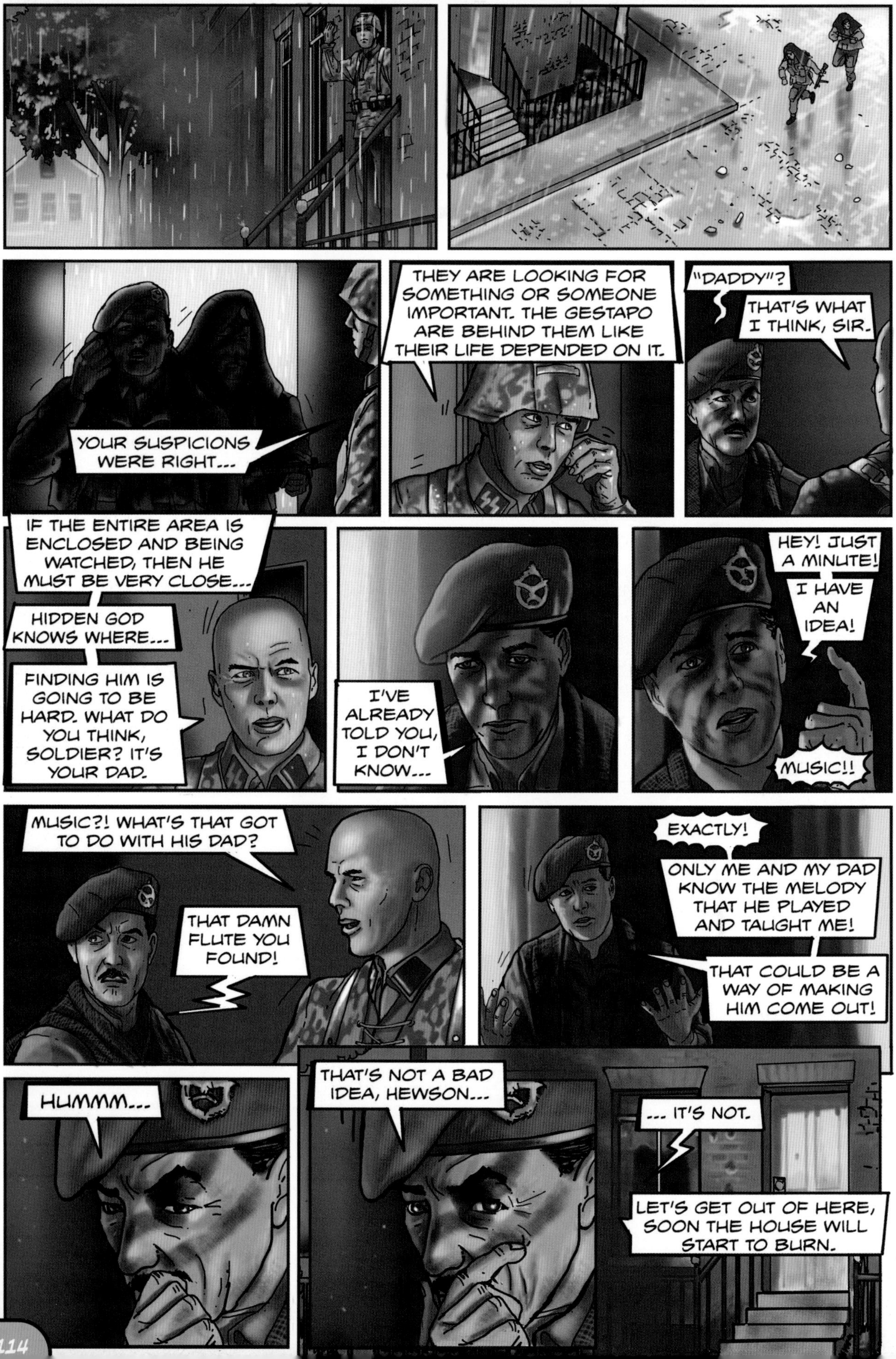

YOUR SUSPICIONS WERE RIGHT...
THEY ARE LOOKING FOR SOMETHING OR SOMEONE IMPORTANT. THE GESTAPO ARE BEHIND THEM LIKE THEIR LIFE DEPENDED ON IT.
"DADDY"?
THAT'S WHAT I THINK, SIR.
IF THE ENTIRE AREA IS ENCLOSED AND BEING WATCHED, THEN HE MUST BE VERY CLOSE...
HIDDEN GOD KNOWS WHERE...
FINDING HIM IS GOING TO BE HARD. WHAT DO YOU THINK, SOLDIER? IT'S YOUR DAD.
I'VE ALREADY TOLD YOU, I DON'T KNOW...
HEY! JUST A MINUTE!
I HAVE AN IDEA!
MUSIC!!
MUSIC?! WHAT'S THAT GOT TO DO WITH HIS DAD?
THAT DAMN FLUTE YOU FOUND!
EXACTLY!
ONLY ME AND MY DAD KNOW THE MELODY THAT HE PLAYED AND TAUGHT ME!
THAT COULD BE A WAY OF MAKING HIM COME OUT!
HUMMM...
THAT'S NOT A BAD IDEA, HEWSON...
... IT'S NOT.
LET'S GET OUT OF HERE, SOON THE HOUSE WILL START TO BURN.

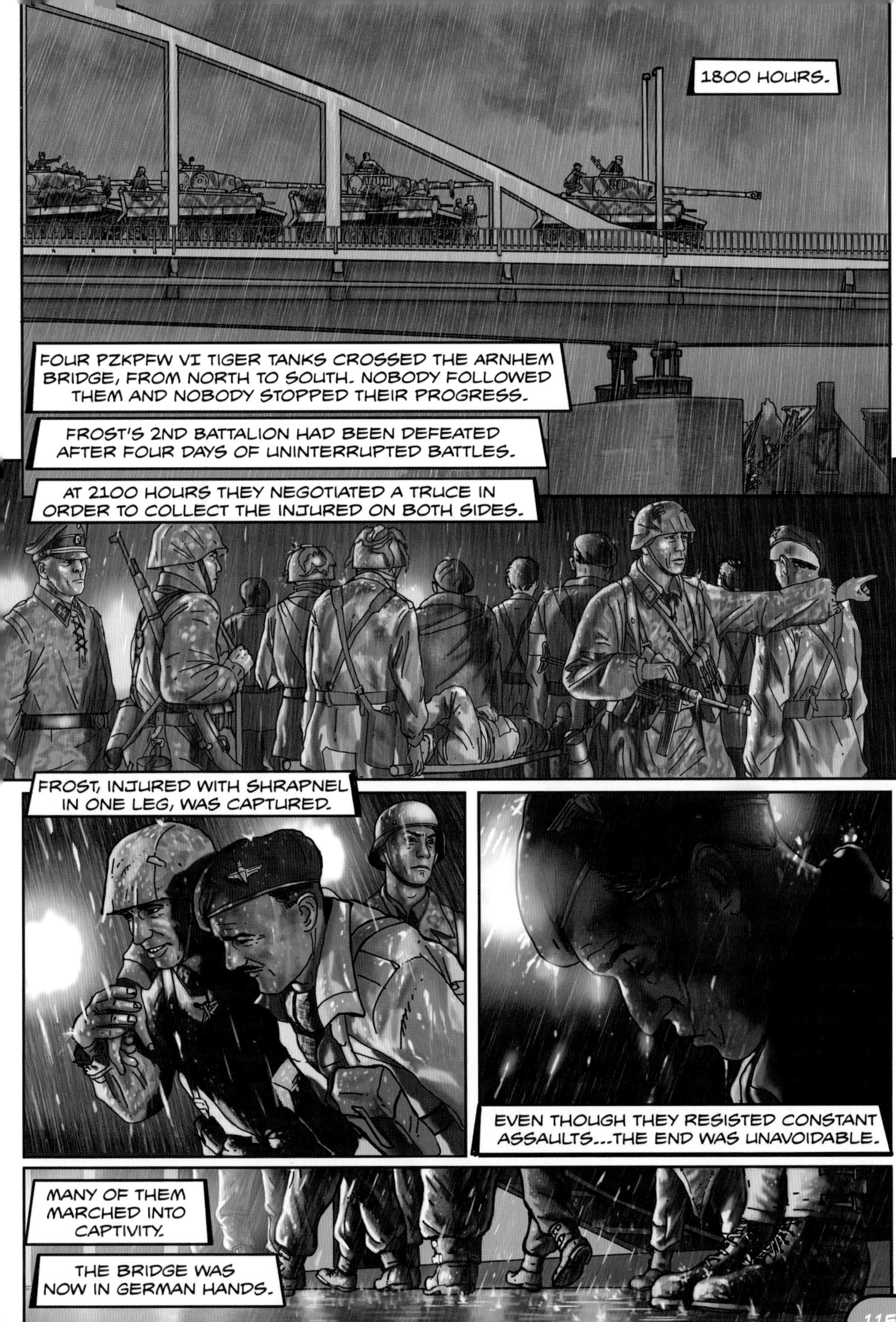
1800 HOURS.
FOUR PZKPFW VI TIGER TANKS CROSSED THE ARNHEM BRIDGE, FROM NORTH TO SOUTH. NOBODY FOLLOWED THEM AND NOBODY STOPPED THEIR PROGRESS.
FROST'S 2ND BATTALION HAD BEEN DEFEATED AFTER FOUR DAYS OF UNINTERRUPTED BATTLES.
AT 2100 HOURS THEY NEGOTIATED A TRUCE IN ORDER TO COLLECT THE INJURED ON BOTH SIDES.
FROST, INJURED WITH SHRAPNEL IN ONE LEG, WAS CAPTURED.
EVEN THOUGH THEY RESISTED CONSTANT ASSAULTS...THE END WAS UNAVOIDABLE.
MANY OF THEM MARCHED INTO CAPTIVITY.
THE BRIDGE WAS NOW IN GERMAN HANDS.

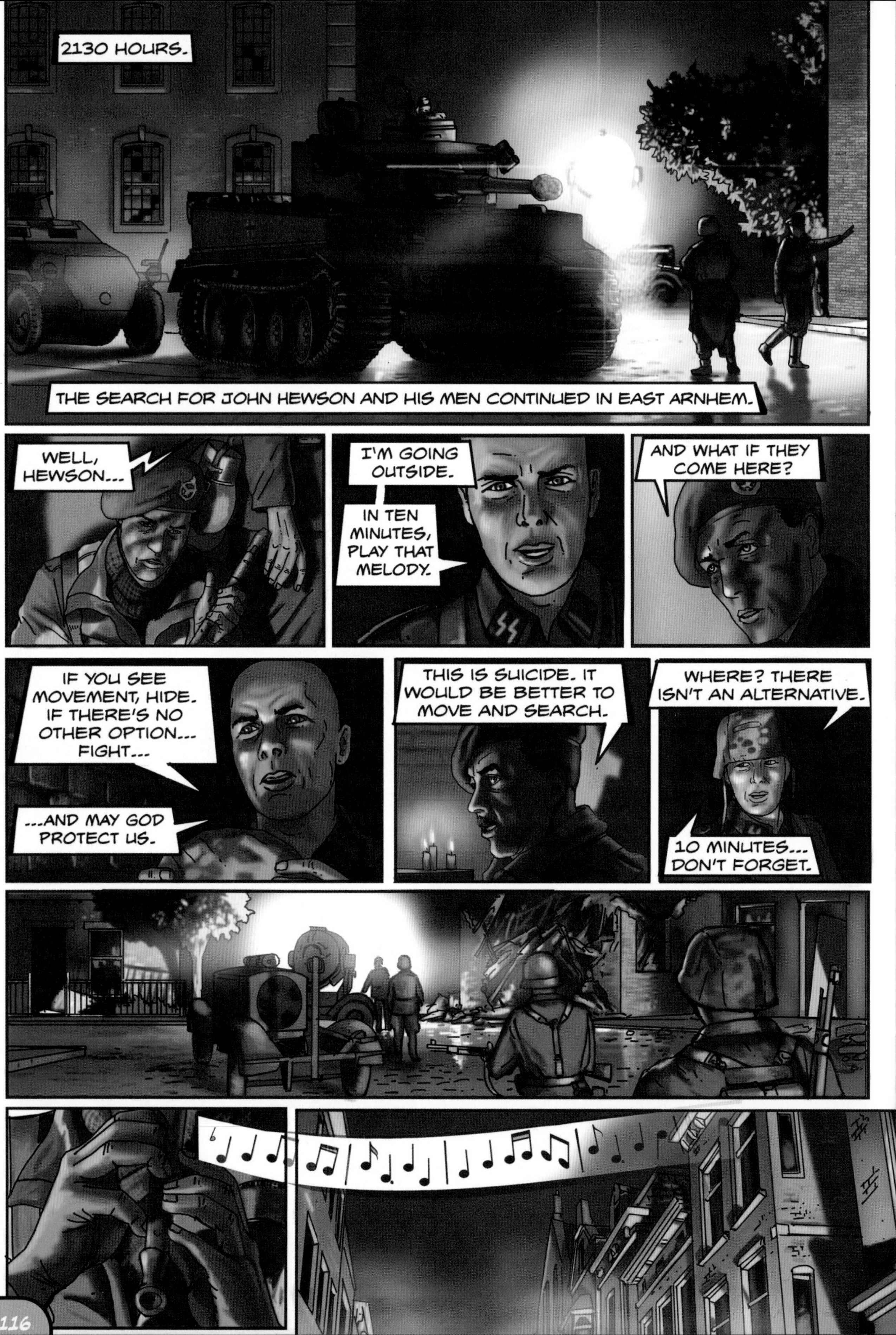
2130 HOURS.
THE SEARCH FOR JOHN HEWSON AND HIS MEN CONTINUED IN EAST ARNHEM.
WELL, HEWSON...
I'M GOING OUTSIDE.
IN TEN MINUTES, PLAY THAT MELODY.
AND WHAT IF THEY COME HERE?
IF YOU SEE MOVEMENT, HIDE. IF THERE'S NO OTHER OPTION... FIGHT...
...AND MAY GOD PROTECT US.
THIS IS SUICIDE. IT WOULD BE BETTER TO MOVE AND SEARCH.
WHERE? THERE ISN'T AN ALTERNATIVE.
10 MINUTES... DON'T FORGET.

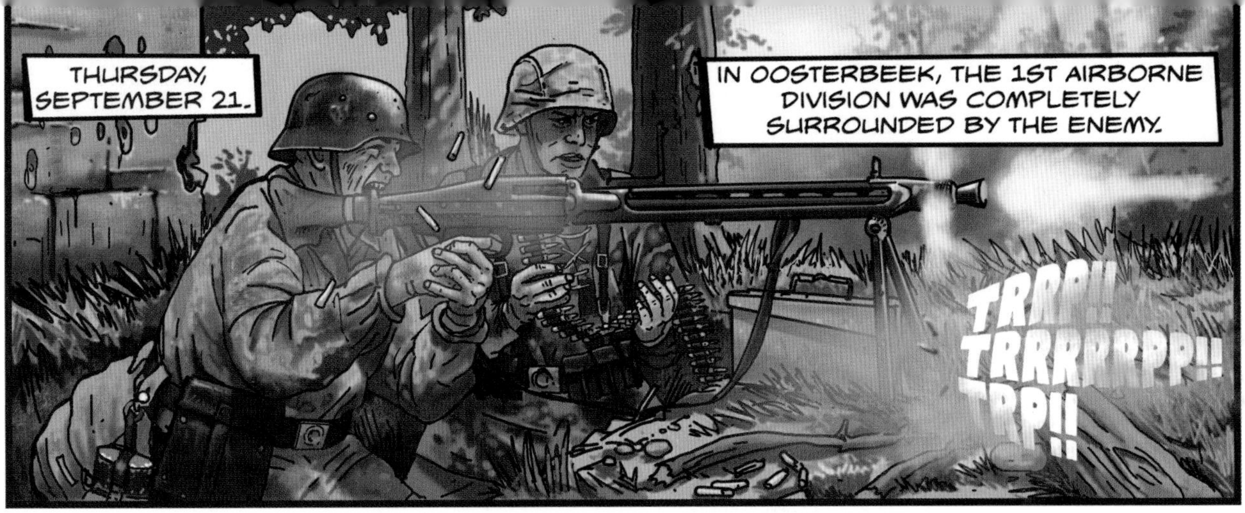
THURSDAY, SEPTEMBER 21.
IN OOSTERBEEK, THE 1ST AIRBORNE DIVISION WAS COMPLETELY SURROUNDED BY THE ENEMY.
TRRRP!! TRRRRRPP!! TRP!!

MAJOR-GENERAL URQUHART'S DIVISION WAS POWERLESS TO RESIST. ALL THEY COULD DO WAS WAIT FOR GENERALFELDMARSCHALL WALTER MODEL TO DEAL THE COUP DE GRÂCE.

ALL OF THIS HAPPENED THE SAME DAY THE GENERAL HEADQUARTERS OF SHAEF MOVED FROM GRANVILLE TO PARIS, IMPROVING COMMUNICATIONS WITH THE FRONT. BUT IT WAS OBVIOUS THAT EISENHOWER ASSUMED THAT OPERATION MARKET GARDEN HAD FAILED, RESULTING ONLY IN HUNDREDS OF UNACCEPTABLE DEATHS AND A WAR THAT WOULD GO ON FOR EVEN LONGER.

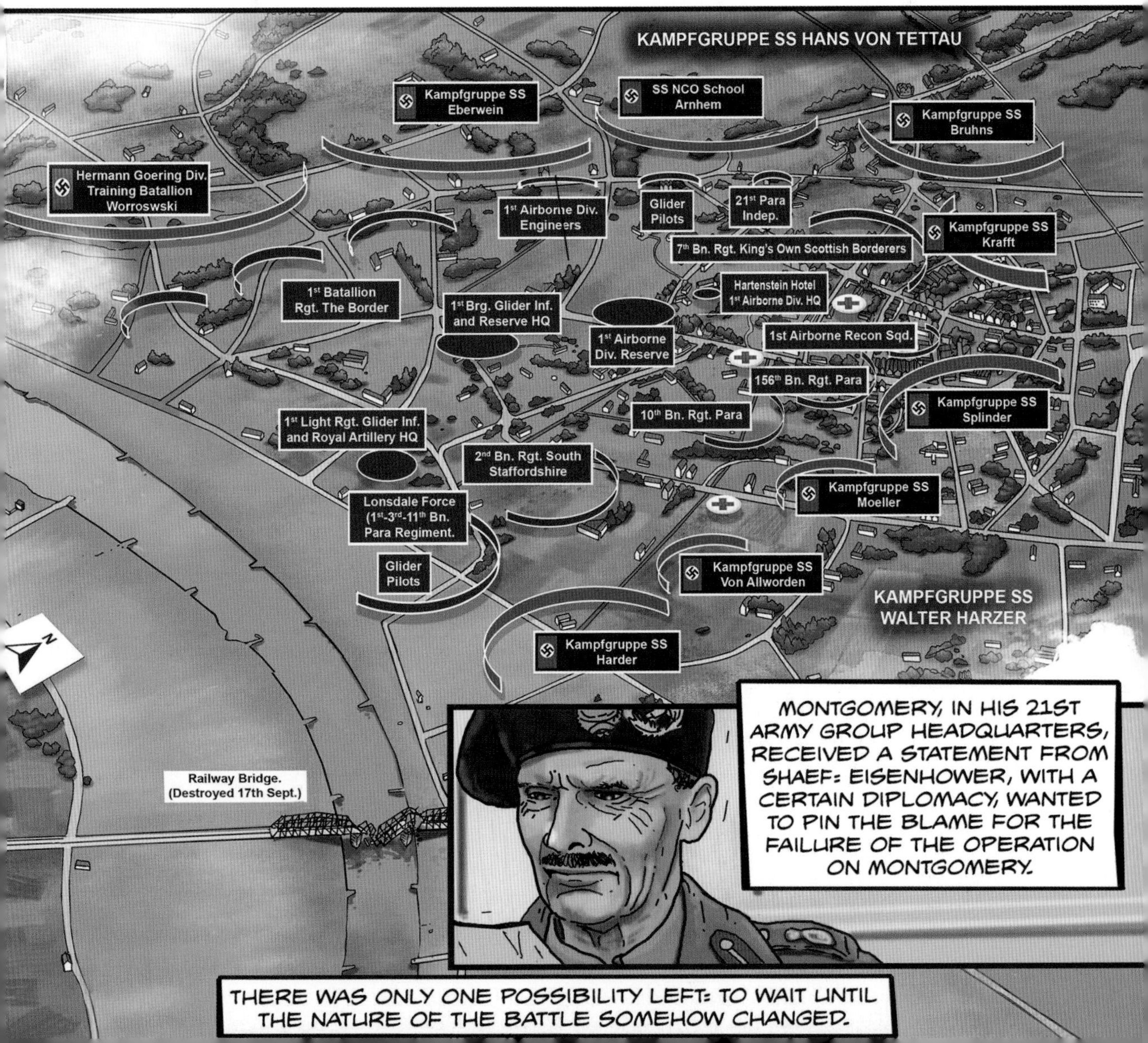
KAMPFGRUPPE SS HANS VON TETTAU
Kampfgruppe SS Eberwein
SS NCO School Arnhem
Kampfgruppe SS Bruhns
Hermann Goering Div. Training Batallion Worroswski
1st Airborne Div. Engineers
Glider Pilots
21st Para Indep.
Kampfgruppe SS Krafft
7th Bn. Rgt. King's Own Scottish Borderers
1st Batallion Rgt. The Border
1st Brg. Glider Inf. and Reserve HQ
Hartenstein Hotel 1st Airborne Div. HQ
1st Airborne Div. Reserve
1st Airborne Recon Sqd.
156th Bn. Rgt. Para
10th Bn. Rgt. Para
Kampfgruppe SS Splinder
1st Light Rgt. Glider Inf. and Royal Artillery HQ
2nd Bn. Rgt. South Staffordshire
Kampfgruppe SS Moeller
Lonsdale Force (1st-3rd-11th Bn. Para Regiment.
Glider Pilots
Kampfgruppe SS Von Allworden
KAMPFGRUPPE SS WALTER HARZER
Kampfgruppe SS Harder
N
Railway Bridge. (Destroyed 17th Sept.)
MONTGOMERY, IN HIS 21ST ARMY GROUP HEADQUARTERS, RECEIVED A STATEMENT FROM SHAEF: EISENHOWER, WITH A CERTAIN DIPLOMACY, WANTED TO PIN THE BLAME FOR THE FAILURE OF THE OPERATION ON MONTGOMERY.
THERE WAS ONLY ONE POSSIBILITY LEFT: TO WAIT UNTIL THE NATURE OF THE BATTLE SOMEHOW CHANGED.

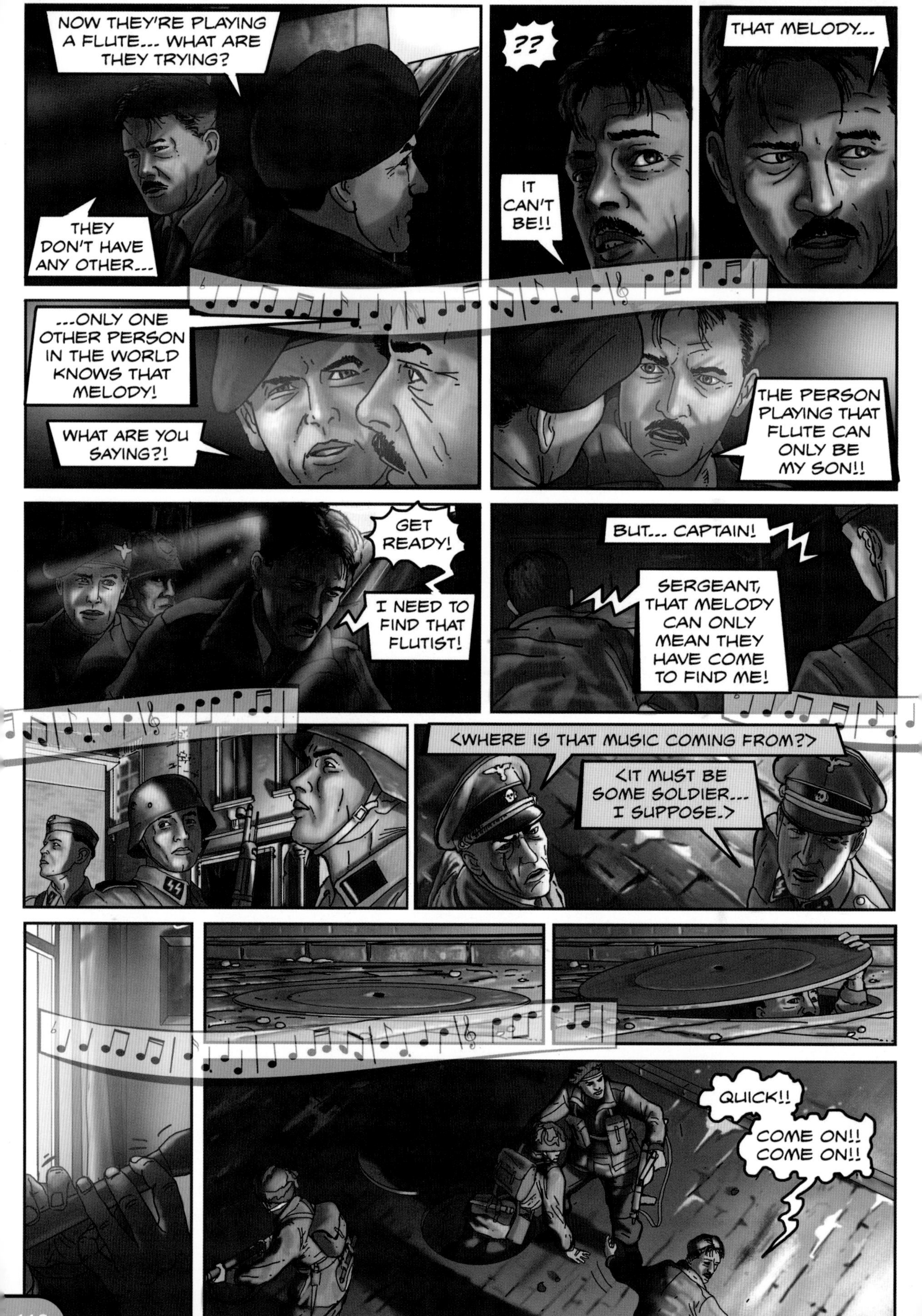
NOW THEY'RE PLAYING A FLUTE... WHAT ARE THEY TRYING?
THEY DON'T HAVE ANY OTHER...
??
IT CAN'T BE!!
THAT MELODY...
...ONLY ONE OTHER PERSON IN THE WORLD KNOWS THAT MELODY!
WHAT ARE YOU SAYING?!
THE PERSON PLAYING THAT FLUTE CAN ONLY BE MY SON!!
GET READY!
I NEED TO FIND THAT FLUTIST!
BUT... CAPTAIN!
SERGEANT, THAT MELODY CAN ONLY MEAN THEY HAVE COME TO FIND ME!
<WHERE IS THAT MUSIC COMING FROM?>
<IT MUST BE SOME SOLDIER... I SUPPOSE.>
QUICK!!
COME ON!! COME ON!!

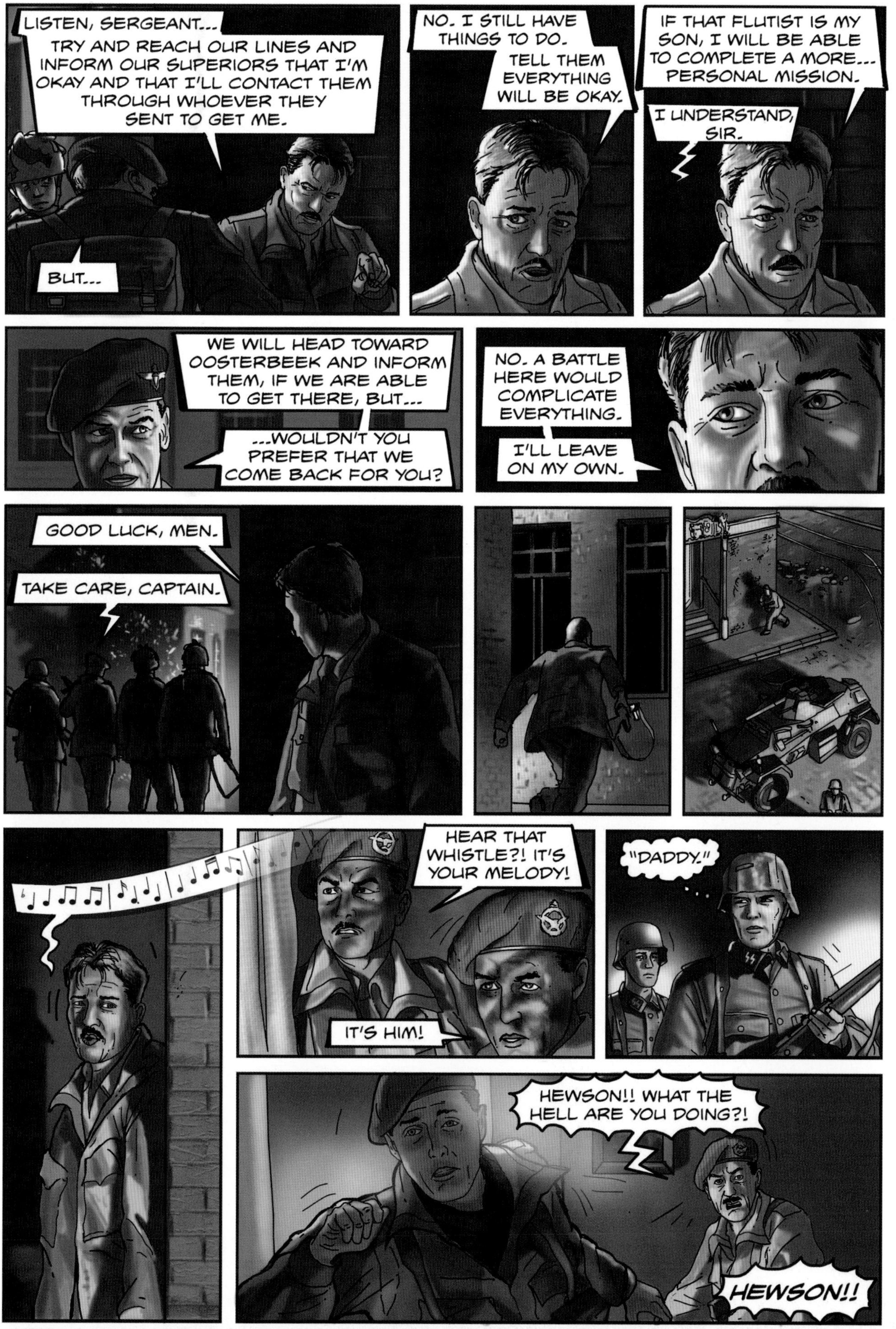

LISTEN, SERGEANT...
TRY AND REACH OUR LINES AND INFORM OUR SUPERIORS THAT I'M OKAY AND THAT I'LL CONTACT THEM THROUGH WHOEVER THEY SENT TO GET ME.
BUT...
NO. I STILL HAVE THINGS TO DO.
TELL THEM EVERYTHING WILL BE OKAY.
IF THAT FLUTIST IS MY SON, I WILL BE ABLE TO COMPLETE A MORE... PERSONAL MISSION.
I UNDERSTAND, SIR.
WE WILL HEAD TOWARD OOSTERBEEK AND INFORM THEM, IF WE ARE ABLE TO GET THERE, BUT...
...WOULDN'T YOU PREFER THAT WE COME BACK FOR YOU?
NO. A BATTLE HERE WOULD COMPLICATE EVERYTHING.
I'LL LEAVE ON MY OWN.
GOOD LUCK, MEN.
TAKE CARE, CAPTAIN.
HEAR THAT WHISTLE?! IT'S YOUR MELODY!
IT'S HIM!
"DADDY."
HEWSON!! WHAT THE HELL ARE YOU DOING?!
HEWSON!!

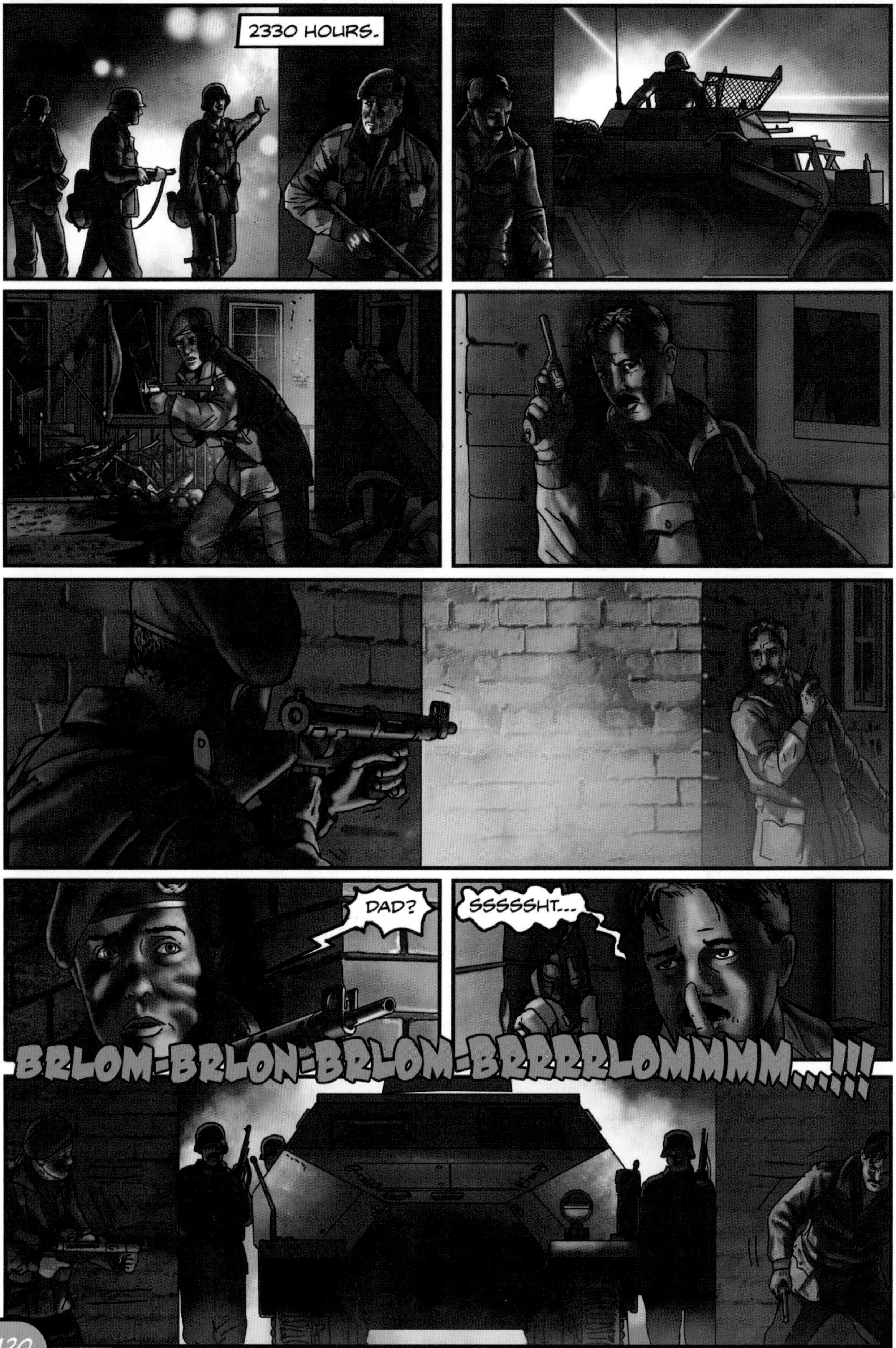

2330 HOURS.
DAD?
SSSSSHT...
BRLOM-BRLON-BRLOM-BRRRRLOMMMM...!!!

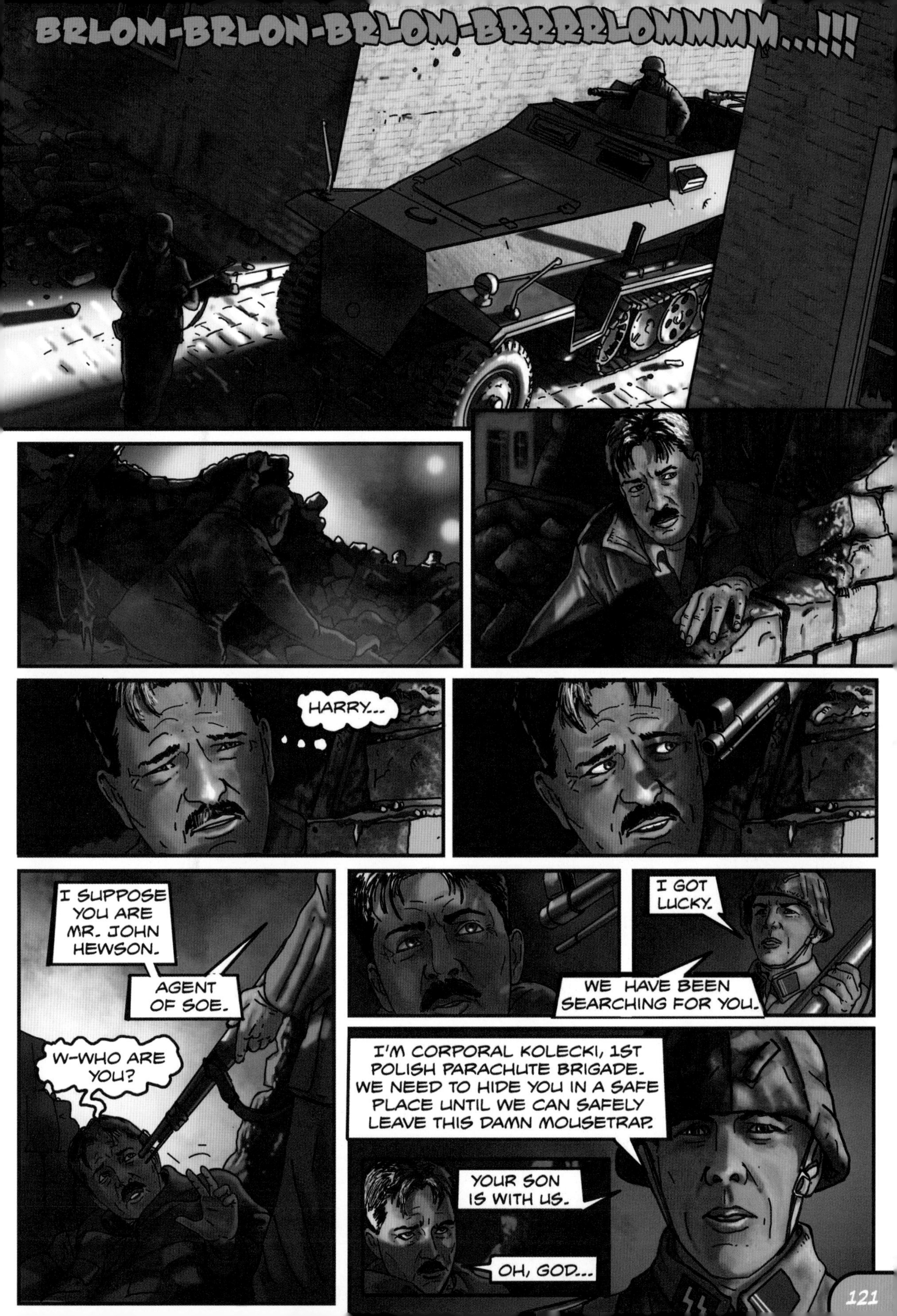

BRLOM-BRLON-BRLOM-BRRRRLOMMMM...!!!
HARRY...
I SUPPOSE YOU ARE MR. JOHN HEWSON.
AGENT OF SOE.
W-WHO ARE YOU?
I GOT LUCKY.
WE HAVE BEEN SEARCHING FOR YOU.
I'M CORPORAL KOLECKI, 1ST POLISH PARACHUTE BRIGADE. WE NEED TO HIDE YOU IN A SAFE PLACE UNTIL WE CAN SAFELY LEAVE THIS DAMN MOUSETRAP.
YOUR SON IS WITH US.
OH, GOD...

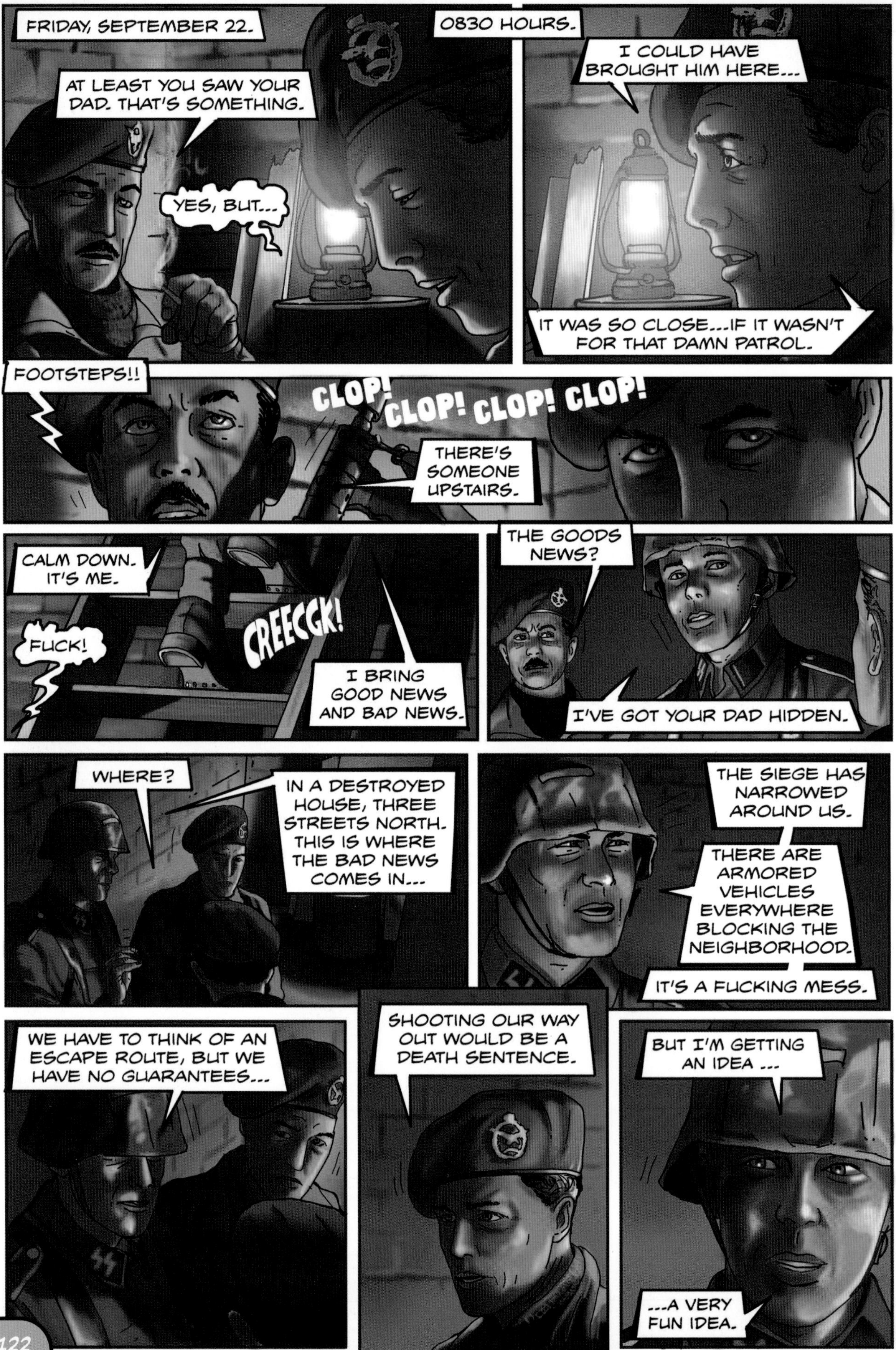
FRIDAY, SEPTEMBER 22.
AT LEAST YOU SAW YOUR DAD. THAT'S SOMETHING.
YES, BUT...
0830 HOURS.
I COULD HAVE BROUGHT HIM HERE...
IT WAS SO CLOSE...IF IT WASN'T FOR THAT DAMN PATROL.
FOOTSTEPS!!
CLOP! CLOP! CLOP! CLOP!
THERE'S SOMEONE UPSTAIRS.
CALM DOWN. IT'S ME.
FUCK!
CREECGK!
I BRING GOOD NEWS AND BAD NEWS.
THE GOODS NEWS?
I'VE GOT YOUR DAD HIDDEN.
WHERE?
IN A DESTROYED HOUSE, THREE STREETS NORTH. THIS IS WHERE THE BAD NEWS COMES IN...
THE SIEGE HAS NARROWED AROUND US.
THERE ARE ARMORED VEHICLES EVERYWHERE BLOCKING THE NEIGHBORHOOD.
IT'S A FUCKING MESS.
WE HAVE TO THINK OF AN ESCAPE ROUTE, BUT WE HAVE NO GUARANTEES...
SHOOTING OUR WAY OUT WOULD BE A DEATH SENTENCE.
BUT I'M GETTING AN IDEA ...
...A VERY FUN IDEA.

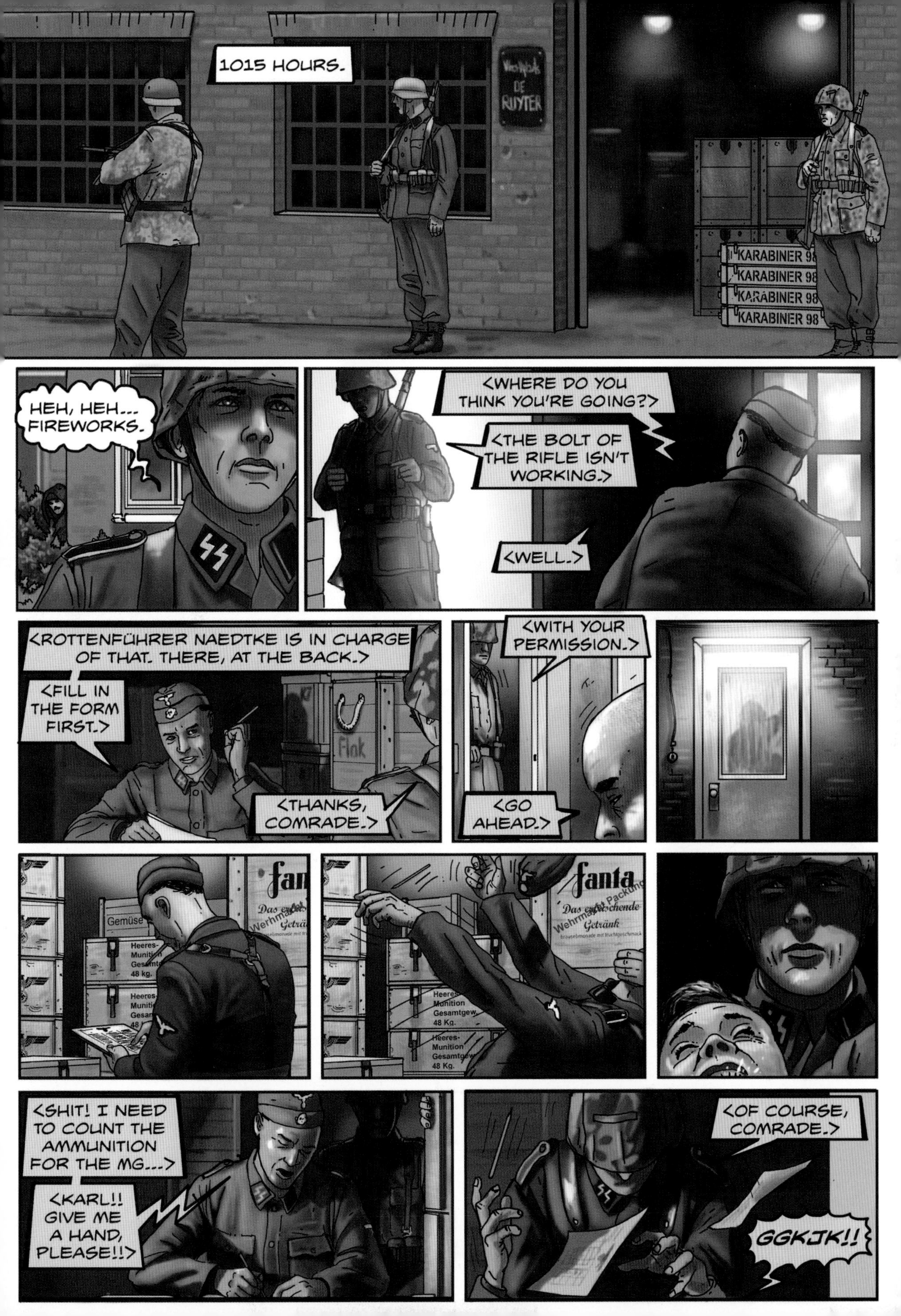
1015 HOURS.
DE RUYTER
KARABINER 98
KARABINER 98
KARABINER 98
KARABINER 98
HEH, HEH... FIREWORKS.
<WHERE DO YOU THINK YOU'RE GOING?>
<THE BOLT OF THE RIFLE ISN'T WORKING.>
<WELL.>
<ROTTENFÜHRER NAEDTKE IS IN CHARGE OF THAT. THERE, AT THE BACK.>
<FILL IN THE FORM FIRST.>
<THANKS, COMRADE.>
<WITH YOUR PERMISSION.>
<GO AHEAD.>
Heeres-Munition Gesamtgew. 48 Kg.
fanta
<SHIT! I NEED TO COUNT THE AMMUNITION FOR THE MG...>
<KARL!! GIVE ME A HAND, PLEASE!!>
<OF COURSE, COMRADE.>
GGKJK!!

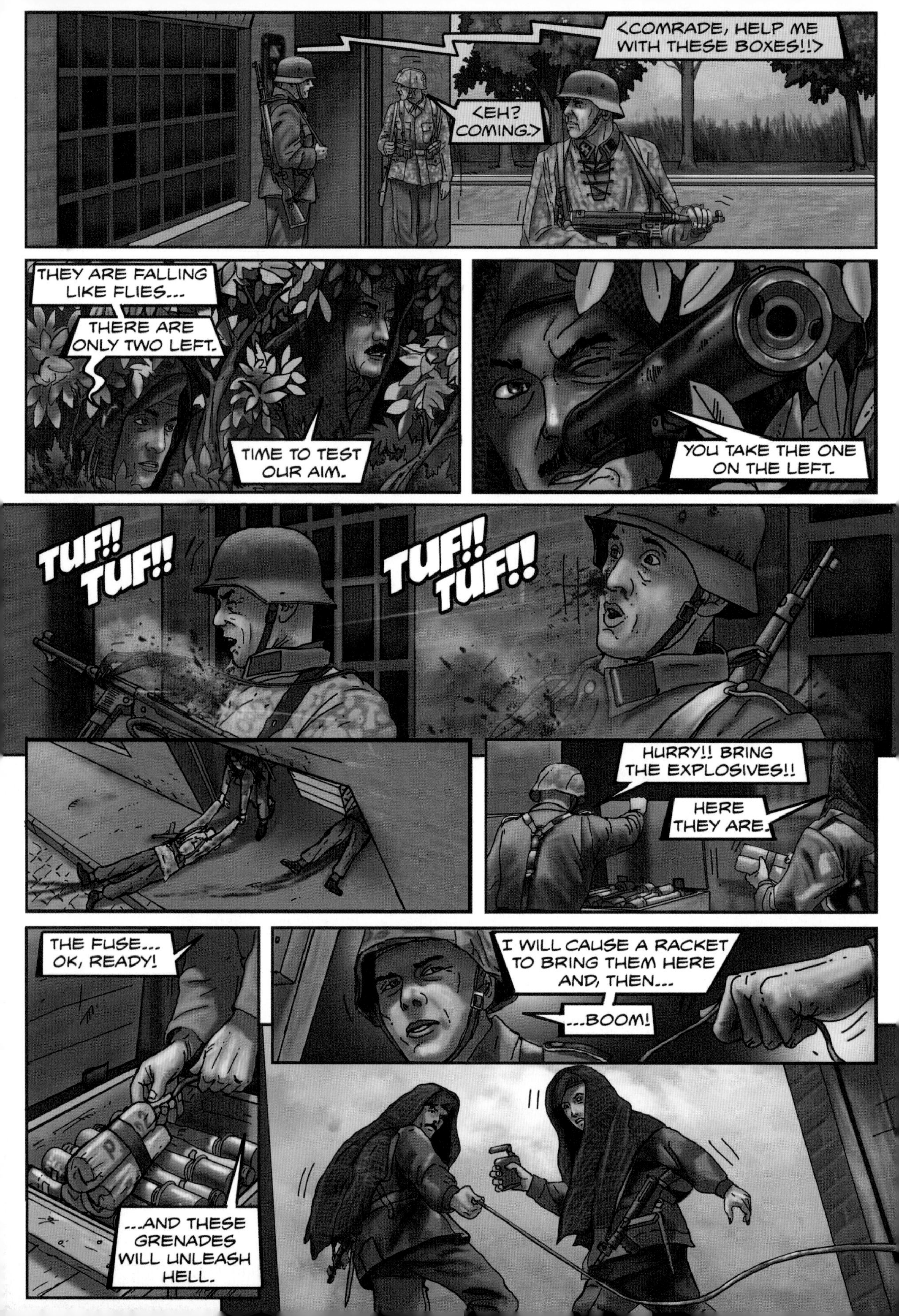
<COMRADE, HELP ME WITH THESE BOXES!!>
<EH? COMING.>
THEY ARE FALLING LIKE FLIES...
THERE ARE ONLY TWO LEFT.
TIME TO TEST OUR AIM.
YOU TAKE THE ONE ON THE LEFT.
TUF!! TUF!!
TUF!! TUF!!
HURRY!! BRING THE EXPLOSIVES!!
HERE THEY ARE.
THE FUSE... OK, READY!
...AND THESE GRENADES WILL UNLEASH HELL.
I WILL CAUSE A RACKET TO BRING THEM HERE AND, THEN...
...BOOM!

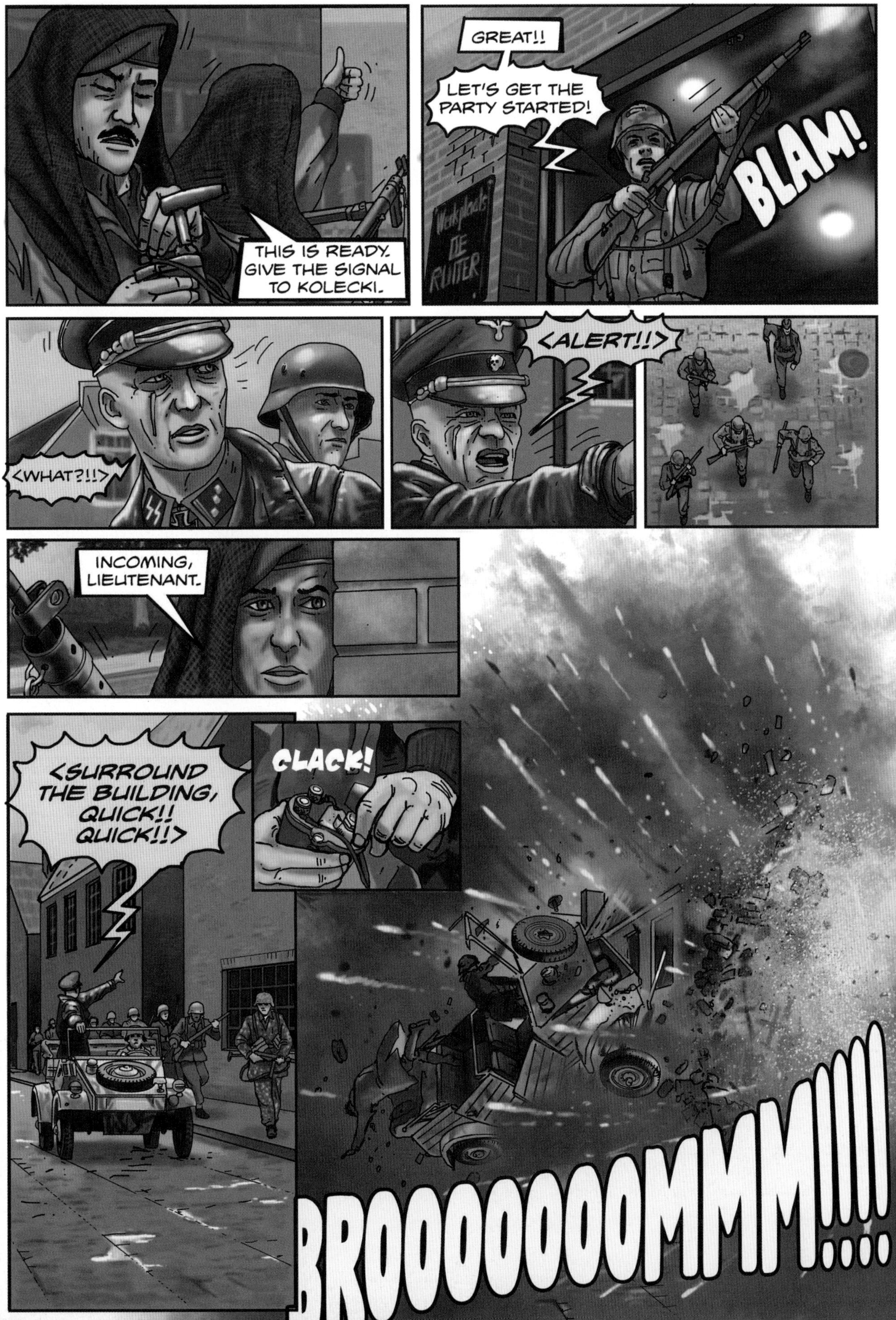
THIS IS READY. GIVE THE SIGNAL TO KOLECKI.
GREAT!!
LET'S GET THE PARTY STARTED!
BLAM!
Werkplaats DE RUITER
<WHAT?!!>
<ALERT!!>
INCOMING, LIEUTENANT.
<SURROUND THE BUILDING, QUICK!! QUICK!!>
CLACK!
BROOOOOOOMMM!!!!....

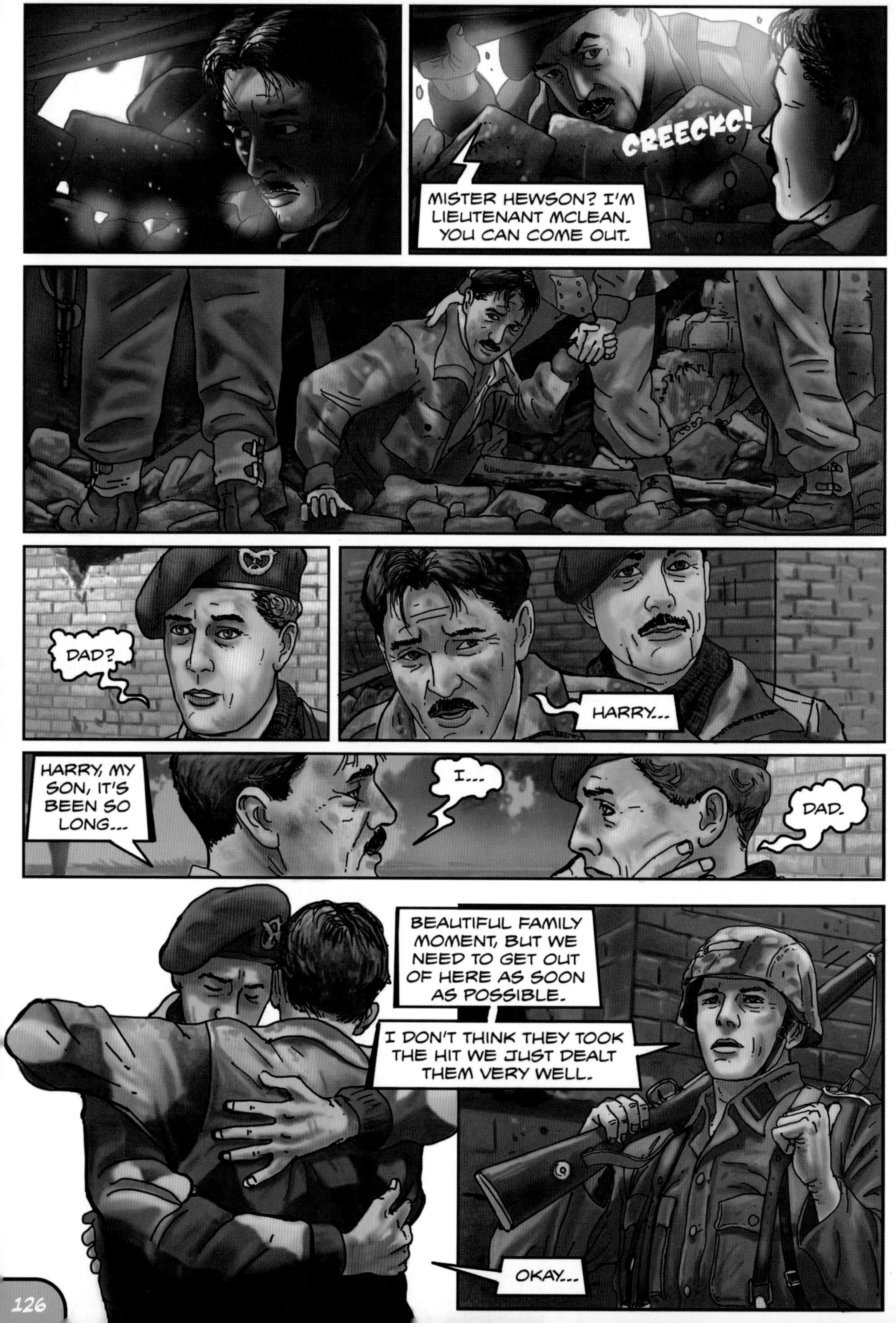

CREECKC!
MISTER HEWSON? I'M LIEUTENANT MCLEAN. YOU CAN COME OUT.
DAD?
HARRY...
HARRY, MY SON, IT'S BEEN SO LONG...
I...
DAD.
BEAUTIFUL FAMILY MOMENT, BUT WE NEED TO GET OUT OF HERE AS SOON AS POSSIBLE.
I DON'T THINK THEY TOOK THE HIT WE JUST DEALT THEM VERY WELL.
OKAY...

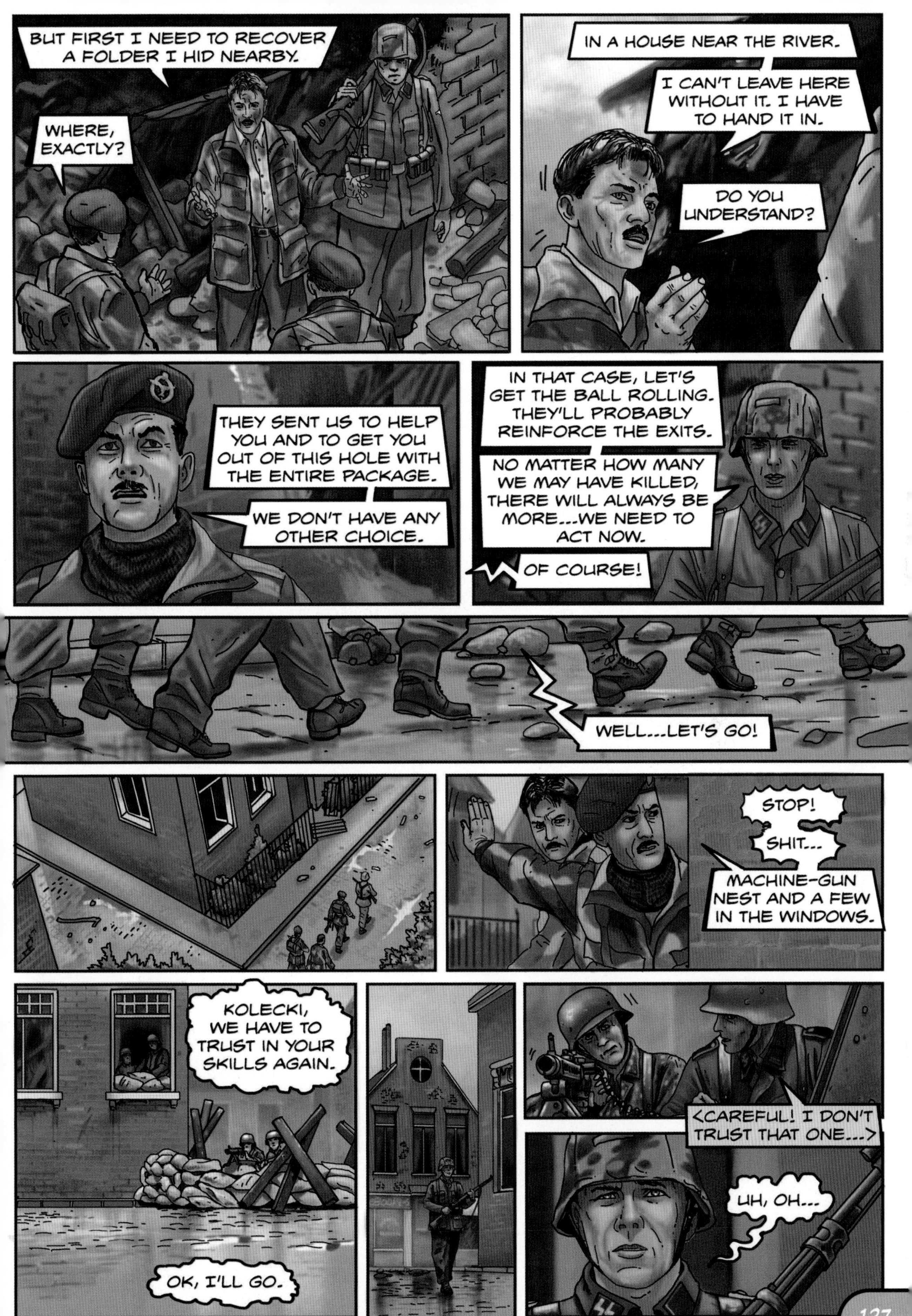
BUT FIRST I NEED TO RECOVER A FOLDER I HID NEARBY.
WHERE, EXACTLY?
IN A HOUSE NEAR THE RIVER.
I CAN'T LEAVE HERE WITHOUT IT. I HAVE TO HAND IT IN.
DO YOU UNDERSTAND?
THEY SENT US TO HELP YOU AND TO GET YOU OUT OF THIS HOLE WITH THE ENTIRE PACKAGE.
WE DON'T HAVE ANY OTHER CHOICE.
IN THAT CASE, LET'S GET THE BALL ROLLING. THEY'LL PROBABLY REINFORCE THE EXITS.
NO MATTER HOW MANY WE MAY HAVE KILLED, THERE WILL ALWAYS BE MORE...WE NEED TO ACT NOW.
OF COURSE!
WELL...LET'S GO!
STOP!
SHIT...
MACHINE-GUN NEST AND A FEW IN THE WINDOWS.
KOLECKI, WE HAVE TO TRUST IN YOUR SKILLS AGAIN.
OK, I'LL GO.
<CAREFUL! I DON'T TRUST THAT ONE...>
UH, OH...

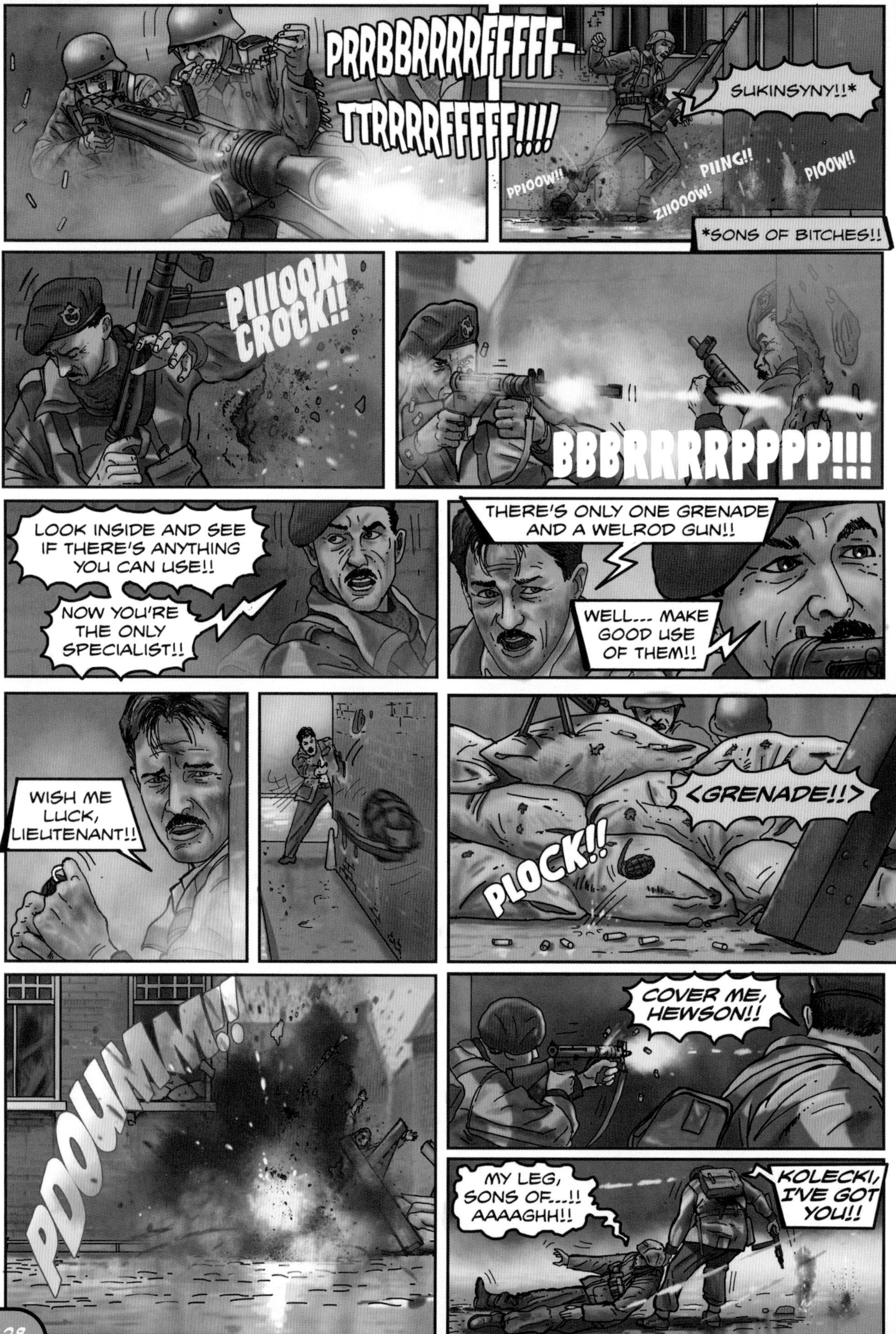
PRRBBRRRRFFFFF-
TTRRRRFFFFF!!!!
SUKINSYNY!!*
PPIOOW!!
ZIIOOOW!
PIING!!
PIOOW!!
*SONS OF BITCHES!!
PIIIOOW
CROCK!!
BBBRRRRRPPPPP!!!
LOOK INSIDE AND SEE IF THERE'S ANYTHING YOU CAN USE!!
NOW YOU'RE THE ONLY SPECIALIST!!
THERE'S ONLY ONE GRENADE AND A WELROD GUN!!
WELL... MAKE GOOD USE OF THEM!!
WISH ME LUCK, LIEUTENANT!!
<GRENADE!!>
PLOCK!!
PDOUMM!!
COVER ME, HEWSON!!
MY LEG, SONS OF...!! AAAAGHH!!
KOLECKI, I'VE GOT YOU!!

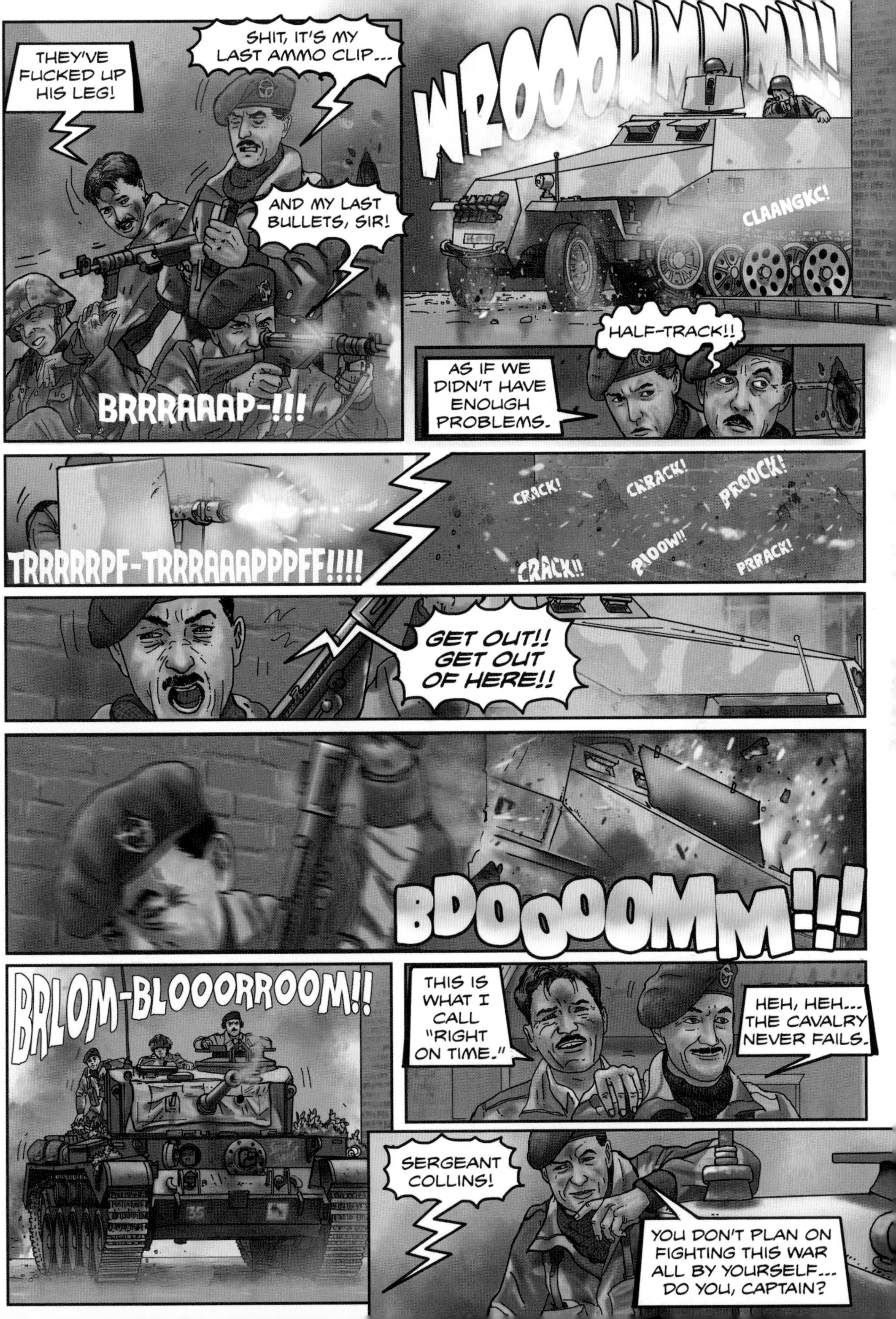
THEY'VE FUCKED UP HIS LEG!
SHIT, IT'S MY LAST AMMO CLIP...
AND MY LAST BULLETS, SIR!
BRRRAAAP-!!!
WROOOMMM!!!
CLAANGKC!
HALF-TRACK!!
AS IF WE DIDN'T HAVE ENOUGH PROBLEMS.
TRRRRRPF-TRRRAAAPPPFF!!!!
CRACK!
CRRACK!
PROOCK!
CRACK!!
PIOOW!!
PRRACK!
GET OUT!! GET OUT OF HERE!!
BDOOOOOMMM!!!
BRLOM-BLOOORROOM!!
THIS IS WHAT I CALL "RIGHT ON TIME."
HEH, HEH... THE CAVALRY NEVER FAILS.
SERGEANT COLLINS!
YOU DON'T PLAN ON FIGHTING THIS WAR ALL BY YOURSELF... DO YOU, CAPTAIN?

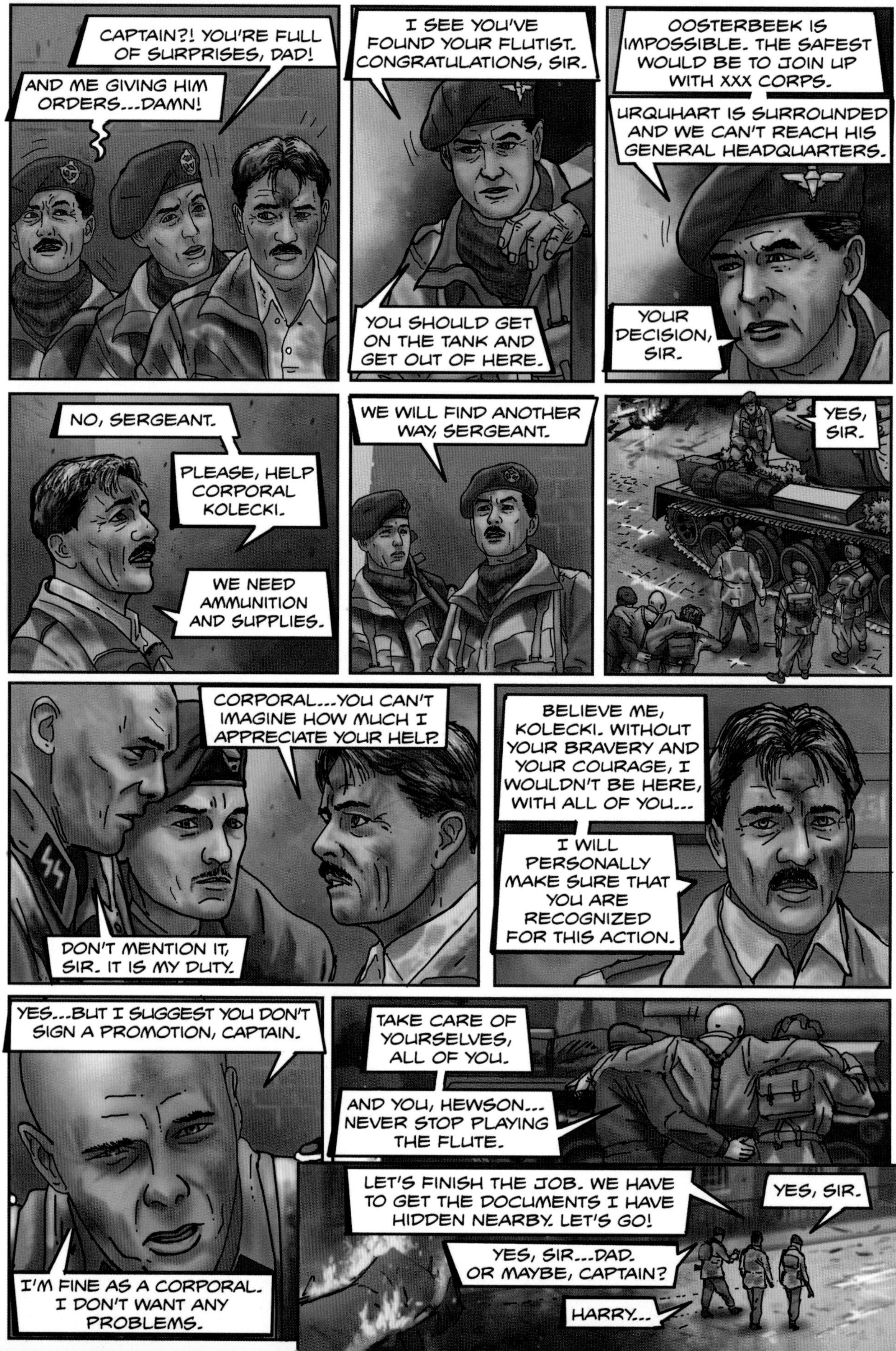
CAPTAIN?! YOU'RE FULL OF SURPRISES, DAD!
AND ME GIVING HIM ORDERS...DAMN!
I SEE YOU'VE FOUND YOUR FLUTIST. CONGRATULATIONS, SIR.
YOU SHOULD GET ON THE TANK AND GET OUT OF HERE.
OOSTERBEEK IS IMPOSSIBLE. THE SAFEST WOULD BE TO JOIN UP WITH XXX CORPS.
URQUHART IS SURROUNDED AND WE CAN'T REACH HIS GENERAL HEADQUARTERS.
YOUR DECISION, SIR.
NO, SERGEANT.
PLEASE, HELP CORPORAL KOLECKI.
WE NEED AMMUNITION AND SUPPLIES.
WE WILL FIND ANOTHER WAY, SERGEANT.
YES, SIR.
CORPORAL...YOU CAN'T IMAGINE HOW MUCH I APPRECIATE YOUR HELP.
DON'T MENTION IT, SIR. IT IS MY DUTY.
BELIEVE ME, KOLECKI. WITHOUT YOUR BRAVERY AND YOUR COURAGE, I WOULDN'T BE HERE, WITH ALL OF YOU...
I WILL PERSONALLY MAKE SURE THAT YOU ARE RECOGNIZED FOR THIS ACTION.
YES...BUT I SUGGEST YOU DON'T SIGN A PROMOTION, CAPTAIN.
I'M FINE AS A CORPORAL. I DON'T WANT ANY PROBLEMS.
TAKE CARE OF YOURSELVES, ALL OF YOU.
AND YOU, HEWSON... NEVER STOP PLAYING THE FLUTE.
LET'S FINISH THE JOB. WE HAVE TO GET THE DOCUMENTS I HAVE HIDDEN NEARBY. LET'S GO!
YES, SIR.
YES, SIR...DAD. OR MAYBE, CAPTAIN?
HARRY...

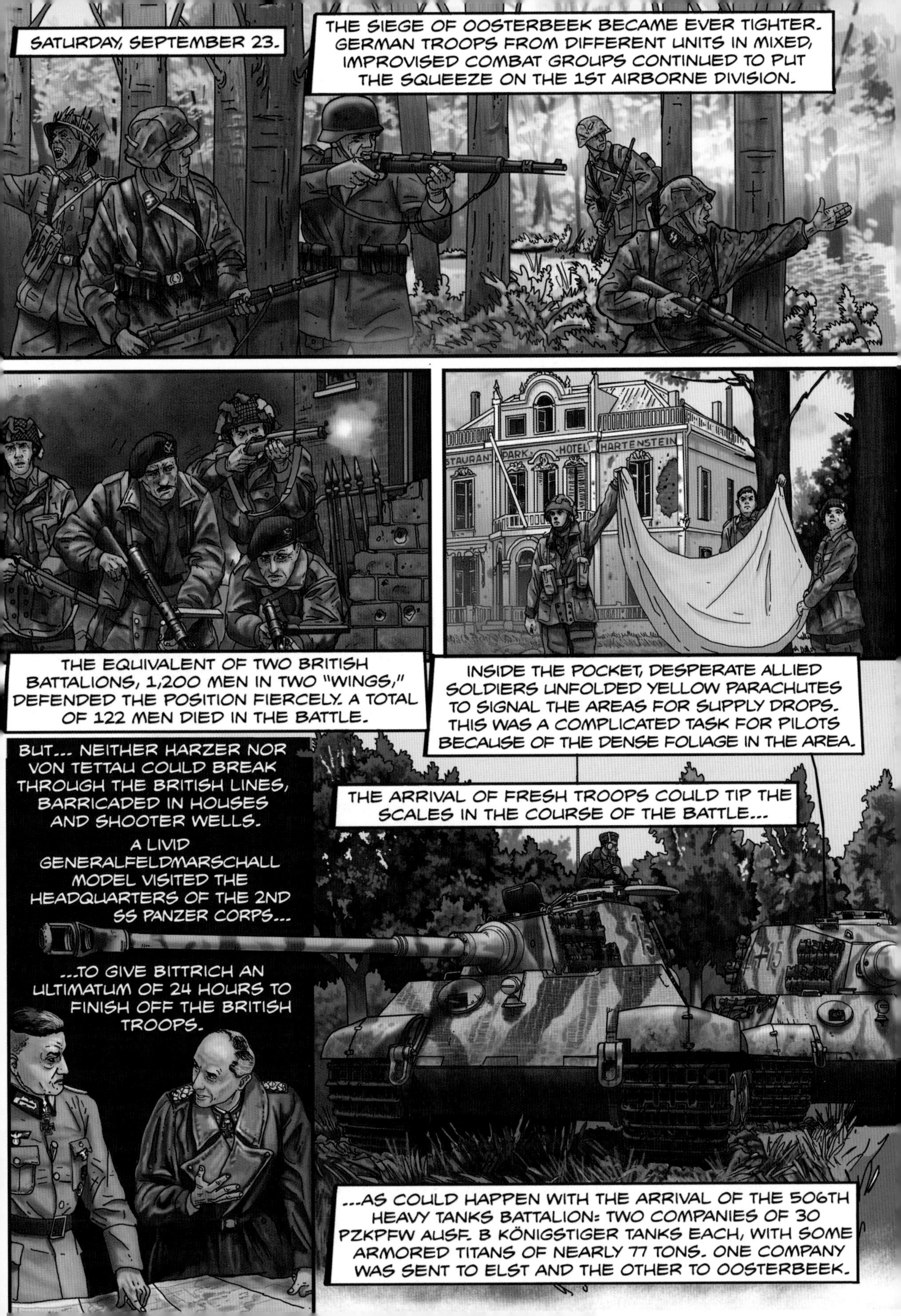
SATURDAY, SEPTEMBER 23.
THE SIEGE OF OOSTERBEEK BECAME EVER TIGHTER. GERMAN TROOPS FROM DIFFERENT UNITS IN MIXED, IMPROVISED COMBAT GROUPS CONTINUED TO PUT THE SQUEEZE ON THE 1ST AIRBORNE DIVISION.
PARK
HOTEL
HARTENSTEIN
THE EQUIVALENT OF TWO BRITISH BATTALIONS, 1,200 MEN IN TWO "WINGS," DEFENDED THE POSITION FIERCELY. A TOTAL OF 122 MEN DIED IN THE BATTLE.
INSIDE THE POCKET, DESPERATE ALLIED SOLDIERS UNFOLDED YELLOW PARACHUTES TO SIGNAL THE AREAS FOR SUPPLY DROPS. THIS WAS A COMPLICATED TASK FOR PILOTS BECAUSE OF THE DENSE FOLIAGE IN THE AREA.
BUT... NEITHER HARZER NOR VON TETTAU COULD BREAK THROUGH THE BRITISH LINES, BARRICADED IN HOUSES AND SHOOTER WELLS.
A LIVID GENERALFELDMARSCHALL MODEL VISITED THE HEADQUARTERS OF THE 2ND SS PANZER CORPS...
...TO GIVE BITTRICH AN ULTIMATUM OF 24 HOURS TO FINISH OFF THE BRITISH TROOPS.
THE ARRIVAL OF FRESH TROOPS COULD TIP THE SCALES IN THE COURSE OF THE BATTLE...
...AS COULD HAPPEN WITH THE ARRIVAL OF THE 506TH HEAVY TANKS BATTALION: TWO COMPANIES OF 30 PZKPFW AUSF. B KÖNIGSTIGER TANKS EACH, WITH SOME ARMORED TITANS OF NEARLY 77 TONS. ONE COMPANY WAS SENT TO ELST AND THE OTHER TO OOSTERBEEK.

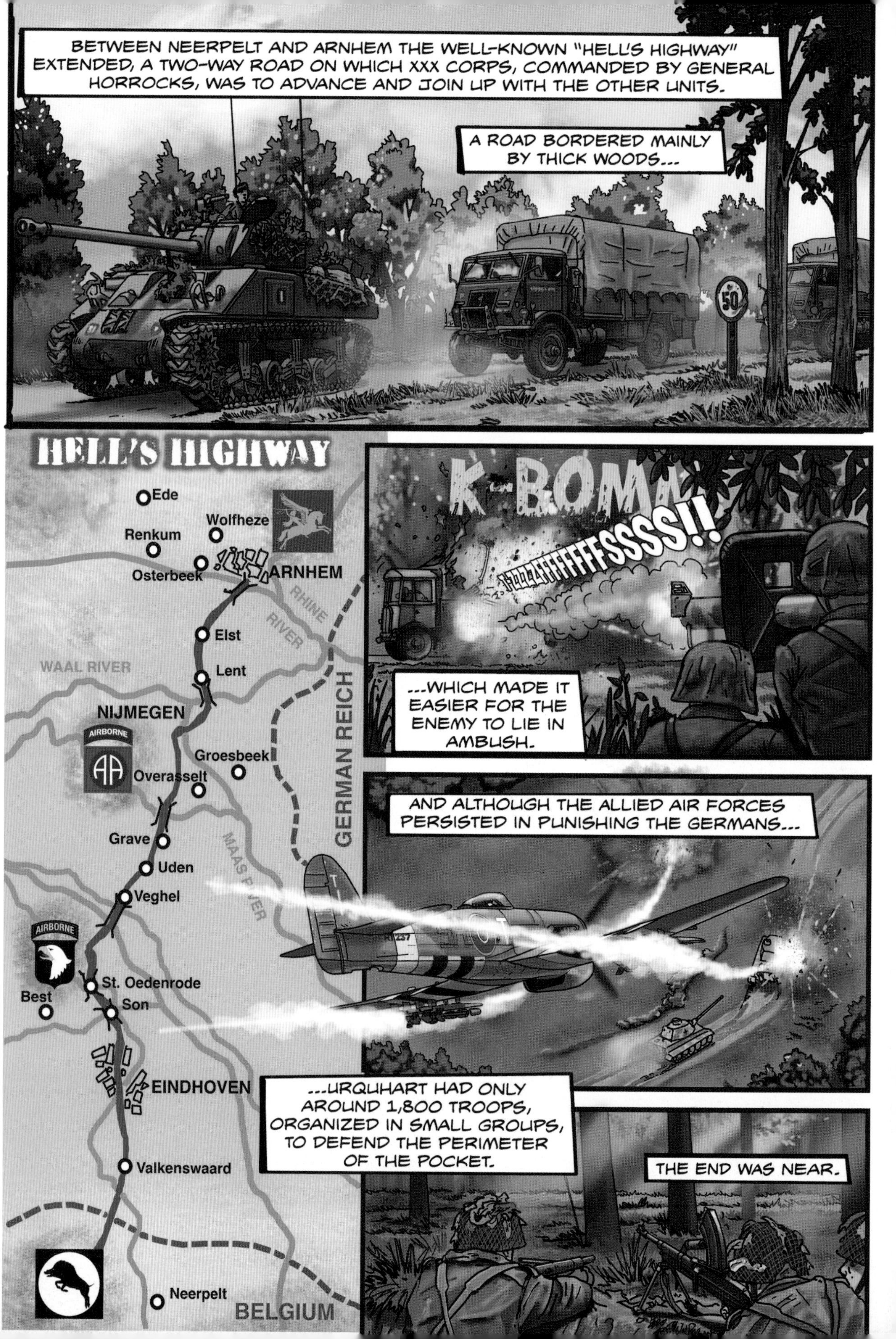
BETWEEN NEERPELT AND ARNHEM THE WELL-KNOWN "HELL'S HIGHWAY" EXTENDED, A TWO-WAY ROAD ON WHICH XXX CORPS, COMMANDED BY GENERAL HORROCKS, WAS TO ADVANCE AND JOIN UP WITH THE OTHER UNITS.
A ROAD BORDERED MAINLY BY THICK WOODS...
50
HELL'S HIGHWAY
Ede
Wolfheze
Renkum
Osterbeek
ARNHEM
RHINE RIVER
Elst
WAAL RIVER
Lent
NIJMEGEN
AIRBORNE
AA
Groesbeek
Overasselt
GERMAN REICH
Grave
MAAS RIVER
Uden
Veghel
AIRBORNE
St. Oedenrode
Best
Son
EINDHOVEN
Valkenswaard
Neerpelt
BELGIUM
K-BOMM
...WHICH MADE IT EASIER FOR THE ENEMY TO LIE IN AMBUSH.
AND ALTHOUGH THE ALLIED AIR FORCES PERSISTED IN PUNISHING THE GERMANS...
...URQUHART HAD ONLY AROUND 1,800 TROOPS, ORGANIZED IN SMALL GROUPS, TO DEFEND THE PERIMETER OF THE POCKET.
THE END WAS NEAR.

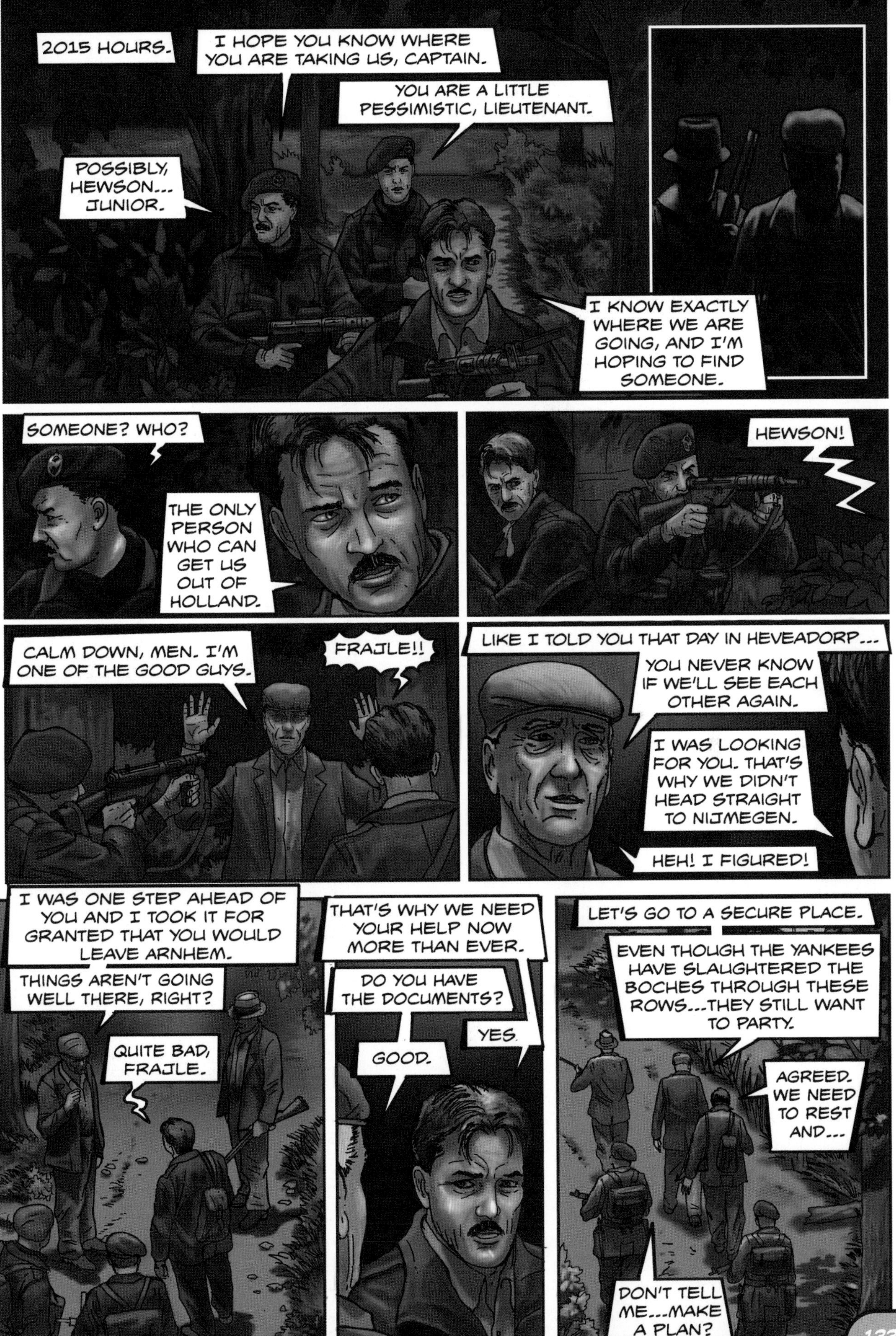

2015 HOURS.
I HOPE YOU KNOW WHERE YOU ARE TAKING US, CAPTAIN.
YOU ARE A LITTLE PESSIMISTIC, LIEUTENANT.
POSSIBLY, HEWSON... JUNIOR.
I KNOW EXACTLY WHERE WE ARE GOING, AND I'M HOPING TO FIND SOMEONE.
SOMEONE? WHO?
THE ONLY PERSON WHO CAN GET US OUT OF HOLLAND.
HEWSON!
CALM DOWN, MEN. I'M ONE OF THE GOOD GUYS.
FRAJLE!!
LIKE I TOLD YOU THAT DAY IN HEVEADORP...
YOU NEVER KNOW IF WE'LL SEE EACH OTHER AGAIN.
I WAS LOOKING FOR YOU. THAT'S WHY WE DIDN'T HEAD STRAIGHT TO NIJMEGEN.
HEH! I FIGURED!
I WAS ONE STEP AHEAD OF YOU AND I TOOK IT FOR GRANTED THAT YOU WOULD LEAVE ARNHEM.
THINGS AREN'T GOING WELL THERE, RIGHT?
QUITE BAD, FRAJLE.
THAT'S WHY WE NEED YOUR HELP NOW MORE THAN EVER.
DO YOU HAVE THE DOCUMENTS?
YES.
GOOD.
LET'S GO TO A SECURE PLACE.
EVEN THOUGH THE YANKEES HAVE SLAUGHTERED THE BOCHES THROUGH THESE ROWS...THEY STILL WANT TO PARTY.
AGREED. WE NEED TO REST AND...
DON'T TELL ME...MAKE A PLAN?

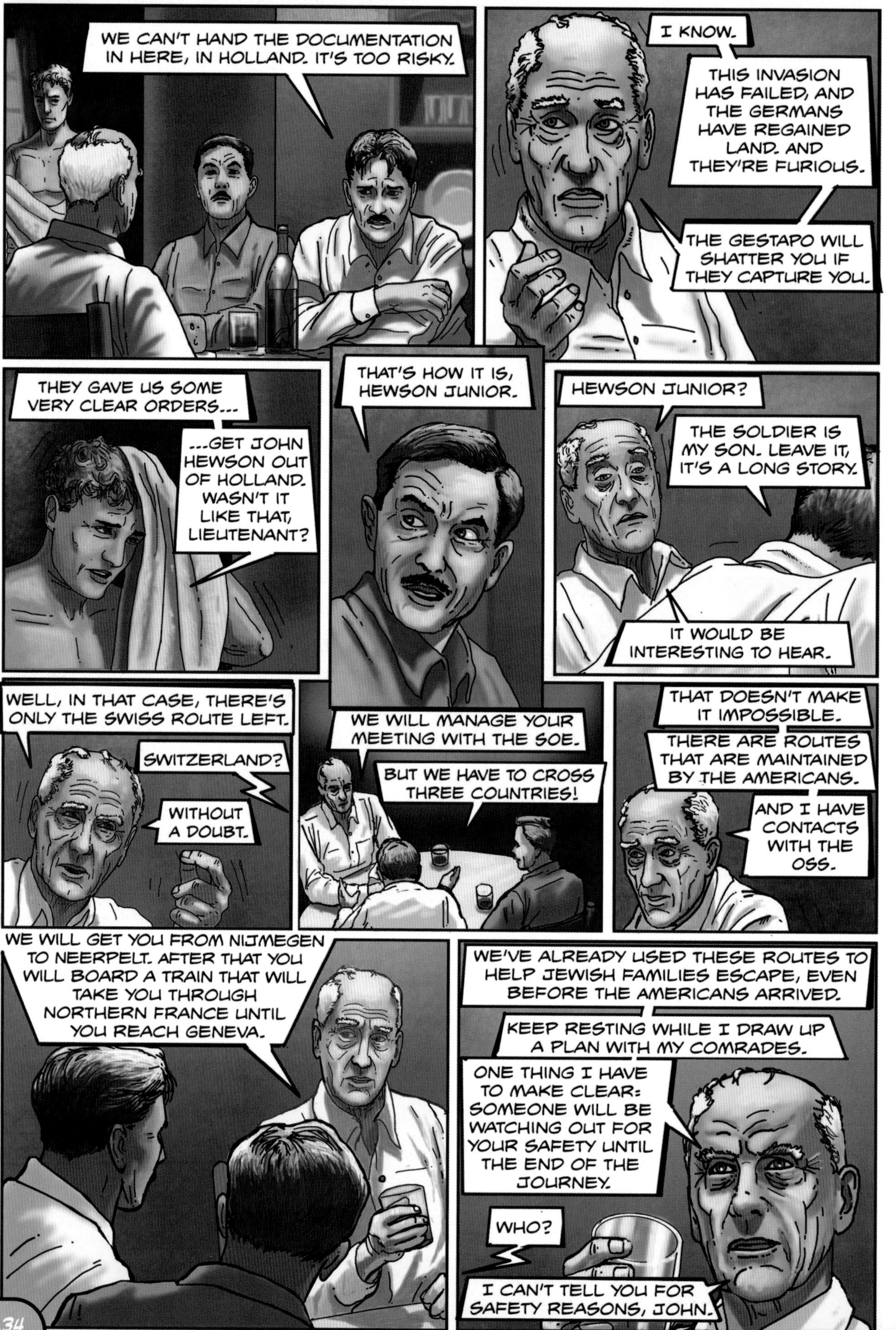
WE CAN'T HAND THE DOCUMENTATION IN HERE, IN HOLLAND. IT'S TOO RISKY.
I KNOW.
THIS INVASION HAS FAILED, AND THE GERMANS HAVE REGAINED LAND. AND THEY'RE FURIOUS.
THE GESTAPO WILL SHATTER YOU IF THEY CAPTURE YOU.
THEY GAVE US SOME VERY CLEAR ORDERS...
...GET JOHN HEWSON OUT OF HOLLAND. WASN'T IT LIKE THAT, LIEUTENANT?
THAT'S HOW IT IS, HEWSON JUNIOR.
HEWSON JUNIOR?
THE SOLDIER IS MY SON. LEAVE IT, IT'S A LONG STORY.
IT WOULD BE INTERESTING TO HEAR.
WELL, IN THAT CASE, THERE'S ONLY THE SWISS ROUTE LEFT.
SWITZERLAND?
WITHOUT A DOUBT.
WE WILL MANAGE YOUR MEETING WITH THE SOE.
BUT WE HAVE TO CROSS THREE COUNTRIES!
THAT DOESN'T MAKE IT IMPOSSIBLE.
THERE ARE ROUTES THAT ARE MAINTAINED BY THE AMERICANS.
AND I HAVE CONTACTS WITH THE OSS.
WE WILL GET YOU FROM NIJMEGEN TO NEERPELT. AFTER THAT YOU WILL BOARD A TRAIN THAT WILL TAKE YOU THROUGH NORTHERN FRANCE UNTIL YOU REACH GENEVA.
WE'VE ALREADY USED THESE ROUTES TO HELP JEWISH FAMILIES ESCAPE, EVEN BEFORE THE AMERICANS ARRIVED.
KEEP RESTING WHILE I DRAW UP A PLAN WITH MY COMRADES.
ONE THING I HAVE TO MAKE CLEAR: SOMEONE WILL BE WATCHING OUT FOR YOUR SAFETY UNTIL THE END OF THE JOURNEY.
WHO?
I CAN'T TELL YOU FOR SAFETY REASONS, JOHN.

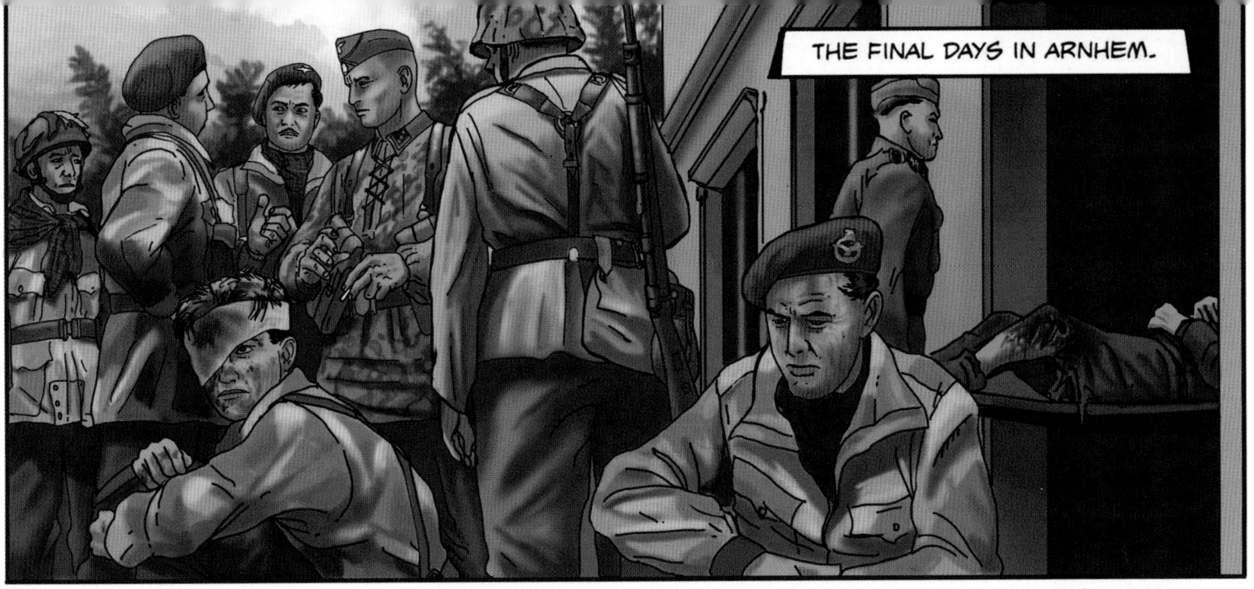
THE FINAL DAYS IN ARNHEM.

AFTER OOSTERBEEK FELL, BRITISH SURVIVORS WERE CAPTURED AND IMPRISONED IN DIFFERENT PARTS OF THE SURROUNDING AREA, SUCH AS THE MISSIONARY SCHOOL IN NIJMEGEN. MEDICS FROM BOTH SIDES COLLABORATED CLOSELY IN AN EFFORT TO SAVE THE LARGE NUMBER OF INJURED SOLDIERS.

IF THE BATTLE WAS EXHAUSTING, THE END WAS WORSE.

THE SURPRISE WAS THE TREATMENT GRANTED TO THE PRISONERS. DESPITE THE WAFFEN-SS' REPUTATION FOR BRUTALITY, ITS MEMBERS BEHAVED WITH AN UNPRECEDENTED MERCY.

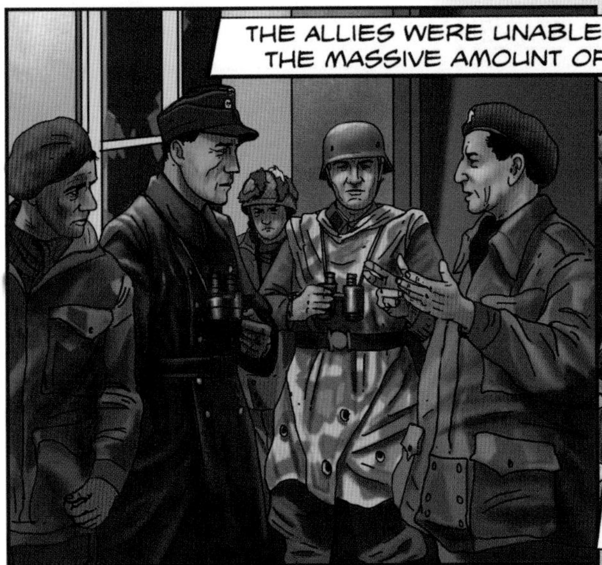
THE ALLIES WERE UNABLE TO TAKE ARNHEM DESPITE THE MASSIVE AMOUNT OF RESOURCES THEY USED.

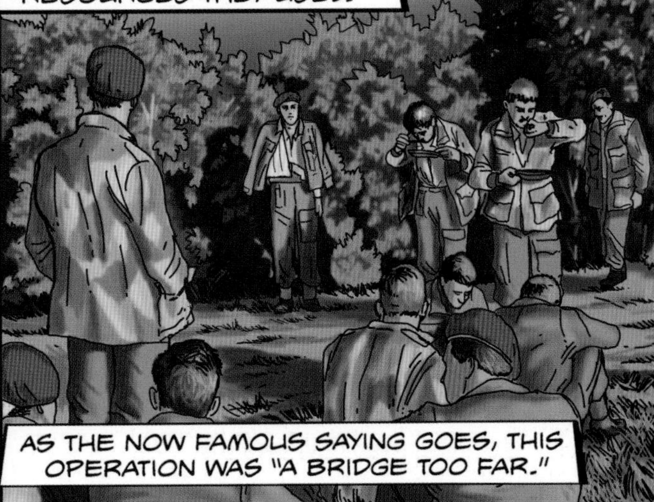
AS THE NOW FAMOUS SAYING GOES, THIS OPERATION WAS "A BRIDGE TOO FAR."

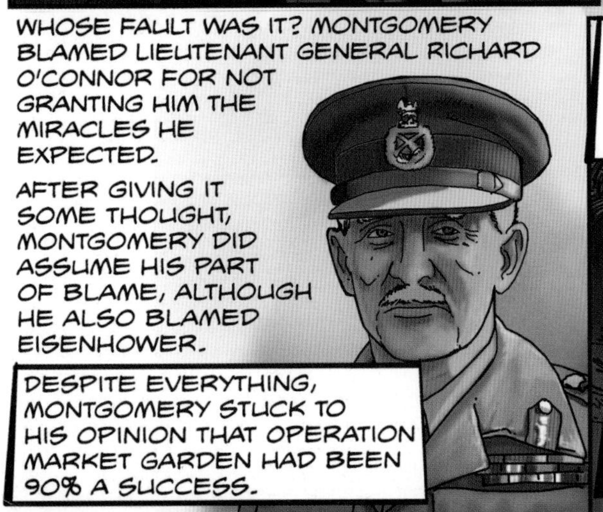
WHOSE FAULT WAS IT? MONTGOMERY BLAMED LIEUTENANT GENERAL RICHARD O'CONNOR FOR NOT GRANTING HIM THE MIRACLES HE EXPECTED.
AFTER GIVING IT SOME THOUGHT, MONTGOMERY DID ASSUME HIS PART OF BLAME, ALTHOUGH HE ALSO BLAMED EISENHOWER.
DESPITE EVERYTHING, MONTGOMERY STUCK TO HIS OPINION THAT OPERATION MARKET GARDEN HAD BEEN 90% A SUCCESS.

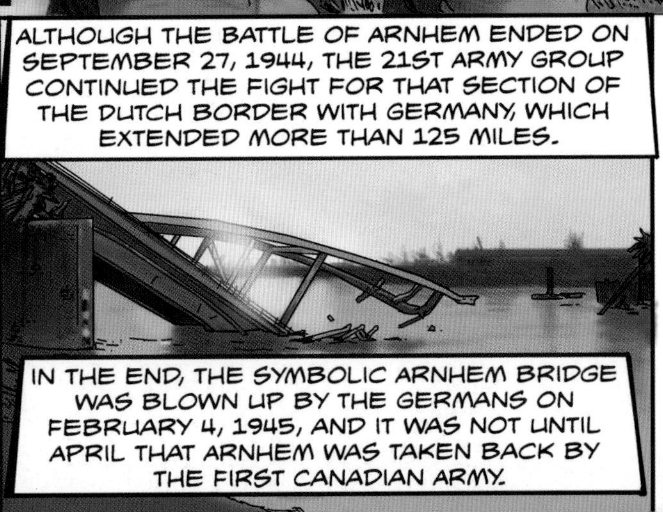
ALTHOUGH THE BATTLE OF ARNHEM ENDED ON SEPTEMBER 27, 1944, THE 21ST ARMY GROUP CONTINUED THE FIGHT FOR THAT SECTION OF THE DUTCH BORDER WITH GERMANY, WHICH EXTENDED MORE THAN 125 MILES.
IN THE END, THE SYMBOLIC ARNHEM BRIDGE WAS BLOWN UP BY THE GERMANS ON FEBRUARY 4, 1945, AND IT WAS NOT UNTIL APRIL THAT ARNHEM WAS TAKEN BACK BY THE FIRST CANADIAN ARMY.

YOU DISAPPEARED OVERNIGHT, WITHOUT A WORD. NOT EVEN A LETTER.

WHY?

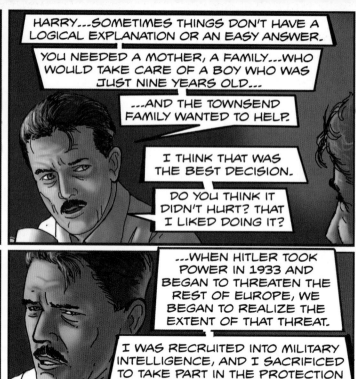

HARRY...SOMETIMES THINGS DON'T HAVE A LOGICAL EXPLANATION OR AN EASY ANSWER.

YOU NEEDED A MOTHER, A FAMILY...WHO WOULD TAKE CARE OF A BOY WHO WAS JUST NINE YEARS OLD...

...AND THE TOWNSEND FAMILY WANTED TO HELP.

I THINK THAT WAS THE BEST DECISION.

DO YOU THINK IT DIDN'T HURT? THAT I LIKED DOING IT?

I NEVER KNEW ANYTHING ABOUT YOU. NEVER...

I WANTED TO QUIT THE WORK, TO COME HOME AND TAKE CARE OF YOU, BUT...

...WHEN HITLER TOOK POWER IN 1933 AND BEGAN TO THREATEN THE REST OF EUROPE, WE BEGAN TO REALIZE THE EXTENT OF THAT THREAT.

I WAS RECRUITED INTO MILITARY INTELLIGENCE, AND I SACRIFICED TO TAKE PART IN THE PROTECTION OF OUR COUNTRY...

...BUT IT CAME AT A VERY HIGH COST.

GIVING UP YOUR PERSONAL LIFE IS VERY HARD, HARRY. THE ONLY THING THAT COMFORTED ME WAS THAT YOU WERE IN SAFE HANDS...

...AND THIS PHOTO.

I REMEMBER IT.

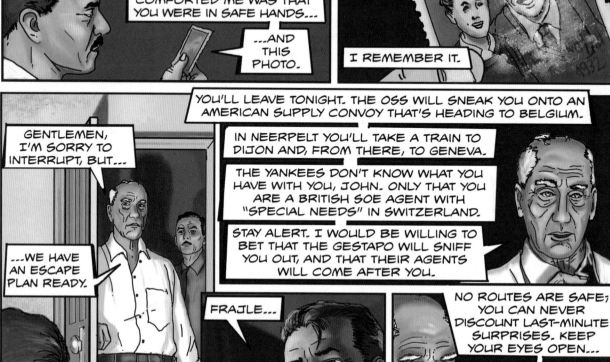

YOU'LL LEAVE TONIGHT. THE OSS WILL SNEAK YOU ONTO AN AMERICAN SUPPLY CONVOY THAT'S HEADING TO BELGIUM.

GENTLEMEN, I'M SORRY TO INTERRUPT, BUT...

...WE HAVE AN ESCAPE PLAN READY.

IN NEERPELT YOU'LL TAKE A TRAIN TO DIJON AND, FROM THERE, TO GENEVA.

THE YANKEES DON'T KNOW WHAT YOU HAVE WITH YOU, JOHN. ONLY THAT YOU ARE A BRITISH SOE AGENT WITH "SPECIAL NEEDS" IN SWITZERLAND.

STAY ALERT. I WOULD BE WILLING TO BET THAT THE GESTAPO WILL SNIFF YOU OUT, AND THAT THEIR AGENTS WILL COME AFTER YOU.

FRAJLE...

HOW SAFE IS THE ROUTE?

NO ROUTES ARE SAFE; YOU CAN NEVER DISCOUNT LAST-MINUTE SURPRISES. KEEP YOUR EYES OPEN...

...EVEN THOUGH I HAVE ALREADY TOLD YOU THAT YOU HAVE A GUARDIAN ANGEL.

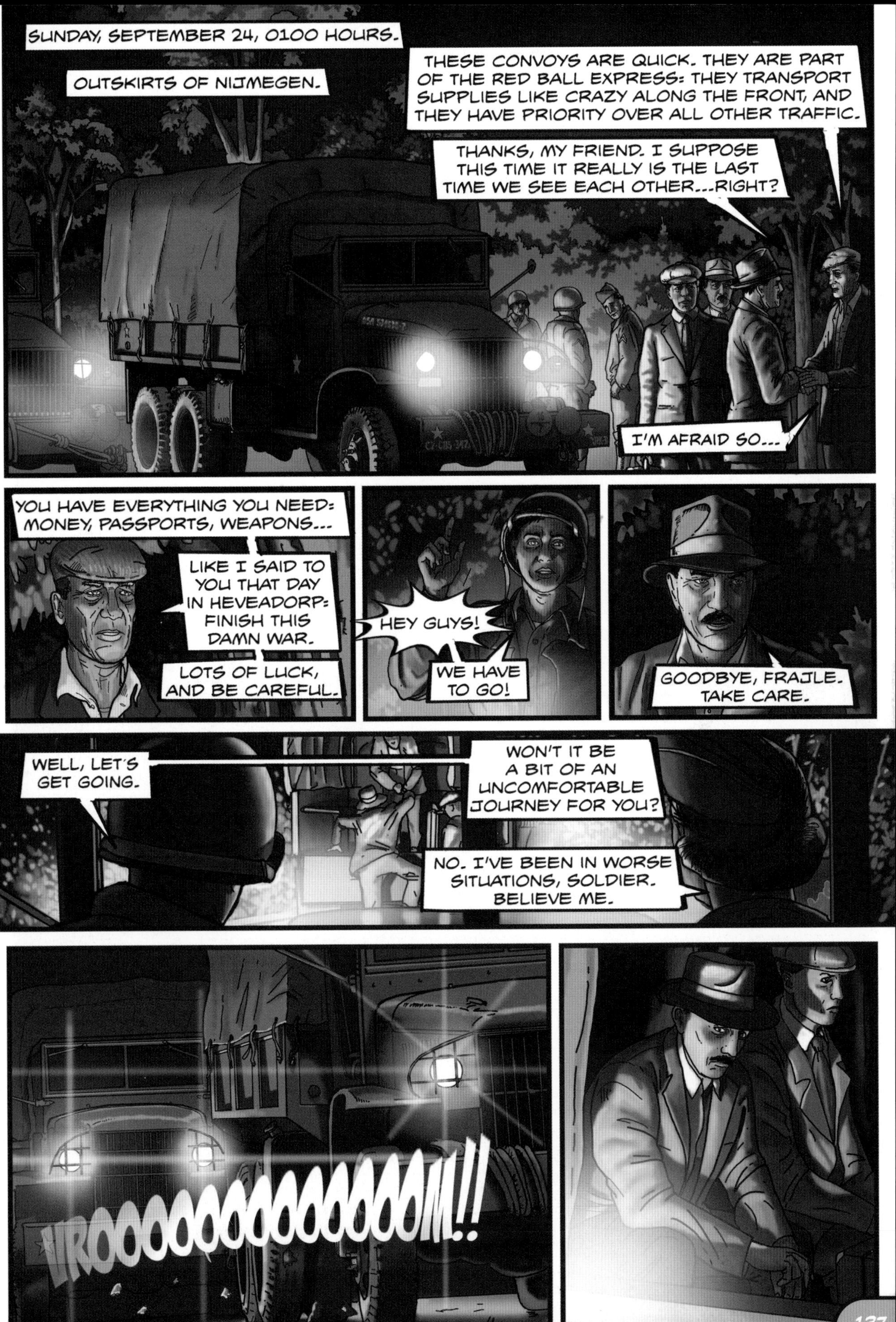
SUNDAY, SEPTEMBER 24, 0100 HOURS.
OUTSKIRTS OF NIJMEGEN.
THESE CONVOYS ARE QUICK. THEY ARE PART OF THE RED BALL EXPRESS: THEY TRANSPORT SUPPLIES LIKE CRAZY ALONG THE FRONT, AND THEY HAVE PRIORITY OVER ALL OTHER TRAFFIC.
THANKS, MY FRIEND. I SUPPOSE THIS TIME IT REALLY IS THE LAST TIME WE SEE EACH OTHER...RIGHT?
I'M AFRAID SO...
YOU HAVE EVERYTHING YOU NEED: MONEY, PASSPORTS, WEAPONS...
LIKE I SAID TO YOU THAT DAY IN HEVEADORP: FINISH THIS DAMN WAR.
LOTS OF LUCK, AND BE CAREFUL.
HEY GUYS!
WE HAVE TO GO!
GOODBYE, FRAJLE. TAKE CARE.
WELL, LET'S GET GOING.
WON'T IT BE A BIT OF AN UNCOMFORTABLE JOURNEY FOR YOU?
NO. I'VE BEEN IN WORSE SITUATIONS, SOLDIER. BELIEVE ME.
VROOOOOOOOOOOOOOM!!

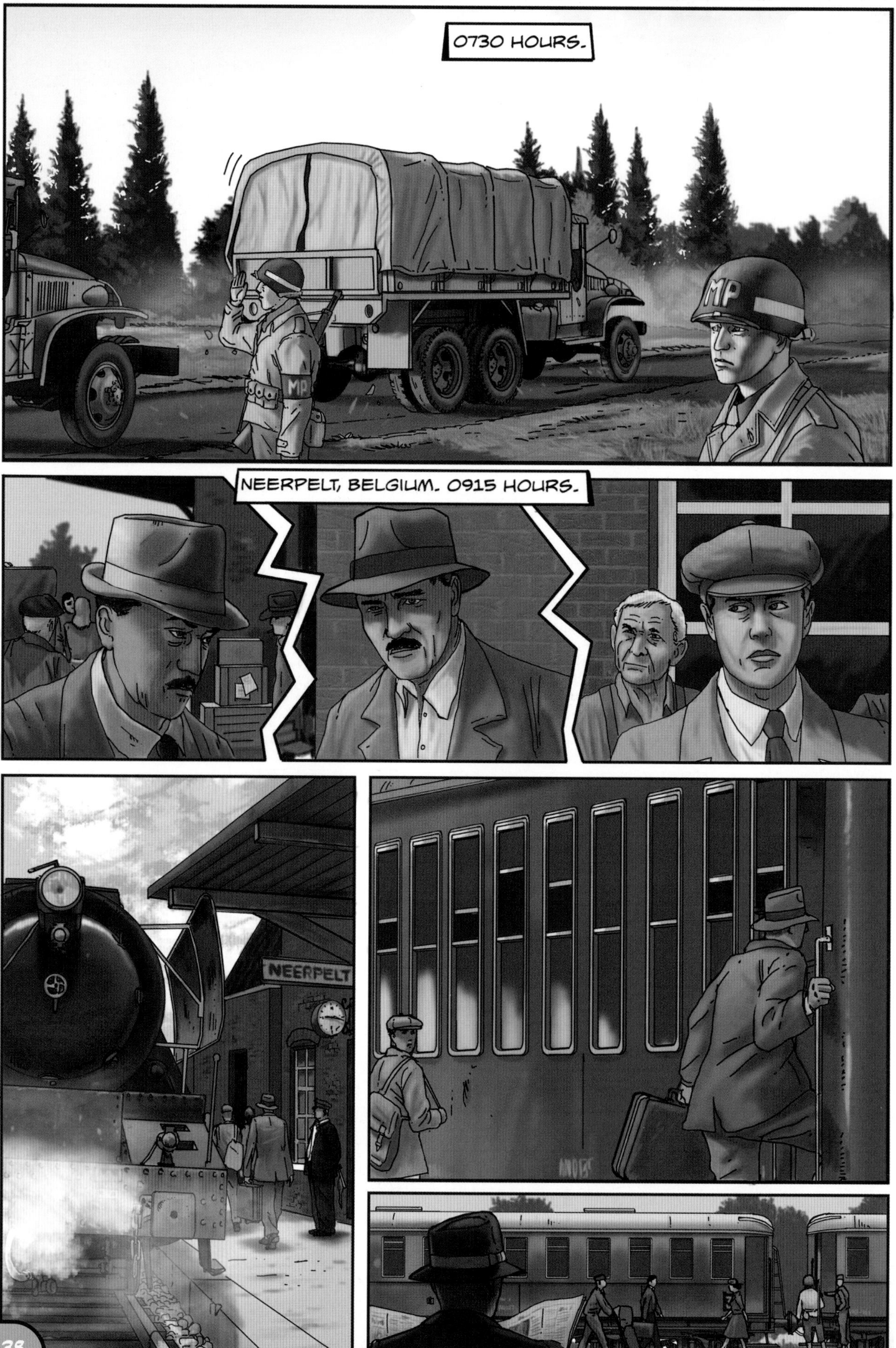
0730 HOURS.
MP
MP
NEERPELT, BELGIUM. 0915 HOURS.
NEERPELT

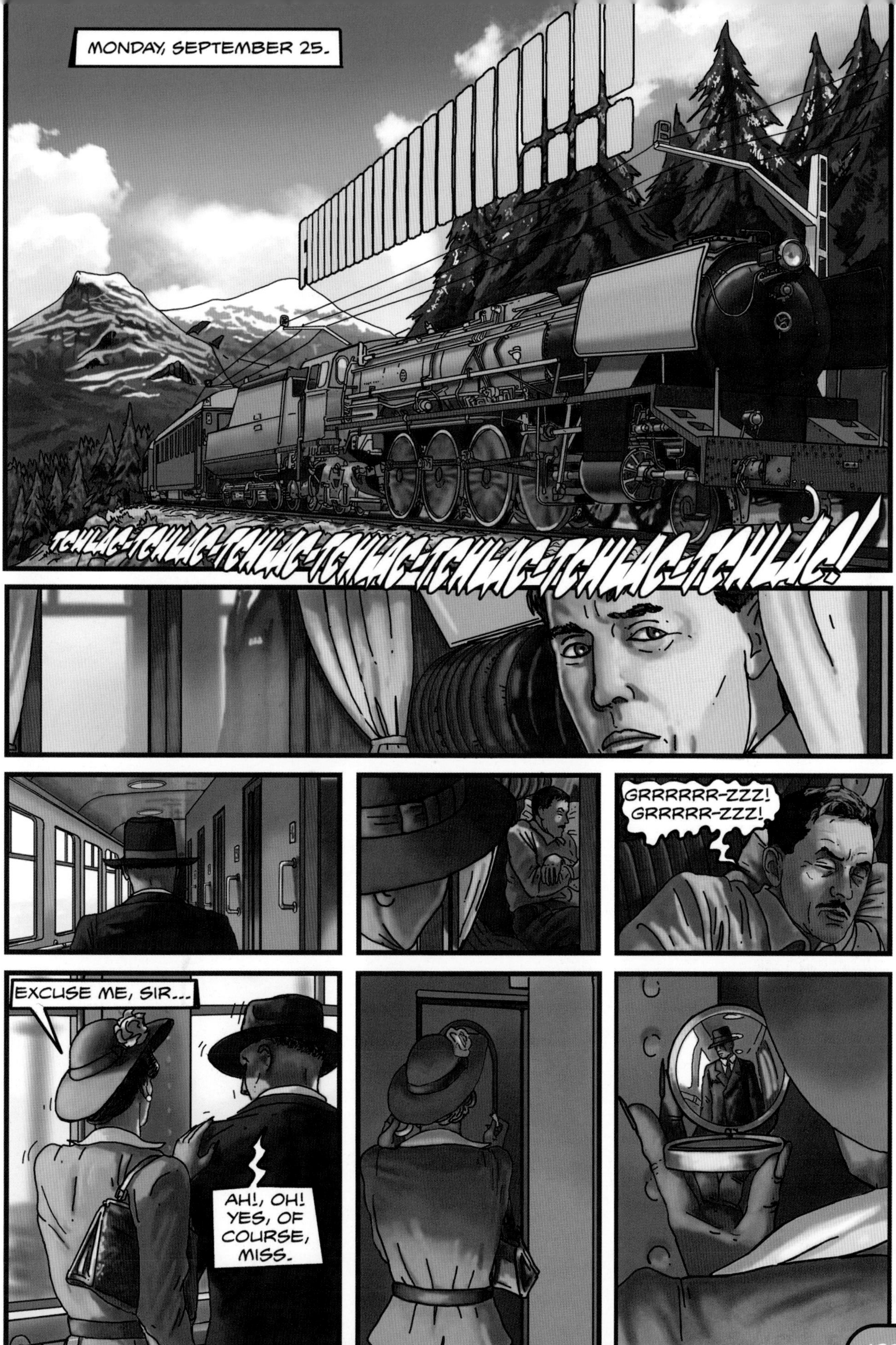
MONDAY, SEPTEMBER 25.
TCHLAC-TCHLAC-TCHLAC-TCHLAC-TCHLAC-TCHLAC-TCHLAC!
GRRRRRR-ZZZ! GRRRRR-ZZZ!
EXCUSE ME, SIR...
AH!, OH! YES, OF COURSE, MISS.

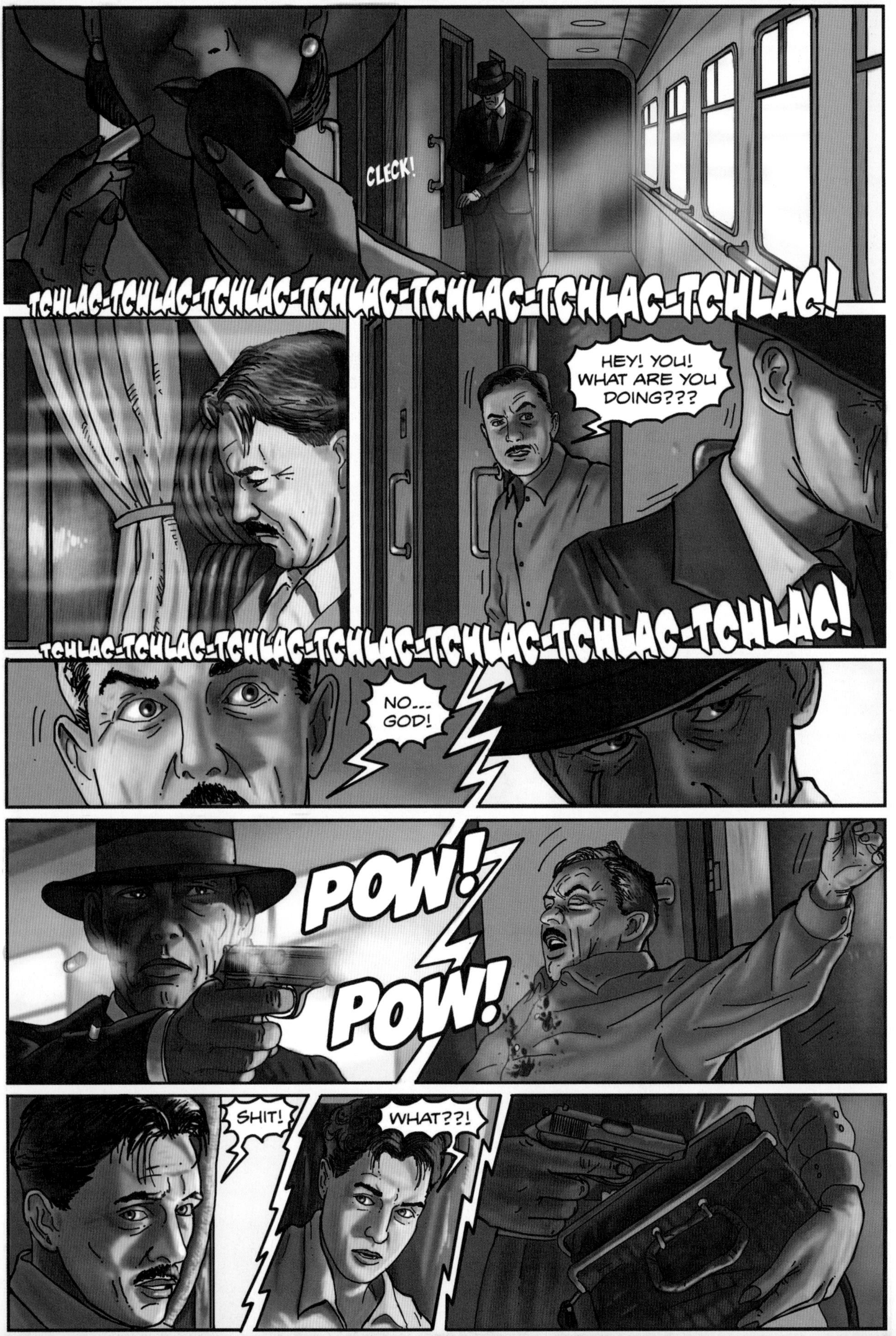
CLECK!
TCHLAC-TCHLAC-TCHLAC-TCHLAC-TCHLAC-TCHLAC-TCHLAC!
HEY! YOU! WHAT ARE YOU DOING???
TCHLAC-TCHLAC-TCHLAC-TCHLAC-TCHLAC-TCHLAC-TCHLAC!
NO... GOD!
POW!
POW!
SHIT!
WHAT??!

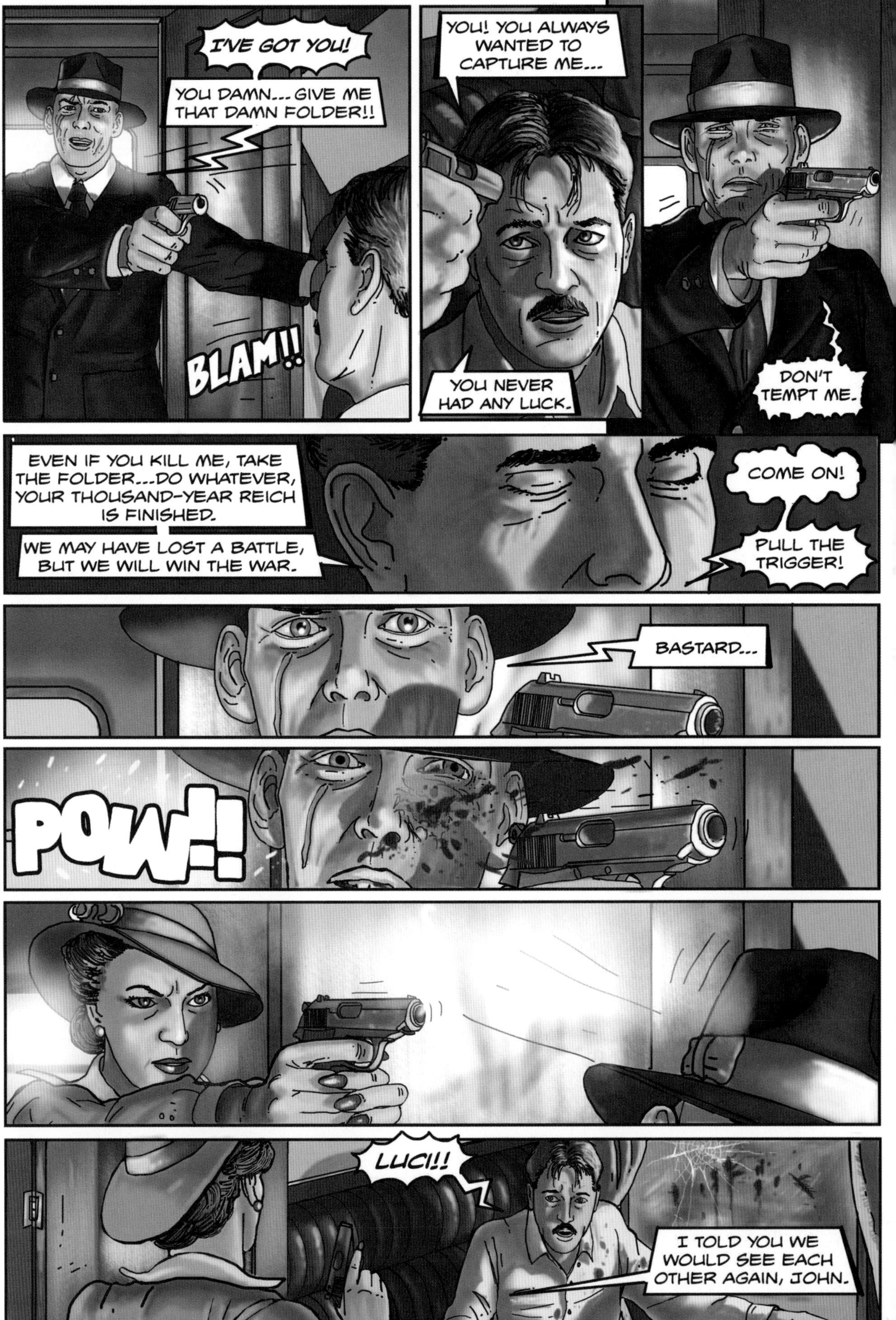
I'VE GOT YOU!
YOU DAMN... GIVE ME THAT DAMN FOLDER!!
BLAM!!
YOU! YOU ALWAYS WANTED TO CAPTURE ME...
YOU NEVER HAD ANY LUCK.
DON'T TEMPT ME.
EVEN IF YOU KILL ME, TAKE THE FOLDER...DO WHATEVER, YOUR THOUSAND-YEAR REICH IS FINISHED.
WE MAY HAVE LOST A BATTLE, BUT WE WILL WIN THE WAR.
COME ON!
PULL THE TRIGGER!
BASTARD...
POW!!
LUCI!!
I TOLD YOU WE WOULD SEE EACH OTHER AGAIN, JOHN.

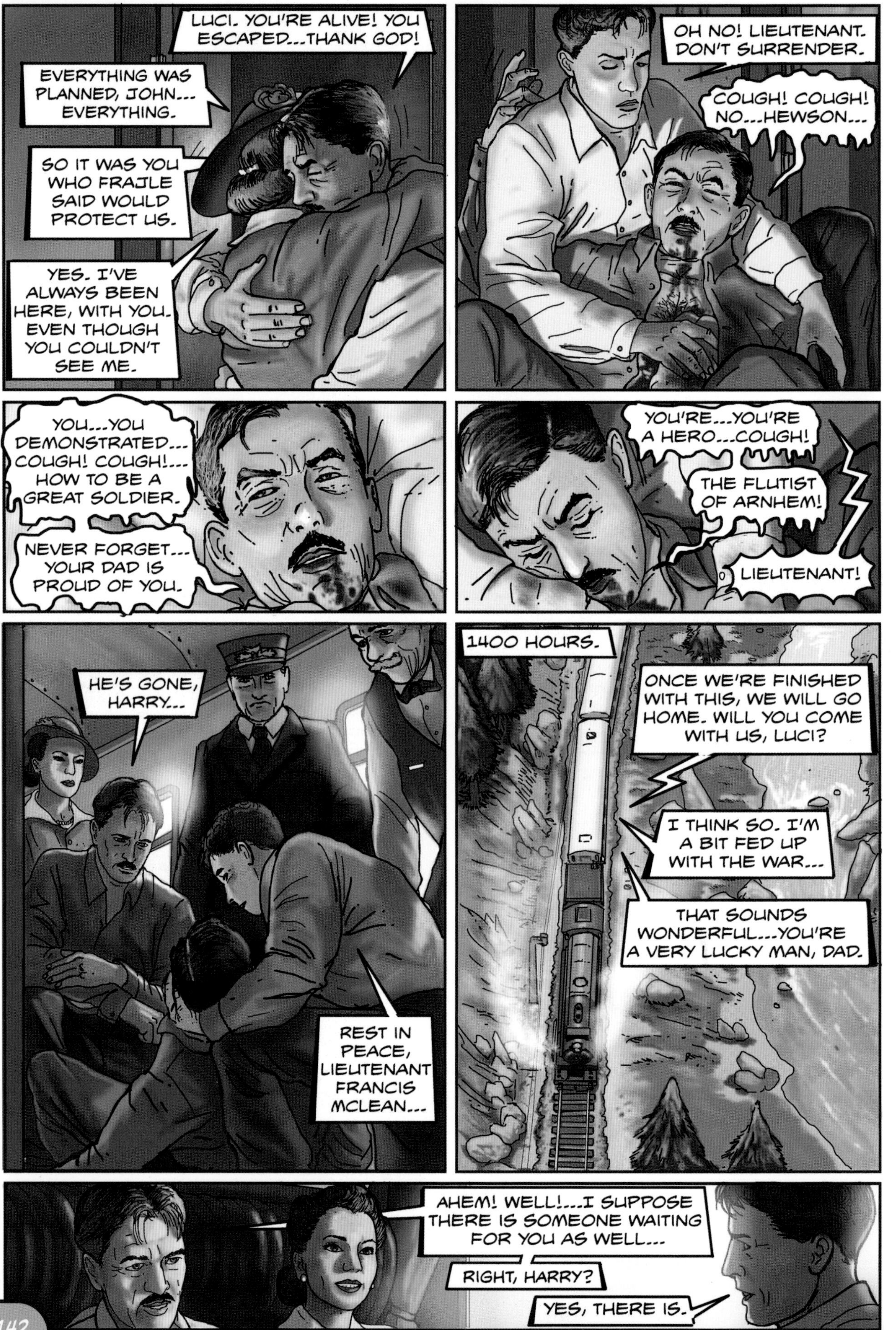
LUCI. YOU'RE ALIVE! YOU ESCAPED...THANK GOD!
EVERYTHING WAS PLANNED, JOHN... EVERYTHING.
SO IT WAS YOU WHO FRAJLE SAID WOULD PROTECT US.
YES. I'VE ALWAYS BEEN HERE, WITH YOU. EVEN THOUGH YOU COULDN'T SEE ME.
OH NO! LIEUTENANT. DON'T SURRENDER.
COUGH! COUGH! NO...HEWSON...
YOU...YOU DEMONSTRATED... COUGH! COUGH!... HOW TO BE A GREAT SOLDIER.
NEVER FORGET... YOUR DAD IS PROUD OF YOU.
YOU'RE...YOU'RE A HERO...COUGH!
THE FLUTIST OF ARNHEM!
LIEUTENANT!
HE'S GONE, HARRY...
REST IN PEACE, LIEUTENANT FRANCIS MCLEAN...
1400 HOURS.
ONCE WE'RE FINISHED WITH THIS, WE WILL GO HOME. WILL YOU COME WITH US, LUCI?
I THINK SO. I'M A BIT FED UP WITH THE WAR...
THAT SOUNDS WONDERFUL...YOU'RE A VERY LUCKY MAN, DAD.
AHEM! WELL!...I SUPPOSE THERE IS SOMEONE WAITING FOR YOU AS WELL...
RIGHT, HARRY?
YES, THERE IS.

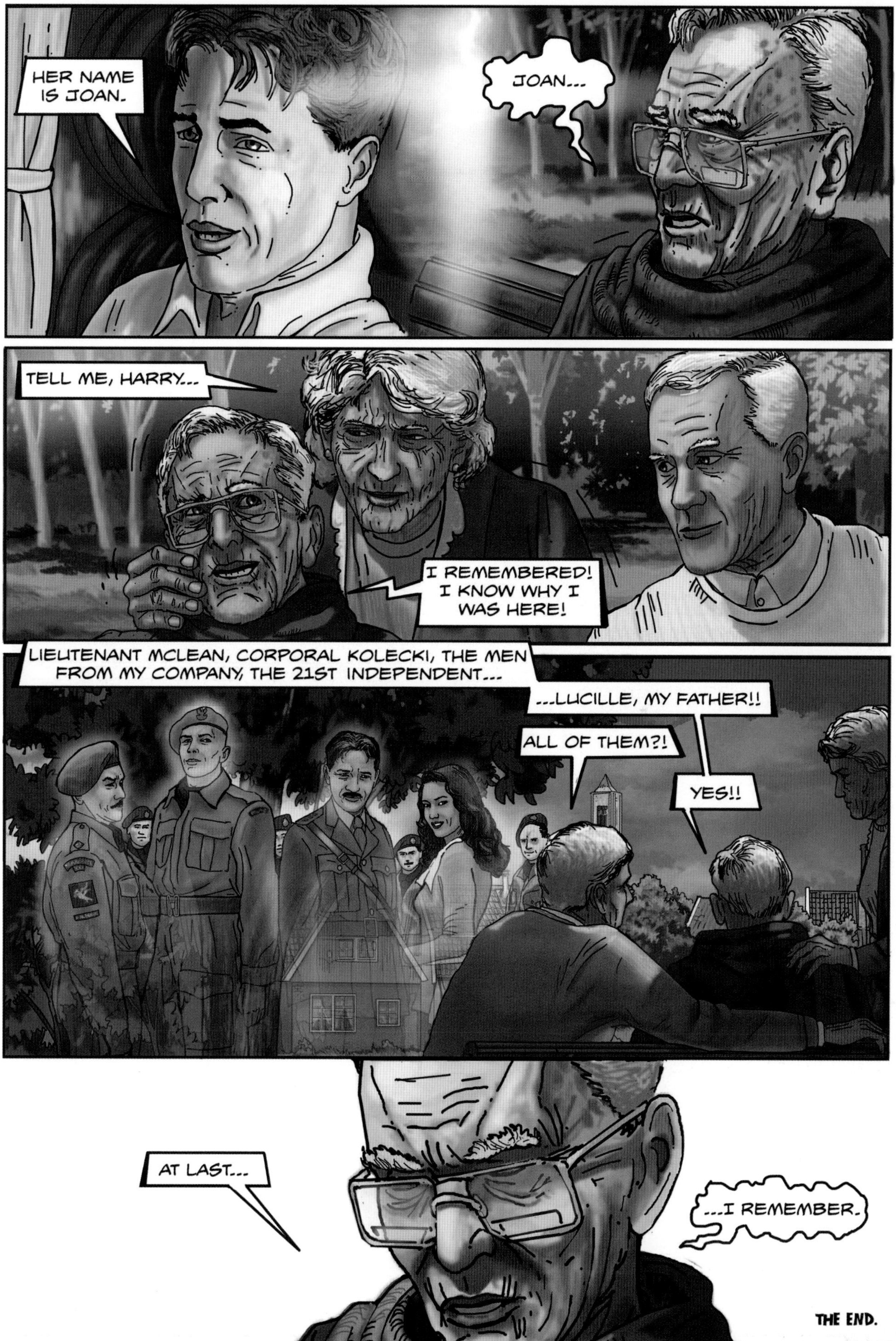
HER NAME IS JOAN.
JOAN...
TELL ME, HARRY...
I REMEMBERED! I KNOW WHY I WAS HERE!
LIEUTENANT MCLEAN, CORPORAL KOLECKI, THE MEN FROM MY COMPANY, THE 21ST INDEPENDENT...
...LUCILLE, MY FATHER!!
ALL OF THEM?!
YES!!
AT LAST...
...I REMEMBER.
THE END.

EPILOGUE

ON MONDAY, SEPTEMBER 25, 1944, AT 2100 HOURS, OPERATION BERLIN BEGAN. THE 43RD DIVISION FROM XXX CORPS BOMBED THE GERMAN POSITIONS IN OOSTERBEEK FOR TWO HOURS, TO OPEN A BREACH ABOUT 765 YARDS TOWARD THE RIVER. THROUGH THIS, THEY WERE ABLE TO EVACUATE ACROSS THE RIVER 1,741 MEN FROM THE 1ST AIRBORNE DIVISION, 422 FROM THE GLIDER PILOT REGIMENT, 160 FROM THE POLISH 1ST INDEPENDENT PARACHUTE BRIGADE, AND 75 FROM THE DORSETSHIRE REGIMENT.

THE GERMANS TOOK 170 PRISONERS.

AT 0130 HOURS ON SEPTEMBER 26, THE EVACUATION OF THE HARTENSTEIN HOTEL WAS COMPLETED.

AT 0200 HOURS ALL AMMUNITION WAS DESTROYED AND THE ARTILLERY WAS DISABLED.

THE SURVIVORS MARCHED FROM DRIEL TO NIJMEGEN.

AT 0530 HOURS THE EVACUATION OPERATION ENDED AND WITH IT, OPERATION MARKET GARDEN.

THE DUTCH RESISTANCE GROUP PAN HELPED 240 MORE MEN ESCAPE.

A TOTAL OF 240 MEDICAL OFFICERS AND CHAPLAINS VOLUNTEERED TO STAY BEHIND WITH THE 1,600 WOUNDED.

THE NUMBER OF ALLIED SOLDIERS TAKEN PRISONER WAS ABOUT 6,450 MEN, ACCORDING TO GERMAN ESTIMATES.

THE TOTAL LOSSES OF THE I AIRBORNE CORPS ADDED UP TO APPROXIMATELY 6,858 MEN. THE 2ND BRITISH ARMY CASUALTIES WERE DIFFICULT TO EVALUATE, BUT WERE AROUND 5,354 MEN, INCLUDING 1,480 FROM XXX CORPS.

LOSSES INCLUDED 164 AIRCRAFT AND 132 GLIDERS.

TOTAL CASUALTIES OF THE BATTLE, INCLUDING THOSE FROM THE U.S. ARMY AIR FORCES, THE RAF, THE 12TH AND 21ST ARMY GROUPS, THE 1ST ALLIED AIRBORNE ARMY, AND THE 1ST BRITISH AIRBORNE CORPS, WERE CALCULATED TO BE AROUND 16,805 MEN.

THE GERMAN LOSSES FROM ARMY GROUP B WERE ESTIMATED TO BE 2,000 KIA AND 6,000 WOUNDED.

THIS IS THE MELODY THAT HARRY WAS PLAYING.

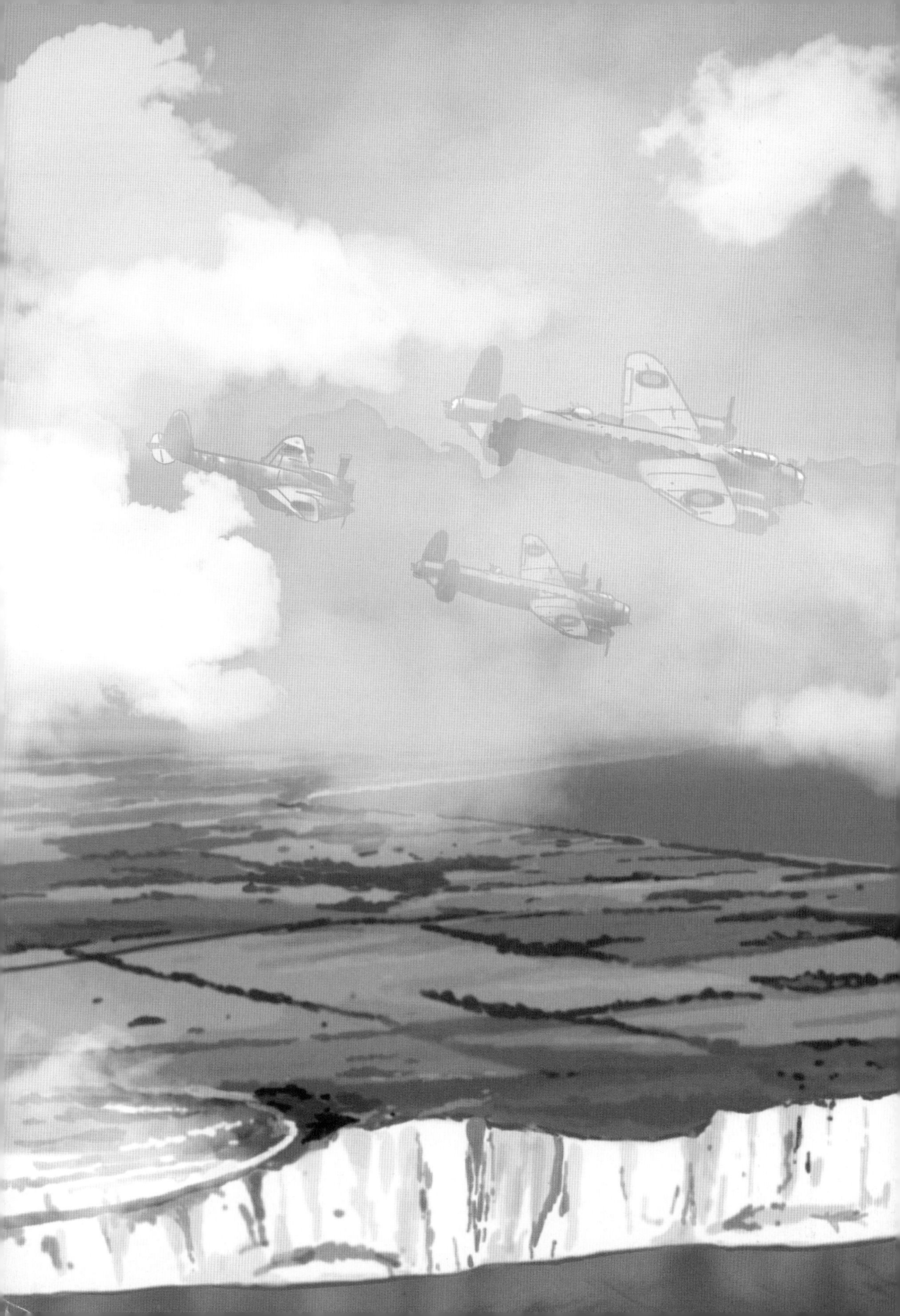

About the Author

Antonio Gil is an illustrator, comic author, and writer specializing in military history, with more than one hundred publications in specialized magazines, books, and comics.

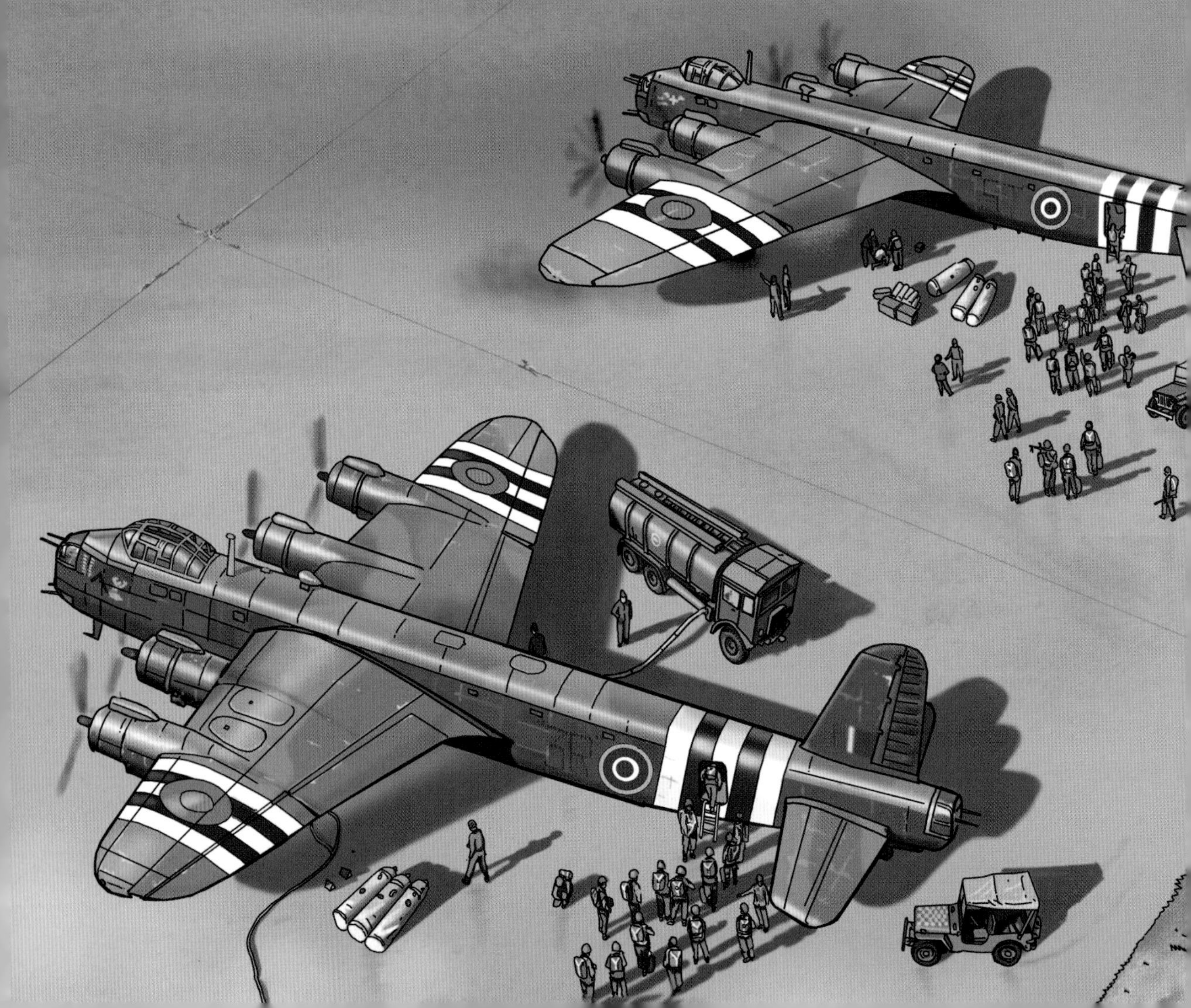